Gratian and me

Tom O'Neill

Grattan and me

DALKEY ARCHIVE PRESS

Copyright © 2017 by Tom O'Neill
First edition, 2017
All rights reserved

Library of Congress Cataloging-in-Publication Data
Identifiers: ISBN 9781628971644
LC record available at https://catalog.loc.gov/

Partially funded by a grant by the Illinois Arts Council, a state agency

www.dalkeyarchive.com
Victoria, TX / McLean, IL / Dublin
Dalkey Archive Press publications are, in part, made possible through the support of the University of Houston-Victoria
and its programs in creative writing, publishing, and translation.
Printed on permanent/durable acid-free paper

Foreword

This book was originally published in 2014 by Blaney Press of 74 Camden Street, under the title '*Lovelessness, Mustard, and miscellany.*' Blaney had apparently been immersed for a while previously in a somewhat less than constructive exchange with the writer. The lingering bitterness of the prior skirmishes, together with a feeling of having been duped into publishing this manuscript, may have been what blinded Blaney to the extraordinary merit of the work. Blaney's publication was undertaken in a spirit of bare minimum compliance with the contractual obligation he felt he had unwittingly entered into. Duly, the book had been printed—with a run of fifty. Blaney personally saw to the contract's distribution stipulation by taking copies to each of the paper recycling depots throughout the greater Dublin area.

The work would undoubtedly have been lost entirely only for the plainness of the faded blue-grey paper cover, which caught the eye of your correspondent one foggy November evening. As my nocturnal jogging route covers most of the North City and much of the South I was familiar enough with the sight of a group of wretched men proceeding down Marrowbone Lane carelessly dragging the insulation materials they had just fished out of the paper recycling bins located there. On this occasion I was arrested by the sight of the tatty tome clutched, rather uselessly to his cause, in the pale knuckles of a small leather-coated member of that entourage, a man with a wide dyed moustache. I jogged on the spot so as not to cool while I expressed an interest in taking possession of the item. I was rewarded with the choice of fighting the wielder, or paying forty-five euro. I bargained the unfortunates down to two and went on my way, immediately engrossed to the point of bumping into lamp posts as I travelled onwards.

Agency being in my RNA I soon fixed up the writer with another publisher, one I thought his match in contrariness and exclusion. I won't feign heroism here. I'll be the first to tell you that I'd be shrewd enough when it comes to the brokerage percentages. Your ideal pairing arises when both end parties are too proud to admit they're in books for the money. That leaves a nice few points for taking the pain in the middle. I first of course went to Blaney for the rights. He appeared tickled to the extent that the Malbec from one of the bottles I had brought him came out his nostrils in spurts. But all credit to the open literary spirit that still survives in Dublin, after a small consideration was received by himself, his mirth eventually subsided and some consideration was given in return to my proposal. One condition he imposed was that the document retain the footnotes. These were the only input his editors had felt able to make under the terms of the reviled contract. He held that the footers at least provided ballast and removed any possibility of a benign misinterpretation of the writer's motivations and "depravities" becoming possible at some time in the future. I found myself with him on that. Conservation rather than restoration. The whole story or none at all.

The rest is history. By the way, the other condition Blaney insisted on was the retention of his cover concept. Complying with this created a little more difficulty for the new crowd. Blaney's peculiar choice of title and the even more peculiar phoneticization he applies to "The compiler's" name, apparently to add further anonymity, were not favoured by the latter. Therefore, in turn, this proviso has been honoured with some economy. The original cover has indeed been retained, but internally (follows).

T Francis Kneel

Lovelessness, Mustard, and miscellany

Being as seeming

Preface

Funny thing, only a week or so previously the great man, Grattan Fletcher, had been talking away lightly on the very subjects of existence and permanence with his associate, Leonard Suck Ryle, whose greatness was less often noted. And now here was Grattan lying in a rather plain pine box in front of an Italian marble altar, stone dead.

In the skulking posture of intellectual underdog, the mould of the small bus-faced, tech-schooled man Ryle, had interrupted the flow that night by saying, 'Of course you'd know better, so explain to me what's superior about the devout atheist's beliefs? For those who spend their lives searching for beliefs like hens scratching in ashes, wouldn't they be better with the meat than the tofu. It's cheaper and more filling.'

'You've got me wrong,' the bigger softer man had responded, looking like a cross between Mary Robinson and Tom Waits, as he leaned his greying black curls into the other's space. It was not that Grattan Fletcher was unable to distinguish comments that were genuinely ignorant from those impelled by an intention to idly rile. It was just that his default setting had always been to respond sincerely, regardless, 'I don't set myself above. Eternity and death are as mysterious to me now as they were when I was a child. I thought understanding would come in time. Instead I now find even life itself almost impossible to believe. I *know* but I can't begin to comprehend the wonderfulness of this earth, this life, this *being*.'

'Answer me this then,' Suck Ryle had responded, 'how does Margot, for example, take it?'

'What do you mean?' Fletcher had asked. He had been registering the recent uptick in Ryle's questions about how his wife *took things*, but was choosing not to embody this uncomfortable phenomenon in a formulated observation.

'I mean having her well-founded faith called a *mental comfort,*'

Ryle had asked, 'Is she game for being de*rided* like that?'

I couldn't tell you how these subjects had come up between them that night so recently preceding the low-key commemoration I was attending. Because I don't know. And I couldn't reveal to you the precise location of the two right men at the time, nor the nature of the mission with which they were engaged, because there are certain areas I don't go and because there are certain matters that remain sub judice. I wouldn't want to subject you to any false promise in this foretaste of what's to come. I can however give you a redacted overview of the circumstances if that's any good to you.

These matters were being threshed out after midnight with our two men bogged down and on the verge. The little road they had made the mistake of driving onto the verge of is one that winds its way in a most unintuitive manner up a certain marshy hill which I am not at liberty to name. Let's just say if you haven't already seen this same dire esker making its absence felt in your news feeds, you most certainly will in the future. You can figure it out for yourself from there.

'I'm just saying,' Ryle had continued, 'They still want to be communing around a set of rules and morals so why not use an off-the-shelf job, millennia in development? Why burn down the cathedrals. We already paid for the thousands of generations of fuckers who sat in soapy water thinking up consolations for every situation you might find yourself in.'

'You never say what your own thing is, Len,' Fletcher had said tenderly, still not accepting that there was no nerve to be touched in his companion. 'What thing it is that you are sure of when you are alone without routines or friends to distract from the brief reality of your situation.' This was indeed a bit presumptuous. The reality of a client such as Ryle is rarely brief.

'And what if you died suddenly,' Ryle had snapped then, with as little respect for the future as for the past, 'And never had time to use all the thoughts you'd wasted your own brief reality home-brewing?'

'You don't sort your ideas out for the rainy day. You sort them out to make better use of every other day,' Fletcher had said.

'The good days.'

Three hours earlier they had made the mistake of putting the two left wheels of the Office of Public Works van over the lip of the little skin of tarmac, on arrival at the GPS coordinates for their rendezvous with the other members of the *Hands-off, Frackers* committee. Fletcher was still insisting that other members would show up and give them a push. To pass the time and to titillate his residual rancour, Ryle liked to see if he could knock a few chips off Fletcher's fundamental beliefs. It was safe turf for him as he had no fixed beliefs of his own as far as I can tell; though if I have to think about it, he was culturally both a little bit Catholic and a little bit Protestant by times, as will become apparent.

Meanwhile, someone's unrushed approach from a copse of conifers two hundred metres across the brow of the hill was illustrated by a beam of torchlight swinging at the end of an arm.

Grattan Fletcher, a man who had been awarded Trinity doctorates in Celtic Studies and the Classics and who had trained himself to become the country's pre-eminent architectural historian, didn't have the stomach for the meat apparently or for the ready-made consolations. The same Fletcher did not think in binary and did not even believe in evil, only in people who had lost their way. 'Sometimes it's not that I don't understand what you are saying, Len,' Fletcher had responded politely, 'it's just that sometimes you are wrong.'

'Take yourself, boss,' Ryle had continued in the slow delivery which was about the only way ire showed up in the man's monotone, 'you hope your spirit will survive through the trees you planted and in the memories people will have of you, memories of your much practiced philosophy of harmlessness.'

'Doing as little harm as possible,' Fletcher had corrected, not for the first time. 'And in a general imprint on the environment, rather than in expecting trees to talk of me! If we really must be reductionist about everything.'

'But you surely know how bad people's memories are. And if the trees started talking again there's no grounds for assuming it would be something pleasant they'd say about the compatriot who transplanted them, the seed preferring naturally never to fall far from the tree.'

Note: I later took it on myself to go online to see if there was any substance to this implication emanating from Ryle. Assuming that he didn't himself remember the time when 'trees stopped talking,' I gave several minutes researching all of the original sources in this regard. I scoured the Four Masters. I forensically scrutinized the Seancas Már. I checked it out in the relevant annals of the Northern Spanish, having had our origins pointed in that direction by the Lebor Gabála as corroborated in the recent genetic research. (My own maternal line being from the Basque village of Licketstown in the South of Kilkenny, I was well ahead of the posse on this one.) All in the vernacular, I add, to avoid any risk of losing one nucleotide of meaning. I can stake my reputation on the conclusion that Ryle is wrong here. The trees never gave up talking. The mere fact that we have no recorded evidence of any speech out of them since the foreign imposition of expository language upon our National writing style, does not prove a cessation. It is well-known that you can't prove silence. Those would be my own thoughts on the matter anyway. *The compiler* [fn]

[fn] Footnote
Assertions need additional citations for verification and may require editing for cohesion, relevance, and tone. This caution should be read as applying to each and every claim, observation, attribution, note, and allusion provided by 'the compiler' throughout this manuscript.
Oh look, this level of guidance is not going to help at all. It doesn't even touch sides. Let's just be brutally honest here. It would by now be patently obvious to any surviving hypothetical reader that this body of work cries out for liberal use of the editorial scythe. Never would a treatment have so redeemed the arts of expurgation and bowdlerization. The only question, whether anything would remain. Put on pause your self-pity for a moment then, implausible reader, and consider the nail-stripping agonies suffered by a professional editor in your place; sidelined by a contractual imbroglio which we won't embroil you in, and having to sit out with you to the finish. Yet the instinct to duty doesn't yield. Despite recognizing the unlikelihood of you, the 'reader' ever being

material, we nevertheless professionally provide you with the best we can offer under these extraordinary strictures: a basic set of concise footers grounding you at key junctures. *The Editors*

'If I didn't know by your actions that you're a generally reliable person Len, that kind of talk would convince me that you're nothing more than a mocking barracker. I'd suggest other assignments for you. Better travel alone than with a companion waiting for you to fall,' Fletcher had responded then, a little tetchily it has to be said. 'It's not principally about seeking immortality through whatever memories you may leave. It's about your existence right now, in this moment, being no more or less than the sum total of what you have come to mean to others.'

'The old people used to say,' observed Ryle, 'that hope is a good breakfast but a bad supper.' He was apparently in a particular grump that night. He had never been assigned to Fletcher in the first place. Also, the torchbearers approaching the public works van were not the others of the committee as it turned out, but two all-too-familiars of the Garda Community Relations Squadron, the Crusty Squad to you and me.

'Ignore them,' said Fletcher. 'Boredom brings out the worst in them. Let us keep our conversation on a higher plane. That's the best medicine for the likes of them.' One of the Gardaí was laughing as he directed a beam through the windscreen onto Fletcher's face and the other had her skirt lifted and was flattening her arse into two massive pancakes on Fletcher's side window.

'So tell me then,' said Ryle, unable not to think of what Sergeant Meg Geas and Garda Michael Devine (formerly Detective Sergeant Devine of Store St.) might think up to charge him with this time. 'Why is the food of the masses never good enough for your class? What's wrong with a recipe for permanence whereby you are just asked to choose black or white and you don't have to ask anyone at all to remember you accurately or even fondly?'

The cops were apparently held up then by a scheduled tea break. All that could be seen of them in the dark was the wan light of the LED torch being held over baguettes that were being unwrapped on a fold-out picnic table they'd had the forethought to bring.

'I can see the attraction of that in your case,' Grattan had said, skirting the colour question for fear of Ryle's follow through, and apologizing in advance for any offence that his attempt at diversionary humour might cause, by putting his hand on Ryle's arm and laughing in the way of a kindly uncle.

Oddly, Fletcher had never figured out that Ryle didn't like to be touched. But touched he most certainly did not like to be. Not even by himself. Even in interactions with women, Ryle tended not to over-elaborate the flesh contacts. So he was hardly going to make an exception for this man to whom he displayed no loyalty. Promptly clamped, Fletcher's wrist was restored to its own half of the car severely sprained. Fletcher had covered his whimper with a little snort. 'But the fundamental difficulty with established religion is the simple awkward problem of the central figure being absent.'

'The devil too I suppose you say *doesn't exist?* Wasn't it you yourself who told me that questioning the reality of everything died out with *Existentialism* in the fifties?' Ryle had recently discovered the Existentialism button and its impulsive effect on middle-class conversation. He wasn't shy to use it. 'If you occasionally came down to earth yourself, you might have planned this meeting so as not to include me freezing my testicles off in the back of beyonds, waiting again for fellow agents of the State to come up with new ways to make things go even worse for me.'

'With all due respect, my good and reliable man,' Grattan had said then, finally risen and keen to avoid the subjects more immediately at hand, 'I have not heard such a muddle of ideas in a long while.'

'What more proof that the humanists all still crave the holy communion,' returned Ryle then with the unsettling prescience I was to discover in many of his mutterings, 'than setting up their own Sunday gatherings?'

Note: For those illiterati amongst you, those like myself not well enough versed in Confucian philosophy, I gave 'humanism' a look-up. It is a branch of speciesism, placing the homo-sapien species above all others. Dogs have also been known to subscribe to humanism, not being all that fond of each other. Cats, not fond of any species including their own, are agnostics in this regard. (I'd lean towards the cat's position.) Other than these exceptions, each variant of species prejudice offers a hierarchy with the generators thereof at the top. Dolphinism is recognized as a particularly jingoistic variant. *The compiler*

The reason Ryle had recorded parts of this religious conversation in his diary, I will be unable to explain to you later.

The reason he had ended it on a probably false note, giving himself the last word, is rooted in human nature, an allowance you surely can make even for Mr. Ryle.

An explanation of my misfortune in coming into possession of such records, let me briefly now offer to you to be taken or left as pleases you.

Grattan Fletcher's funeral, indeed, wasn't very humanist after all. And a good many went up the aisle for the real Holy Communion. Despite his killer having knelt on his chest depriving him of any last wind with which to recant had he so desired, his wife Margot had assumed that Grattan would have reached for the old reliables in the end, maybe calling out a quick Our Father or at least a Jesus Mary and Joseph if he'd been allowed. And she made the executive decision that survivors are entitled to, that the one panicked final thought she conjectured him to have had, outvoted every other thought that he had expressed on the subject since he was fourteen. He was returned to the house of God. In fact, to reinforce matters, the mass was concelebrated. Five priests and a bishop had come out of respect for his cousin, a Redemptorist, who had not.

'Six funeral masses in one,' I heard Ryle mutter as I happened to be leaning with him against the holy water font out in the side porch, 'a fair slapping down for a man's disbeliefs.'

The family refused the opportunity to come up and say a few words about the dead man at the end of the ceremony, as has become customary at the establishment funeral. Nor were there trained singers brought in. Only the ordinary hymns were wrung from the crowd. The family were acting like visitors at someone else's death.

Maybe Grattan Fletcher did achieve a little bit of permanence though, despite Ryle's loyal criticisms. During the course of the funeral procession I happened into a conversation with a man in Heyns' Hotel, one who struck me as a right prick from the very first glance. He too had thought nobody would notice him slip away from the cortege as it inched through what passed for a square in the formerly blueshirt town of Macroom—with the family continuing to avoid ownership of the funeral, an old woman nobody knew was being allowed to lead the mourners at a slug's pace. Each of us realizing from the other's unsuitability to the location, that we were avoiding the same gig, we nodded to each other. I looked him over. He was tall, I'd say six-four, and prematurely stooped. Nothing a well-placed kick wouldn't buckle completely.

Note: As someone once said, length begets loathing. *The compiler*

He wore a yellow cravat and Steve Buscemi hair tailing over the collar of his black velvet jacket. I put him down as one of these people who dressed up well for a funeral as a triumph over the outlived.

'Poor Grattan,' I said mildly, 'it was a great shock.'

'*Rawthe*,' he said, with the dampened Rs of a person affecting that he has got above the vernacular. He affirmed nonetheless that another small Jameson would not be beneath him.

'The wife is holding up well,' I continued courteously, 'fair play to her.' I didn't know whether that was true at all.

'Do you know Margot?' he asked with sudden gruffness, one wicked, hairy eyebrow cocked now.

'No,' I said, because to partially tell the truth I'd never met Margot. 'She's a very fresh looking person,' I added.

'Why, pray tell, would she not be fresh?' said the mangy buzzard, still scrutinizing me, 'After all, the tool she was married to was rarely home.'

'Anyway. They're picking from our pen now,' I said, showing profound patience in ever guiding the talk back to more appropriate generic funereal patter. 'A great shock indeed, a man so fit and able, hardly past his prime, cut down like that.'

'Spare me the harmless bogman patois, that kind of codology doesn't even ambush Germans anymore,' said the posturing pock, displaying self-awareness of all the unattractive varieties, 'while I detect that you may well be a snake in the grass in your very own right, I can see you're no bumpkin. To take a bit of license with Aeschylus, *be as you wish to seem,* my dear fellow, and *seem as you are.*'

He was right, there is more to me than meets the eye, so I opted to let him off with the calm rejoinder, 'You seem to wish to seem to be a bit of an intellectual.'

'That Ryle goblin,' he said then, looking straight at me for reaction, 'the Ryle runt, you know him don't you? I saw the two of you talking away in the side porch throughout the ceremony. He is the one who is taking most strain there today. What do you think?'

There was a grain of truth in this. Though Ryle was entirely previously unknown to me, I had noted the tough little leatherette faced nut as he leaned next to me at the font. He had marks indicating he may have been crying his share over the preceding hours. Granted, he had the high viz on and after the mass was trying to distract himself with directing cars out of parking in the cathedral yard. And I had heard that he had also been a good help to Margot in supervising a mini-digger man he knew, to ensure that there was a very tidy job done on the family plot. But, true enough too, under Ryle's yellow vest and leather jacket was the blackest suit and under his eyes, the blackest bags. It would be in my own makeup to notice such things. 'Conducting civil discourse during mass signifies only fellow respect and knowledge of tradition,' I pointed out. 'I don't know Ryle from a bar of soap.'

From the way this soon-to-be-old man in the Heyns' Hotel continued to fix me with his look, I could already see that he had more he wanted to tell. I wasn't interested though. I had already shown my face at the occasion, shook what hands needed shaking, and generally done as little as I could get away with. After all, none of them was anything to me, not the man in the box any more than this man who looked not long off being in one while he sat on the barstool next to me entirely oblivious to his own predicament. In another few minutes the procession would have turned the top of the town towards the graveyard and I would finish my pint and make my way back to my car. That was my plan. The other wasn't having it. 'Just hold it right there,' he said, 'how do you fit into the picture?'

'I have to get going,' I said.

'Do you fuck! You do in my hole,' he blurted, pointing the claw at me. I wasn't surprised at the slip into profanity. I'll always know when someone is putting on urbanity. A blue Dub embarrassed at his roots. He regained his posture and continued with a dry laugh, 'I mean to say, what's your hurry my friend. Indulge me for a few minutes longer while I see if I can puzzle out what part of the plot you relate to.'

'I am not any good at plotting,' I said, 'I take each day as a blank page and I have nothing to do with the sorry man making that solitary journey. When enquiring after the reason for the decision to abandon the beloved man in this unnoteworthy stretch of the earth, I learned that his father's people were from Cork. I have a very low toleration for such people, for personal reasons I won't go into. I only came to the ceremony because a half-brother of Ryle is known to me. He owes me a few bob. The funeral can be a good spot to catch such persons off-kilter and remind them how short life can be.'

'Bullshit. You can't fool me. What does he owe you money for then, go on, do tell me.'

'For a little painting he commissioned me to do there last year.'

'Aha, an artist,' he pounced.

'I wouldn't say that,' I said modestly, 'I do it as much for the perspectives as the money.'

Note: it is true that the vantage available from the round roof of an average hayshed is often as good as is available to any person not keen on flying. But the painting was merely a mastered trade for the compiler. His artistic hobbies lay elsewhere. *The compiler*

'An artist. Yes. With that big grey noggin on you, I knew you were unsound in some manner,' he came back, doubt about my authenticity still tinkering with him, 'I'm sure you are involved in this in some way more than you're saying. Besides you're going nowhere with the town gridlocked. The execrable bugger has attracted more old bangers and camper vans than you'd see at a tinker's wedding.

'And a bloody Bugatti Veyron Super Sport,' he added as afterthought, his bitterness momentarily darting off in a slightly different direction, 'Some mystery patron Fletcher acquired. Wouldn't you know it!'

'I was surprised there weren't any musicians to give the deceased a better send-off,' said I lightly, 'I understand the wife is a gifted music teacher. Wouldn't you think she'd at least have got a couple of the pupils to scrawb out the Blackbird on the violin. But there we are. Don't we each deal with these things our own way, I suppose.'

'Never mind that,' said my companion, corrosion reappearing through his thin façade, 'What kind of dignity was there in inviting every kind of mongrel? I even saw some hussy in a hijab, up near the altar. And a nun with no headgear at all. Also, a scatter of Nigerians singing the Come all Ye Faithful to burst their lungs out. A bunch of new agers who looked like they haven't seen the inside of a church or a bathroom in thirty years. And an assortment of our own. Southside Georgians who didn't have the decency to take off the straw boaters, stood next to hairy bogmen who looked like they'd just been dragged backways through gorse, skangers, knackers, sambos, crusties, and a fucking foxy headed outright lunatic; bursting the seams of a shrine of our culture like it was a bleeding circus tent. Daly the little phlegm globule of course there too, dressing as fucking Finius Fogg now. I'm not religious in that way but where is the respect? We were only short of Pussy Riot. What is going on at all in this country? How did Margot allow it?'

Though spoken with authority, the lanky louser was entirely wrong in what he said. The gridlock was not a bother to me, in fact. I was better at these matters than Dubs like I assumed him to be. I had astutely positioned my vehicle in the Lidl car park at the outer extremities of where I had allowed Grattan's motley vehicular tribute might extend to. 'It was a decent turnout alright, fair play to the man,' I said, not to be found wanting in the protocols even if the other was making a show of himself. As I got up to go I let out a burst of the same psalm that had been stuck in my craw since the mass ... *Come let us adore him, joyful and triumphant* ...

'You should never *ever* sing,' he said emphatically. 'You have neither the voice nor the attitude for it.' He wasn't quite right there either. Anyone who feels like singing should be allowed do so to their heart's content. But I let him off with it. Unfortunately I noticed that he already had another pint ordered and settling for me and so I had to politely sit down again and continue the conversation. 'I knew neither of them at all,' I said, 'Grattan Fletcher or Suck Ryle, I mean.'

'I don't believe you,' he said plainly. And he looked like he was used to having his say.

I decided, for amusement, I'd pass a little more time of day with him. To build in an escape valve I made a performance of phoning my dearest, a neighbour's wife who'd lived with me for years. I told her I'd be home in no more than half an hour. It was a habit I had developed since the good person had moved on. But the heinous Dub was not to know the full story and he was now on notice that I was not a bowsy with nothing better to do than to spend the entire afternoon listening to some old stream of nonsense from the likes of him.

After a few hours of silent drinking he lifted his head from an iPad that he was very fond of and said, 'Surely you're not going to drive home now, my good man. The state of you.'

'What kind of old bollix are you anyway, with your hairdo?' I asked. For various reasons that I won't go into, I have very low toleration for this class of Dubliner.

It was then that he decided to tell me that he was Grattan's boss. 'So you're a great fellow,' I observed, 'and why did you come all the way here to pay respects to a departed man you clearly never cared for?'

'Oh I did care for him. I have been monitoring him and trying to steer the jerk right all my adult life, you might say,' said the man.

'I might and I mightn't,' I said.

He was losing his battle with the whiskey as his cheeks reddened and spittle sprayed from his lipless mouth, 'I wanted to ensure that for once in his wretched life, Grattan did what he was scheduled to do.'

'So if you came to make sure he went to ground on time, you've hardly made a good job of your final act of supervision,' I observed. 'While you sat in here all afternoon slobbering over good drink, supervising from your seat, the same Grattan could have gone anywhere other than into the ground.'

That seemed to touch a nerve. While I had him on the back foot, I took another shot in the near dark. 'My guess would be that you stole something of the dead man's?'

That paled him completely as he sucked on it.

'Yes,' I continued, 'that's it. You made a grab for the life's work of the dead fellow.' I had always been an above average marksman in the blind dangerous terrain where a little knowledge is all that is to be got.

With a shaking hand he took out a golden fountain pen of considerable value and ceremoniously took the lid off it. He then also produced a little business card—clearly marking him as a government man. He turned it over to write on the back. Trembling anger in his voice, he said, 'So you think you know something about Grattan and I, eh? You know jack shit.'

In a shock of rattled spite he laboriously lettered the URL to what he didn't yet realize was his own solitary life's work. It was intended as no act of largesse. He put this card in my hand and growled, 'Here then. Go feast on the truth.'

I will say that the soft warmness of the palm that touched my own in that process sent a small shiver of disgust up through my chassis.

According to the front of the thing, *An tÚsail Cathal Mac Gabhann Ph.D.* was the handle the wojious scrotum chose to go by.

Note: let me spell something out upfront in case you feel later that I had concealed a personal short position on this particular stock: I had not developed a great fondness for this Mac Gabhann operative from the get go. Nor would it be a known characteristic of my own to regularly alter my position on such matters as new information comes to light. So you can expect, as life has taught me to expect, that this story in its onward march will prove me right. *The compiler*

'Mac Gabhann?' I observed, 'a primary school teacher told me that that is a civil service hibernicization for the name, son of the devil. Or son of Smith. Something like that.'

The title *Secretary General* was embossed in gold over the logo of the *Department of Heritage and Monuments* and he thought he saw me staring at it. 'Indeed,' he said, used to people being unsure, 'SG, that is top dog.'

I replaced the pen in his pocket. 'That's a knock off, I observe,' I informed him, 'Brave, for a man in your position at a time when our country's patrons are lobbying for capital punishment in relation to IP infringement.'

'Like fuck it is,' he said, retrieving his slender tool, 'how did you get that?' He examined it and then myself in foggy suspicion.

'Mind you don't fall on the way to 166,' I said.

'How do you know which room I'm in?' he said, a further wave of superfluous anxiety bubbling through the arrogant stupefaction. He shook his head at me and took a crooked path to the elevator.

I turned over the antiquated bit of cardboard. It took my merry calloused fingers a few minutes to tap the Montblanc-smudged web address correctly into my phone. I waited for it to load via Heyns' one-star wifi.

Even with the very state of me I began to realize that what was slowly downloading before me was a thing that might interest me. Hiding out in the crowded open under an unpronounceable address, was a blog created by the man just gone to bed. Though started just a month back, there was a mishmash of material manually dated back nearly a year. It was clearly a work prodded to life by obsession and resentment.

The origin of this blog, our primary source? Six weeks back, in circumstances we may get around to, MacGabhann had incidentally acquired a dildo-shaped memory stick while raiding the desk of Leonard C. Ryle, a.k.a. Suck. The stick contained one file, INSURANCE.RTF—a diary of many (all, I don't know) outings undertaken by the two men, Ryle and Fletcher. Fletcher and Ryle. MacGabhann had found himself flummoxed. Fletcher's every movement, every network activity, had been under hawkish scrutiny by Mac Gabhann for years. Yet he'd never before noticed Ryle. Now he was seeing him at every turn. He had thus chanced on a crack in the certainties and instead of sensibly moving on as decent people do, he had become transfixed. MacGabhann thought everything had to fit in one picture, everyone had to have a reason to be in his world.

The crow just ascended to find the bar fridge empty in Room 166 had thought his own life's work had come to a head. His opportunity to fuck Grattan Fletcher over good and proper seemed to have landed right in his lap. In tandem with commencing his final disciplinary processes against Fletcher, he had commenced the blog I was looking at in the hope that some sense would emerge from it. The meat of this blog then: a meticulous correlation of notes from the fat, unactioned disciplinary files of Grattan Fletcher, with entries from Ryle's neatly tabulated document.

I scrolled for many minutes to get to the final entries. In the penultimate, Secretary General Mac Gabhann crowed that he was now ready to bring the motherlode disciplinary hearing together, to be followed by criminal proceedings against Assistant Secretary Grattan Fletcher. In the abrupt last entry however, dated two days prior to the sad occasion of our meeting, Mac Gabhann had simply written, *Just heard. Subject down. That murdering cow let the fucker off light. Case closed.*

As I put the phone away and left that hotel, trying to remember which direction Macroom's Lidl lay in, my mind was already a little bit sucked in. Reading between Mac Gabhann's copious lines I was already galloping towards resolution of the first enigma: the marks of grieving that I'd observed on Ryle. In the chapel porch, I confess, I'd been wondering how the same little buck had laid on the emotion—he not being the type who would ever be woefully moved by any other person's situation. If this blog was right, it turned out I'd wronged Ryle; that his feelings were genuine. His insurance.rtf had not paid up. Whatever reward Ryle had been promised in return for loyal service, had been put out of reach by the untimely passing. Who wouldn't have been grievously upset at that?

The next day I naturally enough took my tablet and returned to the blog. What else would you do if you woke up in a dead quiet house having recently suffered setbacks to your career aspirations, your co-habitation status, and your relationship with a lazy greyhound?

Note: The damage to the career tracks was two-fold. There was a bit of a mobility setback caused not so much by the latest fall from a hayshed roof as by being followed down by a five-gallon drum of red oxide paint. Worse was the recent letter from Dublin trashing my hopes of an imminent breakthrough in my real vocation (providing humanity with clues as to the real nature of their dispensation through a series of roman a clef renditions) [fn]. On top of that, I'd endured the obesity-related death of the greyhound. And not to harp on, there was the moving on of my personal associate. This came out of the blue while I was still in traction. She didn't move back next door. She left with a man who was well-dressed, attentive, and virile. In short, a foreigner; teaching me that in the human relationship there is no dividend accruing to multiple years of cautiously banked servility. *The compiler*

On that peculiarly warm September day the challenge seemed a timely diversion. The arrowhead eyebrow of Cathal Mac Gabhan and creamy cellulite of Sergeant Geas had fixed my life to the service of the story. I took on the challenge of parsing the viciously tedious contending narratives that spoke from the endlessly scrolling blog entitled, '*The ghastly Indiscretions of Assistant Secretary Fletcher and his elusive appurtenance.*'

As disciplined historian, I have kept my own contributions to the minimum. Only where absolutely essential to your quest for sense have I provided suggestions on the meaning or effect of any event. Where events had to be reconstructed, forensic analysis of similar facts and relevant personalities preceded any guesswork. Where liberties were taken with a smidgen of infilling chitchat, it was only to tide you over the most excruciatingly barren entries which nonetheless had to be provided for completeness, and to take the academic edge off the account. In short, true to my other trade, I've applied spots of preparatory putty and unobtrusive undercoat only where it was essential for the overall integrity of the finish. Otherwise, I let the facts speak for themselves. That is how you come to have this true account, a story of the frustrations of ordinary people bent on services to our country and our earth, a story that would otherwise have been lost.

----

^{fn} Footnote

This entirely gratuitous allusion to a lost career in novel writing is apparently directed at ourselves. We are thus forced to abandon the promise not to bother you with details of the sorry contractual debacle that led to us publishing, unedited, the pages from which we address you. The facts then. Each year for nearly a quarter of a century, the person in question submitted four manuscripts for our consideration. That is, 98 reams bound in blue baler twine. While awaiting our declination letter on the 98th, he managed to link with our commissioning editor on social media and filled her with inmails, imprecations for more substantial feedback, should his work be rejected on this occasion. Moved, she canvassed those of us who had seen his previous work. This process yielded the few extra explanatory sentences that she toned down and appended to the usual courteous two-line letter from ourselves.

Therein, the man was collegially advised, inter alia: to find something that he might have some of the basic ingredients for success at; if he did insist on continuing to write, to find a subject with which he had rudimentary familiarity (an outhouse painting manual was mentioned merely as an illustration); and to mercifully ease off on the clutter and tripe, etc. Fatally, our commissioning editor reached out further to the man to add a personal note. She aired a long standing concern of ours: that the familiarity with the modes and motivations of 'the devil' so regularly claimed in his submissions, could be unsettling for the modern reader. Rather than bluntly confronting him with the picture of incipient madness plainly evidenced in this worsening trend, we merely intimated in good faith that there might be something here that he would profit from airing in the company of a health professional. We ought to have known better of course. Every good turn makes an enemy.

Disclaimer on how the current ms. came to be published by ourselves

Nothing was heard from the person for months after this 98th rejection letter. It was hoped that at the very least the part of him which wished to be regarded as a literary player may have died. Then one soft October day, there he was again. He told reception he could wait all day. He sat in the foyer, swinging back and forth on a green plastic chair, occasionally bursting into tuneless song as doors closed along the corridor. Unfortunately nobody had thought to warn our new head of young adult literature. She failed to detect the air of menace. She approached. He spoke of an explosive new manuscript 'about people and purpose'. With a weakness for cetaceans, she heard *porpoise*. We all hear what we wish. He led her to believe that this book had already elicited an offer from a schlock publisher, Boland Books of 74 Pleasants Ave. She perceived an opportunity to impress by stealing a march on the competition. (Hard drugs and mid-life do not mix well.) She rushed to champion life into this project and had a contract signed with him before he clarified that he had a low tolerance for sea creatures and made no exception for the cetaceous, branding them by the company they had chosen, no better than fish. The next day the lawyers looked at the paperwork and confirmed that the counterparty's name reverberated vexatiously amongst their colleagues in litigation. The pragmatic course was for us not to contest the contract but to find the cheapest way in which to minimally comply with it.

On the term 'compiler' and the 'free flowing' narrative style

Our friend classed the manuscript he turned up with the next day, a '*documented novel*, an elemental contribution to the National narrative.' He wished to be referred to as *compiler*, rather than author. Frankly, it is plainly neither novel nor documented. However, we were more than happy not to have to refer to the poor artisan as author. Early terse exchanges demonstrated that each editorial observation would be met only with resentment and recalcitrance. Hence an executive call was made to withdraw all editorial services. Rather than devote our by then depleted editorial resources to a mudwrestle that would serve only to leave us all looking porcine, we were to retreat to the footnotes. We could meet our contractual obligations, just, by publishing an unedited print run of fifty, while flagging the product for our distributors and reviewers as a vanity dirge to be ignored as studiously as they would any MakeSpace fan-fiction. SUMMARY ADVISORY: WHERE INTERVENTION WAS COMPELLING WE TOOK THE PATH OF APPENDING FOOTNOTES SUCH AS THIS, RATHER THAN BREAKING THE SKIN ON THE SEPTIC PIT, TO COIN A PHRASE. You're on your own. *The Editors*

Not being found wanting

Chapter I

GRATTAN T. FLETCHER HAD ALWAYS BEEN well regarded. At work, having his head in the clouds by times was his only offence in most peoples' books. That, and walking around the office in white socks. Also there had been occasional murmurs about his fondness for garlic, scallions, and fetid cheeses.

There were few, if any, who could say that Fletcher had intentionally wronged them. In fact by the time we catch up with him, I understand that he may already have helped the occasional person where they had crossed his path looking for something that it was easy for him to give. Such enjoyment as he had taken in life so far, and that was considerable, he had tried to ensure was not at an obvious expense to anyone else.

Beyond that Fletcher had never made much of a mark on the road, white or black.

Then one Saturday he went into his daughter's room looking for an asthma pump for his granddaughter, who was all dressed up for their weekly outing to Sandycove. (Grattan was the youngest grandfather in the Southside.) He was stopped by the sight of an application form sitting inside the open top drawer of Saoirse's neat desk. He wasn't inclined for spying but Form 1400, issued by the Australian Government, drew him to it. On the front page, his twenty-one-year-old had put her own details neatly in boxes and on the ninth page, those of four-year-old Margot, as the accompanying family member. He developed a heavy pain in his chest.

Note: to set the context for you, this kicked off towards the end of 2013 when the main news items were Higgs getting the Nobel for his boson, a woman finding a leech up her nose after travel in Asia, and the country burning the furniture. *The compiler*

The days went by with Grattan Fletcher silently carrying the bolt in his pericardium, waiting for someone to drive it home with the actual news. Days turned to weeks.

A hyperactive man, Fletcher slowed with the weight of what those he loved were keeping from him. And with wondering how far back they'd decided he needed to be managed. Yet he wasn't going to make it real by asking about it.

His boss, one septic fuck called Cathal Mac Gabhann, always with an eye out for a Fletcher failing, phoned him on observing the slightly drooped gait and the decline in emails requesting assignments. With pleasure he observed, 'You're finally seeing the fifty speed limits ahead eh Grat?' Fletcher and Mac Gabhann were both pushing forty-eight.

Grattan Fletcher's trepidation dragged upon him relentlessly. His spirits were trammelled and his shoulders drooped with the strain. His appetite for conversation declined and his appetite for ice cream blossomed. Days ran into weeks until one evening his granddaughter looked into the kitchen and turned back on seeing him at the table with his head in his hands.

He changed there and then. There and then it was that he resolved, no matter what was to come tomorrow, he would like today to have been useful. Grattan Fletcher would seek to do something every day that might make him feel admired rather than thoughtfully considered by the people he loved. For every remaining day before and after Saoirse did whatever she was going to do, he would do whatever he was going to do. And then he would see.

So his life began to blister into resolutions that were to start him on a course more noble; a path that would quickly become the material of legends and that would elevate him into the kind of person at whose funeral thousands of vehicles of every sort would turn up, and on whose behalf moving graveside ovations would be rendered for the upliftment of anyone who had stuck with the cortege long enough to hear them.

Thus, one morning when Ryle arrived into the office, he found Fletcher back to full glow and bluster, the miasma of the preceding days entirely dissipated. As open as a child, he blurted,

'I'm ashamed to say, Len, that I have been indulging despondent thoughts. And deflecting blame even onto the woman I love to the core. Like a coward I've been avoiding the real opportunities that every new day bring, while dwelling on disappointments and fears. Do you see what I'm saying?'

'To tell the truth of me, boss,' said Ryle in his most upbeat manner, 'I couldn't give a living shit.' Or some words to that effect. Ryle knew his man. Peculiar turns of phrase and new perspectives on the same old situation were merely an indicator that Fletcher was immersed in a new book. It would pass. Though he was a slow reader.

'Loving her is easier than anything I'll ever …' Fletcher paused, grinning like a man who had just discovered one of the more rewarding forms of madness.

'For the love of jesus,' was all Ryle said.

'The fact is that Margot is not a bit less perfect than the day I met her and I know if she's not talking to me about something, she has her reasons. She will manage it the way she sees fit.' To describe Margot as Grattan's better half would have been a bit of an underassessment. It would be apt to say that after several years together, they were still very great with each other. She was the darling daughter of a man who had made a lot of money in pharmaceuticals and a woman who was well known for acting. She herself was a modestly talented musician but an outstanding teacher of music. She had transferred smoothly from an affection-filled and untroubled childhood to an affection-filled adulthood with Fletcher. She had a big crop of red-brown hair, a ready smile, eyes that lingered on you and a sympathetic ear for every sort. It was no accident that things fell right for Margot in her life because Margot got as good as she gave.

'No worse, indeed,' said Ryle, 'and no better for that matter. Still a fair one for the grub I presume? Burly women don't show mileage.' Suck Ryle had never married. Women didn't tend to maintain an affectionate view of him, the few that were initially duped by his strong chin and unnational weathered look, into ever forming one at all.

'And here,' continued Fletcher, more worryingly for Ryle.

He waved his arm towards the rest of the formerly ostentatious pile created by strivers and speculators of the Victorian era, now reduced to serving as an overheated dry-walled out-office for the executive team of the Department of Heritage and Monuments, the musty second-floor return of which he had been consigned to for some years, 'Here? What do you notice here?'

'Nearly lunch time,' said Suck.

'Exactly!' said the big fellow, Assistant Secretary Grattan Fletcher, 'It's past midday and what impact have you and I made here? Notice my good friend that nothing at all has changed. Or rather should I say, WE HAVE CHANGED NOTHING!'

That was just the way Ryle liked it. He had worked hard for years at avoiding the attention of anyone with the means and inclination to lessen the comfort of his tenure. After some ups and downs in his earlier life Leonard Suck Ryle had gone steady as a storeman at an Office of Public Works depot. There he had pared his responsibilities down to attending at 10 am when the trucks went out to worksites, rinsing the dust off one or two shovels when they returned at 4 pm, and being there on Saturdays to help the foreman load up some unwanted heritage items that had been left aside for him. Then some years back Ryle had neglected to return to the stores after a two week secondment to the Heritage and Monuments office to help with trolleying box files between floors. He had made certain observations about Fletcher during those two weeks of furtive scurrying. Mainly, that this airy fount of Irish Times class opinions was for some reason blanked out of the top man Mac Gabhann's roll when it came to assigning responsibilities. Ryle had speculated then, very astutely even for him, that Fletcher might provide a useful screen behind which to hide. Ryle and his trolley had since gathered mould in an alcove off Fletcher's return. That is to say, he was a clinker on the arse of the arse of the building. And Fletcher, having no appreciation of the things that were important in Ryle's life, had concluded that he was a thoroughly loyal understudy. For that, Fletcher was ready to forgive certain of the little man's character flaws; the few that even he, an unashamedly pluralistic sort, was unable to entirely fail to notice. In short, Ryle and Fletcher were united only in each being useless to both God and man.

'Mac Gabhann seems happy enough with what we've achieved,' said Ryle.

'Is that all there is to it in the end?' asked Fletcher staring Suck Ryle in the face. 'Trying to avoid the evil eye of another man? That's all he is, after all, Ryle.'

'I don't know about that,' said Ryle.

'I assure you,' said Fletcher, 'just another man. One whose opinions are not even as valuable as your own. Yet we must now divine his every mood. Why? Merely by dint of him having played the game like the *cutehure* Kerryman that he is, forgive my French, and risen above his station. Yet you and I know he is wrong in most things. A classic bureaucrat. He doesn't care at the end of the day. The difference with people like you and I Ryle is that we *do*.'

Note: The compiler wishes it to be recorded that based on his expertise in accents and regional character traits, drawn from many years painting every corner of the country, and despite what it says in Mac Gabhann's biography, on his LinkedIn profile, and in the birth registry, and despite there not being an imaginable reason why anyone not born in Kerry would claim to have been, the compiler sticks to his assertion that Mac Satan's true spawning ground was somewhere in the sewers of Ballsbridge or Blackrock. *The compiler*

'What?'

'We do care.'

'About what?'

'Why, about it all, Ryle. Let's be men. We care about it all and deep down our most fundamental desire gets subdued by paperwork and directives every day, our desire to tear back all the layers of nonsense and stand up to fight for what's right. You know, the generation before us, they believed they could change the world. And they had the valour to stand up and the audacity to do something about it. When did that age of idealism die out and give way to an epidemic of exhausted irony and ready conforming?'

'*Who?*' said Ryle, 'Fucken *hippies?* They never died out at all. They're all below in Thomastown, preaching away on dal, dole, and dope. Happy as larry.'

It was twelve o'clock and Fletcher took out his foil-wrapped sandwiches as Ryle headed out for the buffet in Dwyer's, believing that the dangerous flutter in Fletcher's thinking would have died down by the time he got back.

But at three o'clock Fletcher was more exercised if anything. 'Listen,' he said, 'I know you're a store man and I don't have a right to call on you for anything other than logistical support.'

'Gormless gobshite. Would you ever fuck off and don't be annoying me,' said Ryle, in not so many words.

'Hear me out,' said Fletcher, 'it will pay you to do so.'

'Oh?' said Ryle, looking up from the Racing Post.

'This may sound far-fetched, but do you know what this country needs?'

'What was it you said about paying?' said Ryle, whose instinct with high-flown types was to nail down any mention of benefits immediately as they arose.

'It needs leadership. An ordinary man or woman who is not afraid. A catalyst, really. When people have been wronged, they know it, they understand it, they feel it to their core. But the certainty of the power stacked against them usually grinds them into doubt, and eventually into accepting their diminished lot, diminished. It sometimes just needs someone outside to tell you that *yes*, you are entitled to feel angry, *enraged!* And that, *yes,* there are things you can do to be heard. You know what Suck, I believe I could provide that voice for some. Everyone expects someone else to step out in front. In fact let me swear this to you here my friend, and you can look back and say that of the many who heard it, you were the first. *Grattan Fletcher will not be found wanting! No sir!* From this day on, he will not shy away from the demands of leadership. He will not wilt in front of doubters. His objectives will not be diluted by cold water pourers. He will leave all the griping to others. He will enable people to be their own agents. He will defend the despondent and lead the confused.'

'Leading the whole Nation then eh, what the fuck is the fat

one putting in your panini these days?' Ryle enquired, interested only in a response to his earlier question.

'*The whole Nation?* Maybe, yes, why not? You look incredulous,' said Fletcher.

'Nation me hole,' said Ryle, 'there never was one. That is the kind of talk when it was stirred up in the past that only ever led to misfortune. We're citizens of the world and there's no world law, only take care of your own interests and avoid revolutions.'

'One man could not do it, I hear you say,' said Fletcher, not hearing anything, 'Well, look at Patrick, or better, Brian Boru.'

'You're not them,' observed Suck Ryle, 'for one thing you don't have any good news for anyone.'

'Or Daniel O'Connell.'

'Wasn't he a rackrent landlord?'

'The point is, it always takes someone from the educated, established classes, someone who knows how the machine works, to turn around and lead the people who are ground down by it. Think of Tone, Lenin, Ghandi …'

'I see your point now,' Ryle cut him off, 'You too don't want an end to ascendency, just yourself to be the one in charge.'

'No no, that's not it. These men's *objectives* are not relevant to my point. It's that one man with the balls to stand up and lead can have the ability to sweep the country along with him. What do you have to say to that?'

Ryle looked out the window. The rain was pissing down and he was keeping an eye out for a break so he wouldn't get soaked on the walk home. Consideration of the size of Fletcher's testicles was unlikely to be granted purchase upon his reverie.

'I know what you're thinking,' said Fletcher mistakenly. 'I've thought the same until this day. But if everyone takes that attitude nothing happens. The great James Fintan Lalor said *Remember this—that somewhere and somehow, and by somebody, a beginning must be made.*'

'I knew a few Lalors but never heard of a Fintan,' said Ryle, 'what the fuck is he to me?'

'He's the man who called a halt; the man but for whom Ireland would now look like Scotland … Never mind. Just think, on the first day that Jim Larkin started talking to a few small groups of people, did he have any idea how many would ultimately row in behind him. No! *No! Mr. Leonard Ryle, he did not.* He just took it one bit at a time. That's the way to do it. Then we'll turn around and see where we are at the end of it. You, my friend, might be surprised. I don't want to say it too loud yet, but I intend to set my targets high for the first time. And why shy away from the highest target, the bloody Park? *Now! What do you have to say to that my friend!*

Ryle looked back at Grattan Fletcher in derision where a normal person would have looked in concern. He had seen the man temporarily transported before. Back when he'd been researching castles he got in the habit of stooping in every doorway and revealing to everyone in the office which chieftaincy their people stemmed from. And back when he'd been reading Brehon law he would give half an hour every day discussing alternative mechanisms of trade and restorative justice with Roshan, a master of the Vedas who stacked shelves in the Spar. Immersion with Fletcher tended to be wholehearted. But never before to this extent, where even grand planning made an appearance. Fletcher might have been many things but this pomposity was a foreign thing out of him. Ryle laughed his sometimes wheezy laugh. 'Maybe you should go home and lie down. Finish up whatever it is you're reading. Or else you will finish up in the park alright. The other end of it.'

'I'm serious,' said Fletcher coming closer, his face intense with chive vapours. He tuned down to a confidential tone. 'You just think about it. Just think of who the people have elected up to now. Think about that, Len! Even before I've started my mission I'd nearly be able to beat the usual suspects: TV celebrities, politicians who have managed never to offend anyone, single-issue campaigners … and forgive me for saying it, but in a couple of cases, fatuous windbags. What does that tell you?'

'It tells me that half the people that vote are gobshites and the other half are only having a laugh.'

'You'll have to abandon that cynicism when you are at my side. And you will. Let me make that promise to you, my little friend. Your hardened shield of negativity will fall away and your eyes will be opened in the innocent enthusiasm I have no doubt you once enjoyed, just as soon as you see the greatness of our people once again unleashed. Just as soon as you see that the reason for all the bad directions we have taken is that the people are just weary and don't know which way to turn. They can see nothing better. There's nobody who has truly purged themselves of self-interest standing up to give them the leadership that they deserve. But by the time our work is done there will be no stopping them. And one side effect of that, though not the main objective needless to say, because doing good and right should need no reward: the people will come out en masse to insist that they have Grattan Fletcher for their President. And let me tell you this, though you know me as a humble man, I will go there as directed. Not for the perks, which I will repudiate. I don't need more than I have. But for the fact that it will give me the forum to do more, to elevate the voices of the voiceless, to demand the reforms that people are crying out for, to cement the gains you and I will have already made by then.'

Ryle said nothing.

'No, I don't need more than I have.' A slightly less assured look had come over Grattan Fletcher's face at the sound of rainwater running down the cast-iron drainpipe outside his window. He was on the bike today. 'But I also don't want less. I will fight every day now, come what may.'

'Come what may, eh?' said Ryle, 'what's that about?'

Had he truly been a friend, Ryle would have been very worried for Fletcher's wellness at this point. But he was still laughing. He eased up with the snorting for a fraction of a second when Grattan added, 'And then you. You, my loyal right hand man, you can be assured that you will not be forgotten. You have my word. I swear to you now, and you know what my honour means to me, I swear to you that I will take you with me. You will become my most senior adviser with your own suite out in Áras. There's precedent. You will be bumped up several grades.

◊

Ryle's principal thought as he walked back towards Donnybrook with the sun making a surprise break through the clouds, remained that Fletcher was having some kind of a flowery mental episode. He was thinking of how he could summarize and tart up the effusions for amusing delivery to two people he would be meeting at the Harold's Cross greyhound track later that evening, people also hanging out in forgotten corners of the city. They had no patience for long stories. *My lad is going for President.* He knew that would give them a rise. He'd already briefly described Fletcher to them, the closest he had to a boss. Ryle's ungracious summary: *a man with his head up his arse; over-educated and unable to do the most basic practical thing; but well able to waffle on for hours about some old nonsense he's latched on to at the historical book club the previous night; still unhealthily devoted to the first woman he ever rode and to the premature grandchild he'd got out of her; but, maybe not the worst of them at the back of it all.*

Yet Suck Ryle felt a faint tingle in his marrow as he quick stepped back towards his lair on Stratford Street with a little patch of blue sky appearing over the lake in Herbert Park. There were very few bones in Suck Ryle's body that were not cute. Of course, Ryle well knew that Fletcher had always been given to temporary flights. He could persuade anyone who'd listen that he was descended from the last kings of Munster. And yes, this departure was only made more far-fetched for being into the future rather than the past. He would give a hundred to one against Fletcher even remembering his Presidential ambitions tomorrow. A million to one against it ever coming to pass. Yet he couldn't see a reason to spurn a bet where the stake was already covered, no matter how long the odds.

When he got into his house he addressed his nameless housemate on the subject. 'I see no harm in giving the man a bit of rope on this,' he mused. He was met with a stoic green gaze.

During the course of the evening he occasionally returned to the thought that a stint in the East Wing of the Presidential mansion with a doubled salary would do him no harm. Maybe he could even consider a uniformed role—aide de camp or such. He would have to ensure that his previous bits of military history remained buried.

As he ambled along by Beggar's Bush the next morning, Ryle saw the situation from another angle. If the lunatic who was his human shield insisted on heading out on whatever missions it was that he envisaged, Ryle in fact had only two options. Back to stores or go along and try to keep out of the firing line. The stores in fact could be draughty in winter and did not have sufficient bandwidth for the various web-based activities to which he was now accustomed.

When Ryle stepped through the return, Fletcher stood from his laptop entirely kitted in Southern Rock extreme sports gear. 'What kept you, Len?' he said impatiently. 'It's ten thirty already. Didn't you know we were starting today?'

'What exactly have you in mind?' said Ryle.

'Bravo!' cried Fletcher. 'Bravo! My loyal man puts his faith in me as I never doubted he would.'

'It's not that so much,' said Ryle, in whom faith had never been a virtue.

'Don't be coy,' said Fletcher. 'There'll be no room for that when we face tough challenges. No. You believe in Grattan Fletcher's ability to lead the people. You believe in me. That is all that counts and even though I didn't really doubt it, let me say that I'm moved.'

'Well sure, you might at least make the Senate,' said Ryle, 'the pail lords. I understand there's a seat there for every kind of pompous old bag who thinks we should pay to hear him express methane through his nasal passages.'

'That's my sarcastic old friend,' said Fletcher laughing, and reaching to touch the little person's back. Undeterred by Ryle shouldering him away, he continued, 'You have now confirmed what I always suspected—that behind the façade you do care. You care like hell.'

At this point Ryle decided on creating a log of all of Fletcher's activities as insurance against any reneging. 'What do you have in mind?' he repeated, flat.

'Can you get an OPW van from the stores?' said Fletcher.

'I can, of course,' said Ryle whose position in many situations was weakened by overreach, him being private about the list of things he couldn't easily do. 'What do you want it for?'

'Carlow seems the obvious place to start,' said Fletcher, ready to share all of the logic that had led up to this conclusion if only Ryle were to ask. 'And should sooner than anywhere allow us to stumble on an occasion that calls for our interventions.'

How anyone with even one or two cylinders firing right could think Carlow a suitable starting place for anything, Ryle did not even wish to think about. Ryle knew it well as a tidy little county wherein very little went astray. Every bone was already picked. But Ryle's head was firing on all three cylinders. He decided that any question he might ask was as meaningless as the next one it would lead to. It was after a quick and not entirely incorrect assessment of the sum total of these circumstances that Suck Ryle shrugged and set out for his old Office of Public Works stores that first day of the saga, equipped with a roller door master key that he had kept for the rainy day.

◊

A lanky shadow stood at the third floor window of Northumberland Manse. Cathal Mac Gabhann barely disturbed one side of the blinds on his window as the blue-with-orange-striped OPW Transit stopped in the bus lane on the road below. His black eyes barely moved as he observed a figure, unmistakable even when togged in the unlikely gear, scurry out across the crunchy pebbles of the front parking area below, like a good kid mitching. The woolly head gave a quick scan behind him before jumping into the waiting vehicle. Mac Gabhann picked up his iPhone and considered making a call. But then he put it back. It made a reassuringly firm noise on the polished cherry-veneered surface of his desk. What would pass for a girlish smile if it were seen on the mug of a normal person, cracked the thin lips of the conniving old Dublin bastard.

Nothing's bad but could be worse

Chapter II

'WITH ALL DUE RESPECT, my dear friend,' said Grattan Fletcher, 'can you not drive a little faster?'

Ryle was keeping the van at a constant twenty-five km/h despite Fletcher's anxiety to get to the doing. 'Don't you understand?' Ryle said. 'This city is full of our people. Some in unmarked vehicles. The basic courtesy is never to overtake another person. That way nobody gets showed up.' They had only just crossed the Dublin county line when Ryle indicated that he needed to stop for a bite to eat. He was heavy on fuel, though showed no signs of where he put it.

At the roadside Embassy Hotel, everything spoke of bankruptcy law reformed too late. There was no recovery in the empty restaurant. Only one candescent bulb was working. Even under such a kindness of light it was clear that the white table cloths could have done with a wash. The carpet had had trapezoidal fading that described the path of the sun across the bay window. The situation was going hard on Fletcher, who could already foresee there being few vegetarian options here.

After Ryle ensured that Fletcher had cash, they put their jackets on the backs of chairs at a table by the door and proceeded to the carvery. At the cash register, Fletcher with one scoop of mash on his plate said to Ryle, who had a tray with a mountain of meat, every boiled veg, and two muffins, 'Do you want to go dutch or will we pay alternately?'

'Are you serious? We're not on a fucking date,' said Ryle, nodding at the chef who had come out to the till. 'Come on now, this woman can't wait all day. He gives twice who gives quickly.'

They had barely started eating when in came a party of tanned fuckers with polished teeth and regularly worn suits. This lot,

five male and a female, sat within overhearing distance for two
men with keen ears and with nothing new to say to each other.
The group's prudence was tempered by excitement at being the
men who were writing the history now. This lot ordered instant
americanos, not having the stomachs for anything the Embassy's
cook might have put her hands to.

Ryle was a pub quiz master and he had a head like a basin
for current affairs trivia. Thus he knew immediately the names
of everyone at the table. A senior man from each of the three
main parties was present. Also reporting for duty were a media
mogul, an independent opinion writer from the Irish Times,
and a person only a few weeks out of RTÉ, now working as a
ministerial press secretary. Grattan Fletcher, whose sensibilities
were cultivated in a more ideal world, did not recognize any.

'So this is the story,' Minister Cooney was saying quietly and
urgently. 'My principal has developed some kind of Padre Pio
complex and is actually serious when he talks about incurring
some suffering in our own diocese in solidarity with the ordinary
person. He is actually genuine in his intent to decommission the
composting chamber. Believe me, all the young colts and old
geldings from our own party are just as alarmed as any of yours'
about this turn of events. We all need to work together to stop
it. Needless to say, we have to be circumspect in our handling
of this matter.'

'I'm not so sure about subterfuge,' said the Labour minister.
'I thought this was going to be an open and frank cross-party
exchange of views. Always a healthy thing to my mind.'

'Would you cop yourself on,' said Cooney, 'your lot are going
to get strafed, next time out. You'll need the refugee centre more
than anyone.'

Grattan Fletcher was all ears. He was a great constitutionalist
and ardent 26 County Republican. As such he had been deeply
affronted in recent times by rumours that the current Taoiseach,
an uncouth bogman with no appreciation for the finer points
of any argument, was planning to ride roughshod through the
sacred institutions. This gathering at the next table, a ghastly
banality to you or I, impacted as a divine affirmation upon the

unstable environment that was extensive within Fletcher's head at that time.

Cooney continued with only minor interruptions. He addressed the nodding opposition senior, 'You go ahead with all guns firing in the campaign for a *No*. We'll float the Yes brand on the back of a couple of red herrings that even you should be able to spear. And we all leave the real arguments unsaid. If any new arguments are to be formulated by the Yes men whom we wheel out, you will get the usual anonymous sms in advance, spelling out how you can trip them up. You get to come out of this looking slightly detoxified with a little victory in the bag. And for us, when the good people finally realize that they've spurned the only opportunity to cull the classes they so detest, when they face up to the fact that the government they get is no slimmer than they deserve, we'll be able to shrug and say at least we tried our best. So there's something in it for everyone.' The others nodded.

'Just as long as you *do* lose,' stammered the opinion writer, 'which, as I often say, is about as likely now as David Norris heading off for a quickie with Regina, or to put it more succinctly ...'

'For fucksake, Quentin,' said the squat media owner. 'Just tell us the numbers.'

'Yes indeed, of course,' he spluttered, 'well right now only twenty percent are committed to saving Seanad Éireann. Even with all of those being of the class who will get out and vote, that is, all the people who themselves have opinions that they'd one day like to be paid sixty grand a year for, it's quite literally an impossible hill to climb.'

'Yes,' said the ex-RTÉ woman with more flourish, 'the masses are sharpening the knives, still not quite believing the turkeys are offering a Christmas lunch.'

'Good enough,' Cooney said.

'That doesn't sound very fucking good to me,' said the doubtful Labour man.

Cooney ignored this and focussed his charm on the media. Well I'm looking at three people here who won't have to struggle to get their pearls of wisdom swallowed by the public, not after the next election. I'm thinking the fucking plebs should be forced to pay each of you that sixty grand for worthy pontification as you eat oysters with Harris and Norris.'

'I personally feel offended by that characterization,' smiled the woman in a familiar kind of way. 'Though I do think there's a lot a woman with my experience could contribute from the second chamber.'

'We'll talk about that later,' said the mogul with a laugh and a buddha-like nudge. Even with all the money in the world there would be no budge out of Vanessa for him.

'So, assuming you're OK with that,' Cooney continued with drive, not a Minister for no reason, 'your job is simple. For the duration of our little alliance, I ask you only to pump two simple points. The first: keep repeating that the polls say it's a done deal. That will keep the lazy sixty percent away thinking there are enough hands on the axe. The second is to feed a few lines about suspicions of a government power grab. That will fire up the *independent thinkers* who are so determined not to be fooled that they'd vote against a nine-month summer if any of the *elites* advocated it to them. That paranoid bunch can always be relied on to snatch defeat from the jaws of victory.' He turned to the mogul again, 'Can we call on you to turn off the Internet for half an hour? If we can get that lot off the comments boards and out in the sunshine on the day we could easily aim to add a couple of notches to the twenty percent. Then with every one of the twenty-two-percent No voters all turning out and a forty-percent total turnout *democracy* will win hands-down.'

'How fortuitous is this?' Fletcher said as he nudged Ryle.

'What do you mean, boss?' asked Ryle.

'Well it was surely fate that stopped us here in this plain, honest-to-goodness establishment only to bump into a fine group of ordinary fellow citizens in desperate need of our assistance. You see and hear as I do. These hard-pressed ordinary folk of the silent middle have stopped in for a hurried break from their working day. Why? Because they care. They have anticipated as have I, the encroaching barbarian assault on the cornerstones of our democratic institutions. Even if some of their discourse in relation to the Senate tends to the pejorative we have to make allowances. This is the language of the regular people. Their hearts are in the right place and they are wanting only of leadership in the constructive channelling of their unrest.'

'That's fucking retarded,' observed Ryle, finally getting concerned as he examined Fletcher's face for loose wires. 'Wait a minute, do you really mean to tell me you don't know who any of those cunts are?'

It was too late. Grattan Fletcher stood and cleared his throat. He stepped over to the other table with his hand extended toward Cooney. Suck Ryle took his plate with him to a further away table, concerned to have a chance to finish his turnips. Though they were cold and leathery, he was not inclined to leave anything paid for on a plate.

'I'm delighted to meet you good people,' said Fletcher.

Cooney nodded and briefly touched the generously soft hand that was offered to him with an unsmiling shake. 'What's your name, my friend?' he said, in the deft manner of an experienced politician quickly assessing whether a person's affection was of any value to him. The others looked down at phones, all hoping the tall, soft man in the blue tracksuit was a crackpot. They had chosen to meet in a zombie hotel precisely because none wanted to have to actually dish out the stewed explanation of a cross-party sound check to chance onlookers.

'The name is Grattan Fletcher. And in the matter that binds us together, as well as in being your fellow Republican, a citizen who will stand, you may regard me also as your humble servant.'

'Well Grafton, that's very good indeed,' said Cooney, putting a hand on the maroon jacket of the mogul. 'Michael here will stand you your drink of choice?'

'Oh? Well since you ask, I do rather approve of what the Chileans have done with merlot,' said Grattan, pulling out a chair, 'but perhaps we can discuss wines another time. Maybe after we've worked out our strategies.'

'No, I insist, go have a drink on us right now,' said Cooney, nodding towards the bar and pushing the spare chair back into the table.

'No no, you don't understand, I am offering to join your good fight. I can provide, if I may say so, strategic insights, a help with putting structure on the raw emotion if you will.'

Cooney looked to a table in the foyer and two big dopy fuckers entered. One came to Grattan and said, 'Come on now buddy, there's a good man. It's a private meeting going on here.' When Grattan failed to respond to their soft words of encouragement, they firmed the words up. Grattan became a little worked up, excitable in his speech, in a panic to explain that his motives were good. The lump men then each took an elbow. Grattan still refused to be moved, struggling with vigour that surprised them all and made Ryle a little bit proud of the man despite his own worse nature. The people at the table looked every other way as Grattan pleaded with them to hear him out. To his credit, even under this duress, he still chose his words finely and did not let an intemperate one come to his lips, not even under the extreme provocation of being called a chipped up fucker by one of his escorts.

They ended up taking him out to a cloakroom. By the sounds of things he still struggled to come back in, still talking. At that stage, he may have received a few digs. He went quiet. When the Garda detail re-entered they cast an eye in the direction of Ryle who was eating the last of the turnip. 'Are you with him?' one of them asked.

'Am I fuck,' said Ryle, 'do I look like a man has time to be talking to gobshites?'

'Oh?' said one of the Guards, annoyed with Ryle's tone. Ryle's most submissive effects were often mistaken as mocking. As it happened, the particular sergeant at hand was already suffering a major toothache, which was not Ryle's fault at all, but caused by a massive rotting hole in his skull. And he had been observing Ryle earlier. Anyway, the net result was that he walked over and picked the phone out of Ryle's hand. 'You do know it's illegal to make digital recordings of people's conversations without their written consent?'

'I was only playing scrabble, your honour,' said Ryle.

The second policeman happened to know how to operate

mobile phone menus and was able to play back Ryle's recording of Cooney's instructions to the team. Fair enough, this had not been made by any other party than Ryle. But in Ryle's defence, it had been made as an idle contingency rather than with any concrete plan for extortion yet in mind. Or, if he had been half thinking of having a quiet word on the subject, the most he would have asked from Cooney in payment for deleting it was a couple of bettable tips for the budget. Instead, the unfortunate low-level public servant, one of the ones who always gets it in the neck, now had the other Garda dribbling Lucosade from his glass into the memory slot on his phone.

A person as genuine and natural to ill temper as Suck Ryle can only strive to seem pleasant for short stretches and Ryle had just exited that particular runway. He'd been a star hurler for Ballyhale under-14's back in a time when you didn't have to train or stop smoking to achieve such glory, and he still retained the agility to pick up the heavy glass Lucosade bottle and crack it off the officer's shaved temple before anyone had even anticipated such a move. He lacked the suppleness, however, to worm his way out of the embrace of the other detective.

When they got him out in the cloakroom he was placed on the floor next to the warm carcass of Grattan Fletcher and there the policemen broke several of his ribs with their patent shoes. They took turns and the activity seemed at least to bring some release of pleasure into their day.

When they left, Fletcher picked himself up and dusted the tracksuit, gallantly saying that it was nothing. 'One has to be braced for the occasional misunderstanding and indeed for a little rough and tumble in first reaching out. I will not be deterred by this. Besides, I know who sent those goons.'

'*Who sent them!*' said Ryle, very sore indeed. 'What the fuck are you on about now you scuttering muppet? Have you no iota of worldly sense inside you whatsofuckingever?'

Grattan headed out towards the van with the bouncing of his silver-tipped curls barely dampened by the persisting shower. Ryle waited in the cloakroom watching the cops and then the bronzed ones leave individually, all bar two. He watched the

Lucosade cop drive off with the Labour minister and Cooney's cop sit into the silver BMW to sullenly tap the wheel. 'Ho ho?' said Ryle to himself, 'what's this crack?' Ryle re-entered the lobby where Cooney, sure enough, was at the counter quietly asking if there was a room that had recently been made up and what it would cost for him and his assistant to avail of it for three or four minutes. Vanessa the liaison woman hung to one side acting like she wasn't a bit worked up, scanning mails on a tablet. Ryle sidled up unnoticed and removed a pencil from the counter. He examined it, a 2H. He knew his pencils, technical drawing being the only subject he got an A for in the Intermediate Certificate Examinations back in '85. Commanding all of his energy to one sweet movement he stabbed Cooney in the arse hole or thereabouts. He couldn't swear to his accuracy but was satisfied that he wasn't far off since most of the pencil had disappeared. It seemed to take a fair bit of twisting and levering for the visibly upset woman to remove it as the Minster lay screaming on the carpet.

As he worked the van out of the car park Ryle refused to give way to an incoming ambulance.

'Do you not even know the most basic fundamental thing about civic responsibility my good man?' asked Fletcher, mortified. 'There may be somebody sick in that hotel. In future, all things considered, I may take the wheel myself.'

Invisibility has some uses and Ryle was in no way worried enough to increase speed as he drove back towards Northumberland Rd. By the time they were on Stephen's Green the Herald already had a late edition headline, 'I'm Fine says Minister' with the sub, 'Cooney in for routine procedure, assures that the Abolitionists have it.'

Stopped in the bus lane again, Fletcher delayed in getting out. 'How are you bearing up, Len?'

'Not very well,' said Ryle who was struggling to breathe and had not suffered this kind of bruising and possible breakage for a good couple of years.

'Me too,' said Fletcher. 'But nobody said it was going to be easy.'

'Would you mind getting out like a good man,' said Ryle, a taxi up his hole with nothing better to do than sit there hooting.

'Still, as my Grandfather used to say, nothing's bad but could be worse. A warm bath and a pleasant evening at home will ease matters and have us fresh as daisies for tomorrow,' said Fletcher through lips that were naturally a lumpy purple, nothing to do with the beating which had not touched his face. 'A little earlier, if I may make so bold.'

'I'm going on a week's sick leave so you can go where you fucking want on your own tomorrow, you daft coot.'

Fletcher got out and Ryle drove on.

The problem was that Ryle never took leave. He didn't like to not go out of his house on weekdays. That was because Suck Ryle had something of a Protestant work ethic, always feeling the need to show up.

◊

Having realized at a young age that he was different, Leonard Ryle had been confronted with this part of his character. A story had been directed for his attention by sixth-class lads on his first day in primary school.

The boys had told him the old story of one Molly Teegan on her first day in the big house. *Old Colonel Cromwell Kox hobbled out of his bed to get a hold of the new chambermaid.* (Kox by this time was no longer the man he had once been; not since the night in '22 when the local IRA flying squad had inflicted some damage while escorting him to his front lawn whereupon to botch his execution.) *Young Molly wriggled and dodged until the old lad had a raging horn. The commotion brought the Scottish housekeeper in to shout, 'Still thee beast and dinay hurt the gentleman!' You should go home ask your father's auld wan did she ever know Molly Teegan?'*

Molly of course was the name of the wizened wonder who had sat in the best chair in Ryle's house watching Coronation Street for decades. So he wasn't slow in putting two and two together. After a short altercation in which he stabbed the bigger lad in the thigh with a junior pocket knife and vomited on the other's shoes (to the current day Ryle has the ability to vomit at will), the fledgling scholar had taken himself home to treat himself to a half day off school.

Staring in the mirror that afternoon, young Leonard had noted unemotionally his yellowish complexion. He then thought of the Christmas hampers that came from a Dowager Millicent Kox in England, addressed to his father, also a placid sallow man. He had then readily accepted that his grandmother had been prodded by the gentry. The circumstances were of no relevance to him. All that mattered was that he knew from that young age that he was going to grow up a level-headed man.

He had later read that Colonel Welbore Cromwell Kox, considered a fair landlord by everyone except tenants and household staff, had died without any issue. The rump of the estate had been left to the English Fox Hound Breeders Society. All that went to the grandson was a confirmation name. Moll had insisted. The Bishop of course suspected that Cromwell was not the name of any saint. And he guessed that the crimson-lipped ancient in the see-through summer frock who glared up from the front pew had not insisted on this name for the yellow-faced boy out of pure love for either Cromwell or the boy. But he was a quiescent man of his kind and he said to the Parish Priest, 'Sure I suppose there's no harm in it, and for that matter she's right in saying that neither Lazarian nor Brigid was too much of a saint either.'

Leonard Patrick Cromwell Ryle had remained an only child, a solitary upbringing that had trained him well for the friendless life he was about to lead. He was left with no official relations on the quality side and far too many unofficial ones, his multiplicity of maternal cousins being stock he couldn't get any value or sense out of.

Anyway, God help the poor man, the Protestant in him would put up with the sore ribs and have him turning up the next morning in the arse of the arse of Northumberland Manse like the bad penny that he was, to see whether the madness had yet been drained out of Fletcher's head.

Life is learning the meaning of old sayings

Chapter III

GRATTAN FLETCHER RECEIVED AN EMAIL from Cathal Mac Gabhann, the first in a while. The drought was broken. He looked at it sitting small-headered in his inbox for a minute before opening, letting himself imagine that it might be good. Or at least an olive branch, an opening which might allow him to reset things and to at last kindle some kind of decent rapport, a fellow-feeling, with the man. This protracted caustic silence, this quarantine, had been hurting Grattan as much as it was intended to; though he hadn't admitted as much to anyone but Margot—and she already regarded him as a big softhearted fool anyway so it made no difference to her.

The email however was not affectionately framed. It assailed him with the modern American formalism of opening without a Dear or a Chara, a poison to the eyesight of an effusive human person like Grattan, an old-timer at heart. And it followed, with similar abruptness: *Kindly furnish by COB today a written explanation for your unsanctioned absence from your workplace yesterday. Subject to your response being unsatisfactory, as I anticipate it will, this request can be regarded as the commencement of a disciplinary process. I will then be handing the case over to Assistant Secretary with responsibilities for HR, Josephine Sloane and I believe you will then have cause to look back on my treatment of your behaviour hitherto as having been lenient.*

'To heck with it,' Fletcher said, picking up the phone. He had addressed Mac Gabhann's message minder thousands of times but a few months had passed since the last time. 'I know you're there, would you please pick up?' he said, still misunderstanding how voicemail worked. 'I saw your car out in the back. Let's just talk, dear fellow.'

Fletcher nearly fell over when his phone rang straight back and it said *Ext 601* on the screen. 'Hello, Cathal,' he said as the phone approached his head, showing that he was ready to be as big as needed. He had up till today insisted on addressing Mac Gabhann as *Charles*, the name he'd introduced himself as when they'd met in the Civil Service Exam back in the 80s.

Note: Fletcher of course had got the highest score in the country in that exam, while our other lanky string of misery, now Secretary General Mac Gabhann, had missed the cutoff. An tÚsail had been engaged to publicly service the Nation only after a number of other candidates had mysteriously turned down their offers. *The compiler*

'I know *everything*,' said Mac Gabhann.

'Excuse me?' said Fletcher.

'I have a long trail documenting your misuse of the Public Service email system to send out circulars about Aung San and Malala and whoever the fuck your current liberal jerk-off idol may be.'

That was fair. Grattan occasionally got confused between his work email account and the one his daughter had set up for his own stuff.

'And starting petitions for increasing government aid to fucking Ethiopia so they can breed more,' growled Mac Gabhann in a tone that did not indicate much reaching out. 'Highly paid by the taxpayer for doing nothing and you still want to have your say about the spending of further tax, is that it?'

'Such piety does not flatter you, Charles,' said Grattan, reverting. 'Glass houses and such?'

'And I know you made a day trip in a government vehicle. So what's the big idea this time, Grattan?' he asked as though Grattan was a teenager. 'What are we now, Grattan, eh? Some kind of caviar socialist?'

Grattan thought he'd said cavalier socialist and was confused as he tried to formulate an answer. He had always suffered a compunction to answer questions sincerely no matter how insincerely they were asked. 'No isms for me, Charles. All isms are mere offshoots of the big one, conformism. They require adoption of a rallying framework through which you must thereafter view every piece of art, literature, and life event. I refuse new orthodoxies as old, Charles. I try to observe the condition of every person I meet, not through the safety of some prescribed ideology, but in simple fellow feeling.' He paused. 'That includes you, Cathal.'

Mac Gabhann laughed an edgy laugh. 'All very laudable, Grattan,' he said, 'if you had any real consideration for me however, you would of course have resigned years ago. So now let me ask you this, Grattan.'

'Yes?'

'This earth has had trillions of tiny single cells bumping into each other for four billion years,' said Mac Gabhann, who had a subscription to The New Scientist and liked to emphasize that, in the hard subjects at least, he was more intelligent than Fletcher. This currency funded quite a few of Mac Gabhann's onslaughts on the composure that so repulsed him in his contemporary. 'Yet only once, Fletch, *only once* in all that time has a collision resulted in a cell with an inner membrane, that singular event that every plant and animal and human stems from. How about that for a Creation moment?'

'Ah, the amazing eukaryotic event, eh?' said Fletcher, never meaning to sound patronizing. 'Bacteria, the glass ceiling of basic life throughout the universe. More complex life, likely to be much rarer than was previously thought and all that. Unique though, Charles? Really? I doubt you buy that, with trillions of planets in the zone … Of course you know the numbers at work here better than I do.'

'Ah. I'm not even worth having an argument with, is that it, Grattan?' said Mac Gabhann, sounding ridiculous in peeve. 'Answer me this then. Since all people apparently like to conjure a hidden agency of evil, a dark *other* against which one's own little expediencies may appear relatively venial, what form does diabolism take for the devout humanist such as yourself? What would the atheist devil say or do if he was conferenced in on this call with us? What do you suppose would be his position on the big questions with which an atheist archdeacon such as yourself, preoccupies himself?'

Note: don't be thrown off the trail by this cur feigning ignorance of the devil's manifestations, would be my advice.
Indeed, if the Fletcher fellow had been due any time in atheist purgatory, he'd surely have clocked up a decent allowance
for time served at this point. *The compiler*

'You'll have to write to Dawkins,' said Grattan, getting onto
another theme, 'because I regard myself more as a lapsed atheist.
I don't preach it. I gave that up when I was fifteen. I don't need
other people to share my lack of belief in deities and nor do I try
to dissuade anyone of whatever personal beliefs help get them
through. The only exception I make ...'

'Answer the question, you heinous windbag,' Mac Gabhann
cut in, not entirely unfairly.

'There is no absolutely good or evil person, Charles. Most of
us do a little of both. The quest for a devil is just as much of a
merry dance of personal abdication as is a quest for a god. But I
sense that is not the answer you want,' said Fletcher.

Mac Gabhann answered himself. 'What he would say,
Fletcher, if he was on the line with us, the devil of your atheistic
humanism, is something like this: *to tell the truth, gentlemen, I
don't care very much. This conversation will be entirely without trace
in a hundred years, and every other truth and lie about you will be
equally unremembered. And so, gentlemen, all the details of works
you amuse yourselves with now do not interest me very much either
way. I just don't care.*'

'Ever since thoughts were recorded, people have tended to
view their own time as the pinnacle of history and a calamitous
end of our species as being imminently attendant upon their
personal demise. But a good man once said to me, *don't under-
estimate the cane rat.* There's a lot we can do to better the odds of
a kinder future,' said Fletcher. 'You and I could talk more about
these things Cathal ...'

'All hot air, that's all you are,' cut in Cathal Mac Gabhann in
a heightened pitch. 'Fucking failed priest. Hear this, you senten-
tious numpty, I exist in the here and now. And I will stop your
shit.' The same Mac Gabhann could be a prickly customer.

After Grattan put down the receiver he responded to the email. *Dear Charles, Thank you for the correspondence. You have your job to do. But know this: regardless of our conversation, everything has changed. Kind regards to Fran and the family, Grattan.*

When Ryle arrived at 10.30 Fletcher was raging for the road. He did a quick toilet dash while he waited for Ryle to gather himself. As Ryle was about to follow out of the return, Fletcher's extension rang. Ryle, passing, picked it up of course.

'Is that Grattan?'

'It is,' said Ryle.

'Well Grattan,' said the voice, 'Josie here. How are things?'

'Fair to middling,' said Ryle, taking a stab at a Rathmines accent.

'*Eh?*' she said, 'Are you feeling alright, Grattan?'

'Why shouldn't I be?' asked Ryle.

'Very well then,' she said, not caring for this new attitude. 'I need to formally flag with you that Cathal Mac Gabhann has asked that we initiate a final disciplinary with you. He's breaking my balls on this. Why the fuck do you have to antagonize the man so, putting me in this awkward position?'

'Josie who now?' said Ryle.

'*Josie, Josephine. Tweety …*' she said, taken aback. After a few seconds she resumed, reverting to the status she had worked hard for and wasn't ashamed of tripping on, 'Josephine Sloane, HR director for this Department. And can you cut the funny voice. Come along now, Grattan, let's don't play silly buggers with me. It won't pay you.'

Note: It is my understanding that the same Josephine Sloane had embraced the name Tweety as a way of killing by absorption the nickname that had followed her since a mistake she'd made some years before. As a premature adopter of Twitter Josephine was behind the now famous (in government circles) illustration of how not to use social media. In a drive to keep her HR subordinates more in tune with her unfolding thought processes, a stream-of-consciousness management style that she was experimenting with, she had set up a Twitter account and got them all to follow her. After a first cautious flirtation with the technology she had got fluid one night, emitting a new brainwave after each glass of prosecco imbibed at a dinner with the Minister. It was the references to the Parliamentary member and her plans for the rest of the evening, broadcast after glass four, that would bring an end to that policy initiative. Her choice of handle, selected to show a human side to her underlings, was TweedyBoyd. It had been intended as a jocular joint reference to her penchant for rapeseed-yellow suit fabric and her literary interests. *The compiler*

Ryle took a very small notebook from a pocket in the inner lining of the Pakistani lamb leather jacket which he always wore under the luminous vest. He spelt out the name Josephine Sloane while she stayed in silent puzzlement on the line. His silence may not have been expressed in a threatening way—though in truth no benign intentions may be inferred from that omission as Ryle did not often issue threats. He saw it a stupid thing for the lesser man such as himself to give advance warning of his intentions.

'OK then, Grattan,' she said eventually, unnerved, 'I was just giving you a heads up. I'd been thinking you could take me to the Winding Stair for lunch and over a glass or two of your favourite merlot we could see how to make it go away. But if you don't want to play it that way this time I'll formally notify you via email.'

'A final disciplinary session, eh?' said Ryle, 'Those can lead to summary dismissal, eh? The last one was in 1944, I believe.'

'Don't be melodramatic,' she snapped, 'but do remember, I have a job to do at the end of the day.'

'Josephine Tweety you say, eh?'

She was silent for a further moment. Then she tried reverting to her unofficious voice, 'If you're taking a tone with me, Grattan, you should know that I don't appreciate it. I haven't got it all figured out either you know, Grattan. Yes, I like the trappings of my achievements and I won't apologise to anyone for that. I happen to be good at the challenges and strategies of management. It's not that I don't see the vacuousness at times. You know that I would have liked to paint. And maybe dedicate my life to helping the homeless. It's just that I'm more realistic about things than you are, Grattan. I recognize the facts on the ground and get on with my career on that realistic basis rather than spending my professional life wishing it had started somewhere else. We are where we are, Grattan. For your information.'

Ryle said nothing as he was sharpening his pencil.

'How did we end up doing this to each other, Grattan?' tried Tweety.

'Jesus give me patience,' said Ryle, 'That'll be grand then, Josephine.'

'Wait a minute,' said Josephine, 'who is this? Who is speaking?'

Ryle had already put down the receiver delicately.

This time Ryle refused to fetch the OPW van. 'You can do your own fucken driving today,' he said, one wheeze per word emphasizing the pains in his chest, 'we're going in your own car.' You might wonder why Ryle wouldn't insist on this every time. But Ryle had to balance discomforts here. The upside of Fletcher's car was that the seats were leather and had many adjustments for back support. The downsides: firstly, there was Fletcher's driving which was shocking, accelerating and braking in harmony with passing thoughts rather than in regard for any features of the road; veering to the left as he stared intensely at a companion with whom he was trying to register a point; looking in awe at every ordinary hill, house, and field; following his companion's eyes to see what else there was to be soaked up (you had to stare straight ahead in the hope that Fletcher would do the same). The other downside of the car was that Fletcher had control of the buttons and Ryle could not stop the music.

Ryle had a modest aversion to music. It was an innate thing of some kind. He had a certain contempt for the way a tune or lyric could get in through side channels, and distort straight thinking with irrational feelings. He liked his thoughts linear, like his driving. Fletcher on the other hand, not given to linearity in any of its forms, was mad into music of every and any sort. In his own car he had an arsenal of music receptacles. He could plug in a memory stick, yoke up his iPhone or pull songs from the CD rack in the boot. Anything from Kris Kristofferson to Pharrell Williams. He never thought the words of any song worth remembering but he would hum along like a washing machine.

Note: Ryle was the most normal of the main subjects I have to deal with at least in this one regard. He merely regarded music as a nuisance. Mac Gabhann, for instance, was like an early teen and had to make music belong exclusively to him and become a mark of him, or dismiss it entirely. Margot was a professional. She understood the dangers and knew how to train the treacherous currents. But Fletcher? There wasn't a tune written that Fletcher was not open to—a trough, he was, never realizing how unwise it is to leave emotions to flap freely in the swill, every corny air and tricky string pluck having free access to his soul. On reflection, how could any person be expected to come out of that the right way up? *The compiler*

Anyway the Lexus was how they chose to do it this time.

'Do you know,' said Grattan, with his seat back and arms stretched to the steering wheel of his three month old car, Paolo Nutini blaring, 'do you know the first thing I was asked by Charles Smyth on the day we both started? He took one look at me and asked me, *are you some kind of fucking relic of hippiedom* or something? He's had a peculiar irritation with me ever since.'

Ryle was trying to sleep as they made their way along the N4, the idea of visiting Carlow thankfully abandoned.

'And what I am going to tell you next, you are going to think is perhaps a bit irrational of me.'

'I'm sure I'll be startled alright,' said Ryle.

'But since we are joined together for the coming adventures you are entitled to know,' said Fletcher.

'What? Spit it fucking out! For the love of Christ why does everything have to have a fucking preamble?'

'OK, well,' said Fletcher looking away from the road with his rich lips aquiver, 'there are times I think he hates me so much he would eliminate me if he weren't concerned for the consequences for himself. What kind of hatred is that?'

'Don't worry,' said Ryle, an expert in these things, 'it's not possible. Even if you were caught copulating with an emu on O'Connell Street they'd still have to follow a long, slow process. And of course no process can be followed if the operators fall into the silo.'

'*What?*' said Grattan. Then he let it pass as he had his own thoughts he wanted to explore. 'I don't know what that's supposed to mean but anyway I wasn't talking about elimination through firing, I mean *altogether.*'

'Would you go away to fuck you dozy bastard,' said Ryle not unkindly, 'that man wouldn't be able to kill his grandmother. He hasn't the hands to wipe his arse.'

'I said to him this morning,' said Grattan, taking some poetic license, 'everything has changed Charles. No more passive lily-arsed campaigning from my cushy swivel chair. Just watch me. That's what I said, Ryle. No going back now.'

'Jesus preserve me,' said Ryle, finding the recliner button on his seat. 'It's not him you need to worry about at all.'

'What do you mean?' said Fletcher.

'For your information, there are people back in that rat hole who would smile in your face before knifing you in a disciplinary.'

'You mean Josie? How do you know about her?'

'So it's true, eh?' Ryle made a mental confirmation, a habit he had developed as a twelve-year-old when he'd been barred from giving true answers to the catechism questions at his actual confirmation. 'Here's a person you know would throw you overboard to see what kind of splash you make and you're still calling her *Josie* like she's your friend.'

'Do you know what my father said to me when my first girlfriend broke my heart?' said Fletcher. 'He said, Don't let it make you cynical. Not for the sake of other people, but for your own. To shield yourself from further disappointment you would have to shut yourself to hope, trust, and charity. Sure, the cynic is more often proven right. But he is not always. The journey would be emotionally safer, but longer in its joylessness.'

'I'm not cynical as much as I am realistic,' said Ryle, well up enough at times. 'Expect nothing from a pig but a grunt.'

'Ah, the sceptical realist,' said Fletcher. 'But Nietzsche missed the point when he called hope the evil of all evils, blaming it for prolonging men's torments. In fact, it is not hope but sturdy animal instinct that prolongs life; hope is in fact what eases the torments. Even those who have sterilized their lives of hope and crystallized the reality of life down to a small futility, keep living anyway. So if we're going along anyway, what's wrong with holding on to the short-term hopes that encourage you to reach for things, as well as the prodigal hopes that let you maybe delude yourself for a minute or two along the way? When you buy a lotto ticket it doesn't mean you don't understand statistics.'

'I don't see what that has to do with anything,' said Ryle.

'What I'm saying is that where there are no answers to know for sure, smug gut scepticism is self-delusion just as much so as are any of the more hopeful dispositions that it derides. And it's not *nice*. The most hollow conceit of all is to base your own footing on debasing others' conceits of comfort and permanence. That truly would be a fearful and futile way to expend one's life. And I know deep down, Len Ryle, that you are with me on the other side of the equation even though you'll never admit it.'

Ryle was more inclined to stick to the point than to engage in Existential discourse on this occasion. 'Forgiving after an event might have some peace-of-mind benefits for the coward with no appetite for revenge. Forgiving in advance ... That's just retarded,' he said, snuffling back snot and holding his head with the pain of the idea. 'There are other ways of getting in at people who might knife you given half a chance, ways that are a bit more effective than hoping they'll get no joy out of reefing you.'

'Anyway, let's put that out of our heads,' said Fletcher airily. 'We can't be sidetracked.'

'Would there be any harm in asking where we're going?' said Ryle, waking a little while later, 'because if you keep driving like the wheels of hell, there's a very real danger we'll soon be across the Shannon. And I can't be there. Connaught goes against my grain.' Though he had mixed with the people in Leopardstown, Fairyhouse, and Listowel in his time, Ryle had spent a lifetime avoiding the Galway races.

'Don't worry, we crossed five minutes ago and you didn't miss a snore my friend,' laughed Fletcher, 'and we don't have much further to go.'

'Fucksake,' said Ryle, snuggling back down with a cold shiver. He didn't have long more to nap. Before they reached Loughrea, Fletcher braked fiercely leaving a lot of his factory fitted Michelins on the tar. He had missed his exit. But he wasn't fazed.

'I see now,' said Ryle, in something close to a sincere feeling. Fear. 'This is how the devil planned to kill you. Getting you to reverse on the fucking M6 motorway.'

But they didn't die then and it's an ongoing mystery that no atheist has explained to me, who it is that looks out from the heavens to protect freestyle drivers like Fletcher, rejecting the car's controls and skitting along our roads like eurythmy dancers. Why is it that they're rarely the ones that get broken up?

There followed about ten miles of backroad into the worst and most depressing terrain that a human being could ever set eyes upon, the finest of land with nothing but furze bushes and stone walls cultivated on it; disadvantaged men in caps driving around in vintage David Brown tractors that were as fresh as the day they were bought. There was nothing pleasing about these scenes. And then didn't the sat nav on Fletcher's phone give up on them. It took him another hour of repeating instructions on the phone with someone called Alex, before he turned the car into a narrow lane and headed up to an asbestos-roofed cottage too miserable even for the East Galway people to be miserable in. No doubt the home of a zealous convert.

Note for the foreigner: I don't know what the people are like where you come from but the National Temperament Index in Ireland is in the bipolarity range. (This has been conclusively determined by myself in a longitudinal study using recursive abstraction methodologies within the naturalistic and heuristic paradigms of qualitative research.) When in its miserable phase, this Nation's mood does not take the form of the romantic miserabilism so often exhibited by the French Nation. It is not a studied melancholy doggedly pursued as a form of pleasure, as Hugo had it. It is not a melancholy stewed in out of conviction that happiness is vulgar, as Baudelaire crowed. It is not composed of any variety of melancholic ennui pursued in slavishness to artistic fad, as

with Sartre and Houellbecq. It does not spit tunefully as
Ferré. No, there's very little chic about it. It is not at all the
kind of misery that company loves. Nor even the steady misery of the Slav himself. It is pure authentic flesh-devouring
miserableness. It lacks the slightest bit of self-regard and offers
very little regard for anyone else for that matter. And when
it lifts for spells, it yields to a great collective unbundling of
frenetic, hysterical activity and nonsensical conversation, so
chaotic that no good can be got of it at all.[fn] In short, this
would be the Nation genetically best adapted to the boom
and bust modalities of the modern economic system and so
it should be no surprise to Forbes that ours is such a success
story so soon again. *The compiler*

[fn] Footnote
How glad one remains not to be tasked with actually editing this ineffable
nonsense! I am reminded of another of the paragraphs in that ninety-
eighth rejection letter, misguidedly providing the requested feedback to
the aspiring littérateur. As context for advising him to find other pur-
suits, he was given advice that you will fully appreciate having waded so
far through this agglomeration of intemperate and ill-considered words.
Advice that he apparently had not the slightest appreciation for. *Your voice
doesn't work.* We stated quite plainly. *The stage Oirishisms are tiresome.
Nobody in modern Dublin has any patience with this kind of paddywhackery.
Be a writer who happens to be Irish rather than trying to be an Irish writer.
Colloquialisms and idiom incorporated into a narrator's voice rarely work at
all, but never when self-consciously interspersed through what one assumes is
the natural voice of the narrator: a stilted formal English that starkly belies
an insecurity in relation to his inferior education. Frankly, your narration
voice is the voice of an apprentice butler in nineteenth-century Offaly. Hence
our recommendation that you read more and write less. The Editors*

Tiny black Dexter cows looked hungrily at them from the
side of the lane. There was a cluster of vehicles in the yard at the
back of the smokeless bothán, some new with Dublin registrations, some old with English registrations, two VW kombis, a
Morris Minor estate, and pony and trap.
'What is it now?' asked Ryle. 'A fucking moonie colony?'

'These good people are anarchists, Ryle,' he said. From a Facebook group that Grattan was signed up with, he had learnt that there was a meeting of the Disband movement taking place in East Galway today.

'Associating with antichrists?' said Ryle, who sometimes let on to be a bit less sharp than he actually was. This could cause some confusion socially because there were times when Ryle was actually not all that sharp to begin with. 'Why then would you suppose the boss with the cloven feet would need to snag you?'

Inside, the dark cold house was lit and heated with a single low energy pendulum bulb. The man of the place welcomed them without asking their names. He had a very long beard, shlurped his words like a Dutchman, and slid over the uneven flagstones in barbaric wooden clogs. He didn't look like he had had anything to eat in a good couple of years. The partner, a homebirth midwife they quickly learned, was the one who kept the light on and looked like she was getting a bite outside. There was a whole assortment in there, some young and shiny, others ropey and incurable. Still nobody asked who they were and Fletcher was gagging to remedy this as he wanted to know all of their names, to establish affinities, and discover something like-able about each of them—his counter-sense way of remembering newly-mets.

Ryle didn't like the situation one bit. He could hardly wait to be away and for some reason he developed a terrible long-ing for a lamb bhuna. Not even the devastating smell of a foxy man who came too close to him could shift the desire. Ryle was very sensitive about human smells. He himself was fastidi-ous. He had a habit of bracing himself in a cold bath at 6 am each morning. Not something he picked up indigenously in Ballyhale where all were out reddening each other with sticks at that time of day. Isn't it funny all the same, the things that can come through in the Y gene. He tried to distract himself with images of falling into the embrace of a widely smiling woman in a navy pinafore but the bhuna wouldn't go. 'We need to be moving on,' he shouted across the kitchen toward Fletcher, 'we're not wanted here.'

When he went outside, instead of Fletcher it was the stumpy woman tented in pinafore who followed. 'Everyone is wanted,' she said seriously. 'What made you think you were not?' She was very kind. Ryle could tell. She could see goodness where there wasn't any and that may have been the nature of the climb that attracted her in Ryle. 'I believe that there is more to you than meets the eye.' Of course there was even less to him than met the eye. I should note at this point that the picture of Ryle that I have accurately painted for you from the outset, is not the same one perceived by some women upon first gazing him over. Put it down to intuition and impulse. Inexplicably, for a short while some saw a mirage of whatever they desired buried deep in that smoldering wreck of a man. Whatever caused that, don't ask me. But Ryle knew that this was a chip that he always needed to cash in quickly. They crossed the yard to a lean-to at the gable end of the cowhouse and in there, they engaged in sexual relations of some sort with the grey sky gaping in at them through the holes in the rusted galvanized roof, a situation that could have been prevented by just an occasional application of any cheap brand of oxide paint, had that Dutchman had the slightest bit of go in him. I don't need to conjure any further detail of the picture for you out of no more than the same consideration as I allow myself in refraining from doing so. Ryle returned to the house with his preference for the direct ways of the free English woman reinforced – for Yorkshire bred she was, albeit the runt of the litter.

When he went back into the kitchen, a sour turn was evident. A shaven-headed young woman with a deep voice and a Castleknock accent was explaining slowly to Grattan that this was a movement that required neither his leadership nor assistance with a program of action. 'In fact, both such concepts are anathema. Do you even understand the basic things that bring us together?' As the woman in pinafore brushed past, giving just the slightest tug on her tent, the foxy guy looked at Ryle like you would look at a long shite curled up on your breakfast plate: in wonder and a degree of disgust. He eventually tried to put a bit of sarcasm in his voice as he said, 'May I introduce my wife to you.' He lifted his arm to gesture the introduction of the pinafore. The man on the other side of him moved away. The bloodcurdling smell finally removed the bhuna from Ryle's head. He couldn't be sure about it afterward but for a minute he may have had a feeling of empathy for people such as kindly pinafored Susannah, people who regularly found themselves in this man's dominion. Maybe she had stirred something good in Ryle after all.

'But I just want to help,' said Fletcher pathetically. Some of the others looked at him understandingly but they were not going to win the day. 'What else is there for a person to do? I like to think that I may bring some useful skills. And maybe even some connections. I have been an insider, if you like, all my life up to now. Myself and my friend Ryle could surely at least give guidance on what kind of reactions you can expect in response to various protest strategies you might be weighing up? Which ones may have the most unsettling impact on established Ireland. And what's more we won't be lurking in the background. We'll be in the front line with you all. What more can I offer?'

'That's a decent offer,' said a voice, 'and heaven knows we can't afford to exclude any ideas about how best to deploy limited resources.'

'This is not a movement for day trippers,' returned the strong shaven-headed voice of the leaderless movement. 'Certainly not one for people who show up from nowhere to ask us all our names and where we come from. We know your type, Mr. Fletcher. Get this into your curly top and take it back to whoever sent you here: you represent the machine and you guys are not welcome here. How can I put it more politely than that?'

'He might be idiotic but he's not stupid,' chirped Ryle, who was already becoming proprietary about the right to be abusive to Grattan. 'There's no call for you to take that tone with him.'

Fletcher was like a poisoned pup when he emerged from that house. He was very shook and not worth tuppence. Ryle was walking the ground at the side of the stony driveway to see if there was anywhere firm enough to turn the car on.

'I'm very shaken,' Fletcher said to Ryle, 'and I won't put a tooth in that.'

No better tonic for Grattan could there have been than what happened next. No worse thing could have happened in terms of Ryle's hopes to retrieve normality to his life.

Several people emerged and came over to the car where Ryle was directing Fletcher to reverse onto the gentle bank of a small slurry pit, forgetting the Lexus was a rear wheel drive and might not come out too easy. Ryle sat back in and slammed the door on them. One knocked and Fletcher let down the window. Joe Cocker was singing from a memory stick, *you can keep your hat on.*

At first Fletcher was unsure what to make of the foxy man's hand, reached across Ryle and offered to him. 'Please stay a bit friend,' said someone behind him.

'It occurs to me,' said the foxy man, slower to find words, 'that the sum total of a human life is about learning the meaning of old sayings. As you left I heard my grandfather's voice saying, *never turn down an offer from good hands.* Today, my friend, you have precipitated a split in the Disband movement.'

Grattan was already out of the car and a jagged black smile as irregular as the Corrib stretched across his soft red face.

Ryle was reeling with disgust. Either the foxy guy had come up with this ploy to detain Ryle while he thought of how to avenge himself or he was genuinely taken by Fletcher's words. It would have been hard to say which possibility upset Ryle's stomach more.

Back inside, the Castleknocker and one other were leaving, taking the official title and the .ORG with them. The breakaways remained and wanted to hear what Fletcher had to say. They were prepared to stay there in that house as long as it took for them to formulate a new reason for existing.

Fletcher needed very little coaxing. 'One of the questions that has affected me for a while is, what has become of us? When I walk around my lovely city, my lovely country, and open my eyes I just wonder. *What has become of us?* Home and person kitted out from Chinese-supplied junk emporiums. Paying for a satellite dish that must be pointed the same direction as everyone else's so we may be collectivized by Rupert Murdoch. Imagining we have opinions that weren't predicted and expressing them with indignation. Imagining we are doing something about it all when we vote. Imagining we have more scope for individuality than in natural times, while most of it now is expressed in brand choice. Diversity is lost not only in species numbers but in every cultural facet of our own species' existence.'

This kind of effluence seemed to make a positive impression on Fletcher's new friends. He had already allayed any lingering concerns about his provenance, as no State plant could have been sent out with such a baroque cover story.

Ryle was watching the time. Though thoughts of lamb bhuna were never to return, he still remembered that he had arrangements made for his tea this evening. Two chicken fillets left out to defrost and a few very nice looking old Queens ready in a saucepan, needing only a drop of scalding water thrown over them and they'd nearly turn into balls of flower instantly. 'If we don't hit the road soon,' he said to Fletcher, 'we'll be making the last part of the journey after-hours. And you know that with the cutbacks it'll be hard enough for me to get overtime payments for that.'

Fletcher was in a trance and didn't pay a blind bit of notice. Susannah moved back in Ryle's direction but when he nodded out the window towards the shed, she just ignored him. Instead she told him he might find happiness if he stopped feeling sorry for himself. 'Why not let go? Join in. I'm sure you have a lot to contribute. Who knows, you might even find joy?'

'Chasing happiness like hounds on a drag hunt has very erratic rewards at the end of it and is of course the biggest con the Americans ever pulled on us,' said Ryle.

'That's an interesting observation,' she said, stepping back and taking a new look at Ryle.

'The pursuit of self-pity on the other hand is underrated,' he added then, his own poeticism slightly lubricated by the moment. 'Like the terrier that learns how to eat rats, you have an endless supply of satisfaction and don't need to thank anyone for it. You can bask rather than strive.' Indeed it has to be noted here that there could have been no better model of a man living his philosophy than Ryle. His average day was filled with events that enabled him to refuel his feelings of sympathy with himself.

The woman however stepped further back, less impressed, possibly misunderstanding the allusion to eating rats and already unable to conceive of how she could have been intimate with the person now biting his nails before her. 'That's a rather asinine observation,' she said, moving on, 'you are not at all like your companion really, are you?'

'Who ever really knows what thoughts go through the mind of the other gender?' said Ryle resignedly to the foxy husband whose return to his side now advertised itself pungently.

Suck Ryle had bigger problems than that to contend with. Fletcher had been provided with a glass and a seat by the hearth. The communing wine that had been brought in from the Morris Minor to mark a new chapter, was no Chilean merlot. The hearth was empty and the draught down the chimney tended to make that an unpopular seat. But Grattan was not chilled. All this was the beginning of what he wanted. The embrace of the good honest people of this country. Fletcher took out his phone. For the first time in his life he was telling his wife that he wouldn't be home that evening. '… but don't worry, buttercup, I am safe in the heart of the country. In the hearth of the heart of the country you might say …' 'That's grand,' she cut him off for all to hear. The volume was always set high on Fletcher's phone as he sometimes didn't listen well despite having no shortage of ear flap to funnel the sounds into himself.

Susannah brought a chipped cup half filled with the stuff to Ryle. When he refused it the dwarfish person in the navy pinafore said with a surprising edge of resentment, 'Oh I suppose real Irish country men only drink stout or whiskey?'

'What are you on about now?' Ryle asked, rolling his eyes like they were twenty years married. To tell the truth of him, back when Ryle had been on the drink he had not been prejudiced against any ethanol-bearing liquid. In fact the acrid smell of the wine triggered a fond nostalgic sensation in his hairy nostrils. He had no more time for a connoisseur of whiskey or stout than he had for Grattan's wine buffery. It was the one molecule they

all were after. No, if Suck Ryle was grim-mannered with the
lovely little person in front of him now it was most certainly not
because of alcoholic snobbery. It was because it was taking every
gristly sinew of contrariness in the awkward, bony sack that was
Suck Ryle, as he stood there with one hand clasping the other
in front of his leather jacket, for him not to grab that cup and
take its contents into him in one swallow. That's how keen he
was for escape from the horrible situation he found himself in,
with Grattan settled in for an unspecified duration, what little
there had ever been of light in East Galway now fading, and
the pigmy's smelly husband balefully approaching again. But
no. Since he'd had to give up the drink, Ryle was a proper little
fucker. No drinking and very little smoking, and a fairly aloof
attitude taken to those who dabbled in those practices at which
he'd been master. 'I don't suppose you have any coke knocking
about?' he asked her pessimistically.

Ryle moved in towards the corner and sat next to Fletcher
long enough to get the keys out of his pocket. 'I'm off,' he said.

'We're staying,' said Fletcher, 'we've hit into a vein of decency
here and we must ride it Ryle, we must if we are serious at all.'

'You can stay and ride if you want,' said Ryle.

'Oh sorry! I get it,' said Fletcher, 'you need to get home to
feed your cat and you don't want to admit it. I respect that. Let's
see if anyone can give you a lift into the bus station in Loughrea.'

'I do in my hole,' said Ryle. The cat's existence had come into
Fletcher's knowledge purely by the accident of the beast's curiosity. He had moved a bay window curtain to take a look out one
day when Fletcher had come to the house looking for Ryle. Ryle
found the mention of him an impertinence.

'That man knows where the food is and is well able to turn
on a tap. If I didn't come home from one end of the week to the
other it would be no skin off his nose. I have other reasons for
needing to be back if you must know.'

'Well if you're not up for a bus ride, there's no way,' said
Fletcher. 'You're not insured to drive that car.'

'Another couple of points'll do me no harm,' said Ryle.

'No!' said Fletcher decisively. The room went quiet.

'You drive then,' said Ryle, 'you're not too far over the limit.'
'No!' said Fletcher again.

◊

'Let me ask you this,' said Ryle to Fletcher later as they settled close on the floor of a camper van, 'how does any of this shit take you a step closer to shaking hands with Brian Cody on All-Ireland Final days and handing out statues of famished people to foreign leaders?'

'A journey is made up of steps,' said Fletcher. 'If you keep looking wistfully toward your destination you will trip and fall.'

'It always helps, I find though,' said Ryle, itching himself and pushing the hosts' German pointer pup away from him, 'if your steps are not in the wrong direction. I don't see how winning the affections of this crew is going to get you anything but fleas.'

'Quiet please!' said Susannah, the miniscule tucked in at the far side of the snoring foxy man on the bed above.

Witnessing the banality of evil

Chapter IV

'Stop in for Christ's sake,' said Ryle as Fletcher drove them past the second Gala shop that looked like it might have a deli counter. 'I'd eat a side of the lamb of God.'

Fletcher's own growling paunch gave the lie to his assurances that he himself was not bothered at not having been offered as much as a stick of rye bread by way of breakfast in the stingy Dutchman's house.

Nor would he stop. He was tailing the camper of foxy man and Susannah who, as promised, were leading them to the site of a bog where there was an unspecified problem of some sort.

Ryle's back was paining worse than his ribs now, the repose on plywood flooring having been worse than getting a new beating. By the crooked way Fletcher held the steering wheel it was clear that he too was as good as paralyzed. But not a squeak that was less than ebullient came out of him. Like a man insistently wrenching a nut that was clearly on the wrong threads, he had taken so long to get a new start in life that he wasn't going to be stopped by one or two bouts of agony.

'Sometimes I'm not sure you're fully committed to our quest, Len,' said Fletcher in a flash of lucidity.

'I'd rather be tied to a bullock's tail and scutterred to death,' said Ryle, but less politely. 'Besides, I wouldn't trust that foxy guy as far as I'd throw him. He's the kind of lad who in TV series turns out to be an alien. Not to mention following him out on bog roads where there's not a sinner to witness whatever he has a mind to do to us. Have you even a few spanners in the boot for us to defend ourselves with?'

'*Alien!*' roared Grattan laughing. 'Even though, he's the only one of all our new friends whose got an accent from this side of the river. He's just from up the road, some part of Mayo, I'd say. What do you reckon?'

'Exactly, Foxford!' said Ryle, realizing that he was allowing his anger about the main subject to be somewhat deflated, yet unable not to be drawn into this. Ryle may have spent one too many nights going to sleep on the couch in front of the Sci Fi channel. 'You'd hardly give an alien anything other than a Foxford accent if you were sending one to Ireland.'

'The lack of glucose really is getting into your brain, my friend. I apologize. But we must soldier on now. We are most definitely not turning around merely because you have decided that a fellow activist, one of the few in our country who takes citizenship seriously, might in fact be an alien.'

'He's just a bit too genuine to be true, is all I'm saying. But to tell God's honest truth I couldn't give a fuck where he's really from,' said Ryle. 'The point that worries me more is that he might be hanging on to … a minor grudge.'

'Indeed,' said Fletcher with a hint of disapproval, having witnessed more than he was letting on it seems. 'And would he have any reason at all for that? Our dignity and reputations are worth something to all of us you know, Leonard.'

'The dignity boat left that lad behind a few years ago, I'd say,' said Ryle.

The van in front of them was slowing. They had been on the narrow famine road for twenty minutes, a skin of tar over a rind of stone and human skeletons sinking unevenly into the bog. 'Isn't that a lovely sight, timeless,' said Fletcher waving his hand to the side. All Ryle saw was a few small ricks of turf scattered across the field of rushes and it had all the look of hardship to him. There was a stoppage ahead. 'This seems interesting,' said Fletcher.

They stopped the car and walked past the queue of vehicles to where a mill of people were chanting and waving placards. Stop the Vandalism, Save our Ecosystems, We bear witness to the banality of Evil, and such like. Ryle thought he had gone straight to hell without his death notice ever having been repudiated by The Kilkenny People.

Fletcher did not have quite the same reaction. He was delighted. Even more so when he realized that many of his new Disband friends were already here. They let him through to the front as if his desire to lead something and their protracted absence of leadership were well matched. Grattan was not inhibited by the fact that he knew fuckall about what was supposed to be worth preserving on a raised bog and even less about the traditional rights claimed by turf-cutters. Or at least, nothing more than any other casual reader of the Irish Times might know.

Despite Ryle saying, 'Hold on there boss for Christsake until we detect what way the wind is blowing here,' Grattan quickly scanned the scene and took the megaphone. 'Good people,' he began, his usual voice shocking when amplified. Fletcher always talked with smacking and sucking sounds like he was moving several strepsils around in his mouth. Everyone went quiet. Even the David Brown men moving their harmless bits of machinery into the bog stopped to take stock.

The Gardaí looked too. Ryle shuddered. He liked the picture less by the minute. His intuition for minding himself was usually good. Before him, though he didn't know them by name yet, were Sergeant Meg Geas and Garda John Devine (formerly Superintendent Devine of Store Street), leaning against a blue-light Transit the side of which announced them as the Community Relations Squadron—the vanguards of the Crusty Squad. Ryle was good at the body language of police. He could see what way they were looking. The woman in the pinafore was beside him then and said, 'You see now? They're not here to prevent the illegal vandalism of our ecosystems but to monitor and harass the good people who have the bottle to protest this harm.'

In the interlude, someone with a bad sense of drama shouted, 'Traditional rights indeed, our forefathers never had great big machinery.' It was the foxy man.

'Fucking Beeblebrox,' muttered Ryle, forgetting how well sound travels over a silent bog. Garda Devine's laugh was muffled by a lump of sandwich going the wrong way, as he strained to see who had issued this.

Grattan Fletcher cleared his throat and resumed his warbling.

'Like all of you, I exist only through the people I touch, through my friends, colleagues, and loved ones. The sum of their perceptions of me is all that I am. There is no other me and if I sully this there is little chance in one lifetime to build a new one. Foremost in my mind right now is a little girl called little Margot. Let me say this unequivocally. I want my beloved granddaughter to be able to come here one day and show the unique fauna and flora of this wonderful habitat to her grandchildren. I don't doubt the deep goodness that lies in every human heart or that anybody on either side of this chevron tape wants anything less for their own grandchildren. But my friends, science tells us that the work being done here makes that aspiration unattainable.'

A sod of turf caught Grattan on the side of his head, a soft shot. Nobody could be seen to have thrown it. He continued, shaken but brave, 'I understand that each cutter is trying to do what is best for his family and traditions, but there is also a greater good. It was Hardin who said *Freedom in a commons brings ruin to all.*'

Ryle got the sense that this could go on awhile and was slinking to the rear of the crowd, his stomach pains overwhelming all others. As he retreated unseen he observed a perfect little basket on the back seat of a Dublin registered Note. There was a flask nosing out of it. He looked back at the crowd and heard the suddenly reassuring sound of Grattan's bolloxology keeping the little congregation rapt. The door opened obligingly after a little fiddling and he removed the items of interest. He went back to the Lexus wherein he stuffed himself to the gills with wild salmon, boiled eggs, homemade soda bread, scones, and potato salad. He threw a bunch of scallions out the window in case Fletcher might get hold of them. The coffee, surprisingly, was sweetened to hell and gone. He thought about what to do with the basket and flask. He couldn't put them back to the owners' car. Evidence of a theft might further complicate departure from this godforsaken place. As Suck Ryle walked back to the melee, he was not seen chucking the items across the far ditch for the bog to preserve.

He arrived as the applause from his side abated and one

of the bog men approached the tape. The man came right up to Fletcher with great primordial anger curling his brow. The Gardaí did nothing. Ryle had Fletcher's back.

'What's this then,' said the bog man straining to look through the crowd, looking at the row of cars behind them. 'The government men are here in a brand new Lexus today. On salaries three times what any person on either side of this line makes, burning more kilojoules of oil in a month than we'd burn turf in a year, and coming here on expenses to give us a lecture about the environment. What injunction papers have you brought this time, lads? Well you can go wipe your arses with them, you pair of parasites.'

This man's gait seemed to Ryle to be underwritten by a more strongly held set of opinions than any held by Fletcher's new friends. Also, he could see that little Sussanah was spot on. The Gardaí were more conversational with the bog men than with the protesters. He was increasingly persuaded now that the best thing for himself would be to side with the bog men.

'No,' said Fletcher unflappable, 'You've got it all wrong. Me and citizen Ryle are not here from the government.'

'Shut up, you glorious gobshite,' whispered Ryle, more loquacious now that his blood sugar was back to normal, 'what's wrong with your cunting head? Don't be throwing my fucking name out to them tribesmen. Besides, you *are* from the fucking government. Where else do you think you're from? Fucking answer me that! Let's get out of here. Fucking blowhard!'

'Not from the government, eh?' said the stout bog man with his black bushy hair covering the fact that he had almost no neck. 'Who else can afford to run a fifty-grand car in these parts in the middle of the week?'

Grattan started talking again and the bog man, Kevin the others were calling him, pulled the megaphone from his hands and smashed it against the wheel hub of the David Brown. 'Look here,' he said quietly to the group on this side of the chevron, 'I don't doubt there are some of you well-intentioned, but you should know this: there are people on my side of the tape who are beyond their load-bearing capacity. People who have lost livelihoods and have the bailiff on their doorsteps. People whose settled sons and daughters have been uprooted and dispersed. Digging this ground here is the only thread they're hanging in this world by. And you'd be wise to move off now that you've had your say. There's nothing more for me to tell you.'

This statement sapped any fervour that Fletcher's speech might have drummed up. In recessionary times more didn't need to be said as all present knew people whose threads had already broken. The crowd stayed an hour or two more, milling and talking in small huddles. Another deflating factor was the question Susannah had asked and had received no answer to: 'How did Geas and Devine know we'd be here today?' The foxy alien was not by her side at that time, Ryle noticed.

Ryle went to the car and fell asleep on the back seat. When he woke, instead of being in Dublin, he was still in the bog. The clock on the dashboard said it was nearly four. The fillets of chicken would be going off. All the other cars were gone. The Gardaí too. This was excessive tenacity to the cause of civic leadership even by Grattan's zealous new standards. When Ryle opened the door all he received was the peaceful sound of machinery working the bog. Where the fuck was Fletcher, that was what Ryle wanted to know?

Ryle walked back toward the entrance to the field, not a sign encountered of Grattan anywhere along the way. Fletcher could be in trouble, Ryle sensed. Maybe fallen down a bog hole or followed a will o'the wisp into a marsh. Ryle started to worry that he might be a while waiting for the lift home. He phoned directory enquiries to see if he could get a taxi to Loughrea. From there he had it in mind to get that bus back across the river he knew he never should have crossed. But he had to hang up on the Loughrea taxi man in the middle of trying to give the GPS coordinates because he heard voices just inside the ditch. He entered the field in time to see four or five tall fellows trotting off next to another one of their kind who was on a wide wheeled quad, away into the bad lands. He did not call after them in case they might hear him. He had no desire for them to do to him what they had apparently done to the simpering carcass at his feet.

Grattan Fletcher was down again. And the men who had punished him for no other crime than preaching to them, trotted and rode in a straight line across the quagmire that they were clearly well inured to the dangers of, headed for a small building in the distance. These hardy boys were bog hooligans. Ryle knew their sort and was wild wary of them.

One of the Davys approached with a pitiful few lumps of turf on the transport box. It stopped next to them. The bog man Kevin descended. 'Is he alive?' he asked. Fletcher groaned his answer. 'What happened?' said the bog man to Ryle.

'Your enforcers,' Ryle nodded in the direction of the retreating party and said, 'as if you didn't know.'

'Christ,' said Kevin. 'The poor man.' He bent over Fletcher and asked him if he wanted an ambulance called. The heroic man said not. He was fine. He proceeded to unfold himself and get slowly back on his feet. Aside from blood clotted in his curls and the makings of some bad bruising on his face, the boys had been as lazy about this task as they apparently were about any other.

'Broadman is my name,' said the bog man, extending his hand, 'and I'm sorry about this. They are nothing to do with the turf cutters, only for stealing a few bits every now and then to keep themselves warm beyond in the haunted house where they stay.'

'Why are you apologizing then?' said Ryle, 'Answer me that.'

'I'm apologizing because that's what I'm accustomed to doing,' said Kevin Broadman after thinking for a minute about this, 'owing to the fact that my own son is one of them. He would not be one that set a finger on you though. The same boy hasn't the hardness even to put a hook in a fish or eat the flesh of any animal. But yet he lives among them and has my heart broken. Dole has their lives robbed. They can give fifty a week for drugs. Fifty for slabs of beer from Tesco. And they have a hundred left over to do what they like with.' A tear came down Broadman's face, proof enough for Fletcher that he was genuine. 'If you won't let me call a doctor, come with me back to Stasia's.'

Stasia was Kevin Broadman's wife.

Back in the best of a bungalow, snug and spacious, Stasia did the best she could with plasters and aloe vera, having first tried the best she could to persuade Fletcher that he needed to go to the Portiuncla for stitches. Fletcher had heard stories of that hospital and besides, he secretly fancied retaining a small scar or two from his travels.

After Stasia transferred pizzas from the freezer to the oven, a bottle of clear liquid was produced. Three of the occupants had a small tot and got talking. Ryle waited, peculiarly silent, for the food to bake. He spoke only to book the bedroom of the son who was abroad in the bog. Fletcher, with drink on him, would be well able for the couch.

Even with two of the four pies in his own belly, Ryle was consumed by restlessness. He had a quiet word with Broadman when Fletcher wandered off looking for the bathroom. 'Don't pay too much heed to that lad,' he said, nodding at the corridor Fletcher had disappeared into, 'he could very easy lead you astray. Clever out, but he hasn't a lick of sense.'

Broadman nodded.

Then Ryle wandered out into the corridor himself. He looked at the laden walls as he waited for Fletcher to offload and emerge. There were school pictures aplenty. Beaming Kevin junior winning prizes. Debating and soccer, seemed the things. When Fletcher walked out into Ryle he said, 'Jesus Christ, how long are you standing at the door like that, you … weird little man.'

'I hope you washed your hands,' said Ryle in a state of distractedness.

'Give me patience,' said Fletcher. 'What's gotten into you?'

'I thought I'd have a word,' said Ryle, 'and then I'll head out for a walk.'

Fletcher looked worried now.

'Your problem,' Ryle said, 'is that you are like that English priest who went to the Blaskets admiring the people like paintings. You are looking romantically, like a grand fellow who is above it all, admiring the manners as if culture is a thing in itself. The problem is you need to look underneath the hood like you would with anyone of your own kind and suspect them of being pricks and fuckwits until proven otherwise. Where does culture end and the fellow himself begin?'

'What's gotten into you Len. You look agitated. But I have to say, that's a very good question,' said Fletcher, 'and by the way you ask it I assume you're of the school that puts everything down to personal responsibility. Or lack thereof. But that ignores the fact that we are social animals and part of our very personality is derived from the group. Therefore the cultural is not just a mask. Though it can change over time it is in fact rooted in the person, a part of them as much as they're part of it. Whether you are part of a football mob or a Hindu monastic culture, the ways of the people around you confer a mental territory for you to exist in. Being embedded in Connemara culture and having it embedded in you, makes you a different person than you would be if your culture was of Clane. It's not all there is about you but neither is it just an overlay. It's part of the way you speak and think and therefore part of who you are and therefore ...'

Ryle couldn't take any more. His need to get out walking was as pressing as nausea. He rushed out into the uncertain darkness against the advice of the two people with local knowledge and the one with none. Hence Ryle would have no alibi.

On his journey that night, Ryle would later claim, he met a person he thought was the devil waltzing along the bog road.

Note: I'm only telling you what Ryle said in his diary so it's no lie of my own on this occasion. *The compiler*

This 'devil' looked nothing like Mac Gabhann (though I do concede that he can take any form he wants). The man Ryle met had a full, neat face, the opposite of Mac Gabhann's. This face was set into a large silvery head. The impressive being, Ryle surprisingly claimed, had the look of a priest about his visage. This was all sat upon what Ryle ungraciously described as a 'frightening gorilla trunk' and stumpy legs. Ryle spuriously claimed that he was greeted by name. 'Well Leonard,' the man purportedly said, as if it was the most natural thing on earth for a person to be out for a midnight stroll in ballygobackwards with the yellow eyes of wolves bobbing along through the reeds only a few hundred yards away. 'That's not a bad evening,' he added in an inoffensive voice. There was a glow of flames in the distance behind him.

'Not too bad at all, thanks be to God,' said Ryle.

Ryle returned intending to go straight to the warm bed of the vagrant son. Stasia, Broadman, and Fletcher were still sitting at the Stanley raiméising, their fondness for each other embalmed in clear poitín fumes emanating from the daisy-printed wedding tumblers. No merlot here either, Fletcher was capable of significant cultural plasticity after all, it seemed. Broadman was telling about a time he was working as a roofer in Manchester when he pissed on the head of a ganger. 'He was in the habit of beating one of Polish chaps and I amn't the kind of man to drop a hammer,' Broadman was saying with a croaky bog laugh when a distant siren broke up the ease. '… Jesus Christ, Anastasia, that sounds like a fire engine.'

They went outside and down the road a little way to observe flames on the landscape where the haunted house used to be. The fire engine of course couldn't get next, nigh, nor near it. A few men picked their way across the thin-skinned fetid swampy cesspool and one reported on his return that there was a strong smell of petrol all about the place. He didn't seem elated to be able to deliver the additional news that none of the hardy boys had been at home to receive a roasting.

The local Gardaí were less well walked than the Crusty Squad. They took Ryle as a decent fellow citizen and believed each word of denial. Even though it was miles to the next house, they drove every inch of that looking for the man that Ryle implausibly described seeing. The only thing they came on was a yoke kneeling in the middle of the road about a mile down from the scene of the crime. It was only the mercy of God that they didn't drive over him. They got out and found one of the hooligans there praying away to the high heavens, 'Please tell me I'm not mad, please tell me I'm not mad.' When they got some good of him he told them he was after seeing some kind of strange person appear and disappear before his eyes just two minutes earlier. 'Get up out of that,' said the Guard kindly. 'Go on home with yourself and give up smoking that stuff you boys smoke or I'll take a torque wrench to you.'

The boy started wandering off in the wrong direction again

with Stasia and Kevin watching him like he was taking the last bits of their hearts with him. Grattan read the situation and stepped up to try to do better than the Guard with advice. 'Son,' he said, 'a very clever man called William James once observed that we are all but a bundle of habits. People rejected that because they had higher ideas of themselves. They didn't see the great news in it – that we can each start to make new habits any day we decide to.'

'Fucksake, leave it be,' said Ryle, 'the chap is confused enough already.'

Ryle, most likely, was right. But at least the chap turned and came home that night. Ryle put up a bit of an argument when it came to forfeiting the bed but in the end he was too drained to fight it out and went to sleep on the sofa, demoting Fletcher to the rug in front of the turf-burning stove.

Regardless of having been up all night worrying to a pale complexion about where her son would go to from here, in the morning Stasia made the visitors a fine bit of food to send them well on their way. And Boardman wouldn't take no for an answer when he produced a freshly poached salmon for them to take home. 'Which of ye does the cooking?' he asked, without missing a beat. He offered a few sprigs of his own thyme to go in the baking tray with the big gaffed fish. Ryle glanced at Fletcher and was overtaken by a shudder.

As Fletcher and Ryle walked back to their car Fletcher declared that he had a problem. What way was he to jump. 'I readily confess that I'm sometimes susceptible to picking sides as much based on the quality of person making an argument as I am by the argument itself,' he readily confessed. 'Am I a complete fraud? How can I hope to maintain fealty of any policy objectives if I'm so easily swayed by fondness for this person or the next? Is this the very weakness of thought that has our country lurching from one humiliating submission to the next?'

'Why do you think anyone gives a lumpy shite what side you come down on?' asked Ryle. 'More important now is that you get back to Dublin and let Margot wash and deodorize you because, if you don't mind me saying so, you are not physically good company in a car.' This kind of talk out of Ryle presumed quite heavily on Fletcher being too high mannered to return the compliment.

'I find myself very drawn to the quality of person caught up on each side of this horrible turf imbroglio, people who ordinarily would have great sympathy with each others' situations.'

'I wouldn't know about that,' said Ryle.

As they made it out onto the main road, Ryle eased somewhat. He added, 'If you're so torn, you could always take the third way.'

'Oh?' said Fletcher interested, 'a third way. I like your thinking, my friend, let's hear more.'

'As long as you keep your fucking eyes on the road,' said Ryle. 'OK then. We're not for either side but instead for restoring the natural fauna and flora of the lakes.'

'You'll have to explain that one,' said Fletcher, who could tend to the patronizing in certain tones he took with Ryle.

'Fucksake,' said Ryle, 'how simple could it be. These so called raised bogs all sit where once we had pristine emerald lakes. Am I right?' Ryle remembered primary school geography like a textbook. 'Unfortunately, as weeds and sallies and the like started to grow up in them, the locals were too lazy to think of dredging them once in a while. Sure enough, as the plants died they didn't rot properly and a huge layer of silage started to build up with the acid out of it killing every decent plant and fish that once thrived there. Eventually we ended up with the slag heaps that only the rare snail and the common rush can abide. So you trump the environmentalists. The campaign slogan relevant to this situation then should be *Unclog Our Loughs*. We can put out a little animation job showing the locals digging out sixty year supplies of turf and then see ducks and salmon once again jumping around in the crystal lakes that the devil and the glaciers meant us to have.'

'So your solution is, instead of adopting one side and offending friends from the other, to offend both parties equally? You tell the environmentalists to go to hell and you pile a new slur on the local people. I am glad to hear you saying *we* though.'

'First may I remind you that we don't owe any of those cunts anything. Besides, you don't blame the locals. You shift it onto their ancestors who are really only very distant relations.' Ryle settled into the leathered springs still sitting upright. The pain furrows on Fletcher's brow caused by too much thinking as much as by the welts and the hangover, seemed to have begun to smooth out. Ryle warmed, 'Think of the jobs. Think of how good you'll look cutting the ribbons. Think of the favour you can curry as you lorry out lake fishing licenses to the likes of Kevin Bogman and the foxy alien, and other such luminaries from both sides. You could even give the right of one rod to the Crusty Squad if you really regard all god's children as beautiful.'

'There may be something wrong with your mind,' said Fletcher, laughing kindly.

'What are you laughing at?' said Ryle, letting his seat back. 'Fucking old donkey.'

'Don't get me wrong,' said Fletcher, 'I do really like the idea of a third way. Just not *that* third way ...'

Without any invitation from the already slumbering Ryle, Fletcher unfolded his fourth way. 'The gombeen politicians are to blame of course. While ninety percent of the bogland is strafed by the State, they nominated a few square miles for the people to squabble over.' His voice had the relief of a man just out of a three-month constipation. 'Why didn't that dawn on me sooner?'

'Ah yeah, shoot down the bold thinking why don't you and go for the soft target,' mumbled Ryle, 'there might be hope for you yet boss.'

◊

It could never be proved that Ryle burnt down that demesne of the hooligans from both realms, the useless little haunted house on the bog. But even if Ryle had been the kind of person prepared to put any effort at all into having a clear name he could never have proved that he didn't. And of course he wasn't that kind. The result was a whisper set travelling the road in front of

Grattan Fletcher. The word was that for those who didn't like the wide embrace of Citizen Fletcher's stirring words, there was a less sweet second verse that might be delivered by a nameless henchman who operated beyond the reach of the law; one who displayed no evidence of having any bit of compassion or moral compass inside himself, nor any limitations on what he wouldn't do to those who crossed the man he called boss.

No help in going out to meet your troubles

Chapter V

WHEN RYLE DRIFTED into the office at 11 the next day, there was no sign of Fletcher. Instead, swivelling in his seat was Margot. Ryle had yet to develop a rose tinted perspective on Margot and at this stage she still just looked to him like a large awkward nuisance. He tried reversing but it was too late. She said 'Hi.' Next he tried ignoring her. He proceeded past her to the alcove, giving a single small nod at her as he went.

'*Leonard!*' she exclaimed (a word that's overused).

'What?' answered Ryle, 'Oh it's yourself. That's not a bad day now, Margot.'

'Don't you talk to me about the weather, if you please,' she said.

'Sorry so,' he said, 'where's himself today? He's not dead or anything?'

'He *slept in*, Leonard,' she said staring straight in his face. 'Grattan Fletcher the man who got up at 5.30 every morning since he was a child, this morning Grattan Fletcher *slept in!* What am I to make of this? Suddenly he's being sent away on field trips. Lasting *three days*. He has never been sent anywhere before. Why now?'

Ryle was disgusted. Fletcher's honour was so precious that he hadn't even stuffed his wife with a few comforting lies. Yet another service Ryle would have to provide for him. 'They're doing snap inspections countrywide,' said Ryle without hesitation, 'making sure nobody has snaked double glazing into the listed buildings to make them too snug. As you know, Grattan is our top man Nationally on the windows.'

'Oh I understand,' she said, clearly a virgin when it came to lies. 'Why didn't he just tell me that?'

Note: though not going the whole hog and telling Margot lies,

Fletcher had barred himself from telling her the truth about recent revelations and departures. He thought she would worry too much about him losing the job. He thought that she would worry too much about the future. *The compiler*

'But …' she said, doubt entering, 'no but that can't be it, Leonard. As I sat waiting for you here I couldn't help notice this note on his keyboard. Charles, *Secretary General Mac Gabhann*,' the title seemed to stick in her craw as much as the name, 'asking for a doctor's cert to cover the past three days.'

Ryle came closer and touched his nose. 'There's a concern, shall we say, that certain owners of the protected structures may have been tipped off in advance of previous inspections. So it all has to be kept secret.'

'What, and they suspect … the Secretary General himself is under suspicion?'

'I'll say no more,' said Ryle.

'Understood. Come to think of it, that shouldn't surprise me,' she responded uncertainly and then remembered the realities that had brought her into the office. 'But no, come along now, Len, that doesn't even begin to explain Grattan coming home battered and bruised while not seeming to remember how he got that way. Just talking vaguely about *taking the lead. Fortitude not being for good times but for adversity. Quoting Mandela on courage.* Last thing he says to me before going to sleep last night is, *my love, it occurs to me that there are tragedies in all lives but only triumphs in some.* And then this morning he has a lie in. *Grattan Fletcher!* There's something wrong.'

'Not at all,' said Ryle. 'He had a little fall is all. He got a little push out of a tower house window and sustained a few scratches. He was probably too embarrassed to tell you about that. And as for the other situations he may mention, it's just people we happened into on the road. Don't worry, Margot. I'm with him and you know I have the two feet well planted on the ground. You can rest assured that nothing will happen him with me at his back.'

'Who pushed him then?' she said.

'Oh,' said Ryle ignoring this quite unnecessary little jibe in the interests of selling her the overall lie of the land, 'the locals say that the dark spirit reigns in Balgeary castle owing to the fact that nobody of that family made it to the funeral of their poorer Balgury cousins. And although I don't believe in that kind of old pisroguery, I wouldn't have gone near the place if it had been up to me. Anyway I'd say it was just the wind pushed him.' Ryle said nothing more. He stood looking at her, barefaced. It was now, as she paused in confusion about what to believe, that he noticed her as the lovely looking woman she remains, very fresh. She was also very soft and refined in her speech.

She still had something she wanted to talk about. 'You look well in the tracksuit,' said Ryle, making another attempt to duck. 'Are you trying to get off a bit of the weight?'

'Ha!' she smiled, momentarily distracted, 'training for a mini-marathon.'

'Why does anyone do that?' he asked.

'I can't answer for anyone else, but raising money for a school in the slums of Maputo is my excuse,' she said. And smiled, 'Care to sponsor me, Len?'

'Fucksake,' said Ryle, 'that's a lot of exercise for a people that isn't civilized.'

'Not *civilized*?' she flushed, 'what's that, Len? Do you see nothing wrong that the most *organized* peoples are regarded the most *advanced* civilizations? Yet all we've really organized around is devouring more than our share of the world's resources. Burning the remains of everything that lived for over three and a half billion years in just a century of popping to the charity shop in Ballsbridge and hopping to an art exhibition in Barcelona. There's something not very civilized about that.'

'Jesus Christ there's a pair of you in it,' said Ryle, horrified. 'OK then, if you have nothing else, go on away with yourself. This is a place of work and I couldn't listen to more of this kind of talk.'

She moved awkwardly. 'He talks about you a lot these days,' she continued. 'Seems like he confides in you more than he does me. I was just wondering is there like something I should know. I am really worried, Leonard. His thoughts seem to be a sequence of frissons, and his moods dangerously elated. Even with all the bruising I've never seen him happier. I am so worried.'

'About what?' said Ryle, impatient because he had thought he had the issue wrapped up. 'Don't look for sympathy if you're having marital problems. When you buy land you buy stones.'

'Well, frankly, that he's having a nervous breakdown or something?'

'Is he fuck!' shouted Ryle with a laugh, forgetting for a minute who he was talking to. 'There isn't a new thing wrong with the daft cunt.'

'I know something is not right,' she said.

'Even if you were correct, what help is it to run out and meet your troubles?' asked Ryle sagely.

She went on her way after a few more questions. Ryle thought the incident interesting as he had never seen the woman in the office before. But he left the thought there.

As Margot Fletcher stepped out to a waiting taxi, she noted the blinds on the top floor move.

Ryle went away to the Argentinian restaurant on Haddington Road to see about his lunch, normality restored, he thought.

◊

The next morning Fletcher was waiting for Ryle. 'Do you think you could get the van again today my friend, the car is in for a service.'

'Holy fuck, surely you have some work to do after four days away from that desk.' said Ryle, who was not always reflective on such matters.

'What work they give me here,' said Fletcher, whose only assigned responsibility was to review the fenestration aspects of applications for restoration of listed buildings (the last of these applications had been submitted at the end of the boom four years back), 'I can have done in my first hour and still have an hour to wait for you to arrive. As a side note, I have sent a memo asking for further responsibilities every day of every year since I started here.'

'*Oh?* That would make you popular, I'd say,' commented Ryle.

'By the way, is Margot still anxious about you?'

'What do you mean?' said Fletcher.

Ryle then made a note that she hadn't told her husband about their conversation. He too retreated from mentioning it. In his own reassessment during the intervening hours, he had got on fairly well with Margot. It occurred to him that he might be able to get a short run with her while she was trying to sort things out with Fletcher. I am not going to say that Ryle felt good for entertaining these thoughts. But he was a man comfortable in his own tanalised skin. He thought it unseemly for a hungry man to be picky when he chanced on a plate of food.

Note: Ryle understood that qualms, like indigestion, could be dealt with afterwards. And Ryle had never had indigestion. Besides, because Ryle tended to somewhat overrate how he was seen by others, his willingness to succumb to lowly impulses far outstripped his opportunities for doing so. And if your crimes were only occasional, it hardly makes a blind bit of difference in the abridged accounts of your life that the reason lay with lack of opportunity rather than lack of inclination. *The compiler*

They took back roads as a preference that day, about the only thing they would consistently agree upon throughout their travels. Their preference for using non-National roads where possible, sprung from different wells. Fletcher felt he could express his residual disapproval for the motorways in this way (rather than by taking the train, which is a little pricy). Ryle was still interested in observing the work of farming now that there was no danger of anyone asking him to pick stones or wash a milking parlour, and he liked inspecting the state of the one-off houses, paralyzed from when the music had stopped. Ryle seemed to find reassurance in wild weedy yards in front of plan-book inspired glass gables and wall ties hanging like rusty tongues from unclad concrete block entranceways with the stone recycled from historic houses still lying in piles, unbuilt. If a person has a true habitat, this was his.

Fletcher, of course, and here we have to make allowances for his socioeconomic origins in South Dublin, saw the countryside as amenity. All evidence of continuing indigent subsistence in it disgusted him just a little, as it had done Ludolf von Münchhausen centuries before, and as it had done every person of sophisticated sensibility since. Landed men sitting bare arsed in makeshift hovels next to their castles; women that would be pretty if they were clean and dressed; all ignorant of the arts and subtle craftsmanship, delighting in idleness, inclined to rebellion, breeders of vicious ducks, producers of muddy pearls; in short, still a countryside that would be splendid if the people that live in other places were living here.

Note: There was a long line of quarrelsome liars that came after Ludolf, one of the more infamous being his nephew, Baron. Is it possible that Ludolf spent more time in Waterford than he let on in his account? Inhaled too much of the local vapours, so to speak? Be that as it may, there would still be a certain amount of nodding recognition for the observations of old Ludolf amongst the real Irish themselves. *The compiler*

'Stop, man!' said Fletcher

'Will I fuck!' said Ryle. 'Will you never accept what I tell you – that I can smell trouble?'

They were leaving Kilcullen via the Athy road. They were not long after having an acrimonious exchange over lunch, consumed from a narrow shelf next to the window of a Thai chipper. The reason for the unrest: just before leaving Dublin they had stopped at GardenWorld from which Grattan had subsequently emerged in possession of two spades, a pick, assorted empty sacks, and two traffic cones. At that point he had confessed to the real reason he had been so keen not to take his own car today. They were going to Athy on a mission that involved digging holes in housing estate common areas and in sports grounds. He had reasoned that they'd be less likely to be assailed by hostile locals when conducting such operations out of the back of an official public works van.

Forking you further into hardly necessary background information ... at a past AGM of the secret society, An Taisce, a person who must remain anonymous had casually revealed to Grattan Fletcher one of the many silent darknesses associated with the pretty little dorp of Athy: that most of the town is built on asbestos heaps. This information had lingered in the back of Fletcher's skull since then. Now, in activist mode, it of course had hobbled to the fore. He had convinced himself that the asbestos was the very cause of things not being right in Athy. Our intrepid man clung to this outlook in gallant disregard of the orthodox view that all which was wrong in that town could be sufficiently explained without any reference to asbestos. The irrefutable real explanations of course lay in the double curse of the hamlet being nestled in the valley of gloom that is the course of the Barrow River on top of it being a Laois town (albeit, marooned uninvited in Kildare).

But Fletcher had been proactive on the thing, so sure was he that his own explanation was the correct one. He had already made contact with a US lawyer who specialized in class actions. Fletcher was absolutely certain already that you just had to *follow the money*; some big company could be got to compensate the Athy people for the state they found themselves in.

'It didn't occur to you at all,' said Ryle, still arguing, 'that none of the similarly afflicted towns along banks of that deep and sullen waterway had anything to do with asbestos factories?'

'Will you make a u-turn, please,' repeated Fletcher.

'Well I can tell you one thing,' said Ryle, 'you'll be doing the digging yourself because I moved above the general operative grade more than ten years ago and besides, that equipment you got does not meet the minimum standards stipulated in the agreements between our union and the employer. Mild steel spades with cheap softwood handles—there's all kinds of health and safety implications there, let me tell you, not the least of which is splinters.' Ryle was very sound on health and safety regulations. His points fell on deaf ears because Grattan's attention had shifted. Athy was another Barrow town that would have to wait. At the far side of the road was this woman, not asking anything at all of them, walking in the opposite direction to them and occasionally sticking out her thumb. A lovely warm afternoon and she was buried in a parka.

'We're giving her a lift,' said Fletcher decisively.

'I'd sooner go to fucking Athy and watch you get your head beaten down to size for digging up the rugby pitch,' said Ryle inoffensively.

'What harm can she do us when there isn't more than a fistful of her in it? She's not in a good way,' said Fletcher.

'Anyone can see she's mad, hitching toward Kilcullen when she's only a hundred yards to walk to the epicentre of it. She will only make trouble for us,' said Ryle.

'I suspect she's going further and wherever that is, it's now where we're going too,' said Fletcher with assurance. 'Turn the van around and see if there's anything we can do for her.' Fletcher was so sure of himself that he grabbed the black knobbed gear stick and crunched it out of third to grate on the reverse and it was only a mercy that he failed as they'd undoubtedly have left the gearbox on the road behind them leaving Ryle with some explaining to do. Ryle swerved across the road as he reached into the door pocket and pulled out a wheel brace. He cracked a few of Fletcher's carpals, simultaneously advising that he keep his hands off the equipment. [fn]

[fn] Footnote

Oh wonderful, we have it all now. A little gratuitous phallicism mulched in with all the rest for good measure. *The Editors*

Ryle obliged only so as not to have to hear the wailing lecture he could see in his immediate future if he followed his own assessment instead. He made a meal of the turning and eventually passed the woman and stopped.

Sure enough it was a mistake.

Fletcher stood out to let her in, asking her where she was going. 'The hospital in Naas, please,' she said in a nice round voice.

'I believe we're going there too,' said Ryle at the wheel. She seemed to give no thought to the improbability of this, to the danger represented by two men doing a u-turn to pick her up, or to Ryle's less than attractive smile. She sat into the middle seat and put the little belt across her neat-skirted lap. At first she gave every indication that she was the type of hitcher who didn't wish to be drawn into the life of the vehicle. Ryle was happy enough to leave it like that as his sense was that she had a story that it wouldn't do them any good to hear. When she took off her thick woollen hat and revealed a bald head, he looked across at Fletcher with a raised eyebrow, demanding acknowledgement that he'd been right.

Fletcher of course couldn't leave well enough alone. 'So my dear,' he started, 'you are a patient rather than visitor.'

'A visiting patient,' she said. 'I'm going in for my poison.'

'I won't pry into why you have nobody to drive you,' said Fletcher, 'but could you not get a bus or taxi?'

'I'm living beyond Dunlavin. That's twenty-seven kilometres. Two buses,' she said, 'can't afford it on the lone parent's allowance.'

'Disgraceful,' said Fletcher genuinely shocked. His exposure to ordinary life was much less than he fancied. He was already fumbling for the right thing to say next.

'That's a lovely, mild day for the time of year,' said Ryle, trying to intervene. She nodded.

'But at least,' Grattan resumed, very feebly even for him, 'you're bearing up well. They say a positive attitude improves the prognosis.'

She stared straight front, very pale and then her lips puckered a little.

'Shite,' muttered Ryle.

'Fortitude and positive attitude my arse,' came the diminished voice. 'Try to maintain a positive attitude when your place in the treatment queue has to fit around the golf schedule of the same person who gave you the all clear six months earlier.'

'At least you have found courage in yourself,' said Fletcher now foundering uselessly in the deep water he'd dived into, 'not everyone finds it and we can't tell until we're under fire.'

'That's more of the bullshit platitudes of the worried well,' she said, not leaving them anywhere at all to turn. She was stuck in the middle of them, each of her hips touching one of theirs, and they were now going to travel every inch of this journey with her thanks to Fletcher. What little colour there had been was gone from her face.

'I'm sorry. You seem like a kind man,' she said turning to Grattan. She had the quivers and sobs of someone crying, but no tears. She was all dried out of them. 'But you don't know anything. I don't know you so I can tell you what I can't tell my loved ones because it would only hurt them more.'

Grattan returned her look, already horrified at what she was going to say, but not looking away. 'Your *courage under fire* is all well and good. But courage comes from a chemical well. You can drain it to get you through a moment. That's what it's for. But if you are under fire every minute of every day and night, the fire only ever getting slowly closer, with no distracting thought of reinforcements coming, then the occasional spurts of resolve are as nothing. I challenge you to find any human heart that can bear it. All around me are relentless forces of cold fact. And I am all alone. Think of the feeling of terror when you got lost in a supermarket as a toddler, the cold sweat of a nightmare, and think of those feelings coming to stay. To have to marshal courage and then renew it every day, every hour staving off the nagging thoughts, the regrets, the loneliness, the grief of leaving everyone you love behind, the plain fear … and still the last thought as you put your head on the pillow is the same as the first one arising when the lovely hues of sunrise peep over the Wicklow hills into your window. A sight I used to love so much that I painted it a hundred times, each time I thought more beautiful than the last. A sight that now makes me nauseous with fear. Nobody knows.'

They were quiet for a while. Fletcher put his hand on hers and she didn't react.

'Good luck,' said Fletcher lamely as Ryle parked the van in the ambulance area. 'May I ask your name?'

She may not have heard him as she stood up straight to face the folding doors of the dreadful building, alone. Ryle had observed the name on a card sticking out of her pocket but he didn't tell Fletcher.

They sat where they were for a minute. Fletcher let the water trickle freely down his face then. Ryle couldn't help noticing.

'Much better not knowing these things,' said Ryle.

'Don't talk rot,' said Fletcher. 'A woman with a young family, she has to grasp any chance to prolong her life.'

'In past times when cancer was an inner pain,' said Ryle, 'you could wake up any morning that the sun was shining and imagine you were going to get better.'

Grattan tried to gather his voice in slowly to this. 'The one thing that I could agree was better in times past,' he said, 'was that people were not insulated from death. By the time you knew anything about life you had seen death close by and felt its chill on your own shoulders. You knew it was integral. There was no hiding from it. So a dying person was still just themselves and was not left alone in the silence of our fears.'

More silence. Ryle started the van.

Grattan announced, 'I'm very badly knocked, Len, very badly knocked. Where's anyone's god or humanity in this?'

Ryle reckoned that this was the hardest hit Fletcher had yet taken. Like someone had pulled on his sternum with a lump hammer. 'Here boss, clear up the snot,' said Ryle offering an oil rag that was in the side pocket of the door. 'The best thing now is to go on home to Margot and forget this whole thing. It's bad for your health.'

'What was it Mitterand said?' asked Fletcher. 'We are all on a plane heading for a mountain, it's just that those with a diagnosis can see the mountain. You and I today, my friend, have had a look at the mountain through that dear woman's eyes. There is no going back. For her, we must redouble our efforts. There is no time to get weak. We live only through the other people we touch.'

'Wouldn't you be much better off,' said Ryle, 'if you didn't care very much about any man or beast? That way when you get your notice of execution you're no great loss.'

'That's easy for you to say,' observed Fletcher more truthfully than he'd intended. 'But there is nobody immune to the relentless fear the woman described. And yours is just another rationalization that will only keep you upright for short bursts.'

'Then what do we have science for?' said Ryle. 'They can tell you that you'll never see sunrise the same way again but give you nothing for that. Neither to cure what they diagnose nor to take the edge off the bald facts. I believe, though of course have no experience of this, that there are chemicals that make you feel so pleasant you dread dying less than not having your next hit. Wouldn't those be what you wanted when the time comes that you need to push death down in the ranking of your dreads?'

The rag left an oily glisten on Fletcher's face.

'Or why can't science at least, in failure,' said Ryle sticking to his own, 'dish out a few chemicals that allow you to set your own agenda so you only have to dredge up courage once rather than every other day.'

'Don't blame science,' said Grattan lured by one of his favourite themes, 'blame religion's archaic grip on legal codes. National morality shackled to Bronze Age knowledge. I'm of the opinion that without that moralistic convolution in debates, human compassion would prevail and all such options would be easily available to those who wish to access them.'

Ryle started the van as a hospital security man knocked on the window. 'Back to inspect holes in Athy then,' said Ryle gallantly, in the most upbeat tone he could muster.

'I think we'll go home,' said Fletcher. He said nothing more for the slow journey back to Northumberland Rd.

Just as he arrived at his desk, Fletcher's phone chirped. He picked it up without greeting. 'Long lunch, Grattan?' came the whine of Mac Gabhann.

Fletcher still said nothing.

'Do you think I don't know?' said Mac Gabhann irate. 'I know everything.'

'You don't,' said Fletcher quietly.

'I'll deal with you,' said Mac Gabhann. 'Just see. You'll come to respect my name and your life will descend into a bundle of regrets.'

'OK,' said Fletcher.

'Did you ever think,' said Mac Gabhann, most aggravated

by Fletcher's failure to rise for him, 'that doomsday for humans may not be in war or plague but pleasure?'

'Not now, Charles,' said Fletcher, slumping in despair, a new snippet of scientific misunderstanding in the air.

'What happens then to us Grat when they find the exact key that can be used on demand? No war on drugs will stop people acquiring that. No fear of losing everything else will stop them getting it. And no indirect quest for pleasure can compete. No accomplishment, no reproductive drive, no food satiation, needs to be pursued when you can go straight to the spot and stimulate it on demand. When rats have a choice, between food and reward centre stimulation, they starve themselves to death. Wouldn't that be amusing, Grattan—your noble species extinguished by pleasure?'

'Just fuck off, Charles,' said Fletcher ungraciously, hanging up.

Ryle and Fletcher left the building separately. They would never see Violet Johnson again, though from that day on Grattan would regularly find excuses to take them on the Naas road out of Kilcullen, his eyes always peeled back for her.

About his father's business

Chapter VI

THE NEXT MORNING, a Friday, Ryle arrived to find Grattan sitting on the wide bull-nosed granite steps out front. The sun was making a showing on the little circular clearing at the back of his head and a bitter wind had the curls flattened on the Easterly side. Two smokers in grey three-quarter-length Ballsbridge overcoats were arranged on the half landing below. Grattan had an empty coffee mug beside him and was staring at the Crossaire crossword.

'Well!' Ryle greeted. 'Would you go inside out of that you clown. You'll get your death.'

'Morning, Len,' said Fletcher, standing and shivering at the sudden reminder that he was back in open necked office shirt and socks, not the kit for outdoor activities. He faced the building but didn't move. His gaze roved slowly upwards as one visiting this place for the first time. 'How lovely is that all the same?' he said in a melancholic note as he reached over the railing to run his finger along a row of the red clay stretchers and headers as if it was sight for sore eyes. 'Flemish bond for strength and elegance. Perfectly cut brick in every arch. Dressed granite for every sill. Millimetre-perfect transverse pediments, ornate architraves, and sawtoothed corbelling. Those men gave a lasting account of themselves, sure and true.'

'What choice had they,' said Ryle, 'with the wolf always at the door.'

They went inside and Ryle proceeded to his alcove expecting to get the call at any minute. But it didn't come.

Eventually he came out and talked to Grattan's back, 'So, what's the plan today, boss?'

'Nothing,' said Grattan, subdued to a level below even that

which Ryle had previously wished for. 'I'm just going to respond to Cathal's request for a disciplinary meeting.'

'*Cathal* now?' said Ryle, 'What happened to Charles? So, no expeditions or anything?'

'No.'

'That's good then,' said Ryle. 'Everything back to normal then eh?'

Fletcher didn't answer.

Ryle left him to it. Before leaving at three Ryle asked, 'So what's on the itinerary for Monday, boss?'

'Nothing,' said Fletcher.

'Fair enough,' said Ryle.

'I'm sorry,' said Fletcher. 'I can see you're disappointed. I know I'm letting you down.'

'*What! Am I fuck disappointed!*' said Ryle, stung. 'I'm fucking delighted. You are some font of shit, I'll give you that.'

'Yes, yes I am, amn't I. That's what it comes down to.'

◊

On Sunday morning Suck Ryle was sitting at his conservatory table cursing. Ryle lived in a four-bed detached house in Donnybrook, appointed in the pristine minimalist style that had been modern in the 90s. The chrome fixtures and solid beech floors still had the look of a show house. That is, it looked like nobody lived here. Neither Ryle nor his cat left much trace of his prowling.

The cat, a big rough tom with a tail cut short and scars of many youthful brawls on his shiny black pelt, often sprawled in the bay window. Nothing but his slitty pupils moving until there were children passing on the road. That sight was like magic mushrooms to him. He'd leap the height of the tall bay window snarling and trying to scrawb his way out, wanting nothing but to get at the throats. Kids tended to stand transfixed in terror. Otherwise he was placid. By mutual agreement he and Ryle never talked or touched though it was not unheard of for the two to have a game of draughts on a Saturday evening.

The beast's name, if it had ever had one, was unknown to Suck as he was not the owner. Ryle was minding it for an aunt. The same lady was a duster in the Thou Shalt Return nursing home out in Bray. She didn't care for people much but was a martyr for misunderstood animals.

There, the cat had revealed its ability to predict death. It would curl up next to the bed of someone and the person would be dead within seven hours. Some people found great comfort in it. But one old gent had developed no fondness for the sight of the cat at all. He thought to prolong his own existence by the expedient of spearing the cat with his blackthorn cane whenever the creature came near him. The cat never took a challenge lying down and would tear into that same veteran tooth and nail.

In the end the cat had to be removed as the man wouldn't budge despite being strafed, striated, and scabrous from the battle of wits. After many attempts to capture the cat for removal, a team of deer hunters from Tipperary shot the tail off him and while he was worrying about that, a tarpaulin was thrown over him. No family could be got to rehome the unfortunate creature as health and safety regulations (gone mad) apparently required the owner (a canny man who also owned the adjoining crematorium and was well thought of in the town) to tell potential cat rescuers about this fellow's attitude to children. Neither would Ryle have offered temporary sanctuary despite sharing the cat's attitude to youngsters – like the cat, he firmly believed that the next generation should be left to sort their own shit out and he saw no obligation on himself to pretend to like them. However, his aunt happened to be the knower of certain parts of Ryle's early biography, parts that had appeared on no CV. She had reminded him of this when she came with the box. It was fifteen years now since Ryle had agreed to mind the brute for a month, the old man apparently getting heartier by the year and showing no sign of ever dying. Much the same as the cat himself.

Once, a few years back Joseph Delaney, a colleague from the OPW stores, had happened into Donnybrook on the hunt for famous people. He was an autograph fanatic, the dick. He had nearly dropped when he spotted Ryle out in front of his house dressed up in the Sunday best, pruning azaleas like there was no tomorrow. Delaney had come into the garden and stared open-mouthed like the worst kind of gobshite, at the man in turtleneck and corduroy holding a very good model of Hasami shears.

Note: a good brand is never a bad investment when it comes to cutting equipment. That is, if you put any value on your time: go Swiss or Japanese and never ever go for stainless. *The compiler*

Ryle had passed it off blithely, 'What the fuck are you gawking at Delaney? Is everyone not entitled to be his own man when off duty?' Delaney kept staring, 'But Suck … but this place must have cost over a million. Well over …' Ryle invited him inside then, where his astonishment had only ballooned. He was offered no refreshments. Ryle instructed him to take one look around and consider what comes to them that are prudent. Whatever way the emphasis fell on Ryle's words, Delaney went quiet. With his eyes fixed on the large unmoved cat seated at the draughts board, he reversed out the door. He never told anyone what he had seen in Donnybrook that day. He had avoided Ryle ever after and gave up on the autographs altogether. An ill wind. [fn]

[fn] Footnote
You are asked to believe that all of this background 'information' on the Ryle character and his cat derives from a small ledger of unsanctioned outings in a public service vehicle? We would suggest you consider the possibility that there are other strands to the compiler's association with Mr. Ryle. *The Editors*

Anyway, back to the day that concerns you. Spread over the large glass table top today were three thousand jigsaw pieces. Ryle was very handy at the jigsaw game but this one was annoying the shite out of him. It was of Guernica and he wasn't finding his colour blindness giving him the advantage he had expected. He stood up to transfer his white shirts from the washer to the drier. His phone vibrated in his tracksuit pocket and he inspected the number. The first three digits were from the Rathmines area. He killed it, as it wasn't his habit to take calls he was not expecting. He remembered too late that Fletcher lived in that neck of the woods. In a three storey over basement nightmare that the estate agents would describe as a lovingly restored Victorian home. (That project had kept Grattan distracted for an early decade of his married life when he should have been out enjoying his good health.)

Then Ryle realized that the call couldn't have been from Fletcher. Fletcher always used the mobile and besides would have been out for his swim in Sandymount, his Sunday mass substitute. Ryle phoned back immediately.

'Well?' he greeted Margot warmly as if he already had the right to be familiar with her. Ryle was inclined to unilaterally shift the status of his relations with other individuals. More commonly however this tended toward a downgrade in familiarity with persons he concluded could be of no further interest or use to him.

'Tell me straight,' she said, 'is he sick?'

'I suppose he is,' said Ryle, 'but this is no way to talk. We should have a couple of mugs of coffee between us to warm us up.'

'OK,' she seemed hesitant, 'where do you suggest?'

'Sure why don't I drop in to your house there to save you getting out of the slippers,' said Ryle.

'What? Er, no, the house is a mess. I'll meet you in the Roma Bistro in Donnybrook. That's near where you live isn't it?'

'Who told you that?' said Ryle, a very private man. 'Where did that curly-mopped bollox get permission to let on to anyone that he knows where I live?'

Ryle didn't take any negative read from Margot not wanting him in her house. To him it confirmed that she was thinking the same way he was. He just surmised that maybe it was all a bit quick for her. If there was one thing he knew about women it was that they didn't understand time as being of the essence. But he would be patient and wouldn't rush her yet.

'You were at mass this morning, Leonard?' was the first thing Margot asked Ryle when she stepped into the coffee shop. She assumed the turtleneck and corduroy slacks were mass gear.

'Yes,' said Ryle, flaming now at how much Fletcher talked to his wife about him. He offered too much detail, 'I was at the 8 o'clock in the Carmelite Priory on Bloomfield Avenue, a lovely little mass celebrated by Father Theodore McCloud SJ.'

'8 o'clock?' she said puzzled, 'they stopped that years ago. And isn't Theo McCloud the priest who plays football for Galway?'

Ryle was surprised. He had assumed her to be an atheist like her husband and had thus never thought that she'd have any basis to scrutinize the portrait of himself that he regularly served up to Fletcher. 'Maybe it was later and another man who sounded like a McCloud. How should I know? I was in the porch and wasn't fucking clock watching was I? Now what ails you?'

'The truth doesn't have much meaning for you, does it Leonard?' said she.

'What did truth ever do for you?' said Ryle. 'It's not truth that gets anyone through life. You are looking great.'

Ryle was native to the faith that all humans (other than himself, if that's relevant) fatten on personal lies. That they gobble news about how they're perceived and are blind to how little notice is actually taken of them one way or the other. Unfounded personal observations could induce short bouts of craven dependence in some, temporarily opening a window for Ryle to climb through. He generally found the belittling observation more effective than the flattering. It was what was delivered most naturally by him and received most readily by the local constituency, instinctively suspicious of plámás. *'You are a fraud really, aren't you?' 'You know you'll never succeed, I can see that in you.'* These were lines that had made some think Ryle had seen into their souls, whereupon brief access to their bodies went without saying and was generally later forgotten without mention. Not everyone of course fell to the rogue, but poaching, he understood, is a numbers game. All that said, here now was the same Suck Ryle allowing a slight fondness for Margot to make him choose the harder route to her affections. What perverse system of logic is it that drives any of us? In niceties, Ryle was prone to the misstep. 'You are still looking like a well-rounded person,' he added smoothly.

'So you're still saying I'm fat?' she said grinning to herself, two or three steps ahead of Suck.

'Not nearly as fat as I used to think you were,' he said quickly. 'Anyway I'd rather a bit of a lard cushion any day than some old bony yoke that has to inspect every morsel before she'll swallow it.'

She ordered a mélange while he asked for a black americano.

'Well, you see now that Grattan revealed information about you?' she said, trying to become smarter in her dealings with Ryle. 'Don't you want to get even by telling me anything you think he wouldn't want me to know about him?'

'I told you all I can think of,' said Ryle, 'but I am susceptible to bribery.'

She ignored this and unbuttoned her latest concerns. Fletcher had spent Friday digging out contacts for the elderly and the distressingly sick. Even distant relatives and people who had not been his friends when they were well. 'He started quoting Christopher Hitchens, and the Bible at me,' she said. 'I'm certain he is not well.'

'What exactly did he say?' Ryle asked with more interest.

'Something like, Hitchens was a very clever man in health. But he only cut to the real heart of matters when he was sick. *Go ahead, make that visit, you have no idea the difference it will make.*'

'Hitchens, eh?' said Ryle, looking at the movement of her breasts as she gave way to a sob. 'Carry on.'

'Grattan is now preaching that we are afraid to visit because we are trying to distance ourselves from the dying even before they are ready to go; the most cruel desertion. He said he had never before thought about the word desertion. Leaving a loved one in the desert to die. You remember that story from the Bible of the man taking his mother into the desert in a barrow? ...'

'Indeed,' said Ryle, 'he sometimes says peculiar things. There's nothing new there. Nothing to worry about would be my diagnosis.'

'I know what you are saying,' she said, not knowing what he was saying. 'It is what makes our daughter and now his grand-daughter too, hang on every tone in his voice, always divining for his approval. They somehow knew from before they could speak that ultimately he had external moorings and no matter how much he loved them he wouldn't always just tell them what they wanted to hear. He would tell them quietly what was right. He ...'

'He wasn't just an average man with a barrow?' said Ryle.

'Something like that, maybe,' she said doubtfully now. 'But this is different, Len. Let me tell you this and then let's see you insist there's nothing to worry about ...' she paused and looked around as if anyone might care. 'Grattan Fletcher is not in Sandymount today. No splashing about in the murky little waves, taking in the wonders of the natural universe. No coming home in blue salty happiness. None of that. Instead he is somewhere on the road to Cobh where he is going to visit a demented grandaunt.'

'A nice drive,' observed Ryle, 'especially the motorway parts of it. Until you get to that poxy town, that is. Did you know there's a curse on it? The best natural deep sea port in the universe and nobody uses it. The Lusitania and the Titanic are only the tips of the iceberg. All the poor bastards need coming in on top of them now is Fletcher, a magnet for misfortune.'

'*What?* No,' she said, staring at Ryle, 'do you realize what I'm saying to you? Suddenly I've lost him in every way. From having him in my face every day. Taking him for granted. And suddenly he's completely gone from me. Weekdays it seems he's going to be away on whatever *field trips* with you. And on weekends he's going to be doing his rounds like an atheist priest bringing succour to the dying. I almost expect him to turn to me and say, *don't you know I must be about my father's business?*

'What did the old boy do anyway, Fletcher's old fella?'

'A salesman for Gouldings,' she said, allowing herself a small laugh that Ryle misread, 'Gouldings Fertilizers.'

'Well the bird must spread his wings. I'm glad to see you're over him. Such is life, as the man says,' said Ryle. 'So tell me this, have you decided yet on any alternative amusements?'

'*Over him?* What?' Suddenly she took a proper look at Suck Ryle, which was never good. 'Christ, don't tell me ...' she said, standing. 'I choose not to think that. I would be too hurt on his behalf and you one of his best friends! And whatever on earth could make you think I'd be interested in you?'

'Best friend, eh,' said Ryle, a little off-balance, 'who told you that? But wait up there ... You can't cod Suck Ryle ... what's the matter with him that he can't get friends of his own kind?' But it was too late. She was gone out the door without even paying her share of the bill. Ryle sat there, with lingering feelings and sorrow at his loss.

'*Don't I know you?*' came the voice of a Bulgarian woman in a fur coat who had come over to his table on her way out. 'And the woman just with you?'

'What the fuck are you on about?' said Ryle, taken off guard, '*loon!*'

'Yes, yes, you're Rod Stewart,' she concluded, too delighted with her find to observe that the likeness weakened on second glance; that aside from jacket taste, the flaps of hair, the bold eyes, and an omelette accent, there wasn't too much similarity. She continued, 'Welcome to Dublin! You look much younger in real life.'

Somebody at another table whispered, 'Oh my God, it *is* him.'

'And her who left, she was, she's ... yes, yes, Amy Belle.'

'Are you fucking nuts?' said Ryle, nonplussed because he happened to have a bit of admiration for the same Belle. He had once watched her busking on Miller St. in Glasgow. The woman pulled out a fancy phone and on YouTube, called up the duet that was corrupting her mind. At full volume the surprisingly good Nokia speaker let the sounds of beauty and beast make everyone in that little restaurant pause.

I don't want to talk about it [fn]

[fn] Footnote
Fifteen verses removed. Essentially, *you broke my heart and if I stick around will you listen to it.* The Belle version has a certain cheesy charm, granted. But if the compiler thinks we are going to battle with the Stewarts on his behalf, well, guess what. *The Editors*

Note: if you haven't seen this one, may I share the advice I gave to a physician who told me years ago that I was dying for the want of tablets: treat yourself. *The compiler*

The sounds had the rapt Bulgarian doing a Charles Aznivore waltz with herself. Ryle, as the accidental vehicle of her transport, would normally have jumped straight in to such a nice person's temporary vulnerability. But he was off-balance. 'Anyone can see,' he said coarsely, determined not to listen for even a little bit longer, 'that woman gone out the door has a good few pounds on Amy Belle. Now fuck off, all of you, and don't be annoying me.' The people just smiled kindly upon him, understanding. Ireland is a good place for celebrities to be left alone.

Yet, the episode had a tinkling of poignancy for Ryle at that moment, another new thing for him. He left that place, in a small degree of discomfort.

◊

On Monday morning Ryle was worried that there might be some awkwardness with Fletcher regarding his wife's perceptions of what had been said the day before, so he walked past without greeting him.

'Come out here, Ryle,' said Fletcher. 'We need to talk.'

When Ryle stayed put, Fletcher looked in. He was smiling. 'I've got one last trip that I promised I'd make.'

'Sound man,' said Ryle, relieved. Margot was still keeping him a secret. 'Let's get a move on then. I'll get a van.'

Fletcher looked very pleased, misinterpreting.

Fletcher carried two placards to the back of the vehicle and asked Ryle to open the back door for him. The one facing up said in blue flip chart ink, 'You don't love or grieve any less just because you can't afford the health insurance premiums.' Windy even in slogan. They were off to a protest at the closure of some hospital in one of the border counties, territory that Ryle had no truck with.

'What's that placard got to do with shutting some small town abattoir?' asked Ryle.

'It's all connected,' said Grattan vaguely. 'Did you know that in this great little country of ours, those with no health insurance have a lower life expectancy?'

'There wasn't so much bother before the bust,' Ryle the tech man responded, never forgetting his roots, 'while all the middle class could afford the VHI. Not a word back then about the people who left school with a cookery and woodwork cert being the sausage meat in hospitals run by professional unions for the leisure of their middle-class memberships.'

'Two wrongs don't make a right,' said Fletcher.

'I usually find they do,' said Ryle, 'but I don't see what that has to do with this.'

'Besides, don't knock the unions,' said Fletcher. 'Just because all decency has been eroded from private sector workplaces doesn't mean it's wrong to continue to demand civilized conditions in public employment. Remember it's the unions that protect our terms and conditions against the likes of Mac Gabhann. They are the ones who have created the space for people like us to use our spare time more constructively.'

They drove quietly toward the border.

The protest went well by the standards of such events. Fletcher was pleased despite getting caught for a minute on a camera.

On the way back he was fiddling with his tablet looking up public transport in the Cavan area. He wanted to document the group's claims about how the closure would hurt. Instead of a train timetable for Cootehill, he pulled out Lisa O'Neill in an Arran cardigan. He shut up instantly when she started:

There's no train, no train to where I come from ... Smuggling wheelbarrows from land to land, cross the border and I'm doing grand.

'My God, Ryle,' he whispered, 'just when you can't be surprised ... the funny little thing comes at you out of nowhere. Wrapped up lovely in a geansaí with a voice that would find the soul in a stone and a verse like Kavanagh. The resilience of life, isn't it wonderful.'

'Will you turn it down to fuck,' said Ryle. 'It's wrecking my head.'

On the way back Ryle pulled into Maynooth looking for a place he could get a bun. As he settled into a plate of muffins in a Starbucks knockoff, Fletcher twiddled. A young person sat close with his tall frap and Ryle was about to tell him to shove off and sit somewhere he was wanted when Fletcher engaged the man in conversation. If that's what you'd call it.

Turned out the chap was from New Orleans and so had no understanding of personal space. Ryle still told him to fuck off but the guy just took it as Irish humour. Fletcher reached out with talk about some kind of music festival he'd attended in the boy's home town. And when he recalled the names of streets, the kid lit up like an LED balloon. Poor little fucker was homesick like any normal person would be, sent thousands of miles to earn his fortunes converting pagans to Mormonism. And all of a sudden he was telling Fletcher how uncertain he was about everything in life. How cold he was finding it over here. How much he missed Mom and Dad.

When he went looking for restrooms, to recite some bit of a prayer or do a bout of chanting I suppose (and what harm is that to anyone), Fletcher whispered to Ryle, 'you see, good spirit lurks everywhere, if we are not afraid to see it.' Ryle was finishing the last muffin and expressed his response with large crumb droppings. The chap came back and took out a Surface to search Maps for the hotel Grattan had stayed in. That, he didn't find of course, as hard as he looked. Washed away no doubt. He got distracted then syncing his poor Outlook Calendar and checking his Facebook like a normal christian. Fletcher was moved to nod his approval, 'when we see past the veneer, just a lovely regular kid.'

Ryle was stuffed. 'Fucken monkey on a typewriter,' he said, for some reason especially rattled by this evangelist. Next the chap went to Tweet all his followers. He showed Fletcher. *Just met more wonderful folk here; my spirits awakened; Alleluia!*

'We should get more tech-savvy,' said Fletcher to Ryle.

'Better to stay offline and be suspected a fool than to Tweet and demonstrate the fact,' said Ryle.

When Fletcher started asking the chap more about his family, Ryle took out a hunting knife to gouge and peel the edge of the table, a behavioural therapy he opted for when boredom was getting the better of him. The two kept talking. Ryle's hand slipped and he gashed the little laptop. '*Jesus!* What the fuck's the matter with you, dude!' exclaimed the lad, surprisingly large when he stood up with the wrestling chest stuck out. But then suppressing his anger with only a moment's effort, he smiled, 'Oh goodness, I'm so sorry for my reaction. You've only scratched my Surface.' Ryle couldn't take any more. He gave the impression he was going to the toilet but instead he drove off and texted Fletcher that he could walk home. Incredulous, Fletcher had recourse to help from the boy with a public transport app, and in turn, took him home for tea.

Let sleeping dogs lie

Chapter VII

AT EXACTLY FIVE THIRTY every evening Mac Gabhann would crack open the first of four boiled eggs set before him by Fran. Other householders would all have retreated to electronics in their rooms by then as it was understood that the hoary progenitor couldn't abide disorder when he was trying to unwind. After the eggs he would have two slices of fruit cake. Then he would take a walk with his two fat jack russells, the hairless witless strain of russell that Dubliners prefer. (Mac Gabhann, it should be borne in mind, was no good to anyone because all his capacity was used up being good to himself.) After that and before going to his den for a blast of Bizet in infra-red (he had recently installed a dry sauna), he would watch a bit of telly. Mainly the local channels though, in fairness to him. He liked the consistency of RTÉ where the same people have been commentating on politics and soccer since independence.

So it was always unlikely that Fletcher's first fleeting appearance on the Nation's wide screens was going to slip by Cathal Mac Gabhann.

There he was sprawled on his brown leather sofa with his legs on a footrest and a glass of Jameson Crested 10 on the armrest. A panel of banking columnists was given an indignation break for a bit of lighter news. A stock clip of a protest about the closure of the psychiatric unit of St. Lazarian's, a hospital somewhere in the bandit counties. The home channels reports are of course stuffed with winks to the middle classes. Rug-headed hints at the real facts that could not be stated baldly because of political correctness gone mad. Mac Gabhann of course instantly divined the real explanation for the closure. Yes, it was a money saving necessity spurred by the loss of a ministerial TD. But no, it wasn't that mandarins thought the number of clients for these services had suddenly declined. Merely that these clients were too far gone to be helped.

Mac Gabhann was cogitating on his inside knowledge of these things when the camera panned and suddenly he yelped in delight, 'Aha! Gotcha!' There was such emotion in his voice that Fran came in to the lounge to see what was the matter. Sure enough, not shying from the camera, in fact looking like one of the displaced patients, was a familiar, goofy form waving a placard that looked like a child had written it.

'Jesus, isn't that Grattan? He's all fired up,' said Mac Gabhann's wife, without thinking. 'He looks as angry as Bono. He's a little bit charming like that, isn't he.' Then putting her hand to her mouth too late as always, she tried to conjure something by way of damage control.

Mac Gabhann stared at her. There was history here that he liked to silently punish her with. One not forgotten night when they were all nineteen, Charles Smith had come back to his tent to see his then girlfriend Francesca Heaton snuggling up to his colleague Grattan Fletcher.

It was their first year in the department and all three were Junior Executive Officers. (The plump duckling Margot had not yet floated into Fletcher's view.) Mac Gabhann was still Smith and Fran was still Francesca.

Note: In case you are still having difficulties ageing the population of this almanac, Fran was a year younger than Fletcher and Mac Gabhann. And she says she went to school with Bono's younger brother. So that'll tell you. They were all shoving on. *The compiler*

Despite having not gotten off to a great start with Smith, Fletcher had reached out—inviting him and Fran (who was at the desk between them) to join a group of Fletcher's friends going in convoy to a Lisdoon festival which no one was to know would be the last. Fletcher, even then, trying to fix things. Smith had not wanted to go. His dislike for Fletcher, already well germinated. But he'd regrouped when Fran had given a puzzled look across the desk and said, 'But Charlie, I thought

you were a purist metal fan, surely you don't include even Rory
and Morrison in your list of lightweights?' He did indeed, so
he did. But he agreed to go, chalking it down to the project he
had set himself: securing Fran for breeding more little sons of
Smith from.

Things hadn't proceeded into quite as reconciliatory a trajec-
tory as Grattan had hoped though. As they'd headed back to the
tents on the second night, Smith, setting himself up as the man,
had strode off to bum a spliff and a toilet roll for them. He didn't
come back for ages. Lost probably in the acres of mucky tents,
but he would never admit that afterward. In the interim Fran
had got drunker and more affectionate towards Grattan. When
she asked him if he wanted to have sex with her, naturally he was
interested. When she almost immediately then closed her eyes
and bared her bottom he became a little alarmed. His reward for
the nuanced decline was having to hear things she hadn't told
anyone. He should have been on guard against such a maudlin
turn as, in musical mood, they'd earlier discovered a shared liking for the Irishmen Johnny Maher and Steven Morrissey (bucks
you'd never have thought had any plans to still be hammering
away at the futility songs thirty years later). Even back then
Fletcher was unfortunate in being in the right place at the wrong
time. Even then, it cost him.

'In truth, I only had sex once before,' she had started.

'Maybe just sleep now,' said Grattan. 'When you're sober I
won't be the person you'll want to have talked to.'

'An engineering student I met in The Baggot Inn,' she
insisted, 'when I was sixteen. I was revelling in my new found
sexiness and thinking the world was before me for the taking.
In a doorway on Pembroke Lane I kissed him and let him touch
me. I was a little drunk then too. And slow to the realization that
I had been wrong all along. That I was not, in fact, every bit as
strong as any man. And I was not in fact well able to take care
of myself everywhere. I discovered this at the point when his
uncomfortably strong hug had turned to a rugby lock, a thick
arm prized under one of my shoulders as he pulled my other
elbow behind. His other hand roaming then, unrestricted. The

caress of my neck turned to a thumb and forefinger digging into arteries and squeezing to a rhythm that was not affected by the urgent sounds I then heard from myself. When he released control there to gather my frock up my voice finally rose. But not enough. And then I went quiet altogether when his practical hand slammed back to choking me for a few seconds. Then he returned to his task. He pulled my underpants down around my knees just like that, saying *easy now, easy there*. He dealt impatiently with the mechanical problem of forcing himself in. That's all there was to it. After he was done he said I was great and that my tears were just of confusion. But not to worry, my head would soon catch up with my hormones. The only stupid thing I could think of saying was that I hadn't wanted that. He said coyness was cute but that my body had told him I'd liked it a lot. He asked if I still wanted him to walk me home.'

'Next day my mother looked at the bruises and asked how much I'd resisted. And then concluded that it wasn't really rape *as such*; that I shouldn't choose to dwell and to be a victim. That I should chalk it down, shut the door on it, go forward and be more careful. More realistic about life.'

'It's not fair,' Grattan had said to her, 'people shouldn't have to make these kinds of choices in order to keep their place in society.'

'It's not fair,' she repeated.

'Charles at least is good to you?' said Fletcher. She didn't reply. After a time she started snoring.

Fletcher had laid awake, shaking, brought up soft and innocent to these kinds of things.

Some time later he had heard her crying, still slurring a little, saying 'I'm not nobody.' He had pulled his sleeping bag closer. What Smith mistook for an amorous embrace when he finally jutted his head back in through the tent flaps, was just an ordinary one. When Fran finally woke groggily, after ten, Smith was still asleep after his night of lost wandering. Grattan who had been up since five-thirty and had everything but the tent packed into the mark 1 Kadett, told her quietly that he knew someone, a counsellor. She looked at him blankly, the door shut on it again.

Mac Gabhann of course hadn't forgotten. To this day he didn't know how much had happened between his wife and Fletcher, the downside of dealing out silent rebuke. It didn't matter though. Mac Gabhann had then had the perfect excuse for cutting off all further friendship overtures from Fletcher and at the same time had a knife carefully stored away for later use in jabbing Fran. He had never realized that he needed to make no effort to punish her. From the outset she had chosen his permanent presence in her life as her punishment.

Now, decades on, she was still playing his game. She said in mock retreat, looking away from the TV, 'But how impulsive of the man! He's impossible. Egging on people who protest in ignorance and fear against their own interests!' With one look Mac Gabhann ran her out of the room before she had managed to spoil his moment altogether. He had developed such skills over the years.

In five minutes flat he was up to his little desk, situated off his bedroom in what was to have been a wife's walk-in wardrobe. He started up the laptop and headed straight onto the RTÉ website. He was deft enough at the technology when it suited him and he had the player up and fifteen fairly similar screenshots taken in a couple of blinks of an eye. He readied himself to phone Josephine Sloane on her mobile. As he alt-tabbed between the stills he found his pleasure abating. He let the phone screen go back to sleep. The reality began to nibble at his testicles.

Cathal Mac Gabhann, if nothing at all else in this world, was a wily old fox. One of the disciplines that had stood him well in his steady ascent to Secretary General, was that before engaging anyone in conversation he would try to predict everything they might say, prepare how he would retort, and assess the chances of a conclusion being reached that was in line with his desires. He would decide on that basis whether to actually go ahead with the conversation or not. What Sloane was going to say was becoming depressingly clear as he engaged in his preparation. After a barrage of the usual snippy remarks about his right to phone her at all hours she would follow with snide allusions to 'unbalanced application' of attention to the work practices of particular employees at the risk of losing sight of the general broader picture. She had had the temerity during their last conversation to use the terms, 'loss of perspective' and 'unhealthy fixations.' Mac Gabhann anticipated what Josephine Sloane would say now. *Let sleeping dogs lie, darling. Colleagues over in Health won't thank us for creating the impression that a senior government official had been cautioned for speaking out against health cuts. Bide your time.* She fascinated and repulsed him for being more politically astute than himself and more naked in her ambition. Prudishness can take peculiar forms.

Fundamentally the most tedious kind of arsehole, a dutiful one, Mac Gabhann settled into writing his notes for another futile counselling session, rather than for the final transgression hearing he so desired. It would become yet another file in the folder that was Grattan Fletcher's disciplinary record. He would of course *bide his time.*

The less said, the easiest mended

Chapter VIII

RYLE WAS SURPRISED TO FIND Fletcher in the Southern Rock gear again, Tuesday morning. 'I thought you were cured, boss,' he said.

'Cured?' asked Fletcher distractedly, as if he was talking to a normal person.

'You look worse if anything,' said Ryle.

'Yes, worse, that's it,' said Fletcher, 'that Wicklow woman opened my eyes. More than ever, there's no going back.'

'I don't think that was her intention,' said Ryle.

'When she invited me back into the lives of those I had abandoned in the cowardice of the *worried well*,' said Fletcher. 'She invited me to come to see the whole truth unveiled. There is no other time for any of us, Leonard. Like her we each only have today. There is only now. Are you with me?'

'No time like the present? That kind of thing?' asked Ryle.

'Sort of,' said Fletcher inclusively, picking up the much larger than usual sandwich box. Margot was already resigning herself that Fletcher would keep going about his father's business.

'I beg to differ then,' said Ryle. 'I find there's quite a lot of time just like the present.'

'Well, I suppose, in some Hegelian sense perhaps,' said Fletcher in tones he still thought accommodating. No matter how far he travelled on his path to virtuosity the man remained unable to refrain entirely from his horrible habit of firing off little hard balls of goat shit every now and then, 'But for you and I as individuals subjectively navigating our pathways through the indeterminably few days in which we will remain able to aspirate our cells, it is principally in the present moment that our responsibilities reside.'

'You could think your way out of any pleasure,' said Ryle, 'and there is one of life's greatest pleasures that you have failed to recognize in all your days. The pleasure of not bothering to scratch your arse. Laziness! Letting someone else worry about your problems as well as their own.'

'Have heart, my faithful friend,' said Fletcher, laughing dismissively.

'You think I'm fucking joking?' said Ryle, thoughts of Margot's spreading braless breasts returning as they had done fairly often since the coffee. The runt had nurtured a fancy to see her sobbing again, ideally in a less controlled way.

It was not that Suck Ryle entirely lacked appreciation of Fletcher's patronage. He perhaps saw himself more as a neutron. If Margot succumbed to his insertion of himself in her orbit, he was merely establishing her disloyalty rather than inducing it. If she dropped her guard for a minute it would be purely on her; indulging herself in a sneaky lick of pleasure with the younger-looking harder man. And if she were never to budge, as a person more grounded in reality would have already predicted from the lack of warmth in their parting words, then Ryle wouldn't begrudge either of them. He would wait for another time just like the present to have another go. Either way, he reasoned, Grattan might be pleased with the knowledge that Ryle was at least not actively doing any real harm.

'Give us this day our mouldy bread,' said Ryle not very respectfully to Daly, arriving then with fairly poor timing.

'Chillax, bro,' said Daly.

Though an assistant secretary, Fletcher had only one genuine report, the minimum required by law. Barely one, given that it was Daly. Mac Gabhann had arranged this, intended as one more humiliation that fell just short of the constructive dismissal benchmark. He didn't realize that not being in seniority over other staff was no hardship for Fletcher. He was glad not to have more than one of Daly to feel responsible for. Glad to be able to pretend that Ryle was under his wing when in truth he knew that he owned no blame at all for the state of Ryle.

But Daly single-handedly kept Fletcher worried. Mercifully,

he appeared only once every few months. Here he was now, pulling a chair presumptuously up to Fletcher's desk, with something
on his mind.

'What the fuck has brought you down off the ceiling,
Richmond?' asked Ryle.

'So, goodly sire,' began the chap, addressing Fletcher. Daly's
only obvious tendency was to happily bob along on the wavelets
of Internet fad. He took off his fedora and said with a new air
of gentility, 'I trust you are well? I believe I may have overheard
you talk once about Sartre and his view on activism and cetera?'
At least the self-pitying language of the misunderstood Internet
gentleman was easier on Fletcher's ears than the circlejerk of
hashtag-awkward globish which had infected Daly's linguistic
effusions last quarter. That had irritated the good man out of all
proportion. As of course it would any Irishman with a sound
knowledge of his history – corrupting the English used to be
solely our preserve.

'Hello to you too, Daly. Perhaps you did,' said Fletcher,
'though it's not a great moment that you've caught me in. And
to tell the truth I can't recall the context.'

'I have news for you,' said Ryle, sagely. 'You're not sixteen
anymore. And whatever shit you're into this time will blow over
without real people like myself or this other clown ever knowing it existed.'

'You durst refer to your liege as a *clown,*' he said, turning to
Ryle. 'That is not alright, knave. But I suppose no man is a hero
to his valet. Well my dear fellow, what I'm *into* this time you
enquire? I'm just a *nice guy* tired of getting disenfranchised. I'm
at the vanguard of an MRA action group. And I've been tasked
with developing theoretical underpinnings from which strategies
for an effective campaign of infiltration and counter-subversion
may be devolved. In fact, you perhaps should consider joining
us, my goodly friend.'

'Would you ever rev up and fuck off,' said Ryle generously.
'You wouldn't infiltrate your way out of a wet paper bag.'

'No,' intervened Fletcher, 'I encourage this. I wish
more young people were socially engaged, fired by ideals.

Republicanism shouldn't be judged by the activities of the previous RAs.' Fletcher apparently was not very up with the Men's Rights Activism. 'It is not in itself always a bad thing. As long as it's inclusive rather than jingoistic or subversive. It imposes a discipline of thought from which more sophisticated expressions of citizenship may blossom.'

'*Republicanism?*' responded the youngish Daly. 'Yes, well, as you will, sire. What was your gig with Sartre though, I must persist in enquiring? Were you in support of his attempts to Trojan his Existentialist coda into the postcolonial metrocentric Marxist canon? Or were you merely trolling?'

'Er … I'm afraid I still can't remember the setting in which you overheard me mention Sartre,' said Fletcher, not as limber as he used to be when it came to jumping between trains of thought.

Ryle intervened decisively at this point. 'Take a hike now, sunshine,' he said, lifting the lad out of the seat by his ear lobe. 'We're busy men in this part of the organization and we don't have time to be delving down into the convoluted excuses idle men like Sartre might have cooked up for themselves to continue existing.'

'By the way,' said Fletcher on a quasi-professional note, 'have you had a chance to look through that reference list on the contention between conservation and preservation in Jacobean structures? I'm so sorry, Brian, that I still don't have an assignment for you. I don't have one for myself. But take this as a tip. Use the time well. I believe the next promotion will be of someone with expertise in that arena and I'm more than happy to help you tease through the issues whenever you wish.'

Daly didn't like this kind of work-related questioning and left in a bit of a grump. He wouldn't be seen again until he had something new on his mind.

After even the hair gel smell of him had gone Ryle asked Fletcher, 'What torments are you looking to add to your wheelbarrow today?'

The look Fletcher gave him wasn't warm. 'Today I'm taking up an invitation from a lovely English warrior woman to come to her home in the county of Westmeath.'

'Oh?' said Ryle, the chemicals stirred up in him at this description, one which ticked a few boxes for him. 'Well I suppose having a bit of a talk can do no harm. Is she that big blondy rake you were skyping the other day?'

'There's been oil company activity on a little hill at the back of her house,' said Fletcher, 'a designated special area of conservation no less. The woman has lived under that hill for thirty years in a bothán that used to be a hippie commune. True to herself she remains and knows every rare plant and every unusual beetle in that eco-system.'

'I understand,' said Ryle limbering up to get into the woman's groove. 'She thought she'd found at least one little corner of the world so horrible that she would never be disturbed in it?'

'I don't think you do,' said Fletcher. 'She is one of the rare ones. Too kind and full of grace for the realities of this world, she has never been able to deviate from the path of honour. She is a true knight from the era of chivalry. The last thing she wants to do is fight. But she is left with no choice. And unfortunately as she reaches out to others in the community, those she thought would equally feel their backs to the wall, she is instead left fighting her own despondency as she mostly is meeting ignorant indifference.'

'A person who can live so long in that county and stay so innocent must surely have some special grace alright,' pondered Ryle. 'That's a people which sleeps with its back to the wall. Of course, British **** [redacted] could frack the shite out of that whole county and no sound-headed person would even notice. Anyway we can't be always relying on foreigners to put petrol in our cars. My advice would be that you let me pretend to be sympathetic to the mad one for a bit. I could gather information on her plans and bed down like a Metro spook until I get to know her little secrets. Then you can come out on the side of the fracker. *Fletcher for energy independence*, would be a slogan that could harvest a right crop of votes in the neighbouring counties. And in all pubs where The Wolfe Tones and Aslan play to the gallery.'

◊

They were now off the N4 and on a less travelled road that takes
you out past Lough Ennell. The loveliness of the sight of course
had Fletcher getting Ryle to stop at a cutting. 'Don't tell me it
doesn't take your breath away, Len,' he said as he stepped down
into rushes and looked out over the calm expanse.

'A decent stretch with no locals on it, that's what's good about
a lake,' said Ryle, agreeably.

'The local people here are as decent as you'll meet anywhere,'
said Grattan vaguely, not turning to his companion who was still
in the van. 'No, the peace this expanse gives is that it's an end
of expectations. You're temporary and small. And that's alright.'

'You're on your own with that,' said Ryle reaching across to
close the passenger door against the breeze. He didn't want to
catch his death of cold while waiting for Fletcher to be ready to
move on.

The next thing they saw on that road was a large, round man
in a tweed jacket and the look of a dressed up farmer about him.
He was leaving a house and about to get into a little Toyota panel
van that was a bit too small for him and that had a poster of
himself plastered on the back panel. They were already aware of
the impending council elections as every electricity post in the
country was keeling over with posters.

'The council posters give the purest image of what Irishness
does to a people,' said Ryle. 'For starters, you can see why your
nation should be banned from wearing suits.'

Note: this was true enough for Ryle. There are two main
phyla of suit makers, the Anglo and the Italian. Neither had
the cut of any variety of Celt in mind. In case you think I'm
one of those writers who trades on doing down my own
Nation, let me tell you I have a balanced view. For example,
in circles of the most hostile National introspection, when
we are on a down cycle, I've often piped up at my peril with
the observation that at least we don't disimprove with age the
way others do. You take a look at any of those then-and-now
sites and you'll see any star with an Irish or Scottish surname

looks no worse now than they did thirty years ago. Not so sure about the Welsh. I may also add that while jumpers are a horrible thing on others, a good jumper can flatter a Celt.

The compiler

'I have an idea,' said Ryle, pulling the van in. 'See if you can weasel any tips on the door to door canvassing game off this old shitehawk. He looks like he's been at it awhile.'

Fletcher wouldn't ask. So Ryle stepped out.

'Hello to you my friend,' said the old gent.

'Hello there, my good fellow,' said Ryle who liked to put on a bit of an air when he was talking to fellow countrymen. He didn't want to have them boring him with trying to place the accent. Trying to figure out where he was originally from and then surmising that they knew relatives of his, the way countrymen tend to. 'My principal here was looking for some advice on the canvassing racket.'

'Oh very good, I'm very pleased to meet the both of you,' said the old man, with a bold smile breaking through his weathered face as he studied Ryle, 'though I can see you're a bit of a rogue.'

Fletcher was caught by surprise at this astuteness and laughed.

'You're with Fianna Fáil are you,' said Ryle.

'Ah, I am and I amn't,' said the man. 'They don't really want an old wreck like me anymore.'

'You've some neck on you, all the same,' said Ryle, 'to be going around asking people to vote you into the county council after the way your lot sank the country and drove thousands to their deaths.'

'Well thanks,' said the man, 'but I still like the canvassing better than any other part of politics.'

'Excuse my friend, sir,' said Fletcher, stepping out now too. 'I am interested though. Do you not find people at their doors accuse you all, all politicians, of duplicitousness?'

'Doesn't our whole nation get accused of that,' said the man, 'but isn't it only outsiders who take a singular view on the matter. I just try to do my job.'

'And the abuse you must get?' said Fletcher. 'How do you brush that off?'

'A pelt as thick as bull's hooves,' said Ryle, 'obviously. And you need to start growing one.'

'I can see by you that you are a person who knows a thing or two,' said the man to Fletcher. 'So you'll understand me. In this country the old manner still prevails. When you go to doors people are very kind despite all they've been through. They don't try to hurt your feelings. There's no duplicity in that. I know they're not going to vote for me. And they know I know. So what more needs to be said about it? They are still able offer me a cup of tea.'

'So …' said Ryle, 'why the fuck are you wasting your time at it?'

'What else would I rather be wasting my time at?' said the man. And then he laughed, 'Besides, they might remember me the next time.' Then he zoned back in on Ryle with the searing look of the old-time politician who searches souls for sustenance, 'you look like a man weighed down by cynicism. What is it you are looking for out of life for yourself?'

'Fair question,' said Grattan as he gave way to a look of smug pleasure which didn't flatter him. I suppose he was entitled to it as it wasn't often that Ryle was the one put on the spot.

'What the fuck are you smirking at, with your shovel of a face on you?' said Ryle to Fletcher, then turning back to deal with the politician. 'My expectations rarely fall short in this world and there's not many can say that.'

'Ah,' said the old man, 'but isn't that just another form of escape and self-delusion? You might call me a gombeen but at least I get to have a say about where a by-pass should be built. And I can help a widower in the house behind us overrule the planners so his grand little niece can build her house next door to him and so they can keep an eye on each other. The cynic gets every decision in life made for them and all they get to do is complain about it. But no matter how clever the sniping out of them, they still have to steer their cars onto the by-pass exactly where I put it.'

'I get things done alright,' said Ryle curtly as he turned the radio on in the car. 'We'd like to talk to you all day, old man, but I'm more interested in racing results.'

'Oh, you're a backing man?' said the incurable gombeen who wouldn't let any soul get away lightly. He leaned in. 'Fair play to you. Do you mind me asking who had you backed in the two-thirty in Limerick?'

'Lie-Low,' said Ryle involuntarily, 'they had her at fifty-to-one. But I happen to think that on the right day she's got better legs than Black Caviar.'

'An excellent choice my friend,' said the old man, offering a big hand for shaking. 'Put it there. I had a tenner on the same little filly, bred only fifteen and three quarters of a mile down the road from where I'm standing, as it happens. And what's more, the race is over. She walked it. I just heard in that house behind me.' Ryle wasn't able to help himself. As the little windfall buzzed his reward centre, he shook the big fellow's hand as soundly as if the old fellow had ridden the horse himself.

'Thanks,' said Grattan, also taking a shake of the man's hand for himself. 'And every good wish to you in your travels.'

'What kind of election are you going for yourself,' said the man, as Grattan rolled down the window and Ryle crunched the gears, 'if you don't mind me asking? And what's your name?'

'Fletcher,' said Ryle officiously, 'and he'll be going for President in due course.'

'Ah, don't mind him,' said Fletcher, embarrassed, 'that was just a passing notion I had.'

'Don't say that,' said the man. 'Aren't you as entitled to go for it as anyone else? You seem like a kind gentleman and I've enjoyed our conversation. You'll have my vote if you ever do go.'

'Now you see,' said Ryle as they left the man looking after them, 'you need to take a leaf out of that buck's book. I'd lay money he's done nothing serious for anyone only himself in a long political career. And that takes very little effort. But he wants to be liked so he throws a few shapes to that end. As a result, people still tolerate him even though they don't really know why. If you could go out of your way a bit more to be all things to all men, you'd be halfway to the top job already.'

Fletcher declined to comment. They got out eventually at the foot of what could only have been Knockbawn, which turned

out to be that most hateful of all things, a boggy hill. Not a
hanging tree to be seen on the slopes, for all the sidkas. Too
much brackish water to drown a man in. And on the brows,
peaty ground so deep that it would bury you itself. As they
later discovered.

In a house full of dogs and horses they were made watery tea
by a woman of lingering natural beauty. Along with the lady
herself, were the apologies from the absent committee members.
Not there were the three farmers from the lands at the butt of the
hill, men who had joined the committee out of concern about
being blamed for effluent. (The owner of the hill itself wanted
nothing to do with the committee—mesmerized that the hill he
had always wanted off his back could be worth a fraction of what
he was being offered.) Apologies were also read from a TD. He
was on the committee because his posters had always promised
to bring pristine tourists to the untouched midlands. As soon as
the hill was turned upside down and the chemicals were being
lorried in, he would need to be able to show that he had opposed
it all along. Also not present was an anti-immigration school
teacher. The lady of the hill confided that she was not so upset at
this no-show, as the person seemed much more cracked than the
much maligned members of the corvidae family who were the
primary inhabitants of these parts. Ryle scratched his head—a
woman to whom crows were lovely but people were regarded
with astuteness, would be a hard nut to crack.

Note: over a number of subsequent trips to this area, the rest
of the committee would remain as consistent in abstinence
as they were in the considerateness of the apologies they sent
through. But let me not jump ahead. *The compiler*

'I'm sorry,' she said, 'I'll try to make sure they're all here the
next time.'

'Ah don't worry,' said Ryle, 'you're alright. But of course there
mightn't be a next time. It doesn't look like there's anything in
this for us. You have no vote and your absent friends are unlikely
to be swung by my candidate's fine words. Unless you have some
other little warmness to keep me interested ...'

She didn't. It was all about the hill with her. There were fruit bats, Iberian pine martins, rare owls, and a species of bog cotton not seen in any other part of the country by all accounts.

'That's very interesting,' said Ryle, 'what has it got to do with you or me?'

'I should warn you, they're listening to everything we say,' she said pointing at the roof.

'What, the hills?' said Ryle.

Fletcher smiled benignly. He was long enough on the road now to begin to admit to what Ryle had told him from the start: that not everyone he was going to meet along the way could reasonably be expected to be one hundred percent right in the head. Too much time spent alone in this kind of countryside can create a certain shortness of breadth in certain punters and leave others stone mad.

'You don't believe me,' she said, looking hurt.

'No,' said Ryle, 'I'd sooner believe a bag of frogs. No disprespect.'

'Right, well do this for yourselves,' she said in a lowered voice and scribbling on the last unused page of a fat diary before tearing it out for them. The note said, *Talk to this man. **** A deepthroat, geologist, works with **** Petrol. Mobile 087246**** ...*

Note: Observe, I never provided you with the name of the man nor indeed the name of the company. *The compiler*

'Let's just say,' she said now very loud addressing the ceiling, 'I have every reason to believe that they are lying about the extent of the damage they themselves anticipate will be caused.'

'*Henry Lawless?*' read Ryle aloud.

Fletcher the malleable put a hand on Ryle's arm, pointing at the ceiling, and winking.

Ryle lowered his voice to humour them, 'The only Lawless I heard of moving to these parts was a lad with one leg. I knew his father well. The lad lost from big toe up to the knee one day when the father was mincing meat for burgers.'

She flushed with anger. She drew a stick figure on the page and put two arms and two full legs on it. She drew three lines under it with such force that her pencil tore the paper. Next to it she wrote, *Fuck you!*

'Well you clearly feel strongly about the issue,' said Fletcher nervously heading for the door, 'which is all that counts. I'm not sure though with so little commitment from any local person … Well, you know sometimes it's not sufficient to be right and to chip away on technicalities, you kind of have to have a constituency. I'm sorry.'

'I see. Right is right though,' she said curtly, speaking volumes as her arms folded against them. 'Am I not a local person, by the way?'

'I didn't mean …' said Fletcher, never able to leave well enough alone, 'you know a lesson I've found it hard to take: when you're fighting a lone fight you are at times forced to put your head down and proceed with blind faith. Anyone who has achieved anything great has done so. But there's no clear line between single-mindedness and tunnel vision. One can become a person one wouldn't have recognized. One sometimes needs to find the extra courage to come up for air. To reassess. To see if you can find a way to change tack just enough so as to bring other people along. To make sure you have not become, well, a belligerent.'

'*Spare me!*' the woman cut him off in a most elegantly dismissive gesture with the palm of a slender hand. And who could blame her. Fletcher didn't like it because he knew he had earned it.

'By Christ that was a lucky escape,' said Ryle when they sat back in the van and waved at the woman standing in her doorway, bursting with tears of frustration that she would hold back till they were gone.

He had spoken too soon, which was a trap that to give Ryle credit, he rarely fell into. They weren't a mile down the same road they had come on when the dreadful silence was relieved by a siren. 'Merciful hour,' Ryle said, bringing them to a halt. Even he was surprised by what his wing mirrors then revealed. Sergeant Meg Geas was in the right flap and Garda John Devine in the left, and thirty more Gardaí were still emerging from the Community Relations Transit, but hanging back, fair play to them. Despite all of Fletcher's agitation, this was the very first time he'd achieved direct personal attention from the vanguards of the Crusty Squad.

The British petrol company of course had no idea how to deal with the Irish. Ryle could have told them straightaway that enforcing the letter of the law was what had always got them in trouble on this island. Up to that moment Fletcher hadn't had an intention in the world of ever coming back to this place because the woman was too noble even for him, too enmeshed in minutae of her lone battle, too sure that the testers' prefabs being a couple of inches larger than approved by planning was going to get a judge to stop the whole thing. Her intensity had left Fletcher no room to get a word in and being speechless always made him uneasy. But now? Now as the officers took their time walking towards the OPW van, leaning down to inspect exhaust soot and tyre depths, Fletcher whispered urgently, 'Hello Suck, what is this about? Someone must have been listening after all. What on earth is going on here?'

Note: for the non-indigent reader, it is well known that in periods of wage depression the RoI Constabulary cannot be got out of the barracks for any official business. They only emerge if the organizer of a concert, a race meeting, or a ploughing match has paid for protection. But even Fletcher knew that this county had no ground that a plough would not disappear in, hadn't enough straight road even for a sulky race, and though its pubs were snug they were barely able to draw their fill to see Daniel O'Donnell or U2 on Sunday nights. And this wasn't a Sunday. *The compiler*

'*Well!*' said Meg warmly, leaning in Ryle's window, a lovely friendly voice on her, 'that's a grand day now. License *le do thoil.*'

'Not too bad at all, officer, thanks be to god,' said Ryle who had a difficulty in relation to a license. 'My cousin is a member and there's been no drink taken. Grattan and me, Mr. Fletcher and myself, we're not looking for any bother.'

'Is that a fact now,' she said, having none of it, 'well I have a bit of news for you Dublin boys. Down these parts it's not as easy as having a cousin in the force to get charges dropped. Have you a brother or sister a member?'

'What is this nonsense?' said Fletcher, offended on behalf of the good people of Ireland. 'We don't use pull. If we've committed an offence, we'll pay the fine.'

'Only those who have no pull say that,' came the rasping voice of the Devine fellow from the other window.

'It's like this,' said Meg getting serious, and handing Ryle a docket. 'Today we're feeling generous and you're only getting one ticket. Take my advice and don't go up against these people. To be frank, they're right pricks and they'll win anyway whether or not you put yourself in harm's way. So the question you'd need to keep at the forefront of your mind is, is there not plenty of harmless dabbling to keep you busy elsewhere?'

'Is that a threat?' asked Fletcher unwisely.

There was silence in the moments it took Sergeant Geas' visage to metamorphose. In this reddening phase she fixed her gaze unnervingly on Fletcher, there and then transformed from being part of Sgt. Geas' solution to being part of her problem.

'It seems these gentlemen regard leniency as a threat, Garda,' she said with dramatic huffiness to Devine. 'Very well, the course is set. Throw the book at them. And then search this one for a driver's license, Leonard Patrick Cromwell Suck Ryle isn't it, and run it through the system to see what comes up.'

'Jesus!' Ryle said, jumping out of the car to avoid any flying paperwork, Devine looking like the literal type, 'there's no need for any of that. Don't mind this other curly knob. Coming here was against my advice and you can be assured I try to make all my mistakes new ones. You won't see us here again and I couldn't give a living shit how prosperous the British petrol crowd want to make this place.'

'I'm glad one of you has sense,' said the sergeant, looking relieved, to tell the truth of her. The stress of confrontation had not been sitting well on a naturally jolly brow. Both of the Gardaí in fact looked much happier now with the need for dirty work seemingly avoided. She nodded back to the crew behind who you would have thought couldn't get more at ease. She even tore up the ticket for littering though she had plainly seen Ryle discard the page of a diary into the ditch. 'Fair play to you both for having the bit of cop on. Between ourselves, the private security lads that they'd have sent in after us would have done stuff we wouldn't even be allowed to. The less said the easiest mended. So now … Your lads are coming on well in the football this year I hear?'

'The Dubs are his lads, not mine,' said Ryle amicably. 'I'd even back a shower of mullockers like Westmeath against them, no offence.'

'None taken,' she said.

'Neither of us is from here anyway,' Devine nodded, adding diplomatically, 'it'll be Kerry or Donegal this time.'

Note: there's very little further I am prepared to say here about the case of Knockbawn as various matters are currently proceeding through the courts. And far be it from me, with so little information at my disposal, to create any implication that I'm coming down on the side of the objectors. I have enough troubles of my own to be going on with. You will already have surmised though, so I'm not telling you anything you don't already know, that Fletcher was determined to make up to the womanly committee for not having believed her on that first meeting. There was also the fact that no Dr. Lawless, either one-legged or two, could ever be contacted again. As a result it is my understanding that there may have been a number of further visits by our two boys to that county. This despite kicking and screaming out of Ryle. Fletcher could be determined enough when he set his mind to a thing. Relations with the Crusty Squad of course went over a ledge. Meg felt she had reached out and taken a risk for peace in being so candid with these men. She would perceive scorn in their return visit. Her wrath was to follow. No further quarter would be given. Over the ensuing period the two government men would get very familiar with the ossified and insane ghosts that inhabited the six by four dungeon under Knockbawn Garda Station. I have expunged all further mention of this particular little saga from the record. But where you notice days that I do not account for, be aware that it's no slip up. You can draw your own conclusions about which pock-marked face of the earth it was that our subjects may have tootled back to on those occasions. *The compiler*

None so adamant as the ignorant

Chapter IX

THE NEXT DAY'S DRIVE was harmless enough by comparison with the fracking debacle. Ryle was only finished undoing Margot's adjustments to the Lexus passenger seat, bringing it up and forward as suited his abrupt posture, when they were slowing past a semi-detached house with Grattan gawking at door numbers. They were in Walkinstown or Crumlin or one of those kinds of places that bogmen and the more Easterly Southsiders alike, are never called on to visit. 'What in the name of Jaysus,' said Ryle, 'neither of us has any business here.'

There was a safety netted trampoline in the front garden and a row of ten-year-old people-carriers on the pavement outside. 'Today, my friend,' said Grattan, 'we are attending a parents' meeting.'

'You are gone rotten inside,' said Ryle.

'There,' said Fletcher, not even hearing Ryle now as they parked at the end of the row of cars and walked back towards the house. 'What is happening inside that happy house, is a movement to not merely change the physical landscape but more importantly the mental landscape of our country. In there is a group of people who do not want their children to fall into the clutches of any of the orthodoxies which run our schools. People who want their children to be put at the centre of their own education where they can learn to *really* think. These people are the quiet heroes, Len. They are prepared to fight for the rights of their children and along with that, for a better future for us all.'

Ryle was looking in the car windows.

'Their objective?' Fletcher continued. 'Simple. They are lobbying for the right to establish a non-denominational secondary school in this area, one in which ongoing consultation with the parent body will mean the curriculum evolves democratically, adapting with the times, and never again calcifies around an archaic set of values, never again becomes anchored in an era unable to adapt to new understandings as the decades roll by. In all aspects of the curriculum, the aim is rolling progressiveness.'

Ryle was already bored sick from listening to this.

Fletcher looked at him, 'You're asking yourself the obvious question,' he said. 'Why, when neither of us is responsible for a child of that age? Am I right?'

'You are not even on the right planet,' said Ryle.

'Well little Margot has just entered approximately such a school for her primary education and there are many like her. However her mother, just a little girl herself really,' Fletcher's voice disappeared in a gulp.

Ryle didn't miss much, 'What's the matter with you now. Pregnant again is she?'

'Like the parents of many other primary going children,' resumed Fletcher, controlling himself, 'Saoirse is doing her best to cope with the day-to-day demands. She doesn't have the bandwidth right now to work for her preferred educational dispensation to continue into secondary. But there's no reason we can't do it on their behalf.'

'*We?*' said Ryle reasonably.

'Yes, remember it's not only about my granddaughter. Though she's my touchstone I realize that she's not yours. But there are many others like her. Any small way in which we could help to get this thing going would have a long term multi-generational impact in the country that I am certain we both love.'

Fletcher's granddaughter, born to his daughter when seventeen, had shocked the Fletchers on her arrival and pleased the Fletchers all the days since. Ryle of course wasn't particularly bothered about her one way or the other. Up to now he had done Fletcher the courtesy of not driving this home very explicitly. He was regretting it. 'I don't give a particular fuck about the education of any of the little over-indulged monkeys,' he said politely. 'What is it to me?'

'It's about the future,' explained Fletcher again.

'And you think you'll be welcomed to this meeting?' said Ryle.

'Absolutely, you too,' Fletcher responded, 'you don't think I'd just land up without phoning ahead?'

'Right, going as an adoptive couple, is that it?'

'You're a funny man, Len Ryle,' said Fletcher, slapping Suck Ryle dangerously on the back of his leather jacket. Ryle shuddered.

'Listen to a bit of sense for once in your life,' growled Ryle, not well humoured by the latest personal incursion. He stopped. He sat onto the lichened concrete capping of a low garden wall. Grattan stood to listen. 'Why can't you send the twerp to fucking Alexandra or some such so she can learn the realities of privilege and how to exercise it. You know the established classes aren't supposed to fanny around with this kind of mollydovey stuff after primary. That's only for hippies and the lower middle classes who think they know how everything works. As adamant as they're ignorant, the reason those people keep getting rode into the ground is because they actually haven't a fucking clue how *anything* works or who is pulling their wires. Send her somewhere she'll acquire contacts and an offer from Trinity even if the little brat is as thick as the soles of my boots.'

That drew a deep scowl from Grattan. His face purpled. Ryle was pleased, if a little unnerved. He had never in all the years seen Grattan angry to the point of being ready to hit someone. The great man spoke slowly trying to control himself, his fists curled up, 'Don't let me hear you talking about my little girl that way again. *Not fucking ever! Do you understand me?*'

'You're the boss,' said Ryle, 'but I'm just saying. On the other hand maybe this class of person is better off not knowing the real nature of their situation. Maybe that's what you're thinking? I could give you that point alright. Let them keep thinking they have the machine on the back foot. Because, says you, there's fuck all they can do about it even with their strongest striving.'

Fletcher looked, bewilderment at the workings of this mind before him eroding his anger.

On they went and Ryle decided to go into the dreary house only because it seemed a less bad idea than standing around in an ageing estate called Beech Larch Lawn or such, a place that even on a fresh sunny day reeked of resignation and death.

They walked straight into a scene that Ryle found both fascinating and horrifying. The remodelled open plan kitchen and dining area was full of people sitting on Ikea chairs, bean bags, and carpet. Books and toys were tidied into piles by the wall. The warm atmosphere enveloped the entrants. 'It's like walking into a uterus or a colon,' grumbled Ryle. The peculiar aroma made Ryle wince. 'Too much oxytocin in the air, I'm allergic.' But Fletcher wasn't for fleeing.

Here were men like no men Ryle had met before. Their voices were soft and caring. And here were women talking like zombies with strong, certain voices. People in the fullest surges of missionary self-assurance that parenthood can bestow on those who have a child at forty.

'Not a clue, fucking lemmings,' Ryle muttered.

Grattan Fletcher seemed instantly very fond of the assembly. They showed more reserve in relation to him. And they looked to Ryle with bared teeth. The instinct for sensing harmful predators had them straining at the leash.

Matters proceeded as was becoming normal. Fletcher couldn't keep his mouth shut. He established a level of bona fides by being superlative in his commendations. He went on to offer to do every chore that nobody else put up their hands for. He seemed surprised when all resistance crumbled. Ryle pulled him to the bathroom and whispered to him, 'Don't be a donkey, man. These people are like spent salmon, all they had is gone into the spawn. You'll soon be like that if you don't get away from them. A sucked dry kelt, prematurely withered like all the previous generations of this country.'

The warning fell on deaf ears. 'I think it's actually going quite well,' said Grattan.

Before long they had voted that Grattan was best suited to approach each of the archbishops from the main sects to see if they could be got to drop their antagonisms. Grattan felt neither the insult nor the injury. He was also to write and produce pamphlets. And host a savoury snack fundraiser. By the time the cold tea and water crackers were handed out, Grattan had everyone's contact details. One of the Dads, consulted by the chairwoman on all technical matters, was setting up a Twitter account via Grattan's Department issue iPad, so he could follow the chairwoman. And he was going to be standing in for the group's PR officer who had sensibly gone to Australia to drive a mine truck.

The chairwoman looked at Ryle over the rim of her mug. She had a small face set in the middle of a torrent of grey hair. She asked Grattan, 'And what about your friend over there? He doesn't have much to say for himself, does he?'

'That's right,' said Ryle.

'Don't worry, I'm sure you'll find us less intimidating next time,' she said, still watching him with a cold wary eye, 'and perhaps offer to get involved.'

Where Ryle was from, the one thing you learnt early was caution around the recently calved. He knew the look of madness that could kill mercilessly. He chose his words carefully, not saying most of what came to his mind. He kept it to, 'I will in my testes.'

She paled and Fletcher stepped to the fore heroically, perhaps not aware that most such killings happen when the dog runs behind you. 'Excuse poor Leonard. He spends too much time on discussion boards where the courtesies, reputedly, are somewhat less formal.'

'What? Was that not the right thing to say?' said Ryle.

Luckily for Grattan the mother was mature and the moment passed as he talked more about his vision for the future and how this movement was just the kind of thing that gave him hope.

They left that housing estate shattered men.

'So anyway,' said Fletcher idly, 'you think that we would be better served helping people understand the true politico-economic nature of their problems so as to empower them to fight, rather than joining them in ad hoc battle, is that the core excuse of your obstructionism now?'

'What!' said Ryle in genuine surprise, 'No. That was just an observation. Why bother giving anyone advice on the problems you see gathering around them when there's fuckall they can do to save themselves anyway, would be my advice. To you.'

Killing may not be murder

Chapter X

NOTE: A SMALL BIT OF PRIVATE research became unavoidable at points such as this, where my sense of duty to you and the truth collided with plausibility gaps in the primary source. I have swum the slurry pit for you and I trust that it will in time be appreciated. *The compiler*

A couple of years prior to the episode I relate, one Cathal Mac Gabhann had extended his musical tastes. Until he was forty-three, going as *Balor*, he had presented himself on rock forums as Dublin's foremost expert and archivist of the first wave sub-genre of black metal, deriding anything up-tempo from Hellhammer as pop. Not that he had strayed from melodrama, he had merely bought a black tuxedo, incubated a repertoire of obscure wine requests that he could regale the Gaeity's interval servers for not having heard of, taken to expounding in long convoluted sentences where one short one would have been quite sufficient, and added opera to his fat list of exclusive histrionic pedantries. The horse's ass. After only six months into the new interest he had already acquired disdain for the casual followers of Verdi and Mozart, referring to them on operatic discussion boards with the contempt he had previously reserved for Meat Loaf fans. A man quick to refinement, he had appropriated a perspective that the only consistently *exquisite* forms were those composed by twentieth-century Romanian composers, Bretan and Caudella.

This had not made much of a noticcable change at home. Fran still had the shoulders drooping from lugging Tesco spoils to the front door in the rain. The roller door of the garage, conspicuously untended-looking from the outside, did not open a crack. Behind it, tÚsail Mac Gabhann remained in his padded den. The wealth of worthless metal CDs remained in the humidity-controlled garage, but were gradually transferred into crates as new CDs began to populate the shelves. (Mac Gabhann had developed a rare brand of media purism, insisting that cadences are lost when you take your digitized sound from online stores instead of from injection-moulded plastic.)

> Note: he being a man of unnaturally long fingers and toes it's understandable that our target would have a natural inclination to the concept that there was such a thing as the more refined digit.

His leave calendar now correlated with the opera festivals of Central Europe. (Fran remained aligned with the breaks at Alexandra and Gonzago where the litter were schooling.) Of an evening that there was any kind of show on in Dublin, he alighted from the 7 Series looking like a man who had just mugged a pizza waiter. People walking past sensed he was a dignitary but couldn't quite name him. He attended at least three evenings of each show and kept a file of OneNote tabs comparing the performances, thinking that he would get the Irish Times or at least the Examiner eventually to ditch their lowbrow reviewers. Fran had only come once. The legend of their marriage. She had found herself unable to sleep well during that performance thanks to the pinching of the black dress he had insisted she wear and thanks to the way her eardrums resonated to tinny emissions from a sopranist informing her that, like with many of her husband's other choices, there was something not quite right here.

Maybe a more reasonable person than yourself might make allowances for the actions of such a rubbery old pig's pizzle as Cathal Mac Gabhann, given these insights into his tightly walked personal life. Perhaps you would be more patient with his penchant for the over-elaborate in his plots given that his brain at that time was pickled, suffering the formaldehyde-like effects of immersion in preposterously orchestrated passions; the artistic pitch favoured by the naturally coldhearted.

> Note: If you understand the latter point you have the kind of intellect that will be able to further understand the peculiar neediness that keeps the Germans feeding the Italians, keeps

the modern English averring that the Irish are great 'craic,' and that underlies much of Europe's history along with that. But this compiler feels professionally restrained from such digressions here. For a deeper exploration of co-dependent inter-communal relationships, I would refer you to the evolutionary sociology blog that I will be producing on this very subject and others once I have faithfully discharged the factual rendition at hand. *The compiler*

So there we are.

The miserable old *Blackrocker* Mac Gabhann (ask yourself again now, how could this be a Kerryman) was very correct also when it came to pursuing wrongs. He was a relentless gourmand of revenge. He was of the slow food school, planning meticulously and getting full enjoyment from the earliest stages of anticipation, long before the first aromas of stewing meat began to tantalize his refined olfactory senses. He appreciated the satisfactions in their totality. He was sure that the corrosive lingering heartache of revenge feebly neglected might make a far worse companion than the mild heartburn of revenge gorged upon. Of course he couldn't say for sure as he had never tried the former. (In this, it is conceded that he had certain trait overlaps with Suck Ryle, though one would have been as disgusted as the other to hear this said out loud.) An unnamed inner voice told him that forgiveness was an alien tenet touted by liberal psychologists and New Testament fundamentalists with social neutering rather than one's individual well-being as their prime objective, and that it would in fact slowly poison your heart like a lost love. Mac Gabhann had not lost his love. He had got her and kept her.

None of this may help you understand what Mac Gabhann did next but I'd have to say respectfully, that's your own problem. When I take on a job you won't find any patch unpainted and if you don't care for that, not to sound too defensive about it, but you can fuck right off with yourself.

Here is where we depart briefly into a bit of a crime mystery in which I present you with all the contending evidence relating to a tragic event and you are then left to figure it out for yourself.

In my own view, the thing that presaged Josephine Sloane's timely demise was a plan that Mac Gabhann came up with in respect of the disposal of Grattan Fletcher. It was not a drastic plan in itself, would be my contention. He initially intended no physical harm to Fletcher. Just to add enough substance to the case against the man that he could be instantly dismissed from the Department, ergo a murder. And if someone had to die to serve those ends, it might as well be Josephine Sloane, with whom Mac Gabhann had issues. That would be the way Mac Gabhann thinks. The plan was to have the head of HR ostensibly driven over by an OPW van and to lay the blame at Fletcher's door. Mac Gabhann would kill her himself, scrape a bit of her onto the bonnet of a van parked out front and throw the remainder underneath it. Fletcher would then alight from the building and climb merrily into the crime scene. There would be no getting away from that.

The difficulties with this reconstruction are minor but in the interests of full disclosure, I set them before you. First, he didn't have time to do it. Second, Mac Gabhann did not know how Fletcher was getting hold of the vans. He knew Fletcher wouldn't be able to cajole OPW men. (Oddly for hawkish Mac Gabhann, he did not yet know of the existence of Suck Ryle, in and out of his building every day for five years. It might have been the high viz vests or possibly just his stature and demeanour that made Ryle invisible to Mac Gabhann's class.) Third, there was no actual record in Mac Gabhann's blog of this plan having existed. (However you'd hardly expect the wily old patriot to have written it down?) And fourthly, there was a fair bit of circumstantial evidence pointing at another character.

All that aside, I would remind you that Mac Gabhann remains the main repository of evil in this account and for as long as I am writing it that will not be wrested from him. Not by you and not by Suck Ryle. More importantly still, some previously unknown information for you: Mac Gabhann had the only important thing in real-life crime detection, an iron clad motive for nominating Sloane as his collateral.

The same Josephine had been a thorn in Mac Gabhann's side

for some time. Nothing to do with her not being quite as active as Mac Gabhann would have liked on the Fletcher disciplinary case. (This compiler has never at any time implied that Mac Gabhann was so unprofessional as to kill someone purely for petty work-related reasons.) No. The reason he would not have baulked at including her death under the incidentals column, had to do with her looking for money from him.

Josephine had been married to a small Jewish man, a failed concert pianist and homemaker. Since the children had gone to college, he had been lost like Lír in a terrible low mood. He took to going each day for a little ramble around the town on the pretext of looking for some suitable employment. He said he was interested in something in the insurance or acting lines. Of course he never got anything. He said it was because he was too old at fifty-two, cast aside by a brash youth-centric society. But really, people suspected, he wasn't looking very hard; that he was in actuality only out and about under the propulsion of loneliness and from a need to pester Turkish barbers and Irish butchers with idle bits of conversation. On week evenings his route always took him, hands in bomber jacket pockets, past the Loreto on Stephen's Green just as the fatted-calved daughters of the comfortable emerged, his thoughts of shifts tempered by realization that these legs too would soon be trousers-clad.

Here's the thing: Rudi was the closest approximation to a friend that Mac Gabhann had ever possessed. They had met one night at a musical review. Josie, who fancied herself a singer, having been a runner up in the X-Factor heats, had been persuaded by Rudi to come along so that she might learn some projection techniques. She had spotted Mac Gabhann regaling the manager in the wine bar at halftime, introduced Rudi to him, and left. Afterwards Mac Gabhann had pumped the plump little man for knowledge on the genre. His specialization in Romanian opera had been born thus. Mac Gabhann had no hang-ups at all about acknowledging the Jewish as culturally erudite. Mac Gabhann, to give him credit, could extract some value from most kinds of people. Except Africans and Arabs. He had no time for them.

When the boom had hit, re-connecting the country with

its heathen roots, Josephine like a lot of her kind, decided she could do better than Rudi and enjoy her life as much as any man. She rode all around her. She overcame any handicap imposed through her having got her looks from her father, by focussing her efforts realistically; targeting men looking for a quick promotion or a ticket out of trouble with HR. (She had been working on Grattan for a while in this regard, optimistic about eventual success but by no means waiting around for it.) Some time back she had taken home a bewildered IT chap who was too interested in 4Chan to be discerning about actual events in his life and she had had Rudi kicked out of the house by means of a solicitor's letter that she hand-delivered to him. What Rudi had departed with fitted in one holdall. But in the flush of the republican state's new separation dispensation, and in the absence of Rudi's financial ability or willingness to hire a lawyer of his own, Josephine's lawyer assured her that she was also entitled to half of Rudi's nothing. Being a person inclined to have no more than what was coming to her, Josephine had duly triggered letters of demand in all directions.

She had sent demands to Rudi's daughter from a previous woman, claiming back half the monetary gifts that Rudi had ever given her. After all, she was the one who had earned more than half of that money. She sent one to Portmarnock golf club in relation to a membership fee that they had received fraudulently, it having left the joint account with only Rudi's signature. There were more letters that are not relevant to you. What is absolutely relevant is that in that hurried flurry of free expression Josephine had made one fatal misjudgement: sending such a letter to a man with a soul twice as dark as hers could ever be, Mr. Cathal Mac Gabhann. In this document her solicitor demanded return of money laid out by Rudi for a share in a horse syndicate, a share sold to him by Mac Gabhann, slyly exiting the syndicate as a function of the same transaction. The letter asked for only half of the money lost on Leather Legs, laid to rest in stroganoff. She had encouraged Mac Gabhann to view this leniency as a goodwill gesture, her contribution to ring-fencing the unblemished professional relations that existed between them.

Mac Gabhann was fairly tight and had taken other views on this matter. The letter had given him a bellyache which returned to nag at him whenever he thought of the woman. So clearly Mac Gabhann had not only opportunity, albeit slim, and capacity, fat, when it came to her demise, but also a nine-and-a-half-thousand-euro motive. No more needs to be said on the guilt of the unscrupulous old bastard. Other than that he is one of the type who brought on all heads in this country the slur that killing is not murder to us.

With the unrelenting neutrality of the absolute historian however, I further present some circumstantial details that some might feel justifies a different conviction: that there was a solitary actor in the killing of Josephine Sloane, one Suck Ryle.

It is not disputed that Josephine Sloane stepped onto Northumberland Road that morning, fully intending to cross it, just as an OPW van was coming around the corner from Haddington Road. The van accelerated over the hundred yards. She started her run too late, realizing only at the last minute that the van was lurching across lanes, not to avoid her.

If these few facts incline you to pointing a finger at Suck Ryle, remember that the same Ryle was a harmless going little rascal, in most ways unlike the gank Mac Gabhann. Also remember that the victim had done nothing to Ryle and Ryle had never before been known to act on anyone else's behalf. That is, there was no motive. Therefore, for him to have been involved, it would have had to be accidental. That implies that Ryle would have had to have been suffering extreme shortsightedness such that he was unable to see a full-sized person from a hundred yards, fifty, five yards—there were no brake marks on the road. Not before or after the first impact or the second (she was lucky enough to go up rather than down the first time). But add then this little fact: there was no previous evidence of Leonard Ryle having anything less than perfect vision. A nighttime habituate of Herbert Park, he could drop squirrels from the hornbeams at a hundred yards using a rifle that lacked sights. Also, he was a man with a five-year no claims bonus at FBD insurance.

Anyway, worrying now about whichever way it happened is

splitting hairs. The main factor of relevance here is that the latter part of Mac Gabhann's plan fell short. He had not got Fletcher into the frame because he had not allowed for the van leaving the scene and going somewhere unknown to allow the driver to give the front bonnet a rub down with a yard brush. Nor could he have predicted that the only witness who might have been able to associate Sloane's mishap with Fletcher was a young tosser on the way to a comic convention. This emblem of the future of our great Nation was dressed in a batman costume and did remember the colour of the public works van correctly but was adamant that the lettering on it said *POW!*

Anyway, in the heel of the hunt, let's also not forget that poor Josephine was a gonner and now there was nobody left to say a good word for her. No amount of speculation can bring her back. May the Lord have mercy on her.

Billions without love, not one without water

Chapter XI

'YOU HAVE TO COME BACK here, Len,' said Fletcher in a very irregular pitch, pressing his mobile phone hard against his head to prevent it shaking. Ryle had been more than an hour gone to get a van.

'Hold your horses,' said Ryle, 'I'll be with you in a while. I have to change the van. The one they gave me has to go in for a bit of body work.'

'No. No van today,' said Fletcher, facts beginning to sink in. 'Terrible news here. There's been a horrific incident.'

'Yeah?' said Ryle.

'Josie ... Josephine Sloane ... Oh my lord,' said Fletcher, his voice disintegrating in his throat. 'Horrible.'

'Dead is she?'

'But ... How did you know that?' asked Fletcher.

'You get to know these things after a while,' said Ryle.

'*What?* Have you seen her?'

'Yeah, yeah, I happened to be passing back that way when the ambulance lads were out with snow shovels scraping up bits of her,' Ryle scrambled. 'I did think it wasn't looking too good for her at that stage, I'd have to say.'

'You are a crass and unfathomable soul,' said Fletcher the devout atheist. 'God forgive me for saying it but sometimes I really think that you are not normal.'

'Well I suppose the little Lebanese penis will get the house back,' said Ryle. 'It's what she would have wanted. The house, I mean.' He was right about that, though how he knew it or how it was any of his business is hard to tell. As it happened, the four-year cooling period since the first separation of Rudi Hotz and Josephine 'Tweety' Sloane had been about to expire the following week, whereupon the divorce settlements would have kicked in, giving her full ownership. Now Josephine was despatched for eternity to the latest Irish incarnation of limbo.

Note: the next cult coming to light a fire on Tara could do worse than reopen the gates to the fourth realm. They'd have half the country signed up overnight. The clearcut conventions of heaven and hell were never an easy sale here. And purgatory conjures only the worst of both offerings. The local mindset is more naturally aligned to limbo. Little punishment is perceived in being stuck in debate with no end in sight. Neither is there a great sense of deprivation imparted by a threat that you may never gaze upon the face of the man above. (True, there's also a fierce reluctance to acknowledge sightings of the man from below.) The front seats are always the last to be filled in this country. *The compiler*

'For goodness sake, Len,' shouted Fletcher into the phone, 'do you ever listen to anything right? It's pianist, *pianist*. And the poor man is Irish, not bloody Lebanese. You know he's going to be devastated despite all. Love is a funny thing, Len. Without it, there is nothing. You think you're immune from all that, don't you, Len? But I know, deep down it's there in you too.'

'There are billions living without love, not one without water,' said Ryle.

'You see? Even when you try to sound callous you reach for the words of poets,' said Fletcher.

Ryle thought it best to ignore Fletcher when he was getting over-excited. Hysteria of any shade was not his cup of tea. Fletcher heard the unmistakable sounds of splashing on a steel urinal and then a hand blower before he had Ryle's full attention back.

'She was no great loss anyway,' said Ryle. 'She was as mean as ditch water. Despite all her fake lovery and embracing all comers, she'd return a favour an inch shorter than she got it.'

'Excuse me?' said Fletcher, 'Don't tell me you are one of those who condemns a woman with power for living her life as so many men with power have always done? A woman can't win, can she? The rules of the game evolved with men so the disposition more average in women is not suited. If she stands aside she is written off. If she goes in softly she is overridden. If she tries to shout the odds it is against her grain and doesn't come off. Every way she forfeits something. And then if she harvests flattery from passing intimacies in betrayal of personal loyalties in the way that only ever enhanced our fascination with men from Mandela to Haughey, she is subjected to the kinds of moral harummphing that I detect in your voice. We should have learnt enough in this country to be beyond judging adults on the intimacy choices they exercise.'

Ryle was offended at this lecture, him a man who, when confronted with big swinging genitalia, had always been better disposed to the pudenda than the prick. It left him feeling a bit raw considering he wouldn't have bothered killing her if his concern for Fletcher hadn't tilted the balance, after that phone call he'd picked up and all that. And of course a worry that Fletcher getting sacked might be a distraction in the campaign.

Note: Assuming Ryle was involved only for the sake of the above argument. *The compiler*

'I think I'll call on him later,' said Fletcher.

'I've already texted him,' said Ryle. 'I'd leave the rest for a few days.'

'Why?' asked Grattan.

'You don't want to be too active on the case,' said Ryle. 'It's the kind of thing can raise suspicions.'

'What on earth do you mean?' asked Grattan.

'A guilty person, in trying to act normal, always puts themselves too prominent in the post-crime happenings, joining searches, consoling the family, all that type of thing. The Guards will be watching closely.'

'That's idiotic,' said Grattan.

'Even if you were never formally convicted,' said Ryle, 'you know what this town is like. More people are persuaded by the whispered word than by anything the Gardaí ever write on a docket. These things are held on to. Not to put too fine a point on it, it wouldn't do the run for the Park any good at all.'

'So in short,' said Fletcher, flabbergasted as he tried to process what he was hearing, 'in short … you are saying what? That I shouldn't call on my friend Rudi in his hour of grief because it might make people conclude, what … *that I had killed my other friend, Josephine!* And that I should furthermore only be concerned by such considerations because of the potential impact on my electoral prospects! Sometimes you are so wrong that I can't even begin to think about it.

Note: given that Fletcher found this small piece of hard-nosed electoral advice hard to swallow, it is not clear how he would have reacted to the actual text Ryle had sent to Rudi shortly after the incident: 'Tweety dead. A long story. Sorry for your loss and all. I know a man has set up a website selling good mattresses – if you want to get rid of that manky water bed she had.' *The compiler*

'It's not logical, true enough, it *shouldn't* have any effect,' said Ryle, letting go of his philosophical self a little, encouraged by what he thought was Fletcher's endorsement of his strategic advice, 'but that's the curse of the Irish. Bloodied thinking. It's what makes systematic progress towards a National agenda impossible. And it's what had the country invaded on so many occasions. The thoughts are always bloodied with emotions, bottled up sulks, retained bitternesses, siding with underdogs and losers out of pure contrariness, anger turned inward. In short, leaving the door wide open for clear cold thinking people to walk in and take charge. The real electorate you will face is not some ideal one you might like to face. If you got your name messed up with this kind of business it could be three or four months before they forgot.'

Note: it was true for him. Ireland's difficulty, England's opportunity. How else could we have been overrun by a people so lacking in guile that they take everything you say to be what you mean, an army of David Beckhams, who you could see coming with set pieces from a mile off. *The compiler*

'Where did all that come from?' said Fletcher, his eyes staring wide, no longer even knowing which part of Ryle's logic to tackle. 'And besides, how can you have such a negative and defeatist view of our own people?'

'Of course, the subjects don't tidy up well. The logical invader ends frustrated, all good intentions falling on barren ground,' old Cromwell's cold eyes looked straight ahead from inside Ryle's square of yellowness as he held the phone firmly to his ear and he reverted to saying no more than was necessary. 'I'm just saying you'd be better off not going there for a day or two. That is my opinion. That's all.'

'What am I thinking!' said Fletcher then. 'I'm sorry, Len. Of course it's just your shock talking. Having come on that harrowing sight your thoughts are probably even more disrupted by shock than my own. You poor man!'

'Be that as it may. No woman, no problem,' said Ryle, misquoting Koba much as he admired him, 'it's still looking like a nice enough day for a bit of a spin.'

'What the heck, friend,' said Fletcher, 'come to think of it, you're right. Let's just go anyway. To hell with everything, there's nothing of use that we can do by hanging around here moping listlessly along with everyone else. Can you get another van?'

'Never let it be said,' said Ryle.

An ill wind

Chapter XII

AN HOUR AFTER THE TRAGIC event on Northumberland Rd., Sectretary General Mac Gabhann sent a memo to all staff projecting the Departmental tone. He indicated that he would not countenance any further moping and staring out the street side windows. The dignified response was to get back to work. That was what Josephine would have wished, he asserted. He would represent the Department at the cremation. (As you know by now, the miserable hound was fond of funerals.)

In the meantime he had his own re-arranging to do. The disciplinary procedures against Fletcher would have to be paused until he saw what the new man in HR was made of.

The cardinal creed for the likes of Mac Gabhann is that the minute one door is shut he expects another to open for him. He sat back and waited.

A moment later his idle hands had delivered unto them just such an opening. It came in the form of an email from Harry Boland. Mac Gabhann interlocked and twisted his carpels filling his office with crackling sounds. 'Ah yes,' he said to himself, 'Indeed. Fortune favours the very bold.'

Boland was MD of a little publishing shed on Pleasants Ave., a service boreen at the back of Blaney Books of Camden St. He wrote:

Dear Dr. Mac Gabhann,
I would like to be referred to a person in your Department who is deeply conversant with the history of the tower house castles. I've got a possible publishing deal for the right person!
A commissioning editor in one of the big three publishers in the US has approached me. She has identified a potentially hugely

lucrative placement into the genealogical
research market. Tens of millions are scour-
ing their roots for evidence of anything more
interesting than themselves—i.e. nobility or
criminality. They fervently seek that one
thousandth of their ancestry which may have
spent a night in a castle ☺.
My correspondent astutely realized that a
country with thousands of castles and a history wherein tenure is upended three times a
century, would have surnames of Chiefs and
murderers growing like grass; that we ought
to be able to provide at least one interesting ancestor to everyone in America.
What we'd need then is a detailed historical
account of each castle and the names of the
major and minor characters associated with
them, all thoroughly indexed. No small task
I realize. This would be an impossible commission for anyone to take up from scratch.
But for the right person, the person who
has eaten and breathed the history of these
wonderful buildings for decades, this will
be both doable and hugely rewarding I am
certain.
It is rumoured that such a person inhabits
your department. A man who was obsessively
dedicated to a research project of just this
sort throughout the noughties. A Mr. Fleshley
I think? I would like to be referred to that
person.
Harry B.

Mac Gabhann the utter professional measured out the time
before replying. He didn't want to seem like he was sitting at
his desk waiting for any old email to come in. But he also did
not want to leave any gap of uncertainty within which Boland
might redirect his enquiry. He spent ten minutes composing
his reply … *One warmly welcomes this long overdue initiative
… have been thinking for a while that the existing books are
inadequate … Leask dated, gappy, and sometimes plain wrong;
Sweetman too given to strong houses … both more interested in
pilasters than people: neither made the slightest effort to recount the
human lives of the castles … being a great advocate of the private*

sector partnering with the public towards the common objective
of recording and preserving our extant built heritage and field
monuments ... could not palm this off on a less qualified person
... will make time in own very demanding schedule to write this
work oneself ... nobody with a better overview of the field ... a
sucker for punishment, but as they say, if you want something done
ask a busy person!

It's barely worth mentioning at this point that Mac Gabhann
was in the Department of Heritage and Monuments only
because it was small. That is, it had offered a thin field in the run
to the top. He was not, however, much consumed by affection
for mossy relics of inglorious eras. When obligated to sojourn
outside Dublin he found the well heated rural bungalow much
more to his taste. In his view, only the pathologically backward-
looking would instead seek out a sinkhole in which to embark
on a lifetime of discomfort and financial ruin.

In fact the bold gentleman had been about to launch a demo-
lition drive that would have given his department star ranking
with the Minister of Finance. Under the fog of patriotic recti-
tude all but one tourist-magnet exemplar of each type of historic
building was to have been de-listed and immediately demol-
ished on a health and safety mandate. The builders of Georgian
townhouses were to have been stripped of their status as the
last aesthetes of Irish architecture. Instead they'd be revealed as
the brash vandals of their era, classically bastardizing without
pediment every rolling gable of the city's Dutch Billy vernacular.
Similarly, he would have illustrated how the Victorians lacked
nostalgia for the town squats of their priors and sought to show
off their own best inventions, conveniences and baubles, in turn
mauling every Georgian they could lay hands on. The manor
houses would have been laid bare as follies, poor ersatz tributes
to the English cousins' manors. The centrepiece though was to
have been his plan for the tower house castles. He would have
kept one modest castle in Meath. *Consolidate around centres of*
excellence would have been the message to the tourism people.
The stone from the remaining 3,251 castles would have been sold
to gateway masons and the proceeds given to the IMF. The castle

demolitions were to have been the centrepiece of course, the cherry, that final flechette bomb that he would lob into Fletcher's greenhouse.

But the luck of Lucifer, you surely can't now deny, was with Mac Gabhann. Had Boland's mail come a day later he would have already broadcast his green paper and given the green flag to the bulldozers. Instead the paper went to his recycle folder, seen by nobody other than the junior executive officers who had written it after an oral briefing that he could easily deny.

Needless to say, Mac Gabhann lacked any of the detailed knowledge that might be necessary to write even the first page of the new Boland publication. However, he had not forgotten Fletcher's reports. Seventeen tomes of flowery detail and rambling reminiscence that Mac Gabhann had dumped in boxes somewhere in the basement.

The *Fleshley* that Boland had heard about of course was Grattan Fletcher. For the first year of this millennium he had argued and agitated to have his department commission a study. Mac Gabhann had received countless memos. 'The extraordinary situation of having a few thousand fantastic memory marks in the country ... hardly a scrap of their individual histories recorded ... people who know the local lore dying off ... what other country has anything like it ... what single other issue could more urgently call out for custodians of built heritage to engage themselves with!'

However Mac Gabhann's inclination to stymie or at least dishearten Fletcher had been deeply ingrained from long before this millennium. He had made it clear back then that if Fletcher wanted to conduct such a study he would have to do it on his own time and on his own dime.

That was what Fletcher had eventually done. Every weekend of his unfortunate daughter's early years had involved family camping trips to various teetering piles of stone. Margot would take Saoirse exploring while Fletcher talked to local grey heads, trying to correlate their yarns with anything that the National Library had to offer on each castle.

In this process Fletcher had broken the country into seventeen regions according to some logic of his own and dutifully handed in a folio on the castles in each region as it was completed, hoping they would one day be digitized and made public. Mac Gabhann had made no secret of his intentions to file them in the basement.

After the seventeenth report Grattan's slip of a daughter, seventeen too, had issued. That was the end of the castle frenzy. Fletcher had become wholly distracted with the little blob, her mother, and once again with her mother's mother. Mac Gabhann had found himself perplexed, never having found anything particularly likeable in any of his own five children.

Today, as Mac Gabhann was drawn back to the present by the sight of yet another Garda taking measurements on the road, he surmised that there was no reason to monitor the window further. He reasoned that Fletcher's weak heart would be stricken, even though the hussy had done him no favours other than dying. Surely, he thought, all the mystery field trips would be suspended for at least a week. Thus he gave himself license to get started on his new project. It's an ill wind.

He took up his phone to affirm his assessment of Fletcher's state.

'... so what do you make of that, Grat old chap?' he said, when Fletcher picked up.

'I'm in bits, to tell the truth,' said Fletcher.

'You're not the only one,' observed Mac Gabhann.

'How are you holding up?' asked Fletcher, missing a beat, 'She was someone you were close to?'

'Anyway,' said Mac Gabhann, 'back to our own discussion ... do you not see that every brainwave a middle aged man has will seem to have been entirely predictable and pointless when he looks back from his decrepitude, just as every twenty-year-old's rebellion seems when they look back on it as a thirty-year-old?'

'What?' said Fletcher, trying to understand, 'do you really believe that no new learning is possible?'

'Sure it's not,' said Mac Gabhann, 'only learning what other people learned before you. New-to-you learning. Pre-owned learning. Roth or Rorty haven't learned anything that Kant or

Hume didn't know. They merely continue to labour for nuances of personal rationalization; churning excuses for their inclination to carry on spouting esoteric nonsense, after they've personally re-*discovered* the same basic truths. The more you flail, Grattan, the more ridiculous you look to others. Remember, the prevailing force doesn't care.'

'What you mean is, *you* don't care,' said Fletcher rather sharply. 'You think this a great insight? One that is not every bit as ennui-laden? I have no time for this, Charles.'

'Well keep the chin up, dear boy,' said Mac Gabhann. 'If I need to send a Department person to convey condolences to anyone I'll give you a holler.'

'OK,' said Fletcher.

'I may be rather busy myself for the next few weeks.'

After he put down the phone Mac Gabhann headed to the basement to retrieve some box files.

We exist together

Chapter XIII

FLETCHER, INNOCENT OF ANY of the transgressions occurring around him, set out on a trip that might have been seminal in an election campaign. Without ever leaving the pale, (venturing further would have been ambitious as the unsolved killing had resulted in a late start), he was to find himself effortlessly ingratiated with three important non-National constituencies.

The first encounter was in Killiney.

The two men had been driving about without much aim. Grattan Fletcher, in a bit of a slump, was curled up in his seat and shaking like an aspen leaf. The tragic road death had made a deep impact on him, it seems, despite his resolve to get on. And despite Ryle's advice not to dwell in the past. Then Fletcher spotted a banner declaring '*Féile OMD.*' This was the first thing that had tickled his interest even the slightest bit in nearly two hours of driving so Ryle pulled up and went with it.

The banner was over an archway that led them into a quiet courtyard. Other than themselves and the pleasantly dressed people on the stalls, there wasn't much of a stir at this festival. Wind-blown drizzle was getting in under the flimsy canopies. Grattan brightened a little when he stopped at a table offering children's books for sale. Ryle picked one up and stared at the colourful and deformed drawings that grinned back at him. The writing was in a language that Ryle failed to recognize. The only intelligible bit was in small print on the back. It declared, *The Arts Council* ☺ *'s An Gaeilge.* 'Typical.' said Ryle. 'Should we not take care of our own first?'

Grattan, no gobshite in many languages, addressed the stall-keeper in what reached Ryle's ears as a series of noises such as would be made by someone with a hot floury rooster potato rolling around in his mouth. Last time Ryle had heard him making such sounds Fletcher had claimed it was nothing but a '*blasht of the blas an Corcaigh.*' Grattan had spent every summer holiday with his grandparents on the farm near Macroom and even though they'd never spoken a word of the old language in that part of Cork in all of human history, this was the dialect Grattan had thereafter discovered was in his bones.

Note: in case you were wondering why we started off this account by interring him in the grey windswept parish down South instead of finding a spot between the OTT protuberances of Glasnevin, along with other minor patriots, here is your explanation. He wanted his bones 'returned.' A small conceit, but I was on for letting him off with it. *The compiler*

Anyway on this occasion, the great man, fair play to him, was not going to be outshone in the culture game. The sweet person of the stall responded in whatever dialect it is they speak themselves. It had all the makings of a lovely occasion like a step back to prehistoric times where everyone was making sounds unintelligible to each other and nobody was being either understood or misunderstood. 'I see she understands the twenty-euro note well enough,' grumbled Ryle loudly when he saw Fletcher part with money and take two books. 'For *sweet angelic little Margot,* I suppose,' Ryle added delicately, recalling Fletcher's sensitivities in regard to plain speaking references to the grandchild.

'*Go deimhin,*' said Fletcher, still in character.

'Whatever you're having yourself,' said Ryle, 'but I'm just going to ask, with all due respects, how in the name of the lord lambing jaysus do you expect her to grow up normal when you're stuffing her with peculiar shite like that?' The nearly empty highwalled yard had an unnaturally amplifying effect on Ryle's words, not soft at the best of times. His opinions bounced around back and forth demanding the attention of even the most downbeat stallholders.

'*Oh?* What have we here?' said one large man eventually, perhaps having other weights on his shoulder. 'Two *geas min,*' he said with an intention of mimicry. 'Two salt of the earth real Irishmen come to mock and knock. Well do you know something? We don't have to put up with that kind of assback-wardness. Not in this century.'

'So you can talk English after all, why aren't you at work?' said Ryle. 'Let me guess, you're a washed up architect or a red-carded solicitor …'

'Why don't you just t-t-t-t-take a hike,' said the guy losing his cool and stepping forward, '*shshshshitbird!*'

'You think I give a fuck about you?' said Ryle, his words now turned to icicles. 'You're nothing special to me. Just another big sack of organic matter. It moves this way and the other and distracts itself with noise. Then in a blink it lies down and goes back to being dung.'

'Where are y-y-y-y-you from anyway?' asked the man getting more worked up. 'From somewhere d-d-d-d-down the country I'd guess by the accent? From somewhere that they think that doing doughnuts on the motorways after drinking off-the-shelf stout gives them a lock on National cu-cu-cu-cu-cu-culture. Well bud, we are immune to your disparagement. I'm not ashamed of my accent and we are not afraid to step out and do our best to reclaim our mother tongue. It's ours too you know.'

'That's a good one,' said Ryle, 'and fucking welcome.'

'I think you might apologize or leave,' continued the man, frustration seeping sweetly from every pore, 'your uncouth ba-ba-ba-ba-ba-barracking of people at least trying to be bilingual is a little disingenuous coming from someone clearly not articulate in even one lalalaaanguage.'

Maybe the drizzle was getting in on him, Ryle reasoned. He knew that some of the Easterners couldn't handle the ambiva-lence of the weather in Ireland. They liked things either one way or the other. He stepped past Fletcher and pointed a short thick finger at the large bald man.

'You're saying I don't know my own language?' said Ryle, 'a little declension of your arse would do you no harm you uptight fuck.'[fn]

[fn] Footnote
Hardly a surprise to have the compiler ascribing a touchy defence to

Ryle on this subject, he himself being an atrocious serial abuser of the language. *The Editors*

'Apologize to Fefefefefefelicity,' said the man, 'that's what I'm saying. And then go elsewhere.'

'Listen here to me, bollicky bill, I am not a bit sorry for anything I've ever said or done in the entirety of my life. In this country, the education we get always ends in tiers, two of them. What education I was entitled to was not as large as what my boss here got. But it was fairly compact. If you run into it, it might hurt you.'

Note: allowances must be made. It's too easy sometimes to forget that you and I have the advantage of being much better educated than Ryle. Ryle was never nourished in the fundamental disciplines of thought; the ploughing, tilling, and manuring of a young mind essential for the bouncy blossoms of a liberal arts harvest to emerge. The exclusion of the likes of Ryle could make him dangerous at times.[fn] *The compiler*

[fn] Footnote
One shudders. Endowed with a college education centred on lactic microbes—a course in dairy science is all the tertiary education his biography refers to, one cut short for non-attendance—and the compiler now wishes to portray himself as being a cut above buttermilk, to coin a phrase. Ryle at least is possessed of raw authenticity. Happily, whatever kind of authenticity may adduce to the compiler himself, remains inscrutable. *The Editors*

Fletcher took offence on Ryle's behalf. 'Friend,' he intervened, looking the big sad man in the eye, 'my colleague can be a little bit gruff at times. And I apologize for that. However, he speaks from shock and grief. Also, we too ought not fall into the trap of belittling others for a perceived lesser command of language. Proust said, there are no certainties, even grammatical ones. Only that which bears the imprint of our taste, our choice, our uncertainty, our desire, our weakness can be beautiful.'

That silenced everyone. The people looked at Fletcher like he had said something of relevance, not knowing of course that the man could dig up a bit of old nonsense for any occasion.

'I'm sorry,' said the big man, extending his hand towards Ryle, 'it's a difficult time for everyone. Will you guys have coffee with us?'

Ryle the runt refused the coffee and ignored the hand. Fletcher made up for it.

'What are you on about?' Ryle turned on Fletcher, confused now about what side he was on. 'I don't have to have read *Proust* to know that the weaknesses of most minds are best left sunk in mystery along with the rest of the contents.'

'It's about valuing truth, palatable or not, rather than living and dying behind a wall of cliché and pretence, I think,' said Fletcher.

'Show me a person whose fundamental truth *is not cliché,*' said Ryle, thinking that the females were looking at him as a little intellectual now too, and were maybe taking that bit more interest in him as a result. He got into his choppy stride, 'It's only them with time on their hands who can talk up their own shite until they have craft marmalade labels made for it. Why make an art of examining the contents of a toilet?'

The big man was ignoring Ryle completely now, sheepish at having lost his cool. Ryle became aggravated at the lack of focus on himself. 'Listen here fido, don't turn your back on me. Do you ever find people getting annoyed with you? With the slow go on of you?'

Fletcher apologized again and took Ryle aside. 'I think you may be missing the point, my friend,' he said quietly. 'The people of Dublin Four, the natives of your very own parish as it happens, are celebrating difference and tolerance.'

'I don't know about that,' said Ryle, who didn't socialize much in the locality of his house. He had inherited this under undisclosed circumstances from a woman who had died at a nursing home in which his aunt worked. The fact of it being in Donnybrook was incidental. It could have been in any of the other areas where property holds its value as far as Ryle was concerned. Therefore, in fairness, he would have looked foolish letting this accident of fortune impact on his identity or causing him to try to get in with the Fours.

'They are only too well aware of how they are perceived,' continued Fletcher, 'and they're having the courage and good humour to embrace it as we should them. Did you not get that? The irony of the OMD tagline? *Oh mo Dhia!* Do you even understand irony? What's actually the matter with you, Len? Why do you have to find a way to antagonize even the nicest of people?'

Ryle, finding himself in a very accommodating mode, assumed Fletcher was still affected by the traffic incident, though several hours had since elapsed.

'Alright, I get it,' said Ryle, recalling words from a workplace conflict workshop he'd been forced to attend many years before, a consequence of a minor altercation in which he had taken a pickaxe to an OPW colleague, 'it's about describing our emotions rather than expressing them. It's about building collaborative environments. I feel this. I was hurt by that. That sort of a thing. I can play that game as good as the next man.'

'Do you get it though?' said Fletcher in a tone bordering on condescension, despite Ryle's best efforts.

'Not a bother,' continued Ryle. 'I recognize that in the preceding events I too may not have always been entirely faultless.'

'Really?' said Fletcher. 'Not wishing to tell you your business or anything, Suck, but if I might make the small suggestion: when people are already being self-deprecating there's, you know, no need for you to join in.'

'When they are, you should be extra wary, would be my experience,' said Ryle wisely. 'You'll find it's usually a decoy for the real things that are wrong with them. The people who are genuinely resigned to a low opinion of themselves can always be known by their quietness.'

No further moves were made to engage with Ryle. Fletcher stayed for refreshments and talk. Ryle heard more of the rollicking potato noise from Fletcher as he himself headed out of that place to see where he could get a chicken kebab.

A good hour later when Fletcher got into the van beside Ryle he said, 'You know something, I don't believe your story,

Leonard Suck Ryle.'

Ryle just looked at him, giving the slightly smoky motor a few more revs to warm it up.

'I know there's good inside you. Maybe you never had any-body to believe in you when you were growing up. Or since. So you hardened into this devil-may-care persona. But I don't buy it.'

Ryle didn't even understand this kind of talk.

'I can see ever more clearly with every person we meet, eve-ryone I am touched by, that this path we have stumbled on is the right one. People are a blessing. And I know that deep down you are with me.'

'A lot of believing out of an atheist,' Ryle pointed out.

'That's all I'm saying,' said Fletcher. 'And what's more, I'm going to say that I believe that you know what I mean.'

The book female of the OMD sect distracted Grattan by giving a delicate bang on the window. Ryle was more focussed on his rearview, waiting for a taxi to go out around him and stop with the horn. The African lads didn't seem to know that when Ryle was out in a public service vehicle he could stop in any lane he wanted. He even had two wheels up on the kerb, as a courtesy, on this occasion. The man had nothing whatsoever to be going on about.

Fletcher let down his window and the hipsterish lady with thick framed glasses and an unkempt styling to her hair, stuck her head in. 'Felicity is the name,' she said taking and holding his hand with shameless felicitousness. She pushed a couple more gawky publications in Fletcher's face. 'Here,' she said, able to speak the local language quite well too, Ryle was not beyond noticing, 'we're not getting any traction with this lark. Good idea badly executed. An irony too premature for the masses perhaps. Your little girl may as well have these too.'

'Thank you,' said Fletcher. This was a change. Before, he had been normal about gifts, saying, 'ah no, I couldn't, really, are you sure,' and various others of the mannerly semi-refusals before taking anything. Here he was just taking things as they came. Ryle was worried. His companion's condition was less stable than he had thought. In fact it was getting a little stranger every day.

'And this,' she said, pausing in embarrassment. She took out of her Brown Thomas shopping bag, a little straw swastika. 'My son made a couple of Brigid's crosses in school. Pre-Christian they say. You keep this one with you. You know, to bring good luck to you and your callow friend in your work. *Agus mar sin de.*'

'*Oh go bhfoir a Dhia orainn,* we'll welcome any luck that Brigid and your son's wonderful handiwork can bring us,' said Fletcher. Nothing would do him only to get straight out of the car and give her a hug. She kissed the flubbery lips and Ryle caught a wink from her, he was pretty sure, over Fletcher's shoulder. She wasn't a bad sort after all. He there and then changed his assessment of her origin. Romania rather than Finland.

When Fletcher sat back in he was slightly uplifted.

'Don't be getting too fucking excited,' shouted Ryle.

'Nothing you can say, my friend,' said Fletcher, crushing a wing of the little straw thing in his fist, 'nothing can dampen this moment. We exist together. All of us.'

Ryle hadn't been trying to dampen anything. His shout had been directed at the taxi man, who had finally pulled out into the traffic but now was going slowly alongside Ryle. He looked like a Somali pirate and was shaking his skinny, toothy head theatrically. But Ryle let Fletcher's perception stand. If the cap fits.

Better the devil you know

Chapter XIV

THE OTHER DEMOGRAPHICS to be touched by the heroic duo in the course of that seminal day were the South Inner City Islamists and the North Outer City Biafrans.

They were back in from Killiney too early to go home. Neither had much desire to return to the office. 'I don't want to deal with it just yet,' confided Fletcher, 'everyone fretting and poor Josic, no more.'

Ryle nodded, 'Caged monkeys all worked up because a small thing different happened today.'

The van containing Fletcher and Ryle was perambulating the South Circular killing time when suddenly before them, from an ordinary looking building, there burst a large throng of men in robes. Many walked on air, displaying the good leavening with which people leave any church worth its salt.

'Pull in, pull in here,' said Fletcher letting down his window in a moment of awe. 'Let's soak up the moment. Feel the joy of these decent people.'

'What the fuck for?' said Ryle. There being not as much as the eye slit of a woman on display, Ryle was not inclined for windscreen gazing at this particular mob. 'You'd give days berating your own mild native religion and yet when you see these bucks bouncing along in soutanes, you get all tolerant.'

'Fair point,' said Fletcher. 'All the same though, isn't it grand?'

'No,' said Ryle. Then he spotted No Profit amongst a group of older men and he considered having a change of heart.

Any love Ryle lacked for the spectacle currently affronting them was outweighed by his love for the intestine fouling abomination that is mackerel. He had discovered some years back that these were to be got cheapest and freshest on a Saturday morning

from a shop in Clanbrassil Street. And it didn't require intuition
of the kind that Ryle lacked, to glean the origin of the nickname
associated with the fat owner of the small busy shop and the
large bushy beard. Pleasant while talking about the weather and
jolly while placing goods in secondhand Spar bags, the man's
demeanour always darkened when the total tinkled up on his
mechanical cash desk. '*No!* This can't be right, you people are
robbing me. There's no profit left for me. No profit!' After a
decade of Saturdays, Ryle's engagement with the man had grown
into a routine exchange of short phrases. He had persuaded Ryle
on occasion to participate in a game of dominoes. It was not that
Ryle liked the company. However, since a stint in Cyprus in his
youth, dominoes was one of Ryle's favourite games and where
else was he going to get to play it.

Note: no details can be made available to you regarding the
Cyprus reference. What Ryle was doing in Cyprus or for
how long he was a Tan, I can't say. However, the belief in the
village of Ballyhale which Ryle has not set foot in since he
thumbed out of it at the age of sixteen, is that he left from
there directly for the British Army. The people of that village
are secretly proud of him, and whisper that he went on to
be a colonel in the SAS. They'd have more manners than to
talk aloud about the matter. (You'll probably have guessed by
now that there is more that could be said by myself about the
goings on in city, continent, and county of Kilkenny but one
has seen too many writers sell their neighbours and their family linen for a publishing deal. The old dog doesn't shit where
he eats. Not more than once anyway. So while your compiler
might let slip the occasional hard-learned prejudicial word in
regard to the residents of other parts of this country, the Cats
will remain someone else's work.) *The compiler*

'Well Cassim,' Ryle shouted, 'how are the balls of your toes?'

No Profit came over to the car with the usual broad smile
and extended hand. 'Well Leonard, you reprobate, I am not too
bad at all, thank God.'

'*As-salamu alaykum*,' said Fletcher leaning across, really
impressed with Ryle for once.

No Profit looked at Ryle, puzzled.

'My boss, Grattan,' explained Ryle, 'don't mind him, he's not quite right in the head. An atheist like yourself.'

'Oh,' said No Profit leaning into the window to examine Grattan, obviously a secret reader. 'How then do you guys explain consciousness? Eh?'

Fletcher lit up and Ryle was overcome with regret, forehearing what might be coming. Having heard it twice too often and fearing the unconsciousness that could surround Grattan Fletcher when allowed to mount a hobby horse unhindered, he decided to cut it short. 'So, consciousness, what is it really?' he aped. 'Well that would be *a few billion cells firing off electrical signals in a pattern sufficiently similar to what they did yesterday that we get a sense of continuity and self.*'

'Yes and that's only part of the story,' said Fletcher undeterred. 'The ability to observe our own individual situations and cogitate morosely thereupon, is merely a regrettable side effect of the only evolutionary advantage of our species. We got ahead not by developing speed or good claws but by refining the ability to observe and predict the movements of other life forms to the extent of being able to take advantage of them. Our cunning unfortunately gave them the last laugh on us, bequeathing us, as a side effect, the bitter ability to observe and predict the course of our own lives too. The ability to realize that we too will wither and die. With that came the propensity to ruminate upon the puzzle of our personal lot.'

'Pleased to make your acquaintance,' said the bewildered foreigner, in a nod to Grattan.

'What has you out praying today?' asked Ryle, aware that Friday was normally the only day he would get nobody at the shop. 'Are you burying or marrying?'

'Burying.'

'Sorry to hear that,' said Ryle putting a spearmint gum in his mouth. 'Will there be a feed when you're done?'

'Yes. Well, thank you,' said No Profit, 'So what is it you want?'

'That's not very polite,' said Ryle who didn't like bluntness so much when it came from others.

'I know you're not much for social conversation,' said No Profit, 'so what is it you want?'

'Fair enough,' said Ryle, getting down to business. He said, pointing to Fletcher, 'Take a look at this man's face.'

'I see it very well,' said No Profit, not flinching.

'Next time you see it may be on a ballot sheet,' said Ryle, 'I'll thank you to put an X beside it. You won't regret it. I might drop off a little poster in the shop on Saturday so any of your lot who have managed to wangle the passport can be familiarizing themselves with him.'

'With all due respects,' asked No Profit, 'why would we want to vote for him?'

'Good question,' said Ryle pushing himself back into the seat so the two big men could make a deal with each other directly.

'I'm so sorry, sir,' said Fletcher who was mortified and flustered at the same time, for once the wrong words coming to him, 'Ryle has the wrong end of the stick. I'm not out canvassing at all.'

'Sure you're not,' said No Profit, 'as if people like you hang around outside the Mosque every day.'

'Really, I'm not within the ball of an ass of getting elected to anything,' said Fletcher, 'and really don't ... am not motivated by that kind of thing.'

No Profit looked puzzled.

'Don't mind him, we are at most that distance from the Presidency,' said Ryle, 'he'll soon enough be going up for election.' He dug his elbow in Fletcher's ribs to no avail at all. 'Every fucking campaign has to start somewhere, it seems to me, even though I know nothing about these things. We're not going to fucking get elected by going around to bring-and-buy sales pretending not to be interested in ruling the country with an iron fist.' (Ryle had not at this stage done a great deal of research into the powers attaching to the role of President.)

'Yes, but the reason I should vote for him?' persisted No Profit. 'Just because he's shaken my hand? Is that how simple you think it is to win favour with people from developing countries?' No Profit occasionally had a political streak in him that Ryle didn't care for.

'The handshake is good enough for the local. You think you're better? Alright, well the reason you should vote for him,' said Ryle, making a fair fist of coming up with a campaign manifesto all on his own, 'since the cat seems to have got his tongue: well let me just put it out there that Fletcher is not the worst of them. As you know me, Cassim, I don't like any sort of person very much?'

'I had noticed that,' said No Profit who had quickly moved their domino sessions to a back room after observing that people tended to put items back on the shelves when Ryle was sitting behind the counter.

'Well,' said Ryle, 'he's gone the other way. He's very fond of all kinds of people. Another thing is he is always giving out about what the Americans are up to abroad so I don't think he'll be making moves to root out whatever young blackguards of your variety may be using this country as a safe house. I don't know whether any of that has any purchasing power with you at all?'

No Profit's complexion darkened but it should be noted that no conclusion about his view on holy wars can be drawn from this. 'So,' he said, trying to think of a thing to stump the politician, 'what is your position on enforced integration versus assimilation? Do you support the school principals who make our daughters take off their scarves?'

He would know for the future that what was a stump to a normal person was fodder to Fletcher. 'I'm so interested in that question,' he said. 'In this country we should know better than anyone. We only have to look at how much more adherent the culturally Catholic in the North remain. When external encroachment on religious practice is made to the accompaniment of the tribal drum, resistance is inevitable. Trumped up calls of tribal distress can invoke troupe huddling in the best of people.'

Cassim nodded uncertainly.

'However,' Fletcher continued, 'integration must surely be the way, don't you agree? The problem with a non-integrating group is that their business and charity tends to direct inwards. When everyone else does business and charity evenly but they continue to do business and charity mostly within, it creates a valve that builds the overall wealth of that sub group and further diminishes the incentive for integration. This can be good for the ever distinct minority most of the time. But it seeds resentments and at crisis times in a country it can be very very bad.'

Cassim scratched his beard and looked at Ryle, who nodded.

'But the main thing is this man you see here is harmless,' Ryle intervened, the words hurting himself even before they came out, 'He doesn't even kill flies. He's what some might call a very nice man. And that should be good enough for a few votes even if the hand shake didn't cod you.'

'Well I suppose that's good,' said No Profit, wanting to move on. 'There are not enough nice people. You bring me his poster, Leonard, and I'll see what to do with it.'

'Remember, better the devil you know,' said Ryle, driving off. 'We won't forget you, Fidel.'

Cassim offered his middle finger.

'You see,' said Ryle to Fletcher, 'no point beating around the bush. That went well.'

Fletcher said nothing for a little while because he did not like to.

Wish, father of thought

Chapter XV

'So you might as well tell me about the father of the *lovely little child*,' said Ryle perceptive in the respect that he had a good eye for exposed nerves and could find harmless amusement in giving a jiggle at them. 'You don't ever talk much about the lad that got your Saoirse up the stick, little Margot's daddy.'

The van jolted over the footing of a roadworks sign at that moment and Fletcher bit his tongue. They were driving on the hard shoulder of the N1 and it was not going easy on the bigger man.

'What does he do?' persisted L.P.C. Ryle.

'Very little these days,' said Fletcher spitting blood into his last tissue. 'He sits on his behind. He had an idea to develop an app. He's been telling everyone about that for five years. How it's going to make him his fortune. Appiness he calls it. Imagine surviving five years on one joke thought. An app that lets you type in your most cherished thoughts and does a web search to show you how many thousands of times similar ideas have been aired. And so, he claims, by showing you that you are just the same as what has gone before, and that there is not in fact some great mission before you, his app will free you to just be satisfied as you are.'

'What's wrong with that,' said Ryle, 'if people knew in advance that all they were going to be doing in life is discovering the meaning of old sayings for themselves, then more might feel entitled to excuse themselves of the bother.'

'*What is fucking wrong with it is that he is father of my grandchild!*' said Fletcher, unfamiliar sulphurous fumes of intolerance making his voice squeak. 'His philosophy may amuse fellow stoners. But defeat embraced does *not amuse me*. And of course he hasn't bothered to actually develop the app. Because of course he's pretty sure others thought of it already. As if irony has sustenance.'

'I take it you never warmed to him then,' said Ryle.

Fletcher flushed. They were on the road to Balbriggan and the traffic was dire so aside from jumping from the van he had no out. 'Right little bollox, may God forgive me for saying it.'

'You harbour negative sentiment,' Ryle said, 'so why didn't you do him in?'

'I'll confess, I thought about it at the time,' said Fletcher, still in rapture to the only indulgence he allowed himself in the bitterness game, 'making him disappear. Nobody would be at any loss. I daresay nobody would even miss him. I don't mean *miss* sentimentally, I mean *miss* as in notice he was gone.'

'You mean you'd have got out your uncle's mini-digger and covered him with seven foot of that right good Macroom grass land?' said Ryle who could never understand why Fletcher wasn't angling to take over the grandparents' farm from the ailing bachelor uncle down near Macroom. 'If you were minding that old man even half right he'd probably even do the digging and burying for you.'

'What? *Kill him? Are you insane?*' said Fletcher. 'But I can't tell you how often my fists have tingled to make contact with his disgustingly smug face. I wanted him to come to *physically* understand that my daughter was not no one. Not a solitary little person hanging out there waiting to be part of some hateful game he has going on with all of womankind. I wanted him to know that my daughter has people behind her. I wanted his emasculated narcissistic interpretation of what it is to be a modern male to crash painfully into the differing opinion of the people whose blood is in her veins.'

'So you just wanted to give him a trimming,' said Ryle. 'But didn't even do that much I take it.'

'Yes that's what I wanted I suppose. And then to give him money to go away.' Presently Fletcher remembered who he was talking to and the reverie began to desert him. 'But ultimately I had to think more about whether my loved ones respect me.

I chose to subdue thoughts about how I wanted him to fear me. And on reflection too I felt sad for Saoirse's generation. Everything is contested. Even the natural right of a young woman to put her trust in a young man.'

'So you didn't want to get your hands dirty,' said Ryle, trying to puzzle this out. 'Oh OK, I have you now, he was probably just sixteen too and you thought it'd look bad, flaking the shite out of a kid. So why then didn't you just get him done for rape and have him put on the sex offender's list? No parent disapproving of their daughter's infatuations needs a shotgun, convent, or a JCB these days, the way I see it.'

'As I said, my instincts stopped short of destroying him,' said Fletcher. Stationary drivers hooted at them as they skirted along. 'Since we're breaking the law anyway, can you not just drive a little faster.'

'*Thanks to the frustrated mother superiors of new wave feminism coming in behind the hand-wringing archbishops of your beloved liberalism,*' said Ryle, who had a very adequate memory palace when it came to storing the little he read. Several of the controversialist columns of Waters and Myers had been stashed in perfect order by him, since he had become aware of how much these writers aggravated Fletcher. And as you'll by now appreciate, getting under the great man's skin was one of Ryle's more harmless ways of keeping the devil's work at bay at moments when he found himself with idle hands.

Note: This kind of trash-talking out of Ryle shouldn't be any surprise to you, as by now you don't need me to tell you that he is a scrappy little article at the best of times.

Fletcher on the other hand remembered only gists and themes and never exact phrases. So he never twigged when Ryle was regurgitating. 'What do you mean? What is new wave feminism?' said Fletcher perplexed, lapsing into other thoughts.

'*... the soundbite re-tweeting by feminist carpet-baggers, people who never experienced discrimination but blog indignantly around the right to retain control over their own terminology,*' parroted Ryle happily.

'Don't be hard on them,' said Fletcher. 'Today's real frontlines for feminism are not appealing. What twenty-one-year-old has the heart to go to bat for Traveller girls pushed as children into consanguine marriages? Or to row in behind the pram pushing Finglas kids caught in the welfare mum trap? Why would she when the adults in her society also fail to show heart on these subjects?'

'*The apex males*,' Ryle continued, entirely ignoring Fletcher's personal reflections, '*are still trying to preserve the virtue of the breeding stock virgins. Only this time around the hymen-breaching outbursts of nature are punished by sending the boys to an institution rather than the girls. Apex man scores again. In approving the mother superiors' sentencing of this generation of young men for sins their grandfathers didn't even know they were committing, today's alpha male ingratiates himself to the alpha matriarchs and sees his own beta contenders castrated.*'

'*Bloody heck!*' said Fletcher, wound up as hell, 'that's crude and ugly talk even for you, Leonard. I had no idea you were so full of seething resentments.'

'What do you say to that, eh?' said Ryle, running low on appropriate references but trying to keep it going on a wing and a prayer, 'You had all *the stockades of the modern liberal State* at your disposal and didn't even have the balls to use that apparatus in pursuit of your righteous instinct to obliterate the chap? Is that what you are barefaced telling me, eh?'

'And by the way this was no *Romeo and Juliet* case,' said Fletcher, wound up and growling again. 'He was twenty-seven. Even still I gave him the benefit of the doubt. Wishfulness over wisdom.'

'The wish is father of the thought,' said Ryle, 'as they say.'

'*What?* Yes, I suppose,' said Fletcher. 'Anyway, I *wished* for my grandchild to have a father she could respect even if they were not together. All fine until I stumbled on the worm's *nom de guerre* on a Boards thread, forgive my language, where he boasts about his 'gaming' and compares notes with other 'players'.'

'Stumbled on?' said Ryle. 'Spit it out. You were stalking him.'

'Yes,' said Fletcher.

'Tell me this,' said Ryle with disgust, 'what's the point of stalking anything if you lack the ability to pull a trigger? That's like fucken bird-watching.'

'You know what, you are bloody right for once. I'm pathetic,' said Fletcher. Then collecting himself and straightening his jacket with a couple of tugs, a tic he had, he added, 'What is any of this to you though? Don't pretend you care about my family.'

'You can rest assured on that score,' said Ryle, his thoughts then equivocating as the bigger Margot stepped elegantly into his mind. Despite the dress size, he now knew what the term *a lady of great poise* meant. 'However, before this campaign hots up it is important for all the skeletons to be known to me. We don't want any handicapped children of disputed motherhood popping up in the middle of the campaign.'

'Good Jesus preserve me,' said Fletcher remembering the picture of a bikini clad carbine-toting Sarah Palin that had remained over Ryle's desk for years.

'What the fuck do we want in *Black*briggan, by the way?' said Ryle. 'Those people have hardly a vote between the lot of them.'

'All God's children,' said Fletcher. 'I have a friend out there who asked for guidance.'

'You mean that old geezer who stopped you with the anti-deportation petition on Northumberland Road the other day?' asked Ryle.

'I've had about enough of your crude cynicism for one day, if you don't mind,' said Fletcher.

'Fair enough, boss,' said Ryle, 'far be it from me to criticize a man for working the system. But someone should have a word with him. When you're pushing forty, you need a better ruse than pretending to be 15 and demanding to be let stay in the country until you retire out of the school system.'

'Enough, thank you,' said Fletcher who had promised the Nigerian scholar that he would call out to his family home to see if there was any help he could offer.

'What's wrong with him anyway?' continued Ryle who had never before given any thought to the subject of immigration and was forced now to ad lib. 'Does the city not have enough slappers that he could not find even one willing to marry him?

Kick his ass out, I say. As my grandfather used to say to his tenants, we must be just before generous.'

'Your grandfather must have been quite the character,'
snapped Fletcher. 'How about you could just be a bit more generous sometimes though, Len?'

'Don't get me wrong,' said Ryle, 'I'm all for letting those
shrewd enough to get through the mesh, to stay and improve
the only genetic advantage this lacklustre Nation possesses, cute-
ness. We might have got away with codding the English for a few
hundred years but codding real Germans indefinitely will take a
virulent new strain of the shrewd breeding. So my only question
is why do we need to let in the really dopey cunts? I fail to see
what objection you could have to returning them to the vendor.'

Note: it has often been observed that the Irish person has a
great willingness to every other person's point of view. In fact
that's only a little over half the story. The country is divided
into two types. The other type, not often mentioned in the
brochures, is unwilling to *any* other person's point of view.
Someone from this side of the divide, Ryle being a prime
specimen, will contradict anything you say to them. They
would disagree with themselves if you left them long enough
in a room on their own. The attributes shared by both sides
of this particular dichotomy of falsehoods is that neither gives
the slightest regard to the foreign notion of there being an
objective reality attaching to any situation. *The compiler*

'Just when I think it's not possible for you be any more base,'
said Fletcher. He paused for a while. A corporation tractor came
up behind them.

'You don't think it's a bit dangerous though,' said Ryle, 'going
into a ghetto unarmed?'

'Don't be ridiculous.'

'Anyway, would you let down your window too,' said Ryle,
rolling his down, 'I'm gasping for fresh air.'

'What do you mean?' said Fletcher.

'Nothing personal,' said Ryle, 'but you are fucken stinking.
Your breath is not something I want in my life. You haven't taken
up the Banting?'

Fletcher's little fault was not ketosis at all. Whenever he had a cold he made his warm foul exhalations worse for those around him by trying to heal himself with garlic.

'Well let's just take a break,' said Fletcher, blanched, but taking no responsibility, instead trying to spread the blame. 'Let's pause in Rush. Maybe the sea air will clear *both* our heads of all this stuff, eh?'

'No need for that. The window down will do,' said Ryle.

'I insist,' Fletcher insisted, 'I just ... really suddenly just want to see the sea.'

'What the fuck,' said Ryle, 'a minute ago you had no such desire at all. Now, it's like your life depends on it.'

Fletcher was not disappointed. It's a good spot enough. Despite the slight glow in the water from Sellafield, you could imagine you were in a beautiful part of the country. The sight of three untroubled fellows, weathered from years trying to kite surf, made Fletcher's heart ease up a bit. Low slung Lambay pleased him too. He took several deep breaths and stared at the little verdescent wavelets like it was the great Atlantic crashing before him. 'Freedom,' he said, 'I think that's behind the mystery of the sea's primordial grip on us. Freedom. Freedom and unity. It's what unites every living thing.'

'Right,' said Ryle, not very moved.

'Did you know that our blood is isotonic with sea water?' said Fletcher. 'Do you think that's what calls us back? Four hundred million years out of it and it's still in our blood, calling us. There is no person who does not feel it. Anyone who has lived on the coast for a while, even if they never so much as walk the beach, feels a huge loss that they can't quite explain when they move inland.'

'Not I, lord,' said Ryle.

'Yes, of course, not you, Len,' laughed Fletcher, once again making the mistake of patting Ryle on the back.

Near the van there were six men sitting on the steps of a restaurant. They were sharing two cans of Royal Dutch. 'You're out to the seaside on a day trip?' observed Ryle.

'What are you mickey lickers gawking at? Fuck off,' said one of them, very short with a wide moustache. '*Fuck off* or I'll beat you.'

A person who looked like Ahmadinejad observed keenly for the reaction as he postulated, 'A bollix in the morning is still a bollix in the evening.'

'You'll be waiting a while for them to feed you,' observed Ryle. The blue paint was faded to grey and the windows of The Village Grill were boarded with MDF sheets.

Another, one with ginger hair and a girlish face, stood up and laughed a high-pitched laugh. The operator of the group, he said to Ryle, 'You're right my friend, but you have to admit we're no slackers. We stick with it where others walk away.'

Two others, Tipperary men by the heads, kept talking away to each other not appearing to give much of a shit either way. The sixth man kept his large spectacled baldy head down, as he sat on the top step with his legs stretched before him. He was staring at one of his Puma trainers resignedly. By the way he was twisting it around, the foot may have been giving him a bit of trouble. He looked like a generally pessimistic man and clearly didn't trouble himself by getting up any hopes about the outcome of the ginger buck's pending sales pitch.

'What's the matter with the big lad?' asked Ryle.

'Staple? Nothing at all, only that he is fierce fond of the drink and it distracts him from the thoughts he'd rather be thinking,' said the gregarious one. 'That and the fact that the foot is rotting off him but he says there's nothing wrong with it. Won't go to the hospital to let them cut it off.'

'Beyond help?' said Ryle, not severely. 'Fuck him so.'

'Com'ere, any chance you could lend us a couple of euro,' said the ginger spokesman, laughing again, 'we're caught a bit short on the price of the dinner for when these people do reopen.'

'Sorry, friend,' said Fletcher like a prick, still walking, 'we have no cash on us.' He stopped and turned when he realized Ryle was not with him.

Suck Ryle was rooting in his pocket, not a thing he could be accused of doing very often. He came out with a wallet and from it he produced a perfect blue note.

The lead generation specialist, astonished that he'd got such a large nibble, moved to close the deal. With his hand swinging to take the paper, he was saying, 'That's very generous of you, sir. I hope you'll come this way again soon.'

'No free lunches,' said Ryle pulling his hand back. 'I just want a small favour.'

Fletcher intervened, 'Yes, my friend is right. In exchange you must give us some assurance that it will go on food or shelter. If you can put your hand on your heart and say that, I'll match his note.'

'Don't mind him,' said Ryle, 'he hasn't a tune in his head. What I want for the money is a chance to give that lad a slap.' He was pointing his finger stub at the short Moussilini.

'Which lad,' said the salesperson mock-innocently, 'Drum? Sure everyone wants that but you'll have to up the money to get us to stop him killing you in return.'

Drum was already standing up and taking off his long leather coat. Even when perched on the top step he remained the smallest man present. His moustache twitched like a trapped rat. 'Bring it on, you yellow headed block of shite. Bring it on! I'll fucken pulverize you.'

'Forty,' said the salesman with his hand out, standing in front of Drum who was making no push to come forward but continued to make a dramatic amount of noise and continued to undress down to a yellow Pixies t-shirt and white underpants with singe marks on the front. He held out his chin and put his hands over the Y of his underwear. He was shivering but only with the cold, still full of shit and attention-seeking. While he was at this one of the Tipp fellows pulled a scalded set of Uileann pipes from a Dunnes bag and started a sound like twenty cats in bother.

'Come to think of it,' said Ryle, a fundamentally tasteful man at times, 'clattering him would be too easy. Instead, get the big lad to tell a joke.'

'There is no money worth that,' said the negotiator. 'I'll tell you two good ones instead.'

'No,' said Ryle, 'him.'

'Tell the cunt a joke,' said Drum, kicking Staple on the bad leg.

'We're not going to let that happen,' insisted the extrovert.

'There was a lad from near Carlow,' started the maudlin priestly voice, bringing astonished silence on all the assembled, 'who allowed he'd wander over to London a few year back to see if there was anything stirring in the line of work. But it wasn't a whole lot better there only whatever worse. After he'd gev three weeks solid traipsing around from one site to the next trying to pretend to be a Mayo man, he was gone a bit downhearted. That wasn't helped at all by the fact that he hadn't et a morsel in three or four days and barely had money left for pints. There he was on Westminister Bridge one day looking like a man shot with a shovel when a lovely Englishman in a suit come over to him, a man even younger and fresher than himself. A decenter man you couldn't wish to meet, he offered our lad the fine turkey sandwich from his tupperware lunch box. Our man grabbed it. No thanks out of him, of course, on account of his people being from the Graigue side and having a natural suspicion of generosity. John Joe leant over the bridge to stop the watering of his mouth from causing a slush on the pavement. He held the bit of a sandwich in the tightest anticipation. Too tight. Didn't the lump of turkey fly out and drop into the river. This was a bridge too far for the lad from the wrong side of the Barrow and he finally broke down in tears, not a thing any true Carlow man would succumb to, other than maybe the rangy emotional sheepmen from Mount Leinster way. He was there slobbering away when he was approached by a fine young Metro policeman with the baton at his side. Straight out of cop college and full of chivalry, he came up and said, 'Hello, my friend, whatever is the matter?' '*Are ye fucken blind or what,*' said our lad still sobbing in his native tongue, '*isn't me fucken mate after fallin inta de wather?*' 'Oh goodness!' Without further ado, didn't the pig throw off the jacket, slide out of the jack boots and lep over the side. The Laois man watched him for a while splashing and flailing in the toxic fluid below, before he let a shout down after him, 'You're takin too fucken long, lad, I have the bread et now.'

Nobody laughed, each for his own reasons.

'Like Rossini's tears at the loss of his truffled turkey into the Seine,' chirped Drum. Like all BA people, his references were ones previously endorsed by others. This particular learnedness came from one short novel he had been given instead of food by a Ballsbridge householder. He thought he was fairly safe in taking its observations as his own, as the same book had been banned for decades. (The publication was one of Flitcroft's less frivolous offerings, a po-faced early work in which he had naïvely thought to blow the lid off the cannibalism going on at Oxford University for centuries.)

'Fuck me,' said the gregarious ginger salesman momentarily losing the cool, forgetting the overall objective (gouging the few bob out of Ryle), 'that's my fucking joke, Staple, you weak hure. You stole my joke! What's worse, you made a bags of it!'

'It's not the first and it won't be the last,' said the big manky-footed monkey with the closest thing to a smile you were ever going to see out of him.

Fletcher was outraged at Ryle by this time. He walked on in utter disgust, failing to produce his twenty. Ryle had to produce another note, sourly this time. The big headed treasurer with the sore foot looked up incredulous as the spokesman passed over the money that Ryle had parted with. Drum was dressing again, though he didn't stop with the threats.

'Despicable,' said Fletcher when Ryle joined him at the car. 'Baiting those poor unfortunates.'

'What the fuck are you on about,' said Ryle, 'he was the one threatened to bate me first.'

'Not funny. Not one bit funny, Mr. Ryle,' said Fletcher in his most disgusted tones. 'And giving them money that is clearly just going to be used on more alcohol, poisoning them further, aggravating their illness.'

'What else would they spend it on?' said Ryle.

'Do you not even stop for a moment to think that there but for the grace of God go you and I?'

'Here without the grace of God, are we instead,' retorted Ryle.

'What is that even supposed to mean?' said Fletcher examining it in his head for a minute. 'Your behaviour is simply inde-fensible. Pouring further misery into unhappy lives.'

'If you don't even know that those are not the kind of men

who like to be told how to spend their money,' said Ryle, 'then you don't know anything at all about this country or any other. Besides, they didn't look as unhappy as a lot you'll meet in Northumberland Road.'

Fletcher said nothing, clicking his seat belt with some force as a way of holding onto his anger. 'There is a thing called basic human dignity, and another called responsibility to our fellows,' he said.

'Responsibility and dignity are not all they're cracked up to be,' said Ryle. 'Why else do you think people who've been through the pain of cleaning it all up, are so often on the brink of going back? What? Do you think they're stupid?'

Fletcher was looking more closely at Ryle now. He could not intuit the whole story of course. Yet he could sniff out that there was something more here.

Note: Fletcher couldn't have known that his companion had nearly buried himself in the streets of Killarney after desertion, not knowing that Ryle had been in the British Army in the first place. *The compiler*

'You know Drum?' he tried in a more subdued tone.

'Drum? Everyone knows Drum,' said Ryle. 'He has no friends.'

'Seriously, Len?' Fletcher tried in welling sympathy. 'It's a long, long way from there to here? Eh?'

'Not that long. It's not a choice between hell and heaven. It's more a choice between rye bread and sour dough. Some days you could go either ways.'

'Somehow I can't imagine you foolish with drink,' said Fletcher.

'In life most people don't need to be sober at all. Only less drunk than your companions. The man in the street has more people at his side than the man who's got ahead of everyone. If that's any good to you. Plus you get respect. Everyone is afraid of what you are and they steer clear.'

'You seem to understand,' said Fletcher forgetting all that had gone before, as a disparate thought wafted out of him on a new wave of garlic, 'how people like those men can forego everything we think valuable in life because they've found a way of short-circuiting the reward centre. Upstream, we see the misdirection of hard earned reward from love and family to the fast-food reward of buying stuff for yourself, eroding the ability of Nations to reproduce. Where does it lead our children?'

'Where there are reeds there is water,' said Ryle, 'that was one thing my father used to say.'

'I suppose …' said Fletcher, extremely puzzled but leaving this moment to Ryle.

In the house of my father there are many rooms

Chapter XVI

FROM THE FRONT, the Balbriggan house of Perseverance the Nigerian was a grey pebble dashed mid-terrace job with not many rooms at all.

When Fletcher and Ryle went to the open door a big strong woman shouted at them to come into her kitchen wherein she stuffed them with sweet tea and ginger biscuits while she battered them with a litany of woes which neither of them wanted to hear at all. Fletcher couldn't stop gazing through the patio doors, out back. The little house had been extended by a series of double-story structures until the multi-visioned architect of this wonder had run the full hundred metres to the back boundary.

'How come the people from Nigeria are so loud?' asked Ryle politely. 'Other parts of your continent seem to produce softer spoken types. Is there a lot of background noise where you come from?'

'What? The good lord blessed me with a set of lungs and you think I must sit quietly in the corner like a little girl!' she said, holding a sandwich toaster over Ryle's head without any explicitly stated threat.

She resumed the complaining. Hard to make ends meet. Three adult daughters, Faith, Hope, and Charity, not one of them any good, only want to do one degree after another. Won't go look for work. Not like the older daughter, Desire, married back in Lagos. Can't get catfish from Tesco. And so on. However, she was polite enough in her own way. She refrained from asking directly what the visitors' business with Perseverance was. All she did by way of interrogation was to stop at the end of every outburst of her own to give a long white-eyed questioning stare at them.

Eventually she got fed up of waiting for them to volunteer any information and said to Ryle, 'Why do you look at me like that? Eh?'

'What?' said Ryle.

'You know, some of you Irish think that if you give us enough dirty looks we'll go away.'

'Please don't misread him,' Fletcher intervened, 'he's like that with everyone.'

'Very well,' she said, making a clucking, sucking noise, 'let me call my husband for you gentlemen.'

'She's a very fine person,' said Fletcher when she went out the back to knock on one of the doors of the extension. 'One of those solid women who keep every poor community together in the worst of circumstances, when the men are falling apart or taking to drink.'

'Fine indeed, I can see where you're coming from on that,' said Ryle, pleased and a little overcome with surprise. It was not so usual for him to find he was seeing something the same way as Fletcher. 'In fact, there's nothing wrong with her at all and when you add the pleasure of nibbling from under another man's nose, I'd nearly always be interested myself. But I'll stand back on this one since you mentioned it first. I'll have to settle for the daughters.' He watched with schoolboy wistfulness as the three virtuous young women emerged from one back door and floated along the concrete apron to go in another. 'Maybe Hope wouldn't be so bad in the end.'

'I don't mean like that, for Christsake!' said Fletcher, utterly scandalized. 'Have you no read on your fellow human beings at all?'

'Ah don't worry,' said Ryle, possibly misreading his compatriot's true feelings again. Though who can really tell in these situations? 'Don't worry at all. I should have said to you before. I'd never tell Margot if you slipped while we're on the road. Man cannot live on bread alone. That's only natural.'

'Lord, give me patience!' said Fletcher.

'But my advice in these situations is that it's best to wait until you see what kind of temperament her countryman is composed of before making any moves. There's no point in taking injuries for love. Those days are gone. If it turns out he's an easy-going codger like yourself, It's a fair bet he'd let matters pass with only a small fuss. In that case, be my guest. Besides, I'd have more work to do to get around her than you would. She certainly was giving you the occasional warm gaze. I can never understand that about women. Looks don't seem to matter to them at all.'

'Just shut it, Len,' said Fletcher.

'Always the bitter word,' said Ryle, offended, 'gormless fucker.'

The woman was an eternity out the back, talking away nine to the dozen with whomever it was that had opened a door for her; whomever it was that now lurked in the heart of the dark interior. Ryle had eaten the last of the biscuits and went to look in the cupboards for anything else he could get. The victim of a terrible sweet tooth, he was forced to start in on a box of Farley's rusks.

'I wouldn't exactly say either of us is *gorm*less here though,' whispered Fletcher with a smile. Barbarous puns being Fletcher's staple in the humour department, Ryle had no chance of uptake at all. Much less so when the pun was in an alien language.

'Come on,' said Fletcher, 'you know the Irish word for Africans?'

The planter antibodies had rejected every word of the wild tongue even before Ryle had left primary school, rejecting it like a bad liver transplant.

'*Gorm*ach,' said Fletcher, '*gorm* being blue! They were never called blacks by our ancestors. And people say blue is ridiculous but it's no more so than black. Nobody knows themselves as black in Africa. I myself have never met either a black person or a white one and see no reason at all that we should adopt the crudities of a colonial narrative that we ourselves were victims of.'

'Whatever you say, boss,' said Ryle. 'Might be better to shut your gob now though.' The woman was waving to them to come out to her.

Fletcher never took instructions when it came to shutting his mouth. 'My own theory on it is that the Irish took cognisance of themselves being labelled the blacks of Europe by the nineteenth-century physiognomists. So maybe they didn't feel like passing on the derogatory tones that they had detected, in describing a fellow oppressed people.'

Note: Fletcher had a habit of throwing out fragments of internal discourse as though they should be perfectly understood by reference to an ongoing public debate; bric-a-brac that in reality could mean nothing to anyone who hadn't been reading the exact same book as him the night before. Globules of the idea world that'd even mean nothing to himself if he could meet himself a week later and happened to be reading something else. (The memory wasn't great with him.) In general the compiler has tried to weed out such talk, as useless to you as it is to myself. However, on this occasion, I have an explanation for the great man's carelessly tossed reference as I happened to be reading the same book at the time I attributed this view to him. The ancient sciences of phrenology and physiognomy when refined by nineteenth-century English men, set out to tell the nature of a people by assessing the gait, facial angles, protrusion of the brow, and various other tell-tale features. Their impressive findings are disregarded as though born of nothing more than the mere triumphalist cawing of the imperialist subjugator. I beg to differ. Were we to discard it for minor excesses of a conjectural variety, then what science would we have left? Let us give credit where it's due. Based on the angle of his face, the elusive chin, and a passion for gambling that was shared only with the Basque, this branch of science went on to label their Irish negro, *Sancho the black Celt*; it correctly identified him as being of lower origin, Iberian to be precise, just North of African. That was long before geneticists came along and proved the same and long after our own forefathers made no bones of the fact in the Lebor Gabala. And what would offend you about it? Other than the sore rub that we missed out on the melanin with the result that a prototype such as Fletcher goes scarlet at the smallest touch of sun on his receding forehead. We may not reject it merely because we know the physiognomists failed to pour any scalding water on the strong chinned Scandinavian mutation that gave rise to their own Norman and Saxon lines. After all, which ethnologist is entirely disinterested in his findings or faultless in his methods? The failure to inspect the subjects closest to hand, is clearly itself explainable by the set of their own faces and prescribed by their own genetics. When long-wintered families intrabred in Scandinavian caves the blond on blond variant that emerged with a face wider than it is long, flattened ears, possessed of short calves and long thighs, to triumph over the treacherous caliban, it did so based on rigid organizational adherence and self-certainty. The progeny that came clearing the lands to conduct ethnic studies in these islands some decades later had already developed a sense of the rest of humanity as its burden. With an ancestral yearning for the Swedish cave expressed in the vintage Volvo and ritual thrift, this extremely moderate, consistent, simple, truthful, straightforward, honest, peaceable, self-reliant, unexcitable, fixed of common purpose, free from extravagance, sound in judgement and generally benevolent human variant, had sadly lost the capacity inherent in mainstream humanity to continue using mental alertness and adaptive temper as the humanoid genetic differentiators; going forward. Nevertheless, the singular application has resulted in many inventions, from the sublime to the ridiculous. That is, from diesel engines to more logical superstitions. The latter absurdity, the plain church, of course spread like wildfire everywhere the genotype had spread and not an inch further. *The compiler*

'So I guess that's why they called them the *blues* instead? A noble race indeed, your ancestors,' said Ryle, as so often before, disowning three-quarters of himself when it suited him. 'So tell me, when did those fair minded progenitors of yours die out and get replaced with the bitter low minded dossers and chancers who run the place now?'

Note: once again, in the interests of fairness, I must stand in on behalf of the voiceless, the proper placid upper crust English person: *This mixed-race character, Ryle, provides tragic evidence of the ills attendant upon mismanaged miscegenation. The cross breeding of Anglo with Sancho has to be handled carefully as with shire and donkey. It has to be remembered that along with our local Sancho's concave nose and absent chin,*

is also frequently associated a headstrong, excitable character,
strong in love and hate, swinging swiftly between liveliness and
sadness, alternating generationally between seeking abatement
in alcohol and total abstinence from it, quick in perception,
deficient in application, wanting of prudence, speaking for affect
rather than to relay truths or even honest misperceptions, with a
propensity of crowding together, and with a tendency to oppose.
When one crosses the wrong way one retains every sinew of the
wilful contrariness, only giving it more stature with which to pull
against you. Instead of a sweet compliant Genet (as evidenced
in the Catelonian-Teutonic hybrid that is the saintly modernish
Frenchman) the product is pure mule. The compiler

'Much like the same feeling that inspired the Choctaw
Indians, and freed slaves,' said Fletcher, not to be interfered with
when he was romanticising, 'in the midst of their own suffering
to send what little they had in a donation to the wretched of the
Famine here. This is a moment that reaches across time. It's a
happening that needs no detail. It's an occurrence that can defeat
in a sentence an entire treatise on Malthusian rationalization by
god fearing men with good coats and diligent habits. A few good
people stood up and bypassed all prudent argument to show
faith in fellow humanity, to offer solace to another outcast people
in their time of deepest despair. It is the same fellow spirit that
later inspired downtrodden people here to go and fight alongside the farmers in South Africa. A solidarity amongst peoples
crushed under the foot of hegemonic Imperialism of that era.
Just the kind of solidarity that you and I feel rallying against the
hegemonic power of today's plutocrats.'

'I'm not sure it'll be as easy to rally soft youngsters with neck
beards and posters of pink ponies on their bedroom walls as it
might have been tribes that were facing extermination,' said Ryle,
apropos of nothing.

Note: Ryle had encountered the phenomenon of *bronies* during the course of certain web searches. He had raised the
subject with a grimace on more than one occasion, leaving
the compiler with no other conclusion than that the man
had unresolved issues of an equine variety. I am not able to

say for certain which of the two possible causes this should be ascribed to. Therefore I hope you'll indulge me a small digression while I set the options before you in a neutral manner. (Given the strenuous efforts to restrict the rest of the manuscript to a singular stream of hard fact, God knows this is not asking much.) First is the very dubious, 'nurture' argument. Ryle hails from a county where cows and dogs are the only beings a man is allowed to love, so this theory goes. An admiring word for the emotionally rounded back half of a little cob from the young Ryle would likely have had him labelled as being already on the road to ruinous horsey notions of grandeur or a gender identity crisis. After all, this argument goes, how else (other than through severe emotional repression of our young men) could it be that 98 percent of those who get up on horses uncompetitively and feel free to express their love of the experience, are of the female inclination? In summary, this theory gives us the jolly conclusion that Suck Ryle might have had more love to give had he been born in a different place, in a different time. I place that argument before you not because it's right. But I recognize that you may suffer the modern disability: perhaps you cannot countenance that badness might be in the nature of some individuals because that would mean they were incurable and you couldn't face that. Breeding in fact, of course, is the main culprit in nearly all examples of malfeasance. How much more likely is it in this case for example, that Ryle's inclination to spend his days studying racing newspapers and bringing unrelated conversations back to bronies, was just the Saxon gene coming out in him again. The attraction in the sangfroid for the warm blood.[fn] Ryle didn't lick it off the pavement. For now, I humbly place before you both the nurture and the nature options without any further comment, as it's not my job to judge. *The compiler*

[fn] Footnote
Firstly, it must be stated emphatically that all but the most backward on this island have gotten over the ancient corrosive fascination with

difference. The underlying preoccupation with the Anglo 'type' evidenced throughout this work (and not lacking in any of our friend's previous submissions as I recall, save for the fiftieth submission in which he dabbled in historical mammy porn [Regency period]) reflects a still colonized mind, a throwback. What we have here is a mental artefact that reflects only on the uncanny capacity of our otherwise beautiful countryside to produce vessels that can transport a grudge across the generations. This Teutonic fixation of the compiler's, just as the demonic one, I assure you is a thing entirely alien to the vast majority of modern cosmopolitan Dublin. In fact of course more than a century ago Joyce spoke for the liberated mind, unabashedly enumerating the fine qualities of our good neighbours. Today we see no difference between ourselves and those who happen to be of Anglo Saxon or Norman ancestry. We feel every bit equal at least in persistence, slow efficient intelligence, calculating taciturnity, and perhaps too in any cruelty being unconscious. Overlooking the embarrassingly puerile contrivances of the compiler, what would the psychoanalysts make of the particular tack he throws over his old theme here one wonders. In his own voice here the compiler patronizingly casts our nation as warm bloods. Not so long ago however, masquerading behind the voice of 'starchy' English strawman, he made asses of the entire Nation. *The Editors* [NB: check with Bing whether donkeys are in fact also warm-blooded and if so re-work this segment prior to going to proofs. *Eds.*]

'Pleased to meet you gentlemen, I am Henry,' said a tall man who met the two explorers at the white PVC triple-glazed door of the extension. He had a pleasant smile and a warm handshake. He laid himself and his people naked in naïve trust that the visitors' word was good. He had the kind of countenance out of which you might get an open hearing for the worst of confessions. 'People call me Uncle Henry. My wife was mistaken. Perseverance does not live here. I'm very sorry that you have had a wasted journey.'

'He himself gave us this address, Henry,' said Fletcher in a sonorous tone he apparently thought apt. 'There's no need to worry. We're not from the government. We're here to help.'

'Hmmm. Well I appreciate that,' said the man slowly, a look of amusement flashing across his eyes though his mannerly smile remained unflinching. 'Do come in. Perseverence Adebe, you say? I have heard of him. He is no good, afraid of work. Only for his wife is my wife's cousin and I am the godfather to his third born, I would go and hand him over myself. But you say you want to help? Where I come from it is said that you should never refuse help from good hands. Come inside. What business is it that you gentlemen are involved in?'

Uncle Henry took them through a warren of rooms where people were listening to iPhones and packing boxes. Thirty years ago, so the man said, he had started selling cheap Rolexes and Adidas runners at car boot sales. Now he had an import export business supplying informal traders all over the country.

'More import than export, I'd guess', said Ryle, sniffing the air like an airport spaniel.

'More export, actually,' he said, taking no offence. He opened another room in which they were assailed by rancid airs emanating from the skinned carcases of old mountain blackface lambs hung up over convection heaters and drying to the point of arrested decay. 'From here we distribute kudu biltong to all South African shops in the UK.' In the next room, a woman was shovelling tea from bags with German labels into bags labelled Kenyan Gold Bond. 'From here we cater to M&S customers with a taste for East Africa.'

Grattan shook his head.

'You see, gentlemen,' said Henry directly, 'the Igbo knows that if he doesn't help himself, nobody else will.'

'Igbo, eh?' said Ryle, remembering his table quiz facts. 'The Biafran siege eh?'

Henry offered them bags of biltong and buckets of tea. Fletcher's face was torn with ambivalence. He wanted to like this man. But he suffered the problem of Jesuitical loftiness when it came to business. He pushed his share of the Lidl tea and Wicklow weather-jerky aside. Ryle took the lot.

Note: Fletcher had become a vegetarian at the age of eight because his parents had failed to harden him to human pre-destination in the matters of slaughter and butchery. Similarly he was a pacifist. He was even more disgusted by the SME. Like many of the glebe class, one step removed from the mechanics of his privilege, he was unable to overcome a visceral disdain for those who still had to fooster in the greasy till. *The compiler*

Ryle on the other hand lacked foibles and was warming to Uncle Henry, allowing that if he'd got away with such practices for thirty years, he was no clown whatsoever, nor any kind of a drain on the State. He thought it unreasonable to ask more of a foreign national.

There was one room that they were not being invited into. The door stayed shut. Until a man, definitely from no part of Africa, emerged. He shut the door firmly behind him again when he saw the strangers abroad in the corridor. 'Don't worry, Nidge, *we're not from the Government,*' Ryle mocked, curious now to see what other industries Uncle Henry dabbled in. The skinny little gouger with the Gollum head on him was very cagey and asked Uncle Henry aside for a private word. Ryle took the opportunity to go into the room and Fletcher, nosiness his fatal flaw, followed.

Several native nationals looked up from a formica topped table, the shock on their faces caught in the blue whiteness of an overhanging LED light fixture. One who was in some kind of spasmodic movement on the rug stopped to look up at them with the wide eyes of a frightened animal. At a desk at the side a young man, a near replica of Uncle Henry, had a 23-inch laptop open in front of him. His smile did not falter at the shock of the intrusion. It was a picture that looked set to confirm Fletcher's worst fears and Ryle's greatest hopes.

Since first glancing at the massive extension in the back garden Fletcher had been trying not to think the obvious—drug money. He had been really hoping not to find evidence that the boy Perseverence needed rescuing from being groomed as a mule by a feudal narcotics overlord even more than he needed to be saved from the National Immigration Bureau. But now it was clear. The tour of the other rooms had been so loudly conducted to give the people in this room time to clear the evidence. He was certain that a swab of the table would yield every kind of chemical a policeman might want. The distressed young Dubliner on the rug, Fletcher was sure, had either been used as a guinea pig for some cocktail cut with rat poison or had been used as a bin into which all the evidence from the table had been swept. Fletcher felt partly responsible and went to touch the afflicted young person, incurring a frenzied, '*gerroffme, gimp!*' for his troubles.

Ryle didn't care about that stuff. He sidled closer to Henry Junior's open laptop expecting that he was writing emails declaring himself the widow of Obasanjo. Ryle was an ardent student of the 419 scam, having extracted many of the best examples from his spam folders. Holding a mirror up to those too stupid to exercise greed safely seemed the perfect business for a man like himself to branch into. It required a low amount of work and carried a low risk of having the cops interfering with him.

Ryle recoiled from the screen like a man shat on by a rat. 'What the fuck do you call that crap!' he shouted at the boy. 'Is your people gone soft? You're not going to hook any German investors with that bullshit.'

Three of the indigenous got up from the table to join the girl who had resumed her jittery, fitful movements on the rug. Young Henry directed some booming beats to a couple of speakers. He picked up a mic and read from the screen:

'We don't give a fuck for de man,
You can shove you condescenshone,
Up your hole,
Up your hole,
Up your hole, hole, hole.'

And so on.

Ryle pulled his severely remorseful man out of the room after he got a dig for trying to hug one of the youngsters in apology. 'My God what is the matter with me,' said Fletcher, 'am I really so bourgeois?'

They thanked the ever gracious Henry, now troubled to know what had upset his guests so. He brought them through to Akiko and they had one more cup of tea in the kitchen before heading back to the car. As they gulped the Kenyan Gold Bond, Ryle had the presence of mind to bring up electoral matters. He asked the great woman if she would have a word with all the other

Biafrans. Remind them that the Irish were the first to bring cameras in on them when they were starving. He dropped in the small political mis-speech that Fletcher, a priest at the time, had commanded several of the pilots of the airbridge.

Akiko hadn't a clue what he was on about. History moves quickly in Africa. Seeing them out the door she graciously granted however that she would vote for nobody other than Fletcher for President if she ever got citizenship and nobody other than Fletcher for the Senate if she ever decided she had use for a degree from Trinity College.

Fletcher was very uncomfortable. He said to Ryle as they closed the front door behind them, 'You have to ease off on banging on about the election thing, friend. A watched kettle never boils.'

'That is wrong. It often does if you put a flame to its arse,' said Ryle. 'More to the point, as the man at your back, I'm giving you the all-clear to pursue your bit of campaign respite with Akiko. Henry is a type they make quite a few of in his part of the world. He is more a philosopher than a husband. The kind of person you could go to in trouble. He would be very disappointed at your incursion on his lovely wife. But he wouldn't do a thing about it. When you apologize afterward he might even forgive you with a few bags of biltong.'

'One thing I can say of myself with confidence, Leonard,' said Fletcher a little pompously, 'is that even if I ever were to find myself in a position of power, I would not feed off supporters. Nothing disgusts me more in human affairs.'

'Don't mind that kind soft talk. It's easy not to take unfair advantage until you've got it,' observed Ryle.

Ryle tried to keep Fletcher talking in this cordial manner as they got into the van, not wanting him to notice the baldy head of Perseverance peeping out at them from the upstairs window. Henry had the boy's back after all, fair play to him.

'I suppose I should be glad to see that level of integration. I suppose so,' mused Fletcher, warming up a little to the rap as the car took him a distance from it. 'In fact, what did I ever imagine multiculturalism would look like? At least it proves Joyce's

Ulsterman was wrong.'

'What the fuck are you ráiméising about now?' said Ryle.

'The bard had his boorish character claim that the only reason we had no Jewish problem in Ireland was because we hadn't let any of them in. In the 80s you'll remember our boors were still rehashing this wisdom, only expanded to all foreigners. Well here we are with the gates wide open and we still have much less of a problem than most other EU nations do.'

'You should maybe widen your dinner party circle,' said Ryle.

'No,' said Fletcher, 'there is no need to grind ourselves into a mire of guilt on every single matter. No member of parliament here, not even those trading in the deepest Nationalist jingoism, stoops to immigrant baiting. What other country in Europe can you say that of? There are some aspects of our public life that we have every right to be proud of. For all the things we have to feel shame about, there are also times when we rise above and can be proud. The whole fascist thing never gets beyond the ranting of a few ignoramuses who have spent a while in Kilburn. I put it down to the high numbers who've volunteered and worked abroad and who understand our own history of oppression.' He stopped as if he was thinking, 'You know, Leonard, Viktor Klemperer when persecuted by the Nazis referred to the Old Testament for the simplest most profound definition of his people's liberal tradition he could lay his hands on. Perhaps we as a Nation can come to think of ourselves as providing a model of that fine appropriation, *in my father's house there are many rooms.*'

'Fine words. If you get to repeat it a hundred times,' said Ryle, resonating more with Goebbels than Klemperer, 'you may even create a new National myth and have the unimaginative strive to conform with it. God's work, you might say. But, between ourselves, complete donkey shite of course. If there is any tolerance at all of the foreigner here it is not that we like them better than other nations do. It is just that we like them better than we like our own, a race we are well positioned to judge and one we rightly hold in the lowest of regards.'

People are not always what they seem

Chapter XVII

INEVITABLY CAME THE VISIT to Northumberland Manse by the Gardaí. It was three or four days after the traffic event. The past can be unrelenting.

Ryle had a nose for such visitors and was at the door to suss them out before they'd got to the steps. His concerns were eased when he observed that the matter was as yet with the Traffic Corps, according to the car that was parked in the bicycle lane. He chatted amiably with them about the undependability of the long range weather forecast and about the great loss that was felt within this building on the day in question. He reassured them that nobody had been looking out their windows on that morning as he'd cross-questioned them all, himself. 'But you can go in and ask them all if you want, of course.' They left it at that. For now.

Thereafter, some weeks passed. That's the best way I can put it because no proper record was kept of the period from Mac Gabhann's side. The observations from the top floor window for the dates and times of Fletcher's departures from Northumberland Rd., if they were made at all, were not tabulated with any regularity. This prevents a reliable fabrication of the record over this period and so, thanks to Mac Gabhann's patent inability to keep his eye on two balls at once, it is lost to history.

Note: Not to get drawn into editorializing, but is it not a telling tale of what is wrong with our public service today, that a man of this calibre can emerge as an apex position holder? *The compiler*

Mac Gabhann the one ball man, was working on another project at that time *like a man possessed.* Not to put too fine a point on it.

The publisher was astonished as well as a little concerned at receiving a 150,000-word first draft of The Castle People, along with a set of plates with curiously flowery captions. The document contained tediously extensive footnotes, academically commendable citations, astonishingly generous crediting of 'oral contributions' by so-called 'local historians,' and paragraph-perfect references to books and family papers only available in the locked off section of the National Library of Ireland. All only three weeks after signing the contract with the busy-man extraordinaire, *Dr.* Cathal Mac Gabhann.

It should be observed here for want of a better place to observe it, that Cathal Mac Gabhann now saw the merits of having parted with fifteen hundred pounds back in '85, to convert his diploma in public administration into a higher degree. He had certainly been reluctant at the time, knowing the value of a few pounds even better than Trinity did. Nor had he been taken in by the flattery, '… acknowledgment of the professional achievements of select graduates …' given that he had not even moved to Senior Executive Officer at that time. But he had been persuaded by his shrewd old caileach of a mother, she herself having almost been from a good family. There were no other doctors in the family, she had said.

Note: His mother's was the hard cold hand on Mac Gabhann's shoulder, the voice steering him right even though it was two decades since her final removal from his life; removed to the Serene Haven retirement home in Tralee. *The compiler*

The publisher thought about his own concerns for a day or two. When he came back to flip through the very large Word file again, the professional alarm bells still refused to be quiet. He had managed to get over the short turnaround by allowing that every sport has its freaks. But the language also jarred. It seemed too considered for the man he had met. There was an elegance of construction and a breadth of vocabulary that was hard for him to picture coming out of such a hatchet-narrow head. There was an ease of transition into flowing Munster Irish alongside sections that unobtrusively suggested an equal ease with archaic Italian and French. There were thought-provoking allusions to the Greek classics. And then there were the errors. Gardens instead of gardes. Banes instead of bawns. They would be easy to fix but hard to explain without thinking of the errors cheap document scanning software makes with unfamiliar words. It was also hard to overlook the fact that the page numbers were entirely out of sync with the fabulous index. Not escaping his sharp attention either, a jarring editorial addendum in which the author seemed to be conflating the Cromwellian calumnies, crediting those of Thomas to Oliver.

Yet, a cautious type, he ran a plagiarism check on several sections of the tome. All came up completely clean. His conscience cleared, he closed his mind to all further patent signs of jiggery pokery.

Note: Remember, Henry Boland was a busy man in an industry that was on its knees. At this time in Irish history, the arrogant forces of publishing were finally croaking toward a hoary demise. Not a day too soon. I do not often lapse into retributive prose, as you will have noticed by now, so I trust you'll indulge me this small note of glee.[fn]

[fn]Footnote
It would be asking too much to let this little diatribe pass without observing that it would be our advice that a writer should never speak disrespectfully of literary society. Only people who can't get into it do that. *The Editors*

He quietly removed the 'mastications' overhanging Ballybur Castle and expertly restored its machicolations. He spent a couple of hours relinking the index references. He removed the couple of peevish footnotes. And he sent it on to the US correspondents for a view. The view came back quickly: *far exceeds wildest expectations ... an intricate artifice of complex human stories woven around intriguing buildings ... an entirely nuanced view of all of the sad epochs which the stories of these buildings reflected ... a goldmine for those in search of their roots ... extensive index linking of so many surnames to each monument ...*

As Boland emailed the document to a freelance proofreader in Cape Town (he was already ahead in the race to the bottom, having outsourced all other functions to remote parts of the world) he was calculating how many years this might keep his own salary paid. He preempted questions he felt that might arise as soon as the sharp young woman interacted with the author, by providing her with a quip that he would reproduce at every subsequent introductions of Mac Gabhann: *people are not always what they seem.*

For every evil there is a good

Chapter XVIII

FLETCHER WOKE UP IN A BED one day (date withheld) with a handy woman touching his cheeks. Calloused yet warm, those big bio-energetic spawgs alone wouldn't have woken him so suddenly, given that he had only a few hours earlier laid into a flagon of homemade elder chartreuse like there was to have been no tomorrow. It was her pressing on the thoracic burns and bruises that had done the sudden waking.

I said I wouldn't risk embroiling myself or yourself in more trouble than either of us already has on the plate before us, by providing any further details of the campaign to save the gas under a slake mound in Westmeath. So all relevant details of this particular visit have been redacted partly for your own good. Also note that we distance ourselves from any suggestions that this compiler might in any way support the activities of the committee that has cost the irate taxpayer hefty penalty money by retarding progress on a contract that had already been through all the proper approval channels. Kept from you also you will note, any suggestion about which members of the Crusty Squad had put Fletcher in the condition he had just awoken in. No implications at all may be inferred about how Devine managed to get demoted from Store Street, no less; or how Geas managed to get booted up out of Cahirciveen.

It's enough for us to say that after sabotaging a fence and being caught red handed with sample bottles of brown water stolen from the hill bog now owned by a certain British petrol company, two men were seen being escorted away by Sergeant Geas and Garda Devine in a red 142 MO reg. Mondeo. Rather than detaining them in the cell beneath the unmanned Knockbawn Garda station on this occasion, certain traditional remedies were applied to Fletcher and Ryle in the back of a chip van. The less said, the easiest mended in that regard. The Mondeo had then courteously enough dropped them back into the care of the rest of the worried committee.

Fletcher had been a somewhat broken man at that point. No bone was broken, true. And he was no worse off than the average player at the finish of a physical game of hurling. But Fletcher had never played for the GAA and so wasn't used to taking the soft tissue and cartilage damage in a manly way.

Back in the little house with the horses and dogs the rest of the committee had been very sympathetic. She had let the hair down and come out of herself with the flagons of noxious elder juice. In what was becoming a slightly too familiar pattern, Ryle found himself stranded, as the more committed committee members talked strategy and related stories that had no currency for a sober person such as himself. That was when he'd vowed that all further visits to this neck of the woods would be in the van with him at the wheel and able to determine the timing of his own retreat.

As the wine had gone in Fletcher had become dull to the danger that lurked in the other person's comforting words. The big man had continued innocently nursing himself, rubbing his side and trying to squeeze the bruising out of his neck. Ryle, sensing danger, kept accounts of his wounds to himself. When she first started talking about the local healer, the 'handy woman,' wondering aloud whether it might do no harm to give her a try, Ryle had got up to go to bed declaring that there wasn't a bother on himself. 'But call her all the same,' he directed. 'That would be a very good idea as the big man is in need of hands on him,' he advised. 'It's important to have him healed and back on the field quickly and I hope she gives him a happy ending.'

There are very few missteps that don't have consequences. And so here now with the morning sun laughing through the window, Fletcher was about to get a reward for letting his thinking be loosened by alcohol. He lay on top of another woman's couch with the layers of bandages being laid on his chest by a further woman.

'Easy love,' said the jowly lady as he jolted up with a howl. 'Take it easy. Don't fight it. Work with me. Get into a good zone. You're going to be alright now.'

It'll tell you what kind of a fellow Fletcher was that he slowly lay back down with every movement worsening the incineration of his chest skin. Though the agony of the poultice had tears flowing from every corner of his eyes, he would still rather grind his teeth and take his medicine than cause offence to the sincere indigenous person.

'What in the name of god are you after doing to the man?' asked Ryle, laughing from the kitchen where he was looking in vain for sausages.

'Boiled buliáns, mustard, and butter,' said the local. 'I got it from my grandmother and I don't mind sharing the old secret recipes now because the danger they face these days is a danger not of theft and misuse but of dying out altogether.'

'*Ragwort?*' said Ryle, no eejit when it came to poisonous weeds. 'I can see where the concern about dying out might arise alright.'

'Mustard?' groaned Fletcher. 'Are you sure about that? What kind? *It's really burning something awful.*'

'Don't worry love, it'll soon be better. There was supposed to be pig's lard in it too,' she explained, 'but this being a vegetarian household I decided it would be more respectful to replace that ingredient with rape seed oil and butter.'

'And is Ryle right? Your buliáns are *ragwort?*' said Fletcher, a slight alarm now starting to come up level with his superficial pains and concerns for the well intentioned healer's feelings. 'If memory serves, that plant is notifiable.'

'With every toxicity nature provides an anti-toxicity,' said the healer wisely. 'The more poisonous the plant the more potent its healing properties when applied in a counter-balancing treatment. This cure has been used for thousands of years. Think how much better than trying to get pain relief from a pharmacy packet. For every evil there is a good. It is our job to spend our lives seeking one and controlling the other.'

Fletcher the gallant gasped, 'I suppose … the good thing … about traditional healing … is that it puts the person front and centre ... of the process.'

'Yes, exactly,' she said, 'unlike conventional medicine where your body becomes the property of the hospital.'

'Are you sure about this?' asked the woman of the house and committee, a look of grave concern growing on her face for this man who she hardly knew at all. She was a clear thinker, sharper than healer or patient, it turned out, when you took away all the trappings. She called Ryle from the kitchen. 'I'm not sure we've done the right thing for your friend,' she said, taking command, 'let's stop this right now.'

'Are you sure?' asked Ryle, finally giving up on his search for any of the elements needed for a fry up. He entered the living room in short strides finally determined to intervene to save his man. 'He could be enjoying it.'

'Absolutely sure,' she said. 'Helen, take those bandages off at once.'

Ryle stepped in to do the honours. 'The good thing about pharmacy drugs is that they take away pain rather than flesh,' said Ryle the barbarian addressing the evil-controlling bandraoí. 'Why do you think your people's ancestors died so young?'

Then he yanked the wad of plasters off with a merciless tug. Grattan howled. The mess came with a significant percentage of the chest hair and a reasonable amount of skin, leaving poor Grattan's chest scarlet and badly plucked like a boiled goose. There was a smell that would lift you out of it.

'I was a bit concerned alright,' admitted the healer, 'about replacing the lard with the butter. But it's hard to be right a hundred percent of the time.'

'Oh, and you think butter is alright in an animal lover's house?' said Ryle, moving to touch shoulders with the house-holder who he could see was biting back a sharp rebuke for the unfortunate handy woman. He was quite taken by this revelation of steely correctness underlying the woolly concerns. I suppose we are all attracted to that which is alien to ourselves and Ryle's instinct was to make a new pitch at ingratiating himself even though the cause was hopeless. One advantage of having no beliefs is that you can easily enough run with hare or hound; or you can put a bullet in either as the situation demands. 'For that butter a peace loving cow was anally assaulted by a shovel-fisted farmer, inseminated, and then left to cry out for a week when the ensuing offspring was whipped away from her. Same every year until she can take no more and is sent to have her throat cut. Just so you can have the butter that she meant for her innocent little calves?'

The other three looked away and Ryle realized he might have gone in a bit hard. But he was not one for turning around. His voice regressed to the dark rhapsodic tongue of his origin, *Indeed didn't I land up in a dairy farm for the early years of my life. And there was no standing back in that way of life let me tell ye's. It's often enough a harmless poor cow had mefistup. Hell, ye's might call that evil, but what choice did I have?*

No harm done though. They had green tea and talked things over before Ryle gave Fletcher some wintergreen to rub up under his jumper. That kept him speechless the whole journey back to Dublin.

To stand idly by

Chapter XIX

SHORTLY AFTER SUBMITTING his manuscript to Boland, Mac Gabhann began his period of phone engagement with young Grawne van den Heever, the editor in Cape Town.

The greedy suckling Mac Gabhann was lapping up his first taste of the fan infatuations that mature authors are inured to. And he was reckoning that it was no more than his due.

Aside from being unnaturally impressed by the manuscript, this first fish of Mac Gabhann's had an additional layer of susceptibility. She had an Irish ancestor on her mother's side; information she had previously taken no notice of since being burdened with it in some parental bout of diasporic hankering. Said buck had come to fight with MacBride on the side of the Boers but had not fled with him. And now van den Heever decided that Mac Gabhann had stirred the deep ancestral connection, a yearning unearthed. She perceived the drumbeat of an alternative rebellious brand of European civilization, one that she herself could almost imagine belonging to. She was a bit fascinated with this person who corrected her when she referred to Britain as the mainland, regaled her for not knowing any Erse, *and her with a mongrel Irish name.* Indeed how could she have been prepared as it is not often foreigners get exposed to the private dignified façade that is the learned Gaeilgóir, variously of the Republican, Workerist, Isolationist, and Social Progressive traditions.

Note: The fatuous flute of course didn't have enough Irish to ask to go to the toilet. However it has to be said, his workerist credentials were solid; astutely established in the 80s. This compiler will not allow a mild personal contempt for Mac Gabhann to result in any understatement of the man's professional achievements. I record without rancour that he had been exceptionally forward thinking in terms of his career. Back then he had attended a few of the clandestine meetings in which a band of Republicans, having abandoned the National question upon their recent arrival at a new appreciation of Stalinism, plotted their infiltration of the mouthpieces of the Established State. Mac Gabhann had copped that it would do him no harm at all to be on friendly terms with those who saw their own secret control of the organs of State as essential to progressive democracy. Nor was he slow to realize that secrecy of membership lists meant that he did not have to restrict himself to only one play in the same general pattern of career advancement operations. *The compiler*

Grawne sat unprotesting, mesmerized, at the dressing downs she received on the phone. The strange fellow her father's age, was abrupt like nobody had ever been toward her. He was proud, hollow voiced, and contemptuous.

Grawne was not entirely beyond noticing that instead of answering requests for clarification on certain arcane points of castle lore, Dr. Mac Gabhann, Cathal to her, always deflected with sharp rebukes at the ignorance her questions betrayed. The ordinarily shrewd young boeress who generally took no shit, came close a few times to twigging that Mac Gabhann was just another variety of the middle aged boors of her home city, men more excited by bullying than fucking. However, what was mesmerizing her a little more each day was her quest for the bridge from this crude personal audacity to the seemingly deep broad pools of text in which her work for him kept her daily immersed. The unhurried enticement of words in which she swam between the phone calls.

The jolly man whose Camp's Bay apartment she shared was bored already. To terminate the raking over of the enigma as he cooked the evening meals she hardly appreciated, he suggested that the discomfiting phone voice might merely indicate a person made socially awkward through having been long misunderstood. Too long in wait of womanly tamping. That she should go investigate. She then recalled her Grandmother's attempts at redemptive words about the Irish father who had ridden off with a cross Khoi Malay maid after five years on the Karoo, and joined Lord Kitchener's forces, 'It is not that the Irishman is duplicitous, it is merely that he is in two minds about everything.'

And tamp Mac Gabhann she thought she would, as she started to make firm her plans for the trip. And return disappointed, she undoubtedly would in the traditional manner of those coming to the old country in search of dignified roots.

Note: you may be expecting the compiler to divert the course of this narrative in order to stave off the tragic disillusionment of one more idealistic young person. However, in the interests of exploring truthfully that tattered corner of the human tableau that one is assigned by fate to describe, there are times when a chronicler must stand idly by, a photographer's lens focussed on a vulture about to eat a child, not allowing his role to extend a millimetre beyond bearing witness. This naturalistic saga of Gráinne agus Mac Ghoul must unfold. The compiler, let me assure you, is very well versed in the theories of truth, art, and literature but has reserved his views on these matters so as to be unconstrained in facing the task at hand. *The compiler*

◊

Bigger picture issues continued to unfold. All we have of them are a few snapshots. Fletcher got on the TV again during these weeks. He appeared in a news bulletin that fell during the interval of a rugby match. Therefore there were a good few people of standing who saw him. This time he was actually interviewed, having been mistaken for a spokesman for an anti-fracking lobby in the midlands. The toothless interviewer sensed she had struck fool's gold. Fletcher, not to be found wanting, had enough everyday knowledge on this subject too, to be able to pass himself as an expert. He displayed an exceptional political touch in narrativizing the problem for her and the rugby audience in perfectly lobbed phrases that made all feel like there was a basic thing wrong in Westmeath that they could join him in caring about without any bad bounce coming back against themselves.

During this period it can also be noted that Ryle was going through a very barren patch on the personal front. He placed a couple more calls requesting meetings with Margot but was finding her very slow on the uptake. He was not one who believed in such a thing as true and dedicated pair bonding outside of jackdaws. But she displayed such ease and experience in the ways in which she fobbed him off, that he was almost beginning to believe that she had no interest in recreational infidelity; that in fact in Fletcher and Margot he might have hit on the exception that proves the rule.

He became so preoccupied with the lack of response at one point that he realized his neutron role was becoming blurred. He didn't quite know what was wrong with him. The feelings he was having were not normal. To re-float himself he went back to trawling the affairs websites. His usual notice went up: *A large debonair man seeks to meet handsome women with a view to giving expression to bodily appetites. No fear of emotional attachment.*

Note: the compiler is well aware how certain schools of psychoanalysis would cast Ryle's loveless desire for Margot as nothing more than a subverted desire to be closer to Grattan. Such woolly flim flam has no place in a crunchy chronicle in which every observation is objective and to the point. Unpalatable as it may be to the emotionally intelligent, to set out in search of deeper emotional bearings in the likes of Suck Ryle is to enter a very short cul de sac. *The compiler*

◊

A further note from this period may be worth recounting: one evening Fletcher chanced on Saoirse's Surface, open on a Tumblr discussion that he found himself unable not to look at. His daughter had left her spot on the couch to go read little Margot a story. (Though he had to admit some pride at the flair Saoirse was showing in this regard, it upset him that his erratic timekeeping had seen him lose his own laureateship.)

It was no surprise that the Tumblr thread was discussing restaurant scenes. Grattan's doted upon daughter had been fixed since she could talk, on owning a bistro. Grattan used to drive her around the city on Sundays looking at failing shops and telling her that when the time was right he'd go with her to make the leaseholder an offer they couldn't refuse. There had been a pause when little Margot came on stage. Recently she'd started at it again, working in pop-ups.

However the waffles being dispensed on this thread were in Melbourne. And now, as Fletcher scrolled, he saw a faceless icon called *un-Saor*, saying *Help! I'm suffocating comfortably here.*

Margot came into the room then and said, 'Grattan, that's terrible! Please don't tell me you're prying into Saoirse's stuff?'

'No,' said Grattan. 'But is there something you're keeping from me?'

'Do you hear yourself? Get a grip!'

Putting a price on help

Chapter XX

FOR SOME FURTHER WEEKS Mac Gabhann neglected his record keeping. That is how intoxicated the low lout became with fantasies of the happiness he thought would accompany his ascension to the status of published author.

Yes, there was a slush pile of surplus summary notes from Ryle alluding to various detentions, hospitalizations, and participation in a sulkie race. It is indeed possible that these miscellaneous items may all belong in the lost epoch. But in the absence of corroborating logs of Fletcher's movements by the negligent and sociopathic Secretary General, I would merely be presenting guesswork as established fact. That is a bridge you may (feel free to interpret the word *may* here in either of its national usages) cross without me.

Therefore, all I can do is regretfully note the gap.

Once the manuscript had gone off to be laid out nicely by the morticians at *dtp r us*, Mac Gabhann's hysteria eased and from then dated entries resumed in his own files, against which he could subsequently correlate Ryle's records and enable us to resume this catalogue of errors.

On the 24th of September Fletcher was observed leaving Northumberland Manse and limping like a man with a hamstring injury. His hesitant embarkation onto a waiting Transit with the now familiar OPW insignia was noted. I understand that you will wish to relate this ligament damage to one of the intervening undated hospitalizations but for all you know it may as well have been that he slipped going down the stairs or took a heavy tackle in a game of tarmac tennis.

The two in the van had reached a don't-ask-don't-tell agreement regarding the intended purpose of each mission. All Ryle wanted to know now was the address. After that he would put in his earphones and listen away to nothing. Fletcher would get on the mobile immediately, making calls to this one and that one. He was not a well enough organized man for all that he was taking on. He was now like a post-it porcupine, so many chores from so many causes having stuck to him, accumulating faster than they were being attended to. Unbeknownst to himself he now walked in the image and likeness of the fertilizer salesman antecedent, an accident waiting to happen.

In the pitch pine panelled refectory of the convent of the Silent Virgins of a Little Order in Chapelizod, Fletcher waited to be received by one of the men whom he intended to enlist to the war-room of the Walkinstown Progressive Secondary School Project. Not the archbishop yet, but his own cousin. Martin Fletcher was a Redemptorist priest, a marshalling sergeant of redemption. Unlike Grattan, Martin's helping hands had been applied a safe distance off shore and he was well regarded by the archbishop.

Ryle hadn't needed to be cajoled to get out of the car for this one. He had a certain peaceful fixation with the architecture of prayer and a level of interest in nuns that bordered on lecherous. High pitched roofs, chants echoing through millennia, pious footsteps on hollow boards, and women bent into decades of servility foregoing every human warmth for the love of a man whose existence, like that of Ryle himself, was doubted by some: these were essences that worked for Suck Ryle.

The silence in the room seemed to judge them and even Ryle breathed quietly through his nose, unnerved with every further minute they were left waiting, feeling like what happened next was out of their hands.

Ryle nearly fell over when the door was pushed in by a big headed, blustery fellow with a mop of curly hair and a smile on his red face as innocent as a lamb. He went straight to Fletcher with outstretched arms. When the identical cousins were finally ready to stop fondling each other and cease exchanging enquiries about the health of people nobody else could be expected to care about, Grattan introduced Ryle. Martin started his approach, again spread wide with the offer of a hug, but quickly scaled down to an extended hand as Ryle retreated towards the door, shivering and curled up in himself. 'Any person my dearest cousin calls a friend,' the cousin said, 'I would trust with my life.'

'Why?' asked Cromwell Ryle, with as much disinterest as he could feign. 'Is there a bit of a bounty to be got on you boys again?'

A woman of indeterminable age entered. She was dressed in a blue skirt and a red cardigan. Ryle was with the few in Irish society who felt great disappointment about the slipping standards amongst the orders. If it wasn't for the soft unwrinkled skin, a giveaway no matter what age they got to, it would have been hard to tell her apart from a civilian. She pointed them to an urn and tea bags in the corner and sat down to talk like a citizen who owed them no civility.

'I suppose ye've dropped the fucken hijab altogether now,' said Ryle, unable to hide the disappointment.

The nun didn't bat an eyelid, her face seeming to be of soft plastic. Fletcher the second however dropped a piece of biscuit from his mouth and sat looking with his big uneven lips trembling, flubbergasted. Fletcher the first just shrugged wearily as if saying, surely I'm not the first who has brought before you one of the less fortunate, a handicapped child of a lesser god.

'So the last time we talked,' said Grattan, trying to get onto a familiar thread with Martin, 'I think you were recommending Berkeley to me?'

Martin looked back without great enthusiasm. Something was eating away at him.

'Logic applied to faulty axioms gives faulty results, no matter how perfect the constructions,' offered Grattan enthusiastically, 'RIRO, rubbish in etc., always applies. If the starting point is an assumption about a supernatural force then all arguments constructed thereupon amount to castles built on sand and they could be interesting only to observers of our extraordinary rationalization capacities.'

'So you can dismiss all of classical philosophy in a sentence?' said Martin with some reserve.

'I no longer set one branch of daydreaming above another,'

laughed Grattan, glancing at Ryle. 'I don't begrudge anyone whether they choose to let horses or Heidegger loose in their circuits. I've met enough of both types of thinker to be cautious about setting one above the other.'

'*A bounty* though?' said Martin, turning back to Ryle, with a note of bitterness that differentiated him from Grattan. He put his hand on the woman's wrist, 'It's funny you should say that. Cassie doesn't go out much when she is based here these days. And the sisters leave the TV off. To be honest I myself can't wait to get back to Manila.'

'Pay no attention to my friend,' said Grattan uncomfortably. He clearly didn't like where this was going. His voice became a little quick and anxious as he tried to re-find a thread, 'Let's stick to the arguments about your phantom deity. So remind me, why would we expect thought that predates understanding of evolution, astrophysics, and equality to have the capacity to reveal any interesting conclusions other than about the mind of the person as he constructed his castles on sand? Don't you think we will …'

'Quite frankly,' Martin Fletcher cut Grattan off, as undeflectable as the other when he had started into a vein, 'I hardly care about any of that right now, Grattan. Go find an evangelical the next time you want to have one of your metaphysical arguments, my friend. We're not schoolboys arguing about Socrates anymore. I don't have that luxury remaining to me.'

That cut Grattan. He was not a schoolboy anymore either. He just wanted his cousin's love. On more than one occasion he had visited upon Ryle stories of the tricks the two of them had got up to when they'd boarded together at Clongowes. They'd been in the same year, taken the same subjects, formed a band together, and vied for selection as out half in the first team. And of course they'd acted like woeful little Clongowes pricks, laying thickly into their postcard knowledge of the classics. As schoolboys.

'But here's a thing that I had to go abroad to discover,' said the serious faced Fletcher, 'the traditional values of those who learnt their Catholicism in Ireland are not all bad. You know the way the last thing any of us wanted to be was a *holy Joe*?

A preachy pious arsehole? Well that remains the essence of it. Our lot don't proselytize. When street kids come into our gym to learn boxing, I don't look for their baptismal certs. The Irish missionary has faults but at least isn't a prig putting a price on help or pretending to have answers. Our lot continue to quietly try to find our own personal way. Through work. And we hope occasionally to set a good example.'

The nun seemed to feel sorry for Grattan in his hour of need. 'It's alright, Martin, let it go. Just have a nice conversation with your nice cousin. Who knows when next you'll see him.' She turned to Grattan, 'He talks about you a lot, you know.' She stood to ask Ryle if he wanted her to make him tea, 'since you don't seem to have the hands to wipe your backside.'

Ryle was pleased enough with this kind of personalized comment and said he would.

'Let me tell you a little about Cassie,' continued Father Martin Fletcher. 'Sister Cassandra was only twenty-one when she was sent to a rural village in Eastern Zambia. She cried every night for a year. But she worked every day. And she set up an orphanage, the same as her sisters before her did in Ireland caring for those cast away by a poverty-racked and superstition-riven society. For going on thirty years she worked, from early morning till late at night, worked herself comatose, in terrible conditions, saving disabled children and burying a piece of her heart with any she couldn't save. In latter years she was recognized by officialdom there but the awards meant nothing to her. All she cherished were the letters from those children now grown up and living lives of dignity. That and her dream of one day retiring at home.'

The nun's cheeks had reddened miraculously. She saw she couldn't stop this and tried to get away from it instead. She stood weakly and addressed Ryle, 'Come on then, I'll give you that tour you asked for.'

'Hold on now,' said Ryle, never having seen his principal so flustered before, and hoping for it to come to blows, 'I want to see who comes out on top. I'll go with you then, gladly.'

'I've never been shy to acknowledge what wonderful

ambassadors some of our religious abroad have been,' said Grattan, grasping again for solid common ground, realizing too late that this made him sound like an even worse dick, 'believe me, Martin. I don't let belief differences get in the way of that. The disclosures closer to home are not something any of us in this room need to talk about.'

'Actually I do, whether you do or not is your own business,' said Martin Fletcher sharply, his lips turning down, 'Your friend is right, there might as well be a bounty on us. And I refuse your offer to desert those who worked at home. There's a cruel mean-ness at large in my country now more pervasive even than any I remember in the 80s. For myself, frankly, I don't give a shit. I am going back on Monday and I will never come home here to live. I will work for the poor until I'm boxed. But by God for Cassie I cannot swallow the anger. She always looked forward to coming home. Though never envisaging she would come so soon ... to be a patient herself long before her own work was handed over in a proper way.' He paused to gather himself.

'I'm sorry,' said Grattan. It was all he could say as his failures to notice piled up on him. A failure to notice that the lovely little sparrow of a woman was even thinner than someone who had worked herself to the bone. That was on top of things he had failed to notice over a long time; things that his cousin, merciless now in his fear and despair, was not going to spare him.

'And this is the way she finds her older sisters. Holed up. Ostracized. Civilized people thinking it's a mercy to speak kindly to them. I am enraged. Cassie is my closest ... my dearest friend for decades. In early years we wrote every week and met every three years on the two week breaks at home. In recent years, email and Skype. With her I have talked about every thing. About all the things that are real to me, Grattan. About faith and doubt. About love and regrets,' he paused again. 'About loneliness and death.'

The nun had to sit down again, weakness running through her.

'If she would come away with me out of this for the end, I would go anywhere with her today,' he said examining his hands. 'But of course she won't, will she? She has seen the situation her older sisters are in and now she will not leave them.'

'It's alright, Martin,' she said, 'don't over dramatize. There are many worse off and there is still much kindness here.'

'It is not alright,' Martin Fletcher banged the table, staring at Grattan as if he was to blame for everything. 'The pillorying by the modern day hierarchy of Irish society, the defamation, the lack of any right to reply, the judging of those who went before by a new canon of heartless enlightenment as if it itself will have nothing to answer for when the time comes, the guilt by common purpose, condemned to take all human sin to death. We feed our aunts and uncles to the bloodhounds because we are too weak to ask our parents the truth. And the kindness where it exists? The Irish kindness of not coming out to your face. Another generation lacking the courage of its convictions. The patronizing tribal contempt expressed in what is not said. Stoning would be more humane.'

Grattan Fletcher was upset. He couldn't bear suddenly realizing he had known so little about Martin all the years he'd thought they were close. That Cassie had never before been mentioned to him. That he had never thought to ask why it was that his cousin, on furlough, always elected to stay in this mid-century concrete monstrosity, dark walls with grey paint peeling, smothered amongst overgrown leylandii trees. The invite to stay in Rathmines always politely turned down. A lifetime of misunderstanding was a fair enough matter for regret.

Ryle tried to puzzle what was wrong with Fletcher. He asked the nun to top up the man's tea to see if that would help get the last of the dirty water off his chest. But he ended up no wiser.

Ryle took his boss out of that place with no progress at all made towards an appointment with the archbishop and not a sod turned on the progressive school.

◊

That evening as Grattan Fletcher was driven by Margot to the bridge lessons she had recently inexplicably insisted they embark upon, he asked her if she would come with him on a trip to

Zambia in the summer. She didn't answer, knowing it was nothing to do with her. He asked her then if maybe she would come with him to visit an old nuns' home in Chapelizod on Saturday. She still did not reply though she might think about that. Instead she said, 'What does it mean to you, being married to me?'

Now Grattan didn't reply.

'I'm asking you a question.'

Grattan thought Margot to be going through a difficult patch and was careful how he answered these kinds of questions. 'Everything?' he tried.

'It's just that you seem very distracted these days,' she said, 'that's all. Like you sometimes would rather not be with me.'

'That's not it,' said Fletcher, lured into truthfulness so easily, the disturbance of what his cousin had said to him not left his veins. He put his hand on hers and pressed it so hard against the wheel that she almost steered into a cyclist. 'Sure, I don't need us to be with each other every minute. No more than you ever did. But the thing that frightens me most about there not being an afterlife is the thought that when I finally shut my eyes I will be parted from you for eternity.'

He tended towards the unscripted and bumbling in his dealings with Margot. He always had done. Luckily she was a person who secretly cherished that about him. She turned on the radio to pretend to be too busy to hear him. But as these things go, the song that came out from 2FM was very much their own. Cohen. It was what they'd played on a tape deck when they signed up for each other in a small stone building in West Cork in 1986. '*Dance me* ...' She gave in to tears and danced the Lexus through a fifteen point turn on Charleston Road.

[fn] *... to the end of love.* They went back home where they spent the night very much in each other's company.

[fn] Footnote
Lyrics removed. Not for fear of Leonard (Cohen) and his money problems, but out of respect. The compiler has no right to shroud his textual inadequacies behind the lovely sad words of a true artist. The removed verses referred to themes of panic; and explored the protagonist's desire to be gathered safely in by a beautiful other. *The Editors*

The sun loses nothing by shining in a puddle

Chapter XXI

'I CONFESS,' SAID FLETCHER, 'that I'm losing my way.' Only when he said it did Ryle become aware that it was the first thing he'd said since they'd got in the Lexus two hours earlier. And that there had been no music and no singing.

'Are you fucking gone blind now too?' said Ryle. 'You're passing the third sign that insists this fucking kip is Strabane.'

'I don't mean like that,' said Fletcher in a flat tone. He had his arms held straight to the same position on the steering wheel since leaving the M50. Always staring straight ahead. 'I mean in general. These trips now are mostly errand running. We are mostly responding.'

This was indeed the case. Too many of his trips were given to quests some of which he didn't appreciate or couldn't get up a caring head of steam about. Surprising only to Fletcher, people were quick to relinquish responsibilities the minute they encountered someone spouting the noises of leadership. There was also the flaw with Fletcher that he was as influenced by the goodness of the people associated with any cause as by its raw merit. A gluttonous approach for someone who overestimates goodness. Ally that with the anthropological difficulty that many humans expect you to align with *all* their causes if you happen to sympathize with one of their causes. Speaking with authentic anger against a wind farm in Dun Laoghaire caused some to assume that he could be expected to join the protest against a nuclear power plant in Greystones, which, may God forgive him, he didn't care so much about.

'I wish I found it simpler for us to weigh unlikes,' explained Fletcher to Ryle. 'CO_2 versus nuclear waste, GM versus starvation in Bangladesh, individual rights versus cultur …'

'What? …' interrupted Ryle, 'what the fuck are you looking at me for with that *us* shit?'

'At times it seems like the primacy of what one does or does not stand for has been overtaken by an old game of *with-us-or-again'-us*,' said Fletcher.

'Indeed as with chimps,' said Ryle who watched *some* amount of David Attenborough, 'everything is about the troupe. Once you don a jersey, the tribe gene competition game is on and the guy in the other jersey is the enemy. The issues and past humiliations are no more than the fodder of team pep talk.'

'That's just more of your defeatism,' said Fletcher. 'By that token all causes are of equally little merit and we might as well stay at home and let things happen to us.'

'True,' said Ryle, never a defeatist. Ryle was simply a person who had never been lost in the embrace of any troupe, so he liked his victories personal. He thought Fletcher was agreeing with him now, and thought it appropriate to share further of his own insights. 'How else do you think a cop can stay embedded, drinking and sleeping with true believers without imbibing sympathy for the ideas or the people? It's not that he has strong ideas of his own. It is just that he is wearing a different jersey underneath.'

'What?' said Fletcher. Suddenly he remembered the surprise of other people at the recent propensity of the Crusty Squad to show up at every protest. And he remembered the incident in the cowshed. 'Good God don't tell me …'

'What?' said Ryle.

'Are you working for … for the Special Branch?'

'Would you go way out of that, I play for no team,' said Ryle with a wheezy laugh. 'I'm just explaining to you how it goes in this world. One day you don't care. The next day you sign up and think everyone who doesn't care is a prick. For all you people it's about communion.'

'True, you wouldn't snitch out of liking the police team colours. But I could see you doing it out of liking the colour of their money,' postulated Fletcher who had been getting tetchy of late about having to pay for every sandwich, every bottle of Lucozade, and every drop of fuel.

'You have a low opinion of me despite all the claims about seeing a bright side,' Ryle noted. 'Do you think they'd pay much?'

'One day one speaks at a forum on the corruption of big finance,' said Fletcher slipping back into his own well of painful reverie, 'and the next it is assumed that you would also care about Letterkenny Town Council's plan to remove three rotting beech trees that are in the way of a bypass. And so on and so forth.'

It was good enough for Fletcher the old day-tripper. He had assumed it would be easy like everything else in his life had been, to just suddenly stand up and be counted. Here he was now with a world of chores to do and a volcanic headache after three or four glasses of merlot too many with Margot the night before.

'Trees you say? What the fuck did you expect, you clown?' asked Ryle not unsympathetically.

'I just feel like it's one day after another with no clear progress,' said Fletcher, 'like I've just managed to create a new humdrum is all, is that it?'

'Aha, so you're re-finding your existential crisis, we might say,' pounced Ryle, linguistically adept in certain respects. He knew how to knock the educated back into a defensive posture, the only way he could stomach them.

'We're just reactive rather than breaking any new ground,' continued Fletcher, not falling for Ryle's verbal three-card-trickery this time.

'The only way to keep breaking new ground,' said Ryle slowly, 'is to bury the plough to the crotch and drive straight as a dye. Your problems are that you only skit along the surface like poor Paddy Maguire's harrow sock and then you steer in loops according to whatever direction the last wayfaring hard case pleaded with you to go in.'

Fletcher looked away from the road trying to see if Ryle was serious. He said, 'You know Len, sometimes you say things with such assurance that for a minute they can sound right.'

'Jesus preserve me though,' said Ryle. 'If you had told me what the mission was, I could have brought the chain saw. Break the old humdrum up a bit.'

'Only the sociopath is exempt in your construction. If I were to accept your advice ...' said Fletcher, '... do you think one can wake up one morning and genuinely not care about anyone else?'

'I am led to believe that it is possible to wake up *every* morning with that outlook,' said Ryle authoritatively. 'Now, whether it is possible to choose to wake up only some days not giving a genuine shit, is a matter for the Existentialists I suppose.'

'Of course,' said Fletcher accommodatingly, 'we are all sociopaths at some level. We have concentric circles of care with the intensity declining as the radius increases. Our families are in the inner and most intense zone and we'd give our lives for them. Then as we move out, there are friends, then associates, communities, cities, Nations, and so on. Earning ever weakening devotion from us. For most people by the time you get out to people from other Nations the feeling has weakened to callousness and at the level of other species, excepting a few cuddly ones, we are cold as stone. At times of crisis, our circles constrict like the vascular system in hypothermia, concentrating on keeping the innermost well. As we've seen recently. Good people cutting fellow countrymen down viciously. What we call a sociopath is surely just someone for whom the intensity of feeling is always like that, reserved for the innermost circle.'

'That would all be very neat if it was true,' said Ryle, perceptively. 'Your circles are not in the same order for everyone however. It's this thing of setting your relations closer than other citizens that ruins Africa, Southern Europe, and this very country. People going out of their way to help their relatives and then talking about corruption as if it was a mystery. But don't tar all with your own brush. There are still a few of us with straight blood who would have one or two loyal animals in the 50-point circle or at least in the 25-point area. A dog or a horse. Or indeed, a cat. After that, anyone claiming special favours on the basis of DNA overlap, has to be left out in the cold to fight fairly for your attention with every other citizen. It's not by accident that cooler breeds of people run efficient countries.'

'For Christsake,' said Grattan foostering with the satnav, ever the optimist.

He that lives in hope danceth without a fiddle, as my

Licketstown grandmother used to say. The two boys may have been in Donegal by the time Fletcher acknowledged that as well as being unsure about his destination, he didn't know where he was going. None of this territory is drawn correctly on Google Maps of course. One supposed National road took them into a boreen and ended at a farmhouse with tall gates and security cameras. Decent looking tarred roads on the other hand, had been kept off the maps altogether and had to be explored like they were the first to discover them. This accomplishment was the handiwork of a stocky frontier tribe whose ancient trades had to be protected against any erosion of the border.

Making things not a bit better, the tree people had given him only softish Donegal directions. At first he tried to turn it into a thing in itself, proclaiming, 'A great friend of mine once said that the shortest and most interesting route between any two points in life is a wavy line.'

'Right,' said Ryle. 'You'd need to have good company for that.'

'You know,' said Fletcher, 'being in these territories … I'm never sure of the right position on the National question.'

'The wise politician doesn't beat bushes hoping to rise something true about his nation,' said Ryle sagely, 'he invents bits of truth to suit himself, ramming it down the people's throats with a stout stick if necessary.'

◊

They carried on, up the road, down the road, over the road and back the road and never getting where they wanted to go at all. The building frustration on top of the hangover and recollections of yesterday, the uncertainty of life, soon had Grattan's composure frayed; in fact had him ready to decompose in lachrymosity again. Then to make things a little worse the petrol warning light came on. 'You'd better find a place to fill that up fairly lively,' said Ryle insensitively, 'or we could be marooned here forever and a day waiting for a normal human being to appear. And nobody wants that.'

'Fuck it, fuck me pink,' said Fletcher finally cracking. He

banged the wheel with his fists.

'Stop, hold up there for a minute,' said Ryle, 'you can ask this buck for directions.'

'There's nobody here,' said Fletcher, the gloom seeping in on him. He slowed down all the same. They were on a narrow border road with a shy grey sky hardly visible between the dying back ash suckers on either side. They weren't even sure whether they were back in Ireland yet. 'Here, here, fucksake,' said Ryle, pulling the wheel and directing the car into the mouth of a laneway with Fletcher jamming the brakes in fright.

Ryle buzzed the window down and shouted at the person that Fletcher still couldn't see, 'Well chief, what's the hold up? That lorry is hardly going to paint itself.'

Fletcher noticed that Ryle's stare was directed upwards and he stood out of the car to see where he was looking. Sure enough, he was rewarded with a glimpse of a fine tall fellow standing like a giant twenty foot in the air with a beam of sun poking through the cloud to spotlight him. With a distinguished, if large, grey bald head balanced on the long, hefty torso that gave him most of his height, supported by two admittedly short legs, he stood out as would such a fine man when perched on the roof of a green forty-foot trailer, one that was attached to an unregistered Scania truck. Along the side there was only a faint image of previous lettering now overlayed boldly with something that looked like KNEEL LOGIS ... The remainder of the new identity, probably tics, was yet to be added. But this man needed no stencilling for his future works. He had clearly taken a break from his re-branding to throw a lick of paint on the roof. It was a mark of how deft a mover he was, that he was not worried about denting it. He was leaning on a long handled roller and gawping around at the countryside.

Note: this character appears so briefly that there's no need for me to overload you with a name that you'd only forget anyway. Also, you might note that the roof he was on was not a hayshed roof so he was not a competitor of my own. His vocation, as I understand it, was in freshening previously owned vehicles for sale in another jurisdiction. And while there might appear to be some overlap, there's a world of difference. *The compiler*

'A wee man of letters, I see,' said Ryle taking a stab at the vernacular. 'Where is the nearest spot that a boy could acquire a few gallons of washed diesel in these parts?'

The impressive being began giving them what Fletcher eventually concluded were directions that would not take them to any petrol station on this earth. It was Fletcher himself that was wrong of course. The paint professional in question may not have known the territory well, only visiting this area for the purpose of honouring a contract to purchase. But neither was there any basis for Fletcher's absolute certainty that the carefully given directions would not eventually lead them to a petrol station somewhere. Unless he was implying that vacuous directions are given not out of the helpful instinct, but out of malice in which case they might include a loop, then the laws of nature dictate they'd surely have hit a hydrocarbon oasis at some point along the suggested route.

That wasn't what Fletcher wanted to talk about anymore, however. He had recovered himself and now wanted to ask if the man knew about the bypass and the beech trees. He had remembered in a flash how beautiful an old beech can be and how its long fragile arms can become part of a person's feeling of belonging and reassurance. He had returned to reasoning that Donegal people were no less entitled, despite their excitable ways and negative style of football, to have consideration given to saving the living landmarks that connect them with great-grandparents. He was recovering an anger too on behalf of the beech itself; anger at the philistine priests of Health and Safety who were condemning trees right around the country without allowance for the early-aging beech being dangerous by its very design, its elegance being awkward, its rooting tenuous. He felt re-aroused anger now too at the high-handed engineers who had reputedly point-blank refused to look at an alternative route without even explaining to people with genuine unprofessional feelings on the matter, what it was that made their counter-proposal 'ludicrous'.

The grey lad was finding it a strain to raise his voice and didn't like talking down to people, so he bummed his way across to where the tips of the ladder leaned precariously against the side curtains of the trailer.

He didn't take long coming down given that he was having to keep one leg straight.

'Anyone would think you wanted to fall,' said Ryle, giving the ladder a shake.

'God knows it wouldn't be the first fall and mightn't be the worst thing ever happened,' the man said, raising the curiosity of the visitors. 'It has been noted that the art gets more attention if the artist draws fatal allure onto himself. People remember Conrad over Madox Ford; Behan over Cronin, Hemingway over Steinbeck; Zweig over Mann, Thompson over MacCarthy. Do you see what I'm getting at? It isn't today or yesterday that it became a good career move for an artist to crash into a mountain. Strindberg, Maupassant, Nietzsche, and that chap of the Tooles snaked ahead of better people of their eras only by self-destructing for attention, going mad in pursuit of the clap. And then you have to remember …'

'I'm not sure I'm entirely at one with you on that summation,' said Fletcher in the sympathetic tone of those who do not understand. And then trying to sidetrack the man with an airy aside, he said, 'And don't knock Nietzsche—like the great Schopenhauer he had in common with the ancient wise ollamhs of our own people, the view that if a thing was worth saying it could be said in an aphorism. They knew the value of sayings.'

'Ancient wisdoms, is right,' said Ryle, 'what would the dead German preachers or any ollamh you care to dig up have given for a bottle of penicillin do you think?'

'Good God man,' Fletcher whispered, distracted for a moment from the attention of the painter, 'is nothing sacred to you?'

'Very little. A peculiar question,' sniped Ryle resentfully, 'from a man who has shown no respect for either Lord or Lucifer.

'Franzen on the other hand,' continued the painter, trying

to block Ryle out.

'What the fuck is this head-banger on? No wonder he has to work alone,' said Ryle to Fletcher discreetly, and then turning back to the man, 'What the fuck are you going on about, you horoborical cunt?'

'I don't tell everyone what I'm about to tell you,' said the man, not taking the slightest offence at Ryle, who was the kind of ignoramus he was well used to not taking the slightest offence at. He was not the kind who needed to respect knockers or conformity vigilantes. He did observe then the wanton kindness in Fletcher. So he continued to share insights, 'But my real job is, writer.'

'A bit of an impressionist, I'd say,' said Ryle, staring at the lettering which, right enough, was smudging a little in the unanticipated drizzle. 'You can't even get one word out straight.'

Fletcher's nodding approval had the effect of inclining a person to say more than they had intended to say, inducing moments of injudicious looseness. It would have been much wiser for the fine art man to have heeded the mantra still prevalent in those parts long after the gun had officially been taken out of their business activities: *whatever you say, say nothing*. And in fact a little of nothing would have served him better than a lot of nothing, as seemed to be the local interpretation of that injunction.

Ryle caused some surprise there at that crossroad gathering when he started off on a bit of a rant about writers. 'What is it anyway that makes you do it?' He seemed to be suddenly boiling with anger, droplets of blood appearing at his nose holes. Inexplicable rage as though all his faults could be pinned on a man he had never met before and wouldn't again, you can be certain. 'Isn't it quite a presumption to think you have some unique insight which it will benefit humanity to receive?'

There was no answer to this. Fletcher let the man stand there picking his ear, maybe thinking of a writerly comeback or maybe just wondering whether he could make a candle with what he was harvesting.

'But the world is full of writers,' continued Ryle, not giving up on his attempts to insult the man and everything that he stood for, 'whose deepest thoughts rightly get thrown on the publisher's floor after one page. They flock to writing workshops to get fleeced. Otherwise they squander the few hours they're allowed on earth, polishing their old chewed cud, sitting dry in their bedrooms letting on they know what it's like to get wet. Useless fuckers who wouldn't stand up for themselves. Do you know who is to blame?'

'Don't pay any attention to this fellow,' said Fletcher. 'He's not himself today. I don't know where this is coming from. At least you have tried to express yourself. That's all a person can do. So much better than the person who is always planning to write but never actually doing so. This way he remains always successful, eternally proud of unhatched ideas that the world has never had a chance to criticize.'

'I blame those Americanized fools who say that no matter what kind of ballsup you have made of everything, you must keep trying,' said Ryle, sensing by the continued silence of his opposite number that he had struck into a reef here. '*No!* If you are told you are no good at something, *stop doing it!*'

'The rain is holding off well all the same,' observed the man, rubbing his fingers breezily through the silvery hair.

'Don't pay the slightest heed to my associate,' repeated Fletcher encouragingly, 'he'd take the good out of a funeral. I think our artists are the true champions of our country. In which other country in the world could you stop to ask directions from a man on a roof and discover that he's written novels?'

You couldn't not be fond of this man Fletcher in ways.

'Rendering a true description of an inner landscape is what a good writer strives to do,' continued Fletcher, 'am I right?'

'I suppose you might be,' said the writer cautiously.

'What good is a true picture of the inside of a man's head,' interrupted Ryle, still beside himself, 'if the landscape in there is baw-ways from the start, his thoughts all illogical, his landscape as dreary as the angelus and dry as an ass shite in June? When someone paints a horrible picture or tells a story that makes you want to strangle them, people think it's just that he hasn't the artistic skill to describe his perspectives nicely. Instead they should jump to the obvious conclusion: that he *is actually* skil-fully describing things precisely as he sees them. Don't encourage them to reveal the truth of their minds. Encourage them to pick up the fucking brush and paint it over!'

The painter writer didn't lose his cool. 'What do you think justifies your own conversion of good food into unwanted heat and foul excrements?' he asked Ryle without any loss of a beat. Then he addressed both of his visitors. 'You know there are two types of asshole in this world,' he said, astutely, 'those who don't know that they are and those who don't care that they are. The first kind, are the vast majority and probably includes you two. You couldn't know since you all take such a kind view of your-selves and since there's only the very occasional person, such as myself, who sees it as his job to tell you what you are really like. The other kind, the ones that truly don't care, they're very rare and to be kept a wary eye out for.'

'And who was it appointed you?' Ryle added without much care. When it came to a fight involving deconstructing the other person, Ryle was a believer in going in hard with angle grinder and blow torch. 'Who told you your thoughts were unusual and worth recording? That's the first question all writers should put to themselves.'

'Let me tell you,' said the head which up close could be noted as to be not so grey at all but to possess quite a timeless winsome-ness under the bristling of green and red speckles, 'I spent years doing all the right things. Lacing my writing with blatant clues that I was as well versed as any of the so-called greats in works from the beginning to the end of every trend of any note. From Socrates to Wittgenstein, Bergson to Faulkner, the Upanishads to Rorty, Byron to Heaney, Thackeray to Sorrentino …'

Note: at the risk of interrupting the flow, I meant to say to you earlier to pay no attention to any footnotes, end notes, addenda, or any other kind of 'referencing' whatsoever as may appear in your edition. These will have been appended to this manuscript after I hand it over. It pains me to have to draw you into any professional discord, which I do understand should not have to be your concern as paid up consumer of

my goods. But you should at least know that the publisher
is not a neutral party and is generally not on the same page
as the compiler. Apparently some remorse was experienced
in relation to the publishing contract after execution thereof.
Even greater consternation was experienced by him on having his attempts to nullify the same repudiated by myself.
He hadn't realized that in my trade you learn the value of
a watertight contract—when you paint for farmers you are
dealing with the wiliest survivors on earth. I pointed out to
him that his seventeen pages of legalese was copied and pasted
from the four corners of the Internet and that for future
reference a layman's line in the sand, a plain-meaning one
line email, was a better defence than a faux castle wall that
dares you to walk around it. In particular I was not remiss in
letting him know that the wording of clause 2.3.1 ('Editing
and Proof Reading'), cast all editorial views as suggestions,
clearly meaning that there was no onus on the compiler to
implement any one of them and the manuscript could stay
in an eternal borderland loop until one party tired of trying
to assert its opinion. Needless to say, I know my way around
loops. The implications of this, as I spelt out for them in a
brief legalistic note, were that they could do no review or ten
and at some point they'd have to go and shite, regardless of
whether I'd accepted or rejected their 'suggestions.' Instead
of taking it out on their own solicitor (since struck off for
having conveyed a widow's funds into an apartment block
in Kiev at the height of the last boom) my sense is that they
turned their bitterness in on me. I noted a certain edge to
the pleasantries we exchanged in our subsequent communica-
tions. Most likely, they will throw every cliché in the book at
me from the margins which they still own. (If they don't it
will only be to make a liar of me.) Hence this brief caution.
Margins, footers, cover, etc.: may contain disrespectful noise.
The compiler

'I'm not sure I'm quite on board with your taxonomy of literature and metaphysics, though I don't doubt you have some
faultless seam of logic underlying it,' said Fletcher, thinking he

was being kind. 'Who else would be in each of those series?'

'Merciful mother of the sweet lambing divine Jaysus,' interrupted Ryle very impudently, turning to his temporal master, 'don't patronize these kinds of people. It only makes them worse. Not a word of my advice has touched sides. I'm for leaving this gibbering wreck as we've found him before people are saying you're as bad as he is.' Then he pointed his finger warningly at the man with futile hostility, 'Grattan and me have no time for going down boreens with the likes of you.' As if he was jealous that his partner was accepting an invitation to a place he could not go.

'Copernicus to Feynman, Pynchon to Proulx, Said to Oz, Achebe to ...' continued the author of his own afflictions. That was the sort of effect Fletcher had. You wanted him with you.

'And what is your own genre?' interrupted Fletcher with a solicitude that to someone who didn't know him, could occasionally come across as the aristocratic scorn of the well set Dubliner, always ready to engage with a considerable sound of erudition about him, in the next person's field.

'I have driven right up to the shores of neo-classical avant-gardism by times. I have rather elegantly danced the moves of the post-structuralist on occasion too. And I've given a fair few nods to brutalism,' blurted the man, so rare was it for him to meet someone he thought he could safely talk this kind of talk with.

'I'd say brutal would be the word alright,' said Ryle.

'But I keep coming back to re-connect with my natural realist roots,' the big generous fellow confided.

'Hmmm, that's ...' said Fletcher, considerate and measured gentlemen, 'that's ...'

'Would you ever fuck off,' said Ryle. 'You wouldn't see the realist train coming even as it was running you over.'

'Well that beats Banagher!' continued Fletcher, sometimes prone to mal-colloquialism. It was one of his less attractive traits. He thought the few summers he'd spent with his grandparents entitled him to get down with the people of the country. 'And I'm sure you are a good writer because I can see you are a person with a lot that you'd like to say.'

'Well I'm not too bad. I'd be better than Banville, you're right there,' said the person, only afterwards realizing that he might have misheard. 'Though Banville can never be written off as he doesn't drop the head. But I'm my own harshest critic and I'll be honest with you, there are times I'd be more worried about Sebastian Barry. When he shows up fully togged out, the same buck has a heart on him the size of Roy Keane.'

'*Beats Banagher!* says old Mr. Brennan,' spat Ryle expectorating disgustingly as if midges had got in through his snout, 'fucking roight! You'll have to cut down on the *I'm an ordinary people* shit if you want anyone outside Dublin 6 to vote for you.'

The writer turned his attention to Ryle for another moment. 'You think it's all a laugh? It could be my life I'm talking about here for all you know,' he said, maybe a little severely. 'So what exactly is it again that are you good at, my little friend?'

'Eating, I'll always help with that. Used to be good at drinking too but I worked too hard at it and ran into a wall,' said Ryle, getting close with his punctiliously shaven jaw protruding in a posture that was inviting a slap. 'The past is easy,' Ryle continued, niggling for trouble, 'anyone could write about that. The main test for a writer is whether you could write the rest of your own life. Can you do that?'

'I have been puzzling to myself,' said the gaunt gent to Fletcher, 'what it is that would make a fine person like yourself choose this calibre of company. But I've got it now. Cute enough. As the old people used to say, the sun loses nothing by shining in a puddle.'

'I must say, I respect what you've done,' tried Fletcher. You took on the painting work that was no challenge to you so you could continue to pursue your real craft, your real passion. Unlike so many of us who put what we really wanted to become, on the backburner.'

'Oh?' said the man, irate. 'No challenge? All work is a challenge, sir.'

'Don't be shitting,' said Ryle, who knew his trades if he knew anything, 'if you can piss you can paint.'

'That's offensive,' intervened Fletcher. 'I apologize for my associate. It's not what I meant.'

'Work is a demanding card game,' said the man, 'you're not *meant* to get soulful feeling and fulfilment out of it. That's most people's mistake. Think about it logically, what are the chances you were ever going to get deep satisfaction out of doing jobs someone else decided need doing? No, in work your amusement is only to be sought in getting one over on the other players while you finance your real enterprise. Whatever that might be. But *no challenge?* You're very wrong there.'

'And ... So ...' began Fletcher splashing around like an alcoholic's husband looking for something to defuse the tension as the writer came closer to giving Ryle a suitable answer to his slightly provocative stance. 'So then where would you categorize, let's say, Woolf?'

'Woolf?' the handyman barked. 'You're trying to trap me with trick questions, eh?'

Note: you can see where the man was coming from here. The same Woolf deftly defied anyone to put her on a shelf. She placed herself way below Proust and way above Jimmy Joyce, knowing full well that mass populism would soon situate the latter well above the former. She deftly thereby put her finest work on a shelf of its own in the realm of literary anti-matter.
[fn] *The compiler*

[fn] Footnote
At last, something from the compiler that only sheer churlishness could see us fail to endorse. On this one occasion he is correct, albeit for the wrong reasons. Woolf needn't have worried because nobody was ever to rival Joyce. But Woolf's tragedy ultimately was that she retreated to the lair, responding in Mrs. Dolloway's Sloane voice in panic at being eclipsed. Even if an argument might have been made for her disdainful assertions about self-taught working men in her dissertation on Joyce, the 'underbred' and 'illiterate' characterizations sadly spoke more of her own unshed baggage. It saddens one to reflect that Virginia Stephen in the end may have been no better than Forster, a class romanticist at heart. One wonders how Leonard Woolf might have soared had he not feared being blackballed Bast-like by the Bloomsbury boys not taking kindly to being outshone by a man they'd elevated above his station in the first place. *The Editors*

'So,' continued Fletcher in a patronizing tone, trying to placate what he misread as paranoia, and stepping in front of Ryle, 'and so, my good man, what's your own particular magic?'

'You needn't intervene on my behalf,' said the man, 'let your runt friend through to me and I'll lock his jaw with a box. As to your question, I understand the essence of everything. That's my gift.' It was also his frustration but he didn't say so as he was the kind of person who more often tried to look on the less negative side of things.

'Well you certainly can't be expected to share that with two people you just met,' said Fletcher, trying for a polite parting statement rather than a question.

'I will share with *you* as I believe your time is limited,' said the man, in a slip up that went unnoticed by Fletcher but raised a Ryle eyebrow. He carried on, 'Besides, I don't believe in private knowledge entirely. To get the perfect little three cylinder Perkins engine purring, the motor of it all, you just have to understand the one key thing about your customer. In my case, that's the literary intellectual.'

'I thought they took the lead out of paint,' said Ryle.

'I don't quite see,' said Fletcher.

'It's simple. They have been conditioned to coyness,' revealed the author generously. 'As children they find pure uninhibited pleasure in reading every class of old yarn they can get their hands on. But then as they grow up society engenders shame, associating reading with idleness and masturbation. [fn] Now if you want to reach out and help them get on board with you, you have to first help them convince themselves that they are tending some higher cognitive essence, transcending common epistemologies, exploring uncharted aspects of ethical estrangement; only then can they guiltlessly roam freely for a while with you in a wonderland of nonsense. Once you have cracked that nut for them, there are no better souls to be tapped, no better companions. They are giving and romantic and will come anywhere with you in pursuit of the far-flung plot, the implausible character and the salacious escapade.'

^{fn} Footnote

I find the compiler's recriminations quite humorous. He loads his own literary woes onto the backs of characters crudely photoshopped into this account. This he does to deflect from the core futility of his own dispensation. Twenty-five years caught in the headlights and it apparently only becomes harder for him to accept what was evident to everyone else from the very first submission: that he was roadkill already. Perhaps it's time our mutual friend, the 'truck' painter, accepted that his own ideal reader, himself, is in fact someone who never reads anything beyond the black ink on a race card or the fine print on a SuperMac's menu. *The Editors*

'So …?' asked Fletcher helpfully.

'So? I have that all taped. All figured out. I just can't get to serve it up. Between me and those fine men and women, my clients, stand the courtesans manning the commissioning gates; the plodders and jaded cynics who live for proximity to greatness but don't recognize it unless it's already labelled. If only I could have got past them. But when you approach with a manuscript that would be like catnip to your elite readers, those dyslexic bouncers look at you as if you've just deposited at their feet, the buff mottled puke of a person after consuming a slab of Grolsch and a quarter-pounder meal. Not that I'm bitter,' said the man looking at Ryle and restraining his feelings towards the little yellow rodent in a show of superhuman forbearance as he reserved his animosity.

'Let me understand,' said Fletcher, not hiding his astonishment well, 'you continued trying the *one publisher* all the while? You never thought of trying another?'

'That's right,' said the man.

'But … But did you not think that amongst the many other small publishers there are many who themselves are in it for the very same plain love of books as the readers you are trying to get to? People who can't find enough of what they really like in print so they go print more of it.'

'Of course, of course,' said the man.

'So …' asked Fletcher, trying not to sound incredulous when he was actually just sounding naïve, 'Why did you not try around?'

The man succumbed momentarily to a look of exasperation

at having to explain the obvious. But then, too considerate of the other person's dignity to rub his nose in the stupidity of his question, he spelled it out, 'Once you choose a door, and the people inside ignore you, you're committed. Your honour is their hostage. If you are to die with it, your empty husk must be laid at their feet for all to see.'

'I never got that,' said Ryle genuinely interested for a second, 'how can a man who cared only about himself, think he'll enjoy revenge stone cold—by framing his enemy for his death? What is wrong with the Irish mind that it can never take the direct path? Why not arrange that you get to sit on the enemy's carcass instead of trying to get him to trip over your own?'

'Aha, interesting, a version of a *troscad*,' said Fletcher, ignoring Ryle as he did once or twice too often.

'What?' said the man, unclear. He was the kind bred into the old patterns of thought rather than contriving to resurrect them. 'Anyway I martyred on with the life's work until they got the better of me and I was forced to give up nearly altogether.'

'That's indeed a tragedy,' said Fletcher. 'What or who did you allow to finally quench your dreams and reduce you to this sorry state?'

'Sorry state? Me? What do you mean?' the fellow said, distracted only fleetingly from his thick ethical thesis, 'Some fat bollocks of an editor. I said to him after the last one line rejection letter, *you know Bob, the smallest bit of feedback mightn't go astray every now and then.* So I got it. Big bucking wheelbarrow full of it.'

'What the fuck did you expect,' said Ryle, 'from someone in your own field – people who have no sympathy for anyone only themselves and whose sole driving force in writing is to malign the character of others who got the better of them in real life?'

'Well to tell the truth,' said the genuine article, a self-taught truly underbred working man writer, lapsing dangerously near actually telling the truth in this unguarded minute, 'I wouldn't mind so much only that by the ninety-ninth submission, which I had been just about to make, my game was peaking. I was writing out of my skin, I feel. What I expected was maybe just a passing observation on my Bakhtinian polyphonisms or perhaps a few tips on how well I was getting on with the multistylistic fragments of post-structural form and the Menippean satire I tended to deploy from time to time, the latter, admittedly, more particularly exhibited in the ninety-second and ninety-seventh submissions.'[fn]

[fn]Footnotes
By the way, it is not as though we are unaware of the genre of ethical alienation, wherein a man (and it is always a man is it not?) becomes estranged from his most fundamental convictions. Nor are we unaware that this is where the compiler sought to pitch his tent before he turned to non-fiction (albeit intruded upon by this thinly painted fictional writer). Indeed I personally am very well aware of many distinguished exponents of this fashion. The compiler just isn't one of them. Dissociated thought, for sure the compiler exhibits in abundance, as I have no doubt does this 'truck painter,' his offerings a veritable mixed fruit bowl of axe-grinding metaphor. We remain entirely satisfied that our overlooking his ninety-second, ninety-seventh, or any other of his submissions has not created any vacuum at all in that field of twenty-first-century poetic metaphor as it applies to the literary depiction of moral scepticism. Meaning, what utter shite! *The Editors*

'And so ...' said Fletcher, looking at the ground to avoid being infected by Ryle's mocking grin, 'so ... er, so tell me then, which of the advice that he gave you had this ... drastic effect on your will to go on expressing your art?'

'Which indeed!' reported the somewhat dashing grey man, still assuming that Fletcher at least was the kind of human being who would understand. 'The nail that sticks up of course gets hammered down. He told me a bunch of twaddle such as revealed his own total ignorance of the creative processes. To that, I would not pay a blind bit of notice. But nestled in there was the grievous offence. He commented that I had developed an unwholesome focus on, shall we say, metaphysical metaphors.'

'What do you mean?' asked Fletcher.

'He said ... I should take a break from the writing to see if that would help me stop looking everywhere for the devil.'

Fletcher retreated a step with his mouth open. He was jolted back to Mac Gabhann's taunt. Apparently the question of how an atheist devil would deport himself had deposited some unpleasant plaque at the back of Fletcher's mind after all. And now the harmless writer was bearing the brunt. No offence was taken at the recoil though. This was an initial response that the silver grey man had grown to forgive in people, regarding it as primal and autonomic rather than intellectual revulsion.

'I'm not a religious nut,' said the man, taking the situation in hand in his easygoing manner. 'Alexander is the only Pope I have any time for.'

'Ah,' said Fletcher, reassured, 'of course we weren't thinking that.'

'On the other hand,' said the man, trying out a thought on them, 'what if it's worse than you think? What if it's not just the one solidly bold person that you have to keep an eye out for? What if he *is* everywhere? Did you ever think of that?'

Note: to be honest, the unwashed-up writer hadn't fully settled on this ubiquitous devil theory just yet. At this stage in the game he was just throwing something out to get the government boys thinking. Most of the time back then he was still conventional enough in thinking, *most of the time*, that they were only likely to walk into the devil once in their lives. Not to land up facing dozens of them on the other side of the badminton net. *The compiler*

'Ah! The search for the one honest man,' pronounced Fletcher approvingly.

'*Honesty?* No,' said the writer, staring at Fletcher in exasperation at his unworldliness, 'what's the matter with you? Everyone knows you have to get over the honesty thing fairly lively or a modern career of spray painting would be a hard road and that of modern literature, a complete impossibility.'[fn]

[fn] Footnote
You'd be quite entitled to ask at this point, what has any of this got to do with anything. Has it progressed the ostensible main characters one millimetre towards Letterkenny? Has the compiler revealed anything new of his heroic ingénu in this passage? No. Instead the piece redlines that one essential truth of this entire document and indeed of everything else

the compiler does. He is all about himself. *The Editors*

'And what will you do now?' asked Fletcher, with worry about what answer he might get.

'I'll probably go write pisrógs,' said the man listlessly. 'At least the audience there doesn't want you to clean every unnatural presence out of their sight.'

'You should be well able for that right enough,' said Ryle, happy with the change of subject.

Note: other pearls were then spread before the visitors, more out of generosity than keen judgement. It would have served them well to pause a while and listen. But an urgency about getting away had them deafened. The moment has passed and we'll leave it to rest but I'll recall just one of those many insights for you. *That's a new one on me*, the writer recounted for them as being the thing that Na Gopaleen had said in response to a judicial question being posed at the same time as he was observing a flea peeping out from under the sleeve of his coat. Everyone knows that of course. But what the two boys could have been hearing for the first time is what the judge said back. The person at the bench was French as it turned out and he came back very quick with the observation, 'We find ourselves unsure whether to pity the man or the parasite.' *The compiler*

'Where are you going once you get your fill of petrol, may I ask?' asked the man, eventually resigned to the ignorant retreat.

'Since you know so much,' retorted Ryle, 'figure it out for yourself.'

As the two drove off they clearly heard the man they left behind laughing and chanting away to himself as loners sometimes have the courage to do. Even though their windows were up, they clearly heard, 'Two geas men, eh.'

Beware those in time with the sea

Chapter XXII

It was dark in Letterkenny. Fletcher was adamant that tree pictures taken in the dark wouldn't do him. Ryle, stuck again, was by this time ill-disposed to nights spent in car seats. As they drove through a hilly suburb he told Fletcher to pull up, indicating that he had a house of his own on that very street.

'Christ, a dark horse you are, my man,' said Fletcher.

Ryle left Fletcher looking out from the quiet hilly avenue admiring the lights of a little boat appearing and disappearing far out on the ocean. He walked up the street and picked one of the many houses with no TV flashes inside and no car outside. He rang the door bell and, impatient in felony, waited only twenty seconds before he nipped around and broke a glass panel to open the back door. He came out the front door and onto the street, with the two outer jackets off him. He gave a stretch in his cardigan, like a man ready to retire in his own castle. This sight retrieved Fletcher from his reverie.

In the perfectly neat living room Fletcher was surprised, given the earlier interactions, to see that Ryle kept several shelves of books. The contents of the top shelf surprised him first, the subject range extending historically only from Orange Supremacism to Southern betrayal and geographically from the anatomy of the Bogside only as far as architecture of the Divis Flats.

'Funny,' he said, as he picked one tome and his left eye scanned the blurb ... *transformed at the stroke of a pen from a majority in their own land where they'd been heading into rule by a post-Edwardian Westminster lurching toward a reflective civilization, to despised minority under reflexive Williamite supremacists with a penchant for pogroms.* 'Funny, I hadn't put you down as a person with views on the Troubles.'

'There you are now,' said Ryle.

'When the dust settles we must not forget Ryle, at the back of the fine words ordinary policemen continued to get shot in the face in front of their families. While Paisley's fine words continued to get ordinary Catholics shot from behind. All in protest at much the same deal that they merrily shook on later.'

'What was the difference,' said Ryle, 'when your man Collins was having policemen shot in the face?'

Note: my research indicates here that Ryle's step-grandfather, the man who had taken on the damage done by Colonel Kox and superimposed the Ryle name on Suck's father, had joined the RIC in 1915, gravely misjudging the pension prospects. The third policeman in his family, he had thought nothing of it and remained in that role until he was shot at a crossroads where he had been invited to rendezvous with the woman he really loved. The remains of the family was partially burnt out. Its failure to burn was put down to the family truck with the devil and that the flying squad hadn't brought enough petrol. Ryle of course didn't give much of a fuck one way or the other, but he knew when to throw these gripes into the ring. *The compiler*

'It's a strange thing isn't it that term, *the Troubles*?' said Fletcher not picking up at all on the cue. Though his own politics were different than those that he still assumed this library revealed of Ryle, he was pleased like a proud father, thinking at last he had uncovered a deeper aspect, something beyond personal contingencies that Ryle had strong views on. Something that he and his companion could *really* talk about in days to come.

'What now?' said Ryle.

'Did your grandparents ever talk about the previous era when we cut each other down just as mercilessly?' said Fletcher. 'Mine rarely did speak of it and then only referred to it similarly as *the Troubled Times*. That soft little word *troubles* has been used to quietly concrete over so many horrible wounds in our country, has it not. So much pain buried under the word.'

'I wouldn't know about that, boss,' said Ryle distractedly. He had his own troubles at that time. He was trying to keep his phone connected to BetFair for a minute as he had decided to cash in his position on England. He had them backed for a win against India and they had just ceased the crease with a decent but not unasssailable 524 for 5 after 158 overs. Ryle was always in credit on his cricket by dint of closing his positions ahead of those with loyalties. And by following fixers.

Note: you thought I knew nothing about cricket. Well you might as well be aware that an estranged cousin of my own played for New York. Ryle of course knew a little about it too, it being the game his home county was reviled for. *The compiler*

Fletcher decided he would come back to the subject another time and removed his focus to the other shelves of the owner's life. Each surprised him more than the last. From one he pulled out soft tomes to inspect images of sunsets and middle aged women beneath titles about spiritualism, Celtic mysticism and that class of a thing. From another, poetry by O'Driscoll, Durkan and Kenelly telling the story of the country in riddles. There were lower shelves of crime novels which Fletcher looked down on. He thought he had no time for fiction. Back to the second shelf he eventually settled on an old thing called 'How can I Help.' Water always finds its own level. He stretched out on the Che Guevara quilt that covered the fouton with the good book spread over his crossed hands. 'You're a dark horse, Suck Ryle,' he repeated, as he settled down.

When the snoring got under way Ryle went to a comfortable bedroom at the end of the corridor, the only place in the god forsaken hillside hovel that he could get decent bars on the phone. He lay on the small double bed without taking off his boots and tried to block out the monotonous sound of waves coming up from the bay surely a mile below. Every seventh he noticed louder than the others.

Note: *beware the person who is in tune with the sea*, that was advice my own father gave me and with a bit of experience behind me now, I'd be inclined to say he might have been right enough in his own way. *The compiler*

Ryle phoned the Rathmines number as he had been finding

Margot wandering into his mind ever since the deliberations of the devil-exposing tradesman had bounced off him earlier that afternoon.

'Hello?' she herself answered.

'Well,' he said in a low voice, 'what way are you?'

'Who is this?' she said, pretending not to know.

'You know very well,' Ryle responded with an unctuous smile, one that it was as well she couldn't see.

'Leonard?' she said in panic. *'Has something happened to Grattan?'*

'No,' he said, 'but for you anything can be arranged.'

'That's not very funny, Len,' she said. 'What is it that you want?'

'It wasn't meant to be funny. I was only phoning to see how you were doing,' said Ryle. 'Is that a crime? And to ask whether there's anything I could do for you maybe this weekend. You know, when Fletcher is off minding other people.'

She said nothing for a minute and Ryle thought he might be after finding a crack.

'You don't hold women in very high regard, do you Leonard?' she eventually said, deciding not to hang up this time.

'That doesn't seem relevant,' said Ryle, pleased that she was still there.

'You feign interest in me only in the hope of gaining physical access to me, and that's about all there is to it for you, I think,' she said. 'You are a little misogynistic.'

'Hey now, hold your horses there,' said Ryle, 'I try to be nice to anyone who has something I want. And why wouldn't I? What kind of fool do you take me for? There is nothing false about that.'

'OK,' she said slowly, treading into a crude category of talk that she was unfamiliar with, 'and so confirm for me, Leonard, if my … my fanny didn't exist would there be any other thing that would make you pretend to like me?'

'Not particularly,' answered Ryle too quickly, suddenly unsure. 'Good christ no! You can fucking bet the house on that.' Ryle had already begun to worry that his thoughts on Margot of late were not entirely appropriate. She seemed to present herself in his head at awkward moments and for no reason at all, even when he was not thinking of how to get access to the aforementioned personal asset. 'Besides,' he said harshly in his distraction, 'it's not balanced to call me a little misogynist, implying that I have any deeper liking for men and children. That's only pity-mongering.'

She laughed and hung up on him, leaving him intangibly dissatisfied.

Catch larks when the sky falls

Chapter XXIII

FLETCHER'S FIRST SLEEP was short and then he couldn't get another. He tossed about and just couldn't find ease despite the couch being soft and forgiving. Ryle had no such problem because his first nap lasted the whole night due to him having a sound constitution and no experience of cares.

He fed himself and Fletcher well enough at breakfast. Fletcher was impressed with the forethought of Ryle. At how he had eggs, brown bread, rye bread, and an unexpired carton of milk laid on. Ryle should have guessed that the real owners might not be lurking too far away, given the freshness of the bread. But he was too busy griping about having missed his weekly seven-card stud game. He was several hundred euro poorer as a result, the game never starting before all of the other players had had a few drinks.

'We'd better go meet the tree protestors while there's a break in the rain,' said Fletcher staring down the hill at the breakers that looked angry even from here. He picked up plates and cups, readying himself to wash them.

'Leave them in the sink,' said Ryle, 'there's a woman comes in to do the wash up.'

The cakes of mud began to drop off Fletcher's brain and he said, 'But ...' He took a slow look around, 'But ... How did she know to have the place ready for us? And ... You didn't even know how to get here? *Len?*'

Ryle gathered his phone off the table, hand-swept crumbs onto the floor, and said they probably should get going. Only then did Fletcher figure out why there was such a draught in the kitchen of the otherwise snug little bungalow. The broken double-glaze panel was not enormous but the mean wind powering down the hill from the East was jetting in through it.

'Christ,' said Fletcher. He stood up to gaze at his nightmare. On the wall of the dining room he now noticed the framed drawing of a rising lark. Under it, a quotation in italics, '*A second class life in your own land is no life. Fly free or die in the effort!*' He went to take a closer look at the pictures on the tiled mantelpiece. '*Oh Christ!*' he repeated quieter. In a whisper. 'What have you gotten us into, Len?' He was picking up picture after blurry black and white picture of smiling, long-haired people in pick-your-nose collars. The one that settled in his hand looked back at him with a big hairdo and a beaming teenager's smile. It had a small white slip with the printed caption 'Volunteer Shane 'Dandy' Henderson, 21 Mar 1965 – 21 Mar 1983, executed by British SAS,' and under the type in tight curly biro writing, 'Mo neart thú.'

'How the fuck did Donny Osmond get roped in?' said Ryle, taking a look. Ryle was more used to the simpler southern county variety of four-green-fielder, the billings baby rabidly dancing the walls of Limerick.

'Only seventeen, Len, and trying to make momentous decisions,' lapsed Fletcher, 'I think of the innocence of my Saoirse at that age …'

'Old enough to get up the pole all the same,' said Ryle.

'Jesus Christ,' said Fletcher taking a hard look at his company, 'what is the matter with me?'

'Too late for you to run,' said Ryle, looking out the front window. A large black twincab had just pulled across the driveway. 'Now is your chance to take a hammering for your convictions. And to talk for your life.'

When Fletcher looked around, Ryle had vanished.

Fletcher sat down at the kitchen table with his head held in his hands. He waited. After an age, the key went in the front door. Nothing suspected yet. There was a putting down of shopping bags. Then quiet steps on the hall parquet. The kitchen door squeaked partly open and then stopped in frozen silence.

'I'm so sorry,' said Fletcher, lifting his gaze across the rye bread crusts that Ryle had left on the bread board.

'So am I,' spoken resignedly. When Ryle heard it was a

woman, he reappeared from behind the bay window curtains.

'You've made yourselves coffee I see,' she said, staring into Ryle's cold face, the recognizing of a British soldier hardcoded into her. 'Have you been waiting a while?'

Her wondering brown eyes and a mouth that cracked downward at the sides, looked out from a tired face. It would already have been clear to any sensible person what she thought. Instead of running, she stepped forward and put her hands on the back of a chair. 'So,' she said.

'Those chairs are brutal,' said Ryle, 'you know you can get cushioned chairs for a kitchen nowadays?'

'I'll bear that in mind,' she said, trying to hold onto the cold soldierly contempt for one's executioners. 'I have one request.'

'Fire away,' said Ryle.

'That we go away from here for this.' She said each word like a short sentence.

Fletcher was still so mortified that all he could say was, 'I'm so so sorry.'

Only then did she show any emotion. She could not sustain the hardness and her words blurted their way out of her. 'I have a niece coming here for the weekend. She is very precious to me. I don't want her to be the one to find me.'

Ryle didn't like this kind of emotional display and consequently paid no attention to the words. 'When the sky falls we'll catch larks. Give me the keys of the Nissan,' he said. 'I presume it has a tracker in it? I'll park it square for you.'

She handed over the shaking keys and he handed her his half drunk mug. She and Fletcher sat in silence as the front door closed. They listened together as Ryle crunched the gears and drove away.

'Why are we waiting?' she said, a little anger rising. 'You want me to know your who and your why? You want to punish me with knowledge of who you are avenging? I have bad news for you. There is nothing you can say that punishes me worse than looking around me every day and seeing what it was all for.'

Nothing but a blank stare from Fletcher.

'I have to guess? You want me to look you in the eye and

know your particular why? Well I don't give a particular crap. How about that?'

Fletcher was quite disorientated.

She further considered his lack of action. 'Not under orders then but not an angry personal mission either?' She thought for a second before pronouncing softly, 'Ex-FRU, is what you are then, coming back freelance. One of Thatcher's boys worried that if the prosecutions start the modern Tories will leave you flapping in the wind. They deny you. And … you've heard it said that I was the fourth person in the house where your squad thought there were only three and where they wore no masks.'

'Excuse me,' said Fletcher, glad of the interruption when his phone tinged.

'Go ahead,' she said, laughing acidly.

He looked at his text as she started to shake, unable for the silent delay. It's not being killed that's hard but waiting for it, they say. Though how anyone would know is hard to tell.

'Got her phone too,' the text said. *'Will abandon both at the beach. That way she won't be able to contact her lads for a while. Get yourself away now. Pick me up down here. You're welcome.'*

'Jesus Christ,' muttered Fletcher again.

'I'm confused,' she said, eventually, feeling in her bag for her phone. It was beginning to dawn on her that the look in the face of the man before her was not steely. He had that Southern mystery of adulthood reached with childlike softness retained. A quality that beguiled people of Belfast for the promise of what their own lives might have been. And infuriated them for its smugness as if all this was nothing to do with them. 'Who exactly sent you here?'

'Nobody,' said Fletcher, surprised, 'my friend just led me to believe that this was his … I mean we were short taken and needed a place to put our heads down for the night.'

She dropped the cup on the floor. It smashed all over the place. 'Here,' said Fletcher standing, 'don't move. A shard could easily go through those soft soles of yours. Just sit down and let me clean this up for you.'

Fletcher pulled a chair behind her knees and she sat and wept.

She cried for Ireland. And then when she was done and Fletcher was done cleaning the floor around her but still on his knees determined to get a glistening fragment that had gone between boards, she put her hands on his cherub curls and hugged the big lump of a head into her breast.

Fletcher could just have left it at that. Letting her think that he was just an unfortunate bum the other cheek of which had stolen her phone and car. But then he would have been a different kind of hero. Instead, he told her about the trees.

When two so open glide alongside, spirits can imprint on each other to surprising depth in the float past. That would be my own observation on the matter but I'll leave you to draw up your own ideas. What I can tell you is that two hours later Fletcher was flayed out on the couch again going on about his guilt for each new thing he learned about how people were struggling; at having lived so long sheltered behind his crass certainties.

'Don't,' she said. 'Each of us has been given talents and only some of us has had the space to grow them. If you have to wait for the world to be fair and for everyone to be able to breathe freely before you can allow yourself to do so, then your breath will be gone too, your talents untended, and the world no fairer. I can feel angry that a child had to be born in the Divis Flats to absorb the concentration of fearful seventeenth-century wrath so that you could call the South a peaceful country.' Fletcher saw her glance towards the mantelpiece. 'But the truth is that while I tread the beautiful beach that you see out that window below, I too rarely manage to think of the woman in Bangladesh who made my lovely, warm pullover and who will never see the sea. And I'm unable to always think of others on all sides here at home who were sacrificed for something better than this. Only my own lost are always with me. We have to keep on for them.'

Then she caught him glancing towards the picture on the mantelpiece.

'You know everyone thinks he was called Dandy because of the hair always being perfect and those psychedelic waistcoats, hell knows where he got them. But that wasn't it. It was me gave him that name. When we were seven. For his choice of reading material. Desperate Dan was still his favourite superhero when he died.'

'He wasn't cut out to be a soldier?'

'Who is? You can only wish to have been born in another time.'

'So, what happens here next?' said Fletcher, offering his phone. 'Do you want to call the Guards? Or someone else?'

'Look,' she said surprised, 'just because I said there has been enough hardness and no need for you to be harder doesn't mean you have to be entirely gormless.' She took the phone and picked up the number from Ryle's text. She phoned.

'Well,' said Ryle, 'how did you get on? Did Sister Snoop take a nail gun to your knee caps? If you're in hospital you know I can't go to see you as visiting the sick is not any kind of pleasure for me.'

'Could you be so kind as to bring my car back,' said the woman.

'Like fuck I will,' said Ryle, re-evaluating his situation. He flung his phone to its death. Not even a Nokia could survive more than five minutes in the intense saltiness of that particular stretch of the Atlantic.

'Your friend is not as badly afflicted with qualms,' she said with a laugh. She was looking out to the sea again. 'But I can see where he has parked my car. Would you mind driving me down there before he makes a run for it? Then you can head back to your lovely life.'

The tree issue was quickly dealt with. Fletcher curtly took a look at the correspondence between the protesters and the council. 'You can injunct them on process … here … and here,' he said, matter of factly running a highlighter through several paragraphs. It turned out that our man, not entirely useless after all, had a quick eye for procedural flaws and had a crank's nose for grounds for objections. Council executives, not good at following their own procedures, were getting not to like the mention of his name – associated now, somewhat unfairly, with an epidemic of injunctivitis that was sweeping the country. The rather efficient committee thanked the two men equally curtly and let them get back to the road after only an hour swinging their legs from the lower branches of the bigger tree.

'Well, spit it out,' said Ryle. 'You are grumpy because I suppose in your own head you have convinced yourself that this is somehow my fault. Myself, a man who lost several hundred euro to be at your side this day.'

Fletcher of course could not give up his innocence because if he had done there would have been nothing left to tell of him. 'It is the accidentality of all, if you must know,' said Fletcher in a dangerous haze, moving out to overtake and only changing his mind after the oncoming truck had screamed past them on the hard shoulder.

'Here, do you want me to drive a bit?' said Ryle, nervous.

'That is what is disturbing me,' continued Fletcher. 'A woman like that, true to the bone, who if born at the other end of the country would have been a doctor or a social worker. A person who would have challenged her own people's abandonment in other ways if her idealist years had not coincided with a decade in which Europe dangled a freedom that must be taken by force or lost entirely.'

'Letting off bombs across Europe was all well and good while it was middle class children doing a stint as red hippies who were at it, eh?' said Ryle, a man, in fairness to him, whose voice was not silent when there was a need to speak against the religious-school educated who still ran the country like it was their own at this time in Irish history. He did also have a personal interest in the European Spring of not so distant decades, the uprising that was not crushed but simply worn down by the devil in the system not caring very much about it.

Note: the basic promise of anarchistic socialism had appealed to the younger Suck Ryle though he hadn't looked into the theoretical underpinnings of it in great detail. His logic: he had nothing to lose and found he always fared better than the next person in times of chaos. This had come to the fore at one time when he had been stationed in Lower Saxony (after Cyprus and before his court martial). Ryle would never have had any truck with the Red Brigade or Action Directe, to tell the truth of him, not taken in by either the French or Italian personality. It was clear to him even at that early age that if anyone could organize anarchy it was the German. And it is true that during the posting in that region as a sweeper with the Royal Air Force he did gather old information relating to the RAF, the Red Army Faction that is. In particular his political awakening had led him to focus his collection on articles containing photos of the tall, broad anarchist called Gudrun Ensslin. He took to prowling the streets of Hanover when he was off duty, attending Scientology personality testing sessions. Nothing was found by the Scientologists but Ryle kept going because a man in an English Bar in Bremen had told him that Ensslin was now embedded in the German branch of Hubbard's outfit and had them retooled as a recruiting front for the Continuity RAF. He kept expecting Ensslin, the Saxon stranger, to come there. It was of course just a youthful phase. If he'd had much of a clue about how the world works he'd have realized that Hubbard's men weren't going to let him have Ensslin and that anyway she'd have been about as interested in him as were her Teutonic foremothers in men like him, women who strangled each other rather than be taken by Romans. But like all such follies of youth, it had left a mark on the impressionable mind, a certain soft spot for strident big framed blonde women that had never left the misfortunate and oft misunderstood little man. *The compiler* 'And, I have to ask myself too, but for the accident of her beauty, would I have been so enthralled by her story, extending myself so comfortably into her terrible troubles?'

'Oh?' said Ryle, 'You're on your own there if you're after getting mixed up with one of that crowd.'

'You're missing the point,' said Fletcher, pointlessly. 'How can it be right that sounds, smells, images, personal strokes, lyrics, and longing can all affect one more powerfully than reason?'

'Strokes, eh?' said Ryle.

'She must remain closed to the thought that her universe was a small cauldron, her entire boiling creed but a contained reaction that the outside only worried about when it occasionally spilled into Monaghan or Birmingham. And what arrogance would it be to imagine that I do not myself live contained, and that the set of feelings and reactions behind which Grattan Fletcher marshals rational-sounding ideas, are not merely a tiny subset of the possible, telling more of my ignorance of a bigger picture than of my wisdom. We have no choice but to act as though what we see is the universe, but when you realize that it couldn't be the universe and that there may be terrible consequences to anything believed absolutely, how can you ever make bold or concentrate on anything beyond trying to do no harm? Trying to leave no footprints at all. What is that then?'

We are at the point now where even a man as removed from the basics as Grattan Fletcher could have predicted what Ryle would say to this. Therefore, I don't think you need me to tell you the course that the vacuous goading followed from here or how he threaded his favourite word into it.

Giving the devil a run

Chapter XXIV

'THIS IS GETTING A LITTLE BIT fucking ridiculous, Fletch,' said Cathal Mac Gabhann, the thundering bollocks, setting half his bony arse onto the edge of his desk in a studied pose. He had been re-watching Madmen the night before. 'This vagrancy.'

'Don't waste my time, what was it you wanted?' said Fletcher in a tone unmistakably leaded with cold scorn. A tone that would have shocked you or anyone else who thought they knew all about Fletcher. I'm afraid you'll have to look elsewhere for your saint now. Of late, one on one, when he thought nobody else was watching, Fletcher was indulging in the sin of impatience, letting Mac Gabhann have a reasonable draught of precisely the aloof disdain Mac Gabhann had always accused him of harbouring.

'You know I've been trying to extend a little leniency—because I know that Margot is concerned.'

'Drop the posturing, Charles,' said Fletcher, sat on the guest carver in Mac Gabhann's office. 'There's nobody else in the room. It's just us. We both know the score. So why did you call me here?'

'Do we though?' said Mac Gabhann with a pleasured smile. 'And don't make like Margot has talked to you.'

The scene was like the office footage RTÉ sets up when a minister is being shot. A pre-constituted image. Neat as a pin with only one book open on the desk and the gold-plated MontBlanc sat beside it on the green leather inlay. Framed certificates on the walls. Photos all including Mac Gabhann. What else would you expect from a fellow trying to pass himself as human? Too good to be true.

A glass-doored bookcase held no books relating to his real interests. He displayed biographies of all the state's men from Pearse to Rabitte, declaring fluid loyalties and readiness to pull a stroke for any of them if it was in his own direct or indirect interests to do so.

Explanatory note (only for the outsider): the clubs that put themselves before the electorate in twenty-six-county Ireland do not distinguish themselves on the usual lines of fiscal, social, or abortion policy. They are all well able to jump whichever way suits on austerity, tax, carbon dioxide, fornication, and immigration. Fine Fáil, Labour, Sinn Féin, the Greens, and various other outfits are differentiated only by the dates at which they became resigned to 'The Treaty' (Churchill's finest gift to ordinary Englishmen after Rhondda and Gallipoli, whereby Londoners were lumbered with another spent Northern town) and turned from shooting those who had already signed it to shooting those who had yet to. The electorate of course is detail-oriented and doesn't often get sidetracked by the National or European issues. You can take that from the horse's mouth. In my own case I gave the last vote to the woman that got me sorted out with Council regarding the little bunker I constructed for myself back in '99. Those are the real issues ordinary people want politicians for. I can respect a representative who doesn't rail against the old ways; one who understands that planning in this country will always have to be done retrospectively, (though recriminations may still be done in advance). Furthermore she will continue to secure my own vote as long as she continues to keep the penalty points lopped off my licence. After that, her spouting on about being a green federalist, environmentalist, and neo-Redmondite doesn't bother me one way or the other.

'Oh *Margot hasn't talked to me then*? Are you sure about that old chap?' said Mac Gabhann a little ridiculously.

'Don't be ridiculous,' said Fletcher.

Fletcher knew that Margot, not to put a tooth in it, wouldn't piss on the man if he was on fire. The depth of the antipathy sometimes scared even Fletcher. It had taken root at a party years before when Margot had witnessed a drunken push after which Fran had gone home quietly with her husband. To fence off the mishap, MacGabhann had immediately inflated the price for Fran's weekly lunches with Margot. Any such outing was from then paid for in demonic sulks that contaminated their children's lives for days. For Fran, the brief relaxed pleasures held out by waldorf salads and Portobello cheesecakes shared with Margot were not worth that. She had cut Margot and other friends adrift, reduced to a three day work week, and focussed her energies on the emerging consequences of her life at home.

That was long ago but Margot didn't forget. These feelings towards Cathal Mac Gabhann had only been manured with each belittlement that she thought her beloved husband failed to perceive at the hands the same well-oiled gent. Margot couldn't hear the name without her best mood being eroded, yielding to agitation. And when angry, Margot was one woman who would give the devil a run for his money.

Note: I know what you are thinking here. The very same as I did. To name it: it was a good job that Suck Ryle hadn't got wind of Margot Hartigan's view on Mac Gabhann at this point in the chronicle. Given Ryle's tiny inklings of affection-like feelings for each of the Fletchers, feelings so totally alien to Ryle that he was simply not equipped to respond to them moderately, proceedings might well have been cut short. To borrow and better use Fletcher's word, there has been enough accidentality around Ryle to already stretch your credulity. Any further at this time would have made you question my own integrity, I have no doubt. *The compiler*

'I see I have your attention. You never did know who your real friends were, did you Grattan?'

Fletcher said nothing. He was anxious to be out of here as he had ideas about how he'd like to spend his day.

'So you see, because we go back, all four of us, and because I remain fond of Margot, I've been putting up this bit of sham disciplinary around you this past while. Just enough that all our asses remain, shall we say, at least mostly unexposed.'

'You don't say, Charles,' said Fletcher.

'What? Surely you didn't think that if I'd been really intent on getting you out, you'd still be here?' Mac Gabhann smiled, a sight that would curdle spring water and make a dead cat sick.

'Can we arrive at wherever you are cannoodling us to, please?' said Fletcher impatiently.

'Oh, in a hurry are we? A hurry to depart your workplace on unsanctioned leave, rushing off to bring your employer into disrepute by making further unauthorized media appearances.' Mac Gabhann had not intended to wade into the usual stuff. But resentfulness could always sidetrack him. His voice rose as his face reddened. He hit his fist on the cherrywood which hurt his carpels, already showing signs of early arthritis. 'You fucking vainglorious gennet.'

Fletcher smiled somewhat ungraciously.

'People say Grattan Fletcher is a prodigiously brainy man. Did you know that?' griped Mac Gabhann, who had intelligence-envy issues ever since school where teachers had branded him a steady worker. 'They say it as if it's praise. But neurons are not digitally connected logical circuits. Every synapse is flooded by chemicals and subject to fluxes of every sort.'

'Keeping up on the science mags still, Charles?' said Fletcher.

'So having a surplus of such electro-chemical activity doesn't make you more logical,' said Mac Gabhann. 'By my reckoning, extra *neurons* simply makes you, well, obviously, more *neurotic*. Isn't that so? Just look at the Ashkenazi Jews. Too many circuits firing simultaneously veers you closer to madness than genius in many cases. It leads to a gaze transfixed on the sensations of your own self in the world. Everything comes to be about your personal struggle for meaning. And that can boil down to being a pain in the ass. Unlike the person of good functional intellect, Grattan, you are unable to just get on with tasks and contribute to the world in humble useful everyday ways like a normal person.'

'Interesting theory,' said Fletcher in an uninterested voice that unintentionally made Mac Gabhann madder. Suddenly Fletcher perked up, seeing Mac Gabhann's laptop turned out for him to see on the side table. It was open on Grawne van den Heever's Skype profile. The Fletcher you are familiar with returned. He thought that here might lie a friendly side path onto which

he could detour Mac Gabhann. 'Don't tell me that's your little Jenny? Lovely how she's grown up. Abroad on a college trip
is she? You must miss her so much. God we haven't met each
other's kids in so long, Cathal. We should all get together and
make a fresh go of rekindling old friendships. Hey?'

'Her?' said Mac Gabhann, swelling with pride at the chance
to talk like a man of the world. 'No, she's someone else's daughter, Grattan. To me she's just a chick I plan to shag.'

'OK. Right then,' said Fletcher looking away.

'Don't give me that false piety. You want to know more, don't
you?' said Mac Gabhann, confusing Fletcher's discomfort for
envy. Though Mac Gabhann had yet to succeed in straying from
Fran, other than with prostitutes, he believed that this was an
arena in which he could hammer Fletcher. 'If you ever man up,
Fletch, you will realize the truth that we all want what we don't
have. That's the nature of want. Only those who haven't properly
secured what they already have, continue to expend desire at
home. To live fully is to look outward from the secured assets, to
survey what else is available, and rise to new challenges.'

'So what was it you wanted?' asked Fletcher.

Mac Gabhann stepped around to his side of the desk, sat
and pulled the recline lever on his Herman Miller aero. He lay
back with his hands across him. He paused a minute, an affect
he believed worked well. Then he said, 'To be frank, Grattan,
when one reaches the pinnacle like me one tends to find only
taedium et vitae in the things others still aspire to. That which
retains the ability to thrill is mostly bad stuff. And don't go off
on a tangent here. I'm not willing to argue about whether there's
an objective list of bad things. I'm using the word here as an
approximation for those things that wring indignant froth from
Joe and Miriam. Yes. Sans the self-destructing. Don't worry, I'm
not planning to go Ian Brady on the hunt for novel experiences.
However I am rather drawn to experiences from the legal but
societally reprehensible side of things.'

'Interesting,' said Fletcher drily.

'And young Saoirse?' asked Mac Gabhann in a different tone.
'She must be, what, twenty-one now?'

Fletcher fixed his interest on the autumnal ambivalence of the light grey sky over the mid nineteenth-century double hipped roof across the street.

'Wild little thing, I should say,' continued Mac Gabhann.

'Watch yourself,' said Fletcher.

'Or what?' said Mac Gabhann after a pause.

'So here we are again,' said Fletcher suddenly, as if he had just thought of something. 'Do you want to know the truth, Charles?'

'What's that?'

'I can't even say you repel me anymore,' said Fletcher genuinely, 'you have just become a bore.'

'A *bore,* eh?' Mac Gabhann fumed. 'Fuck you, sunshine. Just watch me lift the protective curtain and go after your termination with the full force of my responsibilities. Then you'll see.'

'For the love of Pete! Look, you win. I'm sorry. I really can't listen to any more from you,' said Fletcher in a sudden moment of desolation. 'If you want my resignation, it's yours.'

Mac Gabhann was thrown quite off course by this. He was plain disgusted by his opponent's capitulation and he would not have it. Though he would circle back for it. Right now he had to return to how he had planned for this conversation to go.

'You are just overwrought. What I'm trying to say to you is,' he continued, 'that as your erstwhile friend I've been trying to avoid any serious action so as not to precipitate any escalation in your ... mental health situation. Always hopeful that this truancy phase of yours would prove transient and that you would soon return to the rather tedious unambitious price-receiver that we all know and ... well, let's not get carried away.'

'Yes,' said Fletcher, 'let's not, Charles.'

'You know,' said Mac Gabhann, working at his own pace towards the thing he wanted to achieve here, 'You know, like when you see a toddler walking on a ledge, you don't shout at them.'

'*Fucking hell! What, Charles?*' said Fletcher, whose time spent in Ryle's company was having some negative rub off on his language. 'What the fuck is stuck in your miserable gut you ... You, you, you contemptible toad.'

'Ho-ho! That's rather unparliamentary of us,' said Mac Gabhann, lifting his black leather briefcase into view for the first time. He clicked it open like this was an ancient craft. 'Let's all keep our knickers unknotted here shall we?'

He took out a document and slid it along the desk. 'Nothing as melodramatic as a resignation form for now, I'm afraid.'

Fletcher picked it up. The heading included the term Assignments of Intellectual Property. 'What is it?' said Fletcher who didn't feel he had the time in his life for fifteen pages of turgidity, not when he had a fundraiser to go to.

'It's just a bit of housekeeping,' said Mac Gabhann, in a slightly quickened tempo that should have warned Fletcher it was anything but. 'Something I've had the lawyers draw up for all of our assistant secretaries and principal officers to sign.'

'*What is it, Charles?*' Fletcher repeated. 'In summary.'

'Well it … In summary. OK then. Well I have no doubt that you're a supporter of that most admirable of modern concepts, the open source movement. You know, where everything should belong to everyone. So I know you'll be my prime supporter in this initiative. I am trying to place all of our department's documentation other than such personal information as is sheltered by the relevant data protection acts, into the public domain for free access and usage to all who desire that.'

'OK,' said Fletcher trying yet again to be warmer, a bottomless pit of benefit of the doubt. He reminded himself of the thing he reminded others of on a vulgarly regular basis: *You have to always allow that people can change. You have to extend such allowance as you would want for yourself.* And so he bit his cheek as he continued, 'OK then. You're referring to the open data movement. To your credit, you would be ahead of the curve on such an initiative.'

'You know,' said Mac Gabhann, who had not expected such an easy sale and didn't want to let the remainder of his prepared pitch go to waste; almost talking past the close, 'of course you can get independent legal advice on it if you like. But you know, I believe that any work any of us does should ultimately be digitized, made searchable, and have absolutely no copyright restrictions. After all, the public has already paid for our life's work, supported our families, indulged us in a great many comforts that elude the ordinary working person. In a way we are like their philosophers. They have granted us the space in which to formulate their story, if you will.'

Fletcher sighed and Mac Gabhann confused his weariness for wariness. He quickly snapped back to a less alarming version of himself, 'Look, just sign the fucking thing like a good man. Page fifteen, and initial every page. Then get out of my sight.'

'It will be my pleasure, I'm sure,' said Fletcher. He did all of this in haste. Thusly, he executed one of the greatest charities yet in his helpful adventures: relieving an old colleague of a great worry. Cathal Mac Gabhann had been experiencing deepening concerns that he might have to reword large chunks of his masterpiece in order to avoid courtroom unpleasantness. After all, Boland was already predicting the book would be a runaway success.

He picked up the phone and asked to talk to Boland. 'How are the proofs reading?' said Boland.

'Perfectly, if I do say so myself,' said Mac Gabhann.

A little knowledge

Chapter XXV

GRATTAN RETURNED TO HIS DESK.

'Where were you?' asked Ryle. 'You look like you're after puking your guts out.'

Fletcher wasn't looking flush, right enough. 'Nowhere,' he said, refusing to have his thoughts dragged back into the dense dark furze from which he had just extracted them. He proceeded to put on a hat and spectacles.

'Where do you think you're going, looking like that?' asked Ryle. 'No offence but you look like a Shetland's knob.' Hovering in the air between them again, the all too frequently unasked question of what variety of websites Ryle perused in spare moments.

Fletcher failed to respond. He pulled the wide straw hat further over his curls with some some difficulty. Boaters did not come in XXL apparently.

It was of course perfectly plain to Ryle where Fletcher was going. It was November the 24th, mini-Joyce day in aid of the little known South Riding Faction, a splinter group of The Georgian Society. Fletcher had made the acquaintance of these un-National agitators several years previously when he was alerted by them to the existence of unauthorized double-glazing in a building in Mount Street. Looking into old windows was already his portfolio by that time. Professionally, he kept from them his personal doubts about their purist approach to fenestration. Fletcher in fact was not so sure that conservation of lead-caked frames and leaking glass, trumped the conservation of energy.

The fact that he had then befriended and continued meeting them, illuminates effulgently for you the fact that at the back of everything what our Mr. Fletcher had always been and yet remained, above anything else, was an eccentric. You will agree, there were a lot worse things he could have turned out to be.

Note: the compiler happens to possess a little knowledge of his own on this subject. 'Joyce' here refers to one *James* Joyce, an early Irish entrepreneur, rather than the well known boxer, though they shared the proud Traveller ethnicity. This lesser known Joyce wrote in the spare time which he had a lot of due to his career as a Stateless artist, ultimately no more Irish than he was British, cutting fingernails with his hands tied, unable but to observe the happenings on his canvases. Like the extended Joyce clan, he had a gift for convenient truths and convivial lies. Speech that dances around a subject. Continuous speech that is unfurled as a silence filler. Speech that offers and seeks temporal associations. Speech that is set forth primarily with the object of communing rather than of relaying verifiable fact.

In the interests of fair play since there's nobody but Ryle here to speak up for the English '[fn] perspective let me briefly give it voice: *As the more enlightened of your race finally become less enamoured of Joyce, do not for one moment believe you can work your way around to pawning him off on Britain. You may have noticed that while Wilde, Beckett, and the exquisite McIlroy are regularly embraced as British, James Joyce has never been. While you may feel this to be harsh, please remember that he made his own bed. He left one in no doubt that he was no lover of the English. It was not enough for him to remove its stric-tures and disciplines, the only natural elegance it possesses. Nor was he yet satisfied with flagrantly, voyeuristically debauching it, jizzing it up with his lowly pun. No. He felt the need to take the disrespect deeper, blatantly raking it into a brand of Hiberno English so degenerate that the contemporary pluckers of that particular pidgin would have it rather, 'Anglo Irish.' Or to explain in the vernacular, may we refer you to the accidentally well-named 'Molly'-cule theory of the equally Irish Nolan, that other specimen on whose behalf we are only too glad to recognize the 'independent' Nationality of the Free State: the language of*

Joyce is so heavily contaminated by the molecules of the primitive form that it is surely by now more bicycle than man. By which token of course, all critique is rendered idiotic. Quite so. A summary then of Joyce's opus will suffice. A member of the clerical class, a protagonist with biographical similarity to the author, a rather ordinary Castle Catholic, has his first sexual encounter at the whim of a music hall vamp. Then attempting to assuage the guilt of his tribe, he crudely renders the lady's grubby little garter spying husband, as classical hero. All rather humdrum. What astonishes is the subsequent elevation of the writer to the role of National balladeer. This can only be attributed to the indigenization of Trinity College Dublin, originally an adequate provincial school for those who could not gain access to Oxford or Cambridge. In an act of post-colonial self-harm on a scale that even Robert Mugabe would be shocked by, the native continues to sack his only respectable institution, allowing the disciplines of the Humanities to be overrun by tautology tutors, rights rationalizers, gender ideologues, and those generally who believe that the jargon of academia can disguise advocacy as intellectual endeavour. So telling of the self-loathing and deep-seated doubt of the seceding statelet, its academic cheerleaders proceed to elevate particular artists far above their station, merely on the basis of sympathetic disposition and local spawning. There is so much more one could say on this, but where is the audience for home truths?

[fn] Footnote

Not for the first or last time in this book, we must apologize to our neighbours. To explain: there's a type of inverted condescension, a sort of pleasure taken from looking down on people who are above you, unique to the rural Irish mindset. It leads to this type of thing. Indeed these days, Dubliners are often subjected to it as much as England's elite are. Let us be clear that the compiler's recurring strawman of the benignly patronizing English person or the privately condescending person of Anglo Irish heritage, is solely his own. It has no resonance whatsoever for any of us who have had modern real world dealings. *The Editors*

Note (contd.): that Joyce the writer struggled to publish his harmless bits of punning raillery, an homage to Flaubert for those of you unable to read the lovelier languages, didn't do him any harm in the end. A lesson to us all. Like graffiti on his gravestone however, it has become the latter day orthodoxy in the very same *Dubhlinia* whose small town orthodoxies he fled, that this Joyce is now to be revered as the greatest writer in the world. The poor man is now a brand more associated with the same provincial town than even Diageo is. And where is the evidence, by the way, that Joyce ever interfered with the natural rotting and subsidence of crumbling piles? This Joyce indicated no more approval for Georgian architecture than he did for the plastering of planes and ferries with his brand. So let this now be said and said with no pleasure but on the back of much research on the subject: given the same old chancer's fondness for new things and comforts, his modern equivalent is most assuredly not to be found amongst those wobbling the streets on high nelly bicycles with straw hats tied down on their floppy heads. Not to go on about it but, when the man piked Dublin, where I ask you did he step out the derogation for the likes of them? Indeed of course he was a humorous man and hardly said a serious word but immor...[fn] *The compiler*

[fn] Footnote
Contract or not, we had no choice but to intervene at this juncture. Truncation simply becomes a duty in the case of a comment of such encyclopaedic ignorance, replete with dilettantisms posing as danteisms, orthogonal in uncouthness and pretension, and pock-marked with eruptions of peasant-prim verbosity. A little learning, danger and so forth … Pope, I believe. The excised further chapters of resentful onanistic diatribe contained no elements that were constructive or insightful and, in our view, added nothing whatsoever to the extant body of learning and discourse on the subject of the man whom we in Dublin are most assuredly not alone in regarding the founding father of modern literature. The relentlessly dreadful excised prose veers from crass assertions about the master himself, only to indulge in base and slanderous observations in relation to the dedicated people who maintain his spirit and his essence in every thoroughfare of our great city. Others who find Joyce beyond their grasp at least have had the grace to shut up and don the green jersey for the sake of the hard-pressed hospitality workers. *The Editors*

Fletcher and Ryle had had the conversation before and though a tolerant man, Fletcher would prefer not to have Ryle's views on matters either Georgian or Joycean aired in front of others either Georgians or Joyceans. Not ever again.

'Which of you boys is after giving Cathal his hole?' bellowed Connie McLean, appearing in the doorway of the return. 'I just met him skipping out of the building with the briefcase squeezed tight under his arm and a slippery little grin on him that would worry sheep.'

McLean was a big roving field archaeology contractor, a mercenary. He had a great black beard. Whenever he visited Northumberland Manse to deliver unspecified items to Mac Gabhann, he stopped in to say hello to Fletcher. Fletcher never gave McLean enough heed, having found that some things he'd said before were not true. Now this McLean was not a complete liar—he was merely inclined to elaborate in support of his point. You would never want to dismiss what he told you entirely.

'More to the point,' said Fletcher sharply, 'one of these days you may tell me exactly what kind of research it is that you are undertaking on behalf of the man upstairs. Please tell me you're not employed in foreclearance of sites again.'

'Ah now!' said McLean. As an archaeologist for hire, there were some things that McLean would not do. His specialist interest was in the dé Danann. Therefore raths, fairy forts, and fairy bushes would not be plundered on his watch. All else, everything constructed after that day seven thousand years ago when the Danann were banished to their little underground reservations was all mere modernity to this man. And its relics were respected by him as epoxy by a pure carpenter. It was all in a day's work for him to be relocating Viking swords to a place where locals did not want development, clearing Roman coins left by some hoarder who hadn't got around to spending them himself, and keeping the occasional Cistercian chalice for himself. McLean had unwritten contracts coming out the door. Developers, the National Road Association, and Mac Gabhann were his main clients.

'I would have put you down as a more grounded type, a

Myles Day celebrator,' McLean said politely, his stare settling now on the hat with pull-stretched brim and at the round framed glasses that Fletcher had since added to his late Halloween disguise. 'A solidly acculturated Christian Brothers product instinctively keeping the wings of the Jesuitical pneumatologists clipped for them.'

Fletcher made no move to be drawn.

'No allusions to the Hebrew ruach or to Derrida's treatise on windiness help me personally to feel attracted to reading an unfiltered rendition of all of the noise from inside another man's head,' added McLean, a well-read man who preferred to run with the hare. 'The growing whine of metal fatigue from my front right wheel bearing is just as predictable in what it's leading to and less painful to listen to.' The same ignoramus, when he made these intrusions from some Godforsaken unmapped fairy-infested bogland in North West Cork, did so in a vintage Land Cruiser, therefore an allowance could be made here. The bearings issues were ones of emotional meaning to himself. He also had that affliction suffered by Cork people, even ones from an area of Cork that was hardly better than a bit of Limerick, of thinking that everyone could be brought around to his perspective if he talked loud enough and fast enough.

'For Christ's sake, McLean,' Ryle appealed to reason, 'do yourself a favour and don't get him started.' McLean was also one of the select few, visitors to or residents of the Manse, aware of Ryle's painful existence in the rear.

'So you're not telling us what has you here today, Cornelius, old friend?' said Fletcher glad of the excuse to take off the glassless wire frames that were already cutting tracks in his temples. It was too late. 'For me it's not about how well he executed his chosen form or how insightful were his experiments with languages and sounds. Nor is it only about Dublin. For me his is a legend of valour we could all do worse than to emulate. Every small wrong, every trivial misfortune, arresting his attention. He walks alone and does not fall in with the rousing calls of tribe though he hears them loud and knows how it feels to let your heart dance to their laments. And like with Moore, Shakespeare, and

Augustine before him his dedication to his pursuit only becomes more true as he suffers great losses in his own life. Instead of basking in the glow of recognition when that is finally granted him, he is to be found trailing lonely the publishers of Europe trying to persuade someone to publish the poor lettereens of his daughter whose grip is slipping from his fingers, still seeing through the illness only the beauty of her mind. And when he finally can't bring her back he instead tries to travel with her and lets her sad portmanteau-ed voice cry out to all corners of the universe from the prison of her living wake.'

'*Augustine?*' picked upon MacLean. 'Oho? I was always warned that mention of Augustine is the first mocking of madness.'

'So at the back of it all, it's just auld sentimental shite,' said Ryle, more to the point. 'I knew I'd be fully justified in never bothering me hole reading it.'

'What's so dirty about 'sentimental'—in art criticism as in many walks, it seems to be a derogatory appellation.' Fletcher, as too often when drawn into talking about something he cared about, forgot who he was talking to, 'for example too in critiques of Steinbeck and Henry James ... Surely everything worthwhile anyone does is driven by, or at least seasoned by sentiment? Either working with it or, just as much so in self-consciously trying not to.'

'What has that got to do with the price of blow, eh Suck?' said McLean, giving Ryle a dead shoulder with a comradely box. The big loud vessel of opinions so strong and diverse they'd leave Christie Moore looking like a pure angel, gets away with this because it so happened that he and Ryle had been contemporaneously 'previously known to the Gardaí.' They had become previously known to each other during overlapping periods of respite at Her Majesty Robinson's pleasure. Maybe I didn't mention before: our lesser man did a little time. After his army duties, in the period when he was of no fixed abode, he had been harassed by a Garda sergeant determined to link a sum of money that Ryle owned, with a robbery from the Tralee AIB. It was the drink that handicapped Ryle in his defence, the sergeant eventually getting the better of him. The injustices that had led to McLean's curtailment, well you could write those parts yourself. The lives of some are patterned from the day they land into the wrong kind of family and are poisoned by their narrow little educations. The professional writer must move on, hard nosed.

'Us lesser citizens of the lower layers of erudition,' continued McLean with the underskirts of his post grad studies at Berkeley ironed almost invisible beneath his restored bogman persona, 'we don't owe the man anything. It's bad enough to have to see the one photograph of him and his signature plastered to the high heavens and to have to listen to the same small towners he turned his back on in horror, demanding our obeisance to their safely proscribed interpretations of his genius.'

Fletcher became somewhat angry with this lumping, which Ryle could have told McLean was not a path to getting silence from him. 'Like he said of another writer, he himself is never dull, never stupid, never tired, never pedantic, never theatrical! Or not too often anyway,' continued Fletcher en route to his point. 'That's all clever. But for me, it's the way that he sees what he sees that keeps me comfortable in his company. What makes for ease amongst his words is the wide embrace of an unfailingly generous mind. It's the portrait of the man himself that comes through across time. The pulse of the good heart that beats in his work. The courage and the raw openness to life laid bare in his words transcend literary critique. The intensity of feeling that must be expressed in tiny detail is nothing other than love. No amount of clever devices mask it when it's present or make up for it when it's absent. Love in any one of its twisted lonely painful guises is the only thing you need to look for to know which art is true. And Lucia. He never abandoned her. He never began that great betrayal, the separation we make with our loved ones as age or illness pushes them closer to the edge of a cliff. Joyce indeed was our valorous knight of the great tradition.'

'Which great tradition, Grattan?' said McLean obligingly, contrite for having upset his friend and wincing as he now chivalrously drew further painful blows upon his own head.

'The only great tradition there is, liberalism in the proper sense,' pronounced Fletcher, rather more abruptly than Ryle had expected.

'A pity about you, you harmless twat,' said Ryle, suddenly aggravated beyond his station. A dark fiery greyness on his skin, he let slip a speech more alarming for its level of animation than for any freshness or insight contained within. He growled, 'Liberalism is only exhibited by those with full bellies.'

'Well you must admit the runt has a point,' said McLean again. 'Anyone in my trade can't avoid noticing that ferocity of competition is the true consistent enduring feature of our species—no better or worse than in any other enduring species. From all previous to present epochs you see the hunting tools and chainsaws of inter species competition. You see the man-traps, gas chambers, and trade laws of inter-troupe competition. You see the clubs and duelling pistols of sperm competition. You also, as with any troupe animal, see evidence of cooperative endeavour—but only within troupes and only, one feels, when it's to the greater good of inter-troupe competition. The brutal besting is always there. You will only occasionally, however, dig up an ornate silver spoon or see a cave wall doodle. It seems to me that it might be total enforcement that occasionally clears planes on which artistic reflection and squeamish glossing may occur. You won't find too many liberals amongst the shat upon, I'd say. Not amongst Aristotle's slaves, not amongst the Zulus massacred when Gandhi was Sergeant Major, and not amongst our own six million cleansed by cholera and cattle boats while the ascendency offered to the historical record many second sons of fine sensibility, using the silver ladles to dish out thin soup as their estates were made viable. Is that not the ultimate humilia-tion of defeat, having the man standing on your back celebrated for his elevation? Getting accused of churlishness for not admir-ing his high-mindedness as he dons your kilt, and bags your culture for the glass case. But for Lalor there'd have been nothing left of us by now, only the packaging, and they'd be as fond of us as they are of an indigenous Scot or a Cherokee.'

'It's very true for you,' observed Ryle, not listening at all.

'Just as we stand loftily informed by circuitry made in

Cambodia and warmed by scarves knitted in Bangladesh, while the wretched of the earth still toil in ignominy, er,' said Fletcher, a woman's words coming back to him in some muddle. 'But you can't wait to breathe. You can only do your best from where you find yourself, not from any other place.' He paused and then took the silence for himself, for his own relentless pursuit of his point, 'Yours is a saddening way to look at the world, my friend. Ultimately through those lenses, all roads lead to defeat and no human elevation is possible. I choose to believe otherwise and admit it's at times a willful choice. In my father's house ...'

'Not that again!' interrupted Ryle, in an alien growl, a sleety look coming over him as his mask of sweet civility slipped momentarily. 'Listen here, the number of rooms in the house you were born in only effects how soft you turn out. The likes of myself, Stalin, and Haughey had only the one room we ever came out of as children. That's why we'd be the kind of people to go and do what needs to be done. The likes of yourself, Chamberlain or Fitzgerald always knew you had lots of rooms to fall back on when you got your fingers burnt buddying up to ordinary people.'

A short silence followed, the other two staring at Ryle's brief blossom of true belief. Fletcher was the most stressed at the bitter poetry. Finally feeling a cold shakiness about his choice of running mate.

Note: The revelation that there are deeper roots and more grandiosity to Leonard Cromwell Suck Ryle's callousness than had initially met the eye, should not mislead you. Granted, at this point, you couldn't be faulted for assessing that the same gent may not be primarily a good person. But he also falls short in a number of respects, of being the primarily bad one. His role in whatever he undertakes is more at the level of an agent. *The compiler*

McLean on the other hand decided to laugh loud at his own thoughts, saying, 'Yourself and Ryle here are well made for each other, both men of high ideals. The heart of the crab tree as hard as the heart of the oak is strong.'

'Not only,' said Fletcher showing his fluster by circling back to the subject already closed, 'not only was his soul open for his own near and dear, but for every kind of person and creature, and laid eternally bare for us. Through the dots and specks of froth and venality, the fluff and resonances, the wood that some cannot hear for the trees, we are told the truth of regret, humiliation, grief walked minutely in the shoes of a man betrayed and betraying, a man reviled and forgiving, never faltering on the lonely path of unflinching love. Just as with Tolstoy, Charlotte Bronte, Edna O'Brien, and, and Proust himself, it was the deep well of honest living feeling [fn] from which his work came that made it resonate through all time where other immensely clever writing fades with the fashionableness of its form.'

[fn] Footnote
You will indulge a brief editorialization on the premise that we have a rare circumstance at hand. The accidental publication (through an aforementioned contractual contingency) of the work of an unpublishable writer fleetingly creates a forum for that harried minority which must generally bear malign public comment in silence: editors. If, as Fletcher notes, a great love of humanity and tumultuous feeling for fellows is the well of art, then it should be plain to you by now why you have landed up in such droughty, arid terrain under the guidance of our mutual acquaintance, the compiler. No further need we fear to speak of ninety-eight rejection letters, the subject which so unsettles the compiler; no further evidence in mitigation needs to be provided by ourselves in response to his resentful misjudgements in that regard. By his own crass words shall ye hoist him. Suffice it to say that most often the discharge of a commissioning editor's duty to art is a noun rather than a verb. It is evidenced not in the titles put into the public domain but in the mountain of dead skin and septic pus on the floor beside her. *The Editors*

This argument about nothing more significant than the soul of a long dead man was as close as Ryle and Fletcher ever came to falling out, a story that tells its own. That is, all things considered, McLean's observation was timely: the heroic duo was well met.

'Can we count on you to rally the vote in the Mullaghareirk mountains, Rockchapel, and thereabouts?' asked Ryle as McLean gathered himself to leave.

'You can of course,' said McLean. 'For what, might I ask?'

'The Áras,' said Ryle.

'You have bet a few bob on someone for the Park?' said McLean. 'You must have got good odds as it might be ten years till the next election.'

'Maybe, maybe not,' said Ryle. 'It might be no time at all if something happened to the present lad.'

'For heaven's sake, Connie, go on about your business,' said Fletcher. 'There is no election campaign. And for the record, I have the height of respect for the current person and I wish him long life and good health as should every decent person.'

'No? One thing you'll need to get realistic about,' said Ryle turning on his master for a minute, 'is that assassinations are hardly news in the presidency game.' Lincoln, Garfield, McKinley, and Kennedy were specialist subjects for Ryle on the table quiz circuit. 'And as for the man waiting in the wings having eyed out a quick track to the prime seat for himself, he must at all times remain on red alert for it being unexpectedly vacated. That's the difference between winners and losers, boss, and you need to get up on that.'

'All true, no doubt,' said McLean, not fully gathering what was being said. He was still thinking about risks to the life of the incumbent. He considered that he should have the last word on all matters involving the little people, 'though it'd take a good shot in this case.'

'I wouldn't know about that,' said Ryle absurdly, 'they're all the same height lying down.'

The other two scratched their danders simultaneously, and both turned for an examination of Ryle's face. Clearly this is an instinct hardwired in the human brain. Despite each subject's ample previous experience to the contrary, each still entertained hope that a scan of the sallow parchment with its pursed mouth and wide set eye holes would be fruitful this time. There was of course no explanation to be seen there.

Fletcher put the painful glasses frames back into the tracks they'd made in his temples and blocked the other two out in the way he had, busying himself by stuffing various bits of papers into his tablet bag and then putting on his hiking boots.

'They don't mind you walking around the office in the socks?' said McLean momentarily distracted. 'Old Mac Gabhann's growl not as bad as his snarl, eh?'

Fletcher, ignoring even more, busy, busy, humming Handel.

'Who have you the money on anyway?' said the visitor guessing. 'You are aware that in PaddyPower's novelty bets they have Bono down at 500 to 1 for everything from the next Pope to scoring the next goal for Man United? You didn't by any chance fall for that? Just because he's listed as a novelty bet doesn't necessarily mean he's expressed an interest in the Presidency even if the shoes would fit him.'

'I don't make sucker bets,' said Ryle untruthfully. 'But good thinking.' He coughed and reached under the luminosity and deeper, under the soft Pakistani lamb sheath. He retrieved the notebook. He turned to a page with a neat list headed, Dangermen. As he added a name with his pencil he said, 'And he'd be harder to shift out if he did sneak in ahead of us as bullets would only slide off him.'

'Ganley then?' said McLean, memories returning of incarcerated nighttime glimpses into the conservative mind of the insomniac on the top bunk.

'No. The candidate is here in this room,' said Ryle.

The roars of laughter echoed as the big roving archaeologist rumbled out through the main building.

'Not me, you clown,' shouted Ryle after him, apparently no longer concerned about letting various cats out of bags in Northumberland Manse proper, 'the other lad here. Be on the ready. Our office will be sending you a bit of bumf. And a few bob for a suit so you can tidy yourself up when it comes time to go around promising to look into Padjoe's suckler payments and showing your face at MaryJo's funeral.' Ryle was thinking on his feet now, putting in the bit of work that would make him worth the Executive Assistant salary. He trotted after the big swinging púca consorter and held onto him, talking fast in crude street voice unknown to Grattan Fletcher, 'And you can let them know a few other things that Fletcher would be too polite to let be said on a newsfeed. If we get a good turnout in that area we'll close the heroin dealerships from Abbeyfeale to Kanturk. Don't say this too loud yet in case other candidates latch on to it for copycat purposes, but the days of bollixes walking free are nearly over. As a thanks to all areas that supported Fletcher and as a downpayment on the following election, the people in those areas can draw up lists. Then there will be dawn raids on the morning after the coronation. Only in those areas. Examples will be made of the unpatriotic locals. Bankers, bouncers, beef barons, bailiffs, big farmers ... Beano readers. You get the picture? Whatever you're having yourself. They'll be taken to the Curragh and shot before any clever lawyers can get involved. That'll paint a clear picture of which side it is profitable to be on. And it will give the illusion to the people that we take care of our own. All we have to do then is keep our man out of the public eye for the seven years and the second term is assured, giving us a fourteen-year run which takes us as near as dogshit to retirement.'

McLean was looking at Ryle, a policy detail question or two floating through his head, no doubt. Maybe he was wondering about the cut-off acreage for being branded a big farmer. But to his shame, like so many of his tribe, he didn't get up quite enough interest in public affairs to ask for any clarification. 'Grand,' he said, shaking the budding axe wielder by the hand. 'I'd better go on, the battery is low in the angle grinder.' McClean generally had to cut off a clamp before he could get clear of Dublin. Why they wanted to keep him is anybody's guess.

'It's as simple as that,' concluded Ryle.

After Ryle returned Fletcher said to him, 'Listen, sit down there a minute.'

Ryle stood looking at him.

'Let's drop the Presidency thing,' he said.

'You're joking now,' said Ryle.

'To be honest, I don't know what silliness came over me the morning I said that to you,' said Fletcher, not a good man for telling a joke, 'But I have since found no way to mention it to anyone other than you. Not even to Margot. There's a message in that. If you can't find words to fit something, then maybe it was never meant to be said.'

Ryle pretended not to be listening.

'Are you hearing me, Len?' said Fletcher. 'It was a dumb momentary capricious notion. One that faded with the very first sally we made forth. Our work must be its own reward. We must look only into our hearts to find courage to help fellow travellers, reject any further reward that is offered not because of some ascetic purity of spirit, but because it would only get in the way.'

Ryle still said nothing.

'I can see you are wondering why I didn't tell you straightaway. I know. It's not fair. I've kept up a deceit for months.'

Ryle was not wondering that particular thing.

'Well, if you must know, it's that I didn't want you to stop coming with me,' said Fletcher, embarrassed to say it. 'I saw that it had a motivating effect on you and I then didn't know how to replace that without losing you from the missions.'

'That's all good,' said Ryle, shutting him down. Little as he was willing to hear of the cold feet, he was much less wanting to hear any further on the theme of Fletcher's other reasons for wanting to be in a car next to him. 'We can sell that story. The reluctant candidate who had to be pushed into it. That will work.'

'No,' said Fletcher. 'It's not a tactic. I won't be going for the Presidency.'

'Indeed, I agree,' said Ryle, 'it might be better to aim for the Senate first.'

'Or the Senate. None of that. Not ever.'

For an instant, recognition flitted across the yellow face and the look that came with it can fairly be described as murderous. Then it was gone again from view. Stored away in the putrefied inner caverns of the man. Without breaking his stare, an unnatural habit he had, Suck Ryle resumed as if nothing had been noted. He soldiered on as any good mentor should do. 'Any tribe is divided into two types. Those who stand up to talk about doing things and those who whine as they do what they're told. You have been picked as one of the former and you can't unpick yourself.'

'I'm serious, my friend, and there it is,' said Grattan, a man who was in fact a specialist at unpicking himself. 'I only ask you to travel with me for its own sake. And I hope you'll still come.'

Eaten bread is soon forgotten

Chapter XXVI

As LUCK ALONE COULDN'T have had it, the next visit from the Gardaí came the day after Fletcher's assignment of his rights to Mac Gabhann.

'We were looking to have a quick chat with Assistant Sectretary G.T. Fletcher,' they said to Ryle, who again happened to make it to the front door first.

'Why?' asked Ryle.

'Are you him?'

'I could be,' said Ryle.

At this juncture in our history the Garda divisions were carefully policing their own turf. Consequently the intelligence that now brought CID was uncontaminated by knowledge from the Traffic Corps or the Crusty Squad. And hence, the guards took this news with only slightly raised eyebrows.

'We'd like you to come down to the station with us,' said the amiable sergeant.

'Why?' asked Ryle.

'Frankly, Mr. Fletcher, you've become a person of interest in the recent death of a colleague of yours,' said the other.

'Not to worry,' assured the sergeant, 'I'm sure that an hour or two will set the entire matter straight.'

'If you're so sure why don't you sort it out yourself.'

'Amusing, Mr. Fletcher,' smiled the sergeant. 'I'd quite happily be doing other things, if you must know. But we have to follow up on tip-offs.'

'*A tip-off eh?* Do you now? I've often given tip-offs and seen no results. Who made the tip-off?'

The sergeant laughed now. 'Well perhaps if you too were a *Secretary General* and friends with the Commissioner, your tips might also result in us being sent on fool's errands, my friend.'

'Mac Gabhann, eh?' noted Ryle.

The obliging sergeant just kept smiling.

'If you're treating every road accident as murder,' observed Ryle reasonably, 'is it any fucking wonder the real cowboys are riding high.'

'*Murder?*' said the junior cop, suddenly taking notes. 'Who said anything about murder?'

The sergeant's demeanour changed too.

'Have you found the Transit?' said Ryle.

'Was it a Transit?' said the suddenly serious sergeant, 'What do you know about the vehicle, sir? I do think you had better come along with us straightaway, Mr. Fletcher.'

'Will I fuck,' said Ryle genuinely. Anything not in his interests was never done by him voluntarily. 'Get a bit of evidence and then come with an arrest warrant. See how well you get on.'

'Make no mistake,' said the sergeant very seriously, 'finding that van has suddenly become a high priority. A Transit you say? We will find it. And when we do, Mr. Fletcher, you will indeed be coming with us, I feel.'

'Tell the commissioner to advise his friend that he'll get a closer look at the next accident that happens round here if he's not careful about the slander,' said Ryle to the men of unnatural forbearance.

With that disturbance put to bed Ryle came back in rubbing his hands. 'We'll need to step up the tempo with the elections. You need to be in power and changing laws sooner than you thought. Get the controls before the controls get you.'

'What have you done now?' asked Fletcher.

'Not a bother,' said Ryle, 'you take care of your end of the campaign and leave me to mine.'

◊

There was a pause in the dialogue for about two hours until Vesty McClaferty walked up the two steps to the return of the manse and spouted out his business like he had been bursting for a piss.

Fletcher called Ryle to come out of the alcove. He had the feeling that this was to be a landmark on his journey. It was the first time someone had actually come looking for their help. The visitor was a freckle faced fellow with a full head of non-descript hair on him and a bit of a belly starting, more noodles than beer by the innocent look of him. He was after losing an uncle-in-law in circumstances some in the family thought unjust. The local TD wouldn't touch them. But some rogue in the Citizen's Information Centre had helped him find the contact information of the man he had heard speaking passionately at an anti-poverty rally in Roscommon town.

Ryle had an instinct on such matters. He could see this chap was hard as the road. Ryle knew the look of a stray dog used to taking care of himself, his eyes flicking back and forth between the men of the return, weighing them up, slow to put trust in either of them. Aside from this unusual insightfulness, there was also the detail that Ryle already knew the chap. 'You should fuck off away with yourself, young McClaferty,' he said, 'you have no business here.' In case his view was not clear, he turned to Fletcher and said, 'Show this chap the door.'

The young lurcher took a step back like you would when someone makes a kick at you.

Fletcher was more gullible about these sorts of things. As if there were no deeper levels of depravity below the one that was immediately below his own.

'I know your father,' said Ryle to him when Fletcher refused to shift him on. 'He's a decent hardworking fellow by the name of Jimmy McClaferty, am I right?'

The look changed from an attitude of belligerence to one of paranoia. 'You're wrong. How do you know that?'

'He has a father who is half settled,' said Ryle turning to Fletcher, 'but still has the heartbeat of a Traveller. He'd tarmac Ireland. He has struck the last blow in a few rows but is rarely accused of striking the first. The chap gawking at us here is probably as innocent as him. But you should have nothing to do with him. Theirs are the kind of problems that are so deep and wide that if you get roped into them you might never re-emerge.

And at the finish there'd be no percentage in it. Not a single vote and they'd still never respect you, only see you as a harmless, softheaded countryman.'

Fletcher's restlessness for road won the day. Soon enough the three of them were in the Lexus heading out the N4. While Ryle tried to rest himself, Vesty edged forward with his thin knees between the seats, confessing to Fletcher.

'My uncle was never down a day in his life,' he started. 'But on Thursday he … On Thursday morning he was got dead in his shed. Even though everything they said about him was lies. It's not fair.'

'Into children, was he?' said Ryle sitting up in disgust.

'No,' said Vesty, 'he makes gates.'

What came out was that the uncle had been getting by until the downturn. He hadn't understood that in such times the tradesman's bill goes to the bottom of the pile. He kept at it, buying trefoils and welding sticks from deposits for new gates. Naturally this scheme saw him falling a bit behind. He wouldn't even let Vesty go out at night to pull down gates and break windows to make examples of defaulters.

Note: the boy had that one right. In a country where nobody respects the law and people behave only under the rules of freewill (there's no country on earth with the possible exception of Sao Tome and Principe in which there is a greater surplus of free will than in this island), you get a good look at how the human being, unconstrained, really wants to behave. And from my own studies on the matter, what is revealed is that it boils down to there being only two types of personality in the world: those who would knock down your door to pay and those who will look for every evasion. The lad was also dead right that you have to set the tone with the latter kind of person. Half the haysheds in Meath have acid holes in their roofs just because their owners thought paint was free. (It is true though that the big men are often the stingiest.) If there is one thing the compiler is good at it is keeping books straight. *The compiler*

Ordinary decent nurses and guards around the country had

deposits paid and granite piers erected only to have to wait and wait for their Victorian-style gates. One of them picked up the phone.

First the uncle had a woman from Revenue visiting. She wanted to see books going back twenty years and told the uncle, who hadn't even a single screed of paper to his name, that she'd be nailing him to the cross. The self-employeds' days of lording it over the likes of her were finally done, she indicated. That had knocked some of the happy-go-luckiness off the man. But a worse blow came when he got a call from Sam Keane of the Sunday Herald. Sam was that paper's indignation investigator and ran a popular column called Builder Scumbags Busted. The same journalist was zealous, needing to put clear water between himself and the decade he had spent as a socialite reporter embedded in a developer's helicopter.

The uncle had tried to explain his side to the journalist who came wearing a cravat. But it touched no sides with the committed convert, a man always fingering the squeezed middle for a pulse. When the uncle had turned to straight pleading and crying like a baby, Vesty had finally walked out in disgust on the man who had taught him to weld spearheads onto box iron. An hour after the paper came out Uncle John Joe took the gun to himself.

Nobody bats an eye these days. There is no give left in people.

Ryle, a man who had never had much give to give up, was sitting quietly thinking that not even Fletcher would imagine there was anything could be done with this kettle of fish. They'd be heading straight back to Dublin after dropping this sad lad home.

It seemed that the chap himself began to reach the same realization as they ate into the road. With the repeated recounting of the situation, he was starting to hear the concluded reality of it himself. Eventually he stopped dredging up further details of the wrong and sat back into himself with wrinkling lips, starting to digest its whole.

'So what did you have in mind?' said Fletcher awkwardly, seeing the boy slipping away and trying to bring him back on board, 'I mean we'll get stuck in whatever you'd like for us to do, won't we, Len.'

Vesty was hardly twenty and, brought up in a loving family, had still somehow thought the worst wrongs could be sorted out. He had made the trip to Dublin because he had thought he might get away with fighting instead of grieving. Doing something instead of sitting around moping. He had never grieved before and he had been running away from it. Now though he was gone quiet.

'You should slip the old seat belt on you there like a good man,' said Ryle, when he was satisfied that Vesty was staying sat back. 'Our chief here got the license the year of the amnesty.'

◊

'I'm starting to get a funny feeling,' said Fletcher, driving back.

'Let me be clear,' interrupted Ryle, 'I do not fucking want to know about that.'

'A feeling,' continued Fletcher fighting off a tone that was alien to his voice, a fearful, maudlin quaking. It was very late and they had just escaped after a night spent sitting on a hard bench in a snug council house, shaking hands with a stream of people all of whom they had to be introduced to. To make conditions for maintenance of a sweet easy disposition even less favourable, it was the kind of winter evening that can strip the firmest mind bare. There wasn't another car on the road. Walls of freezing hail swept the countryside leaving no place for illusions of nature having any care or even benign intention for us. Even with the foglights on they had hardly ten metres of visibility. The track shuffler app picked "The Streets of Philadelphia" from Fletcher's phone. Sounds of blood in veins, black rains, and vanished friends suddenly haunted the car.

Such conditions could spring no surprises on the routinely low-spirited, such as Leonard Ryle. However, a spritely soul such as that ordinarily possessed by Grattan Fletcher, can be caught with his sails open. This glimpse of eternal reality was not a visage he was equipped for. 'I am suddenly feeling that for every step I take, every effort I make to stand with people against the worst, I am being stalked, closed in upon, by … by …' He stopped.

'By death?' said Ryle, the better grounded. 'Well what the fuck did you expect?'

'Suffering, is what I was going to say,' said Fletcher.

And this foreboding, I should note, was even before the second visit to the convent. And before anything happened to himself. That of course is how foreboding should occur.

This was not perhaps the best time for Ryle to have brought up the image that he was now waving in front of Fletcher. But he was of that type who could not restrain himself from small bursts of celebration on the occasion of a triumph. He had done an image search from his half-smart phone and he couldn't wait for a better time to show the peculiar results. Not even fear of distracting Fletcher's eyes from the ten visible metres in front could restrain him. 'Come here,' he said, 'who does this remind you of?'

Fletcher didn't need to say. He knew that Ryle had got to this picture by searching the photos he had removed from the house in Letterkenny. Some clever cloud program had found the same image on a Republican Facebook page. And there, alongside Dandy Henderson, was an image of the woman whose brown bread Fletcher had eaten a few days back. At least twenty years younger, but unmistakably the same eyes and smile.

'Nice woman,' said Fletcher.

'You think?' Ryle continued, eager to get to his point. 'Helen Kelly is her name.'

'Fine,' said Fletcher not wishing Ryle to see that he retained any interest.

'*Fine?* said Ryle. 'Yes, fine. You know what it says about her, then?'

'Nothing can change my view of her. They were young in a different universe. The horrors of their time were part of a shock wave across Europe, just as previous uprisings had international momentum behind them. '98, The Fenians, 1916 … terrible beauties more terrible than beautiful. Even in that, the most isolationist of us is more connected to the rest of humanity than he thinks. We …'

'Shut the fuck up,' Ryle said. 'You really don't know, then? You are right about the different universe part, *Volunteer Helen*

Kelly, 23 Mar 1965 – 21 Mar 1983, executed by British SAS.'

Fletcher was overtaken by a slight shake and they had to pull in, him asking Ryle to take over the driving. He gaped at Ryle with various questions.

'No, she is unlikely to have got away,' said Ryle with some authority. They were stopped with one front wheel on the hard shoulder and the other three still on the road. 'As shown in the movie made for a Raoul something or other on the SAS. That is a unit renowned for being extremely prejudiced. They turned down applications from solid men with neutral feelings on all matters …' Ryle remembered himself, and corrected, 'So I've been told by a 'tan I met once in Belfast.'

Fletcher just looked at him with the pleading eyes of the drowning. 'Will you drive us back,' he asked eventually, 'I'm a bit dizzy.'

'Fifty-seven bullets it says here,' Ryle was pulling up another website as he climbed across the gear stick, Fletcher having come around the car in the relentless spills. 'Two less than in Dandy Henderson and ten more than in the third one ambushed. There have always been rumours that a fourth person escaped while the soldiers concentrated on emptying their clips.'

'Must have been a twin,' said Fletcher.

'With the same first name?' said Ryle, not in the habit of leaving defeated opponents any room for interpretative escape. 'And her an only child? Whatever you think yourself, boss.'

Fletcher lost all colour, a big lot of loss for him. He pushed himself back in his seat. He made a repeating click like he was trying to clear his nose.

Ryle switched on the car radio for them to be told that ebola had shown up in West Africa and there was nothing being done. Mention was made of orphans, poverty, and indifference. This may have been what tweaked Fletcher's parasympathetic orifices and made him yield to a good cry. Everything has a context.

'But don't worry,' said Ryle, not liking this turn of events. 'Eaten bread is soon forgotten.'

It did no good.

'Best we get you back to your *lovely life*,' said Ryle presently with an air of conclusion.

All that glitters is not gold

Chapter XXVII

GRATTAN THE INDEFATIGABLE. Surely it would not be far-fetched for us to brand him thus at this stage in the account. When Ryle rocked up in the return the morning after the wretched wake, he was not expecting to see more than a shadow. He had no doubt that the unfortunate events of yesterday had permanently derailed his candidate.

Ryle had never accepted any of Fletcher's previous resignations from the race. He had been thinking that when the time came to submit the application form it would only take a bit of cajoling to set the train back on track. Failing that, blackmail or some other sort of browbeating would not have been far beneath Ryle's reach.

But since leaving him in Rathmines at five thirty this morning, all expectation of an electoral bounce back was flushed from Ryle's mind. Fletcher had sat shaking icily for the entire journey back to Dublin. Ryle had scraped the wing of the Lexus on bollards in Athlone and pulled the exhaust on speed ramps in Santry without succeeding in getting a rise out of the man. On entering Lower Rathmines Road, he had asked Fletcher to tell him again the stupid theory about how the accent of ordinary Dubs had retained a truer rendering of the place name, Rath de Moines. Fletcher had still just stared blankly. And when Ryle had stooped, after stopping, to asking Fletcher to remind him yet again how he'd managed to reinstate the original cornicing on the gable façade of his angular home, Fletcher had just given one or two sobs. Ryle had instructed the sorry state of a man to go inside and take aspirins to see if that would thicken his blood up a bit. And Ryle had then gone home planning to wash hands of Fletcher, perceiving him to be suffering from his nerves. Ryle had no time for that kind of thing.

Yet, in the here and now, Ryle was most pleasantly surprised to see that the show was most resoundingly still on the road. The road from the arse to the Áras. For it was no broken wreck sitting at the desk with the Irish Times spread in front of him, literally twiddling his thumbs (something Ryle had never seen elsewhere in real life). 'Here Len,' Fletcher said, so near recovered that Ryle could only conclude there was something extra magical in that lovely life, some potion that Margot was administering, something new under the sun and therefore a valid unemotional justification for Ryle resuming his plans to have a little sup of her. All good news.

'Here my friend, while I've been sitting here waiting for you, I read this email from Daly.' Though Fletcher was near recovered, there was still a wobble in the voice. With that Ryle knew to expect an appetite for conversation that was loose and wide-ranging, that is to say, deranged. Ryle, the semi-loyal, decided it best to humour this. I won't serve it all up to you but I'll dish up a fair bit of it as it goes to my case. Any little man who could sit through this kind of pontification from a person who was never appointed an editor of any sort, surely could not have been all bad.

'You know it's never good to read Daly's mail,' said Ryle. 'Is he still on the manchild gig or has he moved on?'

'Listen to this … *the management female hams the role of Fredericka Flinstone, like 1950s suitboy, enlarging herself by diminishing subordinates and publicly belittling her husband, tied to her now only by a marriage contract that will take his children if he leaves. The new woman is told she can have all through lethal control and that a day will never come when she herself will need loyal cherishing. So the loyal man becomes a stooge in her drama. Feminism falling like many noble movements into creating grotesque reflections of the caricatured enemy …* He's a bold brat. What is it about me that he presumes he can send his stuff to me, his supposed manager? What makes him so sure I won't rap him over the knuckles?'

'What indeed,' observed Ryle wryly.

'But I suppose even a crank sometimes makes one or two

points worth noting,' said Fletcher too kindly, and continued reading, '... *80% of sitcoms and TV ads casually portray men as infantile and light-headed, in tow to strong sensible women* ... I don't watch TV. Is that true Len?'

'Boo fucken hoo,' said Ryle. 'So advertisers know their audience. Tell Daly he was not employed by us for the use of his brain.'

'Fair women don't buy that, I'm sure,' said Fletcher.

'Fair women,' drifted Ryle.

'What about this one ... *gender balance is a National concern – only where the balance is not already tilting against males. So, balance no longer required in education, health, law, public administration, and most levels of management.* A little overwrought.'

'What? Women doing all the management?' said Ryle. 'Of course. That was always going to happen. What planet does Daly think he was born in? Don't tell me whatever little scrap of farm or sweet shop his people crawled out of weren't run by his grandmothers. The women always did the management jobs in this country and left the little bit of directing to a couple of men and the whole lot of dirty work to all the rest of the boys. The women always managed the morals too while the few top men argued about the theology. Who do you think it was asked for adulteresses to be stoned and hookers to be hung out to dry?'

'The latter at least touches an interesting point, if I understand you,' rambled Fletcher aimlessly. 'I take it you support the argument that there's a whiff of a new establishment morality here? An implied prejudice that all males and only males are capable of enjoying and benefiting from casual intimacies. Or alternatively that an overriding imperative to protect trafficked workers rings hollow unless it also calls for prosecution of customers at Bangladeshi restaurants. A long day's argument indeed. But let me say this for now. I'm really just interested to hear you defend sex workers. I wouldn't have put you down as a client. Then I suppose, you do have a lonely private life ...'

'Would you ever fuck off,' said Ryle in genuine revulsion. 'Don't presume you know the first fucking thing about my real life and do not ever make any enquiries. You'll be a very sorry little fucking soldier. Also, I never in my long life looked sideways at a hooker.' This part was true. Private though Ryle had been, he had always managed to forage for himself and never felt the slightest urge to pay someone to pretend they liked him. This was not a matter of pride or prejudice. It was that he perceived that a relationship with a prostitute would entail too many expectations. Not least objectionable amongst these, the expectation of him parting with money.

'Oh dear, a touchy subject, eh?' said Fletcher.

'And what's more, the matriarchy were the ones who selected the soft mammy's boys to run the church for them too. They're not getting out from under that. And then they were the ones on Sunday mornings shouting at the bottom of the stairs to wake every normal man, woman, and child out of their beds at unnatural hours to go look at the same soft boys standing on the altar all dressed up in robes embroidered for them by the same mammies.'

'So families' management losses are capitalism's gains kind of thing?' said Fletcher, giving too much credit. 'That would be your take?'

'What else would you expect. There's no hop in managing families anymore. The women had to move on.'

'What about this then, have I had my head in the sand ... he claims sixty-four percent of the students at my alma, my old university, are women? That can't be correct. Did you know that? Is the school system now that tilted against lads? What does that tell you?'

'That university is still a den of pussies?' said Ryle, who while never moving to the newer theory that universities are where the reptilian overlords finally colonize the minds of the weak, yet had never abandoned his traditional disdain for college boys nor his distrust of the motives behind liberal education.

So, unhindered, Fletcher continued his watery meander, dismissing several other outrages enumerated by Daly until he got to one about family. 'And here, he quotes Geldof on family courts. Is there not at least something of the law of unintended consequences at work in marriage legislation?'

'Agreed. Only clowns get married,' said Ryle. 'Nothing new there.'

'Jesus. That's not what I'm saying at all,' said Fletcher, and then darted off into middle space. 'In marriage as in any friendship you just need to be with someone who likes you and not someone who is competing with you or resenting you. Every time you falter you need someone who will pick you up, not someone who's been waiting for you to fail. I can honestly say I haven't regretted a minute of it.'

'Is that how Margot sees it, eh?' asked Ryle casually. 'There's always one party with regrets, so I'm told. It's not today or yesterday they came up with the old saying, marry and be happy for a week, kill a pig and be happy for a month …' Ryle stopped short, leaving out the last bit of that particular old saying. He was circumspect when it came to advertising the location of his own goldmines.

Note: credit where it's due, Ryle was an extraordinary technician in certain aspects of horticulture. The cutthroat world of snow drop growing for example was divided down the middle in relation to L.C. Ryle and his winning exhibits. Some looked with innocent awe upon his arrival from nowhere to the position of total dominance in all competition. The more canny looked murderously, aware that the rare *giant galanthus anastasia* and the elongated *krasnovii* bulbs had not been dropped in his garden by magpies. And they certainly had not been given to him by any of themselves. Furthermore, though they didn't know enough about Ryle's other nocturnal roles to suspect him fully of the yellowing of their own gardens each spring, there was a primitive instinct to blame the only competitor who appeared to have no difficulty with Roundup drift. *The compiler*

'Good old Ryle, unflappable,' said Fletcher, touching his back again. Ryle's flesh crawled a little more than usual. 'I'd been thinking the episodes yesterday might have knocked you off kilter and that I'd maybe lose you from our expeditionary exploits.'

'*What!*' said Ryle, truly knocked for words. 'You were thinking *I was the one a bit knocked!* You're shitting me.'

'Are we even leaving any space for boys to become the men we ask them to be?' Fletcher wandered again. 'I'm starting to think that in my anger with the father of my grandchild, thirty-two years old and his life still not gone beyond his Xbox, weed, and his futile "shift and drift" bravado, I have been blinded.'

'So you've been sneaking an old look up the PUA and incel websites, eh?' said Ryle, who kept a wary eye out for what the younger men were doing to get sex, those who still wanted it.

'What is that?' said Grattan, flapping. 'No. Feminism is the closest I've been to any ism. And so I remain. [fn] Being born girl, gay, darker or … or whatever, shouldn't mean you have to wait till people get over themselves and decide they are finally ready to give you the full light of day. Remember the sad lines of Forster. *They said in their hundred voices, "No, not yet."* Choice in our lives is the privilege of our freedom. The key dispensation of liberty unavailable to most in our past and still most in our present world, is the simple right to seem as you are. Not as others wish you were. Your chance on earth is gone in a flash and having to hesitate means losing out. It's just that I always saw feminism merely as a necessary tool for the journey. Like Black Consciousness on the road to non-racialism, a counter-prejudice, invoked as a corrective expedient, as a device for crashing barricades extant and internalized. But never as a destination. It seems to me, a wave of young men pushed to the peripheries is also not what was wanted by anyone genuinely in search of fairness …'

[fn] Footnote
As a publishing house we would like to distance ourselves from the compiler's blatantly patronizing sops to the feminist critique. We are only too well aware that there is no review from any school of feminism that would ever in a million years flatter any aspect of this publication other than the limits of its distribution. As you will have realized if you have made it this far, all women in this diatribe are divided into good and bad, as in any bog-standard patriarchally incepted discourse. Here the good are crudely turned into nurturing and hapless figures. The bad woman is mown down by a van. One is only glad to have avoided the compiler's endeavours in the field of female portraiture. But we are where we are. *The Editors*

'I never saw the benefit in that,' practical experience muttering its way out of Ryle. 'Following the feminists, I mean. Granted, a box is a box and I prefer the raw woman. But the feminist can be lacking in respect for a man telling her he wishes he could feel her pain. You must remember, the only man who gets a foothold in that kind of person's thoughts is a right prick. Being vagina-envy-boy can amount to a thankless two days of door holding and sympathizing, waiting in vain for her to consider giving you a little comfort.'

'Do you ever look at any kind of person without your first thought being of what you'd like to get from them?' asked Fletcher irritated but only momentarily sidetracked from his homily. 'But we can't level the tables by turning them. The cult pursuit of products and services that has hijacked our civilization is agnostic. The equal *right* to work has been quietly hijacked by the *pressure* to. The call to full workforce participation marches on and the right now is to freeze eggs and to equally tend the spreadsheets. It is anti-woman and anti-society. The richness and intangibles get eroded ever further, even below the nuclear family level now, to solitary system-serving protons with friend circles managed around lifestyle products, the new social construct. Diminishing any working person who decreases their purchasing potential by staying home to mind children or their elderly, even if that's what their heart yearns to do. Only the wealthy, above the system, or poor, disregarded by it, are free to do that without sacrifice. No pat on the back for loyalty to a partner who is failing. No recognition for taking time to do things for your neighbours or friends when they need help. Friendship in a manager is weakness. Empathy succumbed to is tantamount to standing aside. Tending where you're needed puts you in breach rather than in credit. Squashing people who have non-commercial ideas or voices is TV entertainment. Prioritizing anything outside of career will get you whispered about. What is respected, only, is *self*-fulfilment, achieving personal goals, getting your *self* ahead. Other cultures like the one we're losing at least placed premium value on feminine roles and those who cared and nurtured were respected deeply. Unjustly those societies prescribed that each and every woman act these roles. And that only women could act them. But capitalism unharnessed will always tap into the lifeblood of societies it is supposed to serve. Instead of removing the prescriptions about who could take on the central roles of nurturing family and community, those roles were dialled right down in value, thus activating a whole new army of earning spenders. And if feminism has made any mistake in battle weariness, it is in accepting this as a milestone of victory. After a battle against *having to* express nurturing traits, *wishing to* express them also got diminished. Each now is encouraged to shout louder than the next person. So each can become equal and unhappy and lonely and buy more.'

'I see what you're on about now,' said Ryle, 'it's gone the way that only the gay man can show off the bit of femininity and flaunt the desire to be a homemaker these days. They're fairly good at it too, I believe. You should consider striking up with one of them. I wouldn't say Margot would mind as she's not the type would be much good around the house.'

'Excuse me!'

'I'm just saying. You could keep it plutonic,' mused Ryle. 'Anyway. But isn't the country a lot better off as a result of all the things you think are wrong?'

'What does it profit a society if it gains the whole world and loses its soul ...' continued Fletcher.

'Mother of god,' said Ryle.

'OK, sorry. But I do truly believe a society without nurture at the centre of everything can be no good to anyone in the end. We are responsible. We should be forcing the values we want, not leaving it to mindless commerce. We should be placing hard value on the more soft-spoken qualities that we want restored. The solution is not in trying to jimmy all education and State employment towards counter-swings. That is not facing the problem but introducing new exclusions.'

'Nearly everything you are saying now, for once in your life, is just common sense,' said Ryle. 'Loyalty is for mugs. They say the reward for disloyalty is loneliness, as if being left alone is lonely. Men and women are not, on average, the same. And if the attempts to level them get serious it will take the good out of them both. But you can't be saying these kinds of thing out in public. It never pays to tell voters the truth about themselves.'

'What? That is not what I was saying at all, not one scrap of it,' said Fletcher, to whom appeals to common sense were like a fire alarm. 'All I'm saying is that there's danger of getting blinded in battle. We only further delay our arrival at de Beauvoir's humble appeal for men and women to move beyond their natural differentiations so as to unequivocally affirm each other. The young people deserve better leadership from us. How many families will lose sons to this?'

'*Deserve?* What good is that to anyone? Those women who have moved into the mahogany long ago realized that whining on about rights is just loser juice. Like in 1984 where the people turned into pigs and so on. The woman who gets power will abuse it,' Ryle said, now that they were into territory where his opinions were as wide-ranging as those of any college boy. 'What else would she do? That's what you get power for. You rile people up about their rights so they kick out the old fellow and put you in charge of abusing them instead. Power always makes itself heard and somehow people are disappointed every time it does. Don't tell me you thought that women would be nicer?'

'Actually,' said Grattan, 'yes I did, and I do.'

'Fucksake, I thought you believed in equality. Were there no girls where you went to school?'

'Granted, there are those who share your cynical view of human governance.' said Fletcher, 'that the only model is to infiltrate it like a Marxist and then run it like a Stalinist. But I never gave an ear to weak men whispering secret knowledge about women, so why now would I respect conspiratorial whispers between women? I believe we are all capable of better.'

'I'm glad you're talking again,' said Ryle. 'I am indeed. However, I am worried about what is coming out of your mouth. How am I ever going to harden you for the job that lies ahead?' said Ryle. 'I strongly advise you not to get your knickers twisted on this matter. The few males like myself that get on well in their chosen activities will always be well served by the head women who just want a seat at the top table. They want to bear in on the man at the top. As you've finally noticed, family is fucked, so now Obama, the Zuckerburgs, and the Cowells are the great patriarchs—the ones it pays to mind and manage.'

'Well you certainly won't be thanked for minding women,' said Fletcher.

'Indeed I won't,' said Ryle. 'I don't mind them at all. Smart, relentless movers, what else would they do only reposition ruthlessly. That way they control the few lunatics tearing around at the top, working night and day for a bit of praise. Meanwhile they settle their work-life balance and count out exact change at Aldi. Nothing new. Just like of old. Wasn't the warlord Niall of the nine sausages courted by the eight great-great-grandmothers of your lowbred Irish people? And once seated at the top table those bossy bean-an-tís, leaning in on their front man, got the boys sent off fighting wars to identify the two percent of next-generation alphas, leaving the surplus to rob cattle, follow sheep around the hills, and flail their willies to within an inch of their lives. Just like today. Every female can be a woman if she wants to but being a man is enjoyed by only a few males. The rest just get run ragged. It's all written in the book of nature and we don't have to blame ourselves for that. Just go with it, boss, would be my recommendation.'

'With all due respect,' said Fletcher, distracted, 'that kind of pop evolutionism or whatever that is, is just cop-out. Brothers and sisters pitted against each other is the worst kind of civil war imaginable. Surely we can't afford the distraction when all of humanity faces challenges needing us all to work together. Gender-based solidarity set above natural relationships based on intellect, temper, or spirit is unsustainable because it represents a cleft in humanity. What was it that charming Afrikaner Pik Botha said in a fleeting wisdom? It doesn't matter if you shoot a zebra in the black meat or the white meat, it will surely die.'

Ryle's stomach grumbled loud.

'Actually … That's … Not forgetting,' said Fletcher, as he always did when starting a new sidetrack.

'For fucksake,' said Ryle getting desperate, 'I'll even go to fucking Carlow with you if you'll just shut your gob. Put on that jacket there like a good man, the wind outside is after turning harsh again.'

'Not forgetting ... I can't remember what I was going to say. But tell me this, my friend, do you think the grim certainties endured by most of the poor world have been displaced by a happier dispensation in the case of our privileged boys and girls? That ours are really so much better off than people who never get to contemplate any right beyond bare survival?' said Fletcher, wandering wantonly onwards.

Ryle let the Fletcher stream continue. '... Everyone dutifully seeks to be indulged, to get the most for themselves. In the new amorphism of social and personal roles, the more basic want is unmet. To have a sure role in your community and to be loved without qualification in your family.'

'Indeed,' said Ryle, thinking a bit of mutton would be just up his street for lunch today, 'is it any wonder the women are all turning to Islam? Now Angela Merkel, there's a fine woman who got on well, fair play. There's a good buffet in Kilcullen, I believe.'

'A corollary,' said Fletcher, 'of self-reward being accepted by us as the overriding virtue – the art of giving love has been lost by many. Replaced only by a search for ephemeral reciprocity of flattery and epithelial stimulation. And the maths dictate that if there are a lot of us out there who only want to receive love but don't know how to give, very few are going to receive it and very many are condemned to a longing they can't name. Such thoughts sometimes make me sad for our children.'

'Your cousin didn't lick the Redemptorist genes off the pavement, then.' said Ryle. 'Don't fucking worry a bit about them. They can take care of themselves, no happier than any generation before them, would be my opinion.'

'Seriously though, Len,' said Fletcher, unfathomably still not having noticed that Ryle was never anything other than serious, 'the rich and harder to win reward of family, responsibility and bigger love are being forfeited without note. Can there be something like the slow food movement for love?'

'The problem of the spoilt child is as old as the hills,' Ryle turned on him. 'The 1.3-child policy just means we are now overrun by little empresses and emperors.'

'A rather abrupt put-down of a whole generation, don't you feel?' said Fletcher, an only child.

'I wouldn't worry a bit about them. Just keep expecting nothing from them.'

'Maybe in a broader sense I see what you're getting at though, Len,' said Fletcher, still talking rather liberally. 'So in a globalized society everyone in the West is like the Victorian ascendency, some poorer than others but all lording it over serfs and tenant classes kept out of sight now in faraway countries instead of in neighbouring slums. Kept locked in the undeveloping world through bullying trade deals, inferior education, intellectual property strangleholds, debt entrapment, and naval blockades. That's what you're saying? And that in *the West* we're *all* indulged to some degree. All navel-gazing like the later Victorians?'

'You'd make fucking vegetable soup out of bulrushes,' said Ryle. 'No, all spoilt, is all. Most don't even have the excuse of a single drop of landlord blood in their veins.'

'But I don't accept that an entire class or Nation can suddenly become narcissistic,' said Fletcher, half listening. 'The innate need in the majority of any community to give and share and to build others doesn't go away just because it's been untended.'

'All that glitters is not gold,' said Ryle mildly, still nervous that yesterday's gnashing of teeth could resume at one wrong word from him. That was a sound he could do without for a while.

'What do you mean?' said Fletcher. 'What has that to do with anything?'

'Strike while the iron is still hot,' added Ryle. 'A bird in the hand.'

'Well, yes,' said Fletcher doubtfully, 'I suppose. So you see where I'm coming from?'

He was talking to the wrong person. 'For fucksake,' said Ryle, still in conversational tones, 'you know, they berate the likes of myself for pulling the ladder up after me? Sooner or later, boss, you too will have to decide. Do you take the primary pleasures due to the winner or settle for the dung-warm pleasure of whining in solidarity with the rest – imagining they'd do the same for you if the tables were turned. Just ask your feminist friends about that one.'

'You don't care?' said Fletcher infuriated. 'Not even when the system is so broken that neither women nor men can find their way and when many people are feeling they're not wanted, they're surplus; to the point even that ending it all seems the only respite?'

Ryle continued picking his teeth with a fingernail. After some time he took his fingers from his mouth to examine a chunk of breakfast bacon that he had speared, and said, 'Everyone dies at least once. When he runs out of road it's a matter for the individual whether he closes his eyes to wait for nature or does away with himself.'

'There are times, Leonard Ryle, when I find it hard to still believe that there is someone decent lost to us behind your defensive shield of cynicism,' said Fletcher. 'Times that I declare to Christ, I can't help thinking you are actually a wholly deplorable human being with not a single decent thing that can be said about you. Will you go and see if you can get a van?'

'You think that's bad,' said Ryle, putting on the yellow jacket, 'but it's neither good nor bad. It's just how things are.'

Fletcher left the return in a huff, making out he had people to talk to in the mainstream sectors of the building.

Ryle took the opportunity to sit into Fletcher's Inbox and opened Daly's mail. He clicked Reply.

A Chara,

Stop your whining. If you want to fix your problem with women, get lessons from my vice executive, Mr. L.C. Ryle. In the meantime if you have no work to do, meet V.E. Ryle in the basement at 5 pm. He always finds work for idle hands. Do not ever bother me again.

Is mise,

GT Fletcher

Note: I'll grant that Ryle continues to periodically exhibit some depression of empathy levels. However, I'm around long enough to know that being accused of having a narcissistic disorder doesn't make you a bad person. It's not what you think of doing but what you do that defines you. It's the consummation that marks only a few NPDs as full-blown sociopaths, stallions rather than colts in the world of the uncaring. Only amongst this select group should we look for the true source of pure evil—what other population would he rationally hide out in? Getting sympathy from progressive psychologists who believe he suffers a lonely misunderstood anguish, and facilitation from admirers. Suspicions may fall on enlisted men like Suck Ryle every day of the week. It's up the ranks you find the root. Don't take your eye off Charles Smyth at this stage. *The compiler*

The abyss staring back

Chapter XXVIII

WHEN FLETCHER JOINED A GROUP marching from his alma mater to Spencer Dock in the Financial Services Centre one glorious autumn day in early winter, he walked with his head held high in the thin blue air like a person lacking a worry in the world.

'What was that you were saying the other day?' Ryle asked him loudly, pissed off at having to drag spare placards along the ground for the group. Ryle's scrupulous memory cells, a curse to himself and all around him, 'Weren't you giving out about *bias reversal in education* and *dubious gender advocacy masters* being printed like pamphlets in Trinity?'

The young women who led looked sideways at Fletcher. But this didn't make them any more suspicious of the support of two misfits than they had already been. They all continued inclusively on their way to their day out.

Ryle had never marched so close to the sin of despondency. He slumped under a glass building watching the self-conscious alternative circulate with bold banter outside the temple of Price, Waterhouse, and Cooper, a curiosity to those coming and going about their business in suits.

To surmise from the posters and chants, the great young humanities-immersed luminaries, and Fletcher, were there to call out the great young engineers who had recently gone over to financial services. Not to design the robots and antibodies they'd dreamt of as boys, but to design shelters, skimmers, and siphons, apparently.

No good would come of it.

As Fletcher's familiars from TV6 arrived, Ryle walked across the quay road causing car and van brakes to yelp and a congestion to be reported on the air. He went to stand at a recently cut limestone bollard. There, he looked at the choppy dock water for a while without comment. Presently he took off his patent Italian shoes. He took off his luminous jacket. He had the presence of mind to transfer his mobile and wallet from his trousers to the inner pocket of his lamb leather jacket with the notebook. He took that jacket off too and folded it with careful fondness and placed it on top of the other jacket and shoes. Mercifully, he stopped the undressing there. He tucked his white shirt neatly and straightened his paisley tie. He then leapt into the high tide.

The splash caused no stir as all eyes were on the camera at the other side. Eventually the captain of a yacht came over to ask if anyone knew the man who had just disappeared. The horrible reality that falsely dawned on Fletcher as his eyes followed the captain's pointing finger to the neat little pile of leather and luminosity on the other side of the road, caused his cheeks to go cold. His blood stagnated with horror. He bounded across the road with traffic having to brake again. When the TV people saw the Maltese flag on the yacht, the camera was put down.

Fletcher didn't have the sense of Ryle. He just dived straight in, overcoat, shoes, phone, and all. He was an elegant diver, let it be said. But after he came up to the surface he duly started to sink again as the sports shoes and clothing became sodden and heavy. His flailing began to look pointless.

A tall one of the women threw down her placard and ran after Fletcher, stripping a heavy overcoat and other layers to surprised eyes as she went. Revealing herself as one of those compelled to go around hidden in plain clothes, as the only way she could reject the burden of being admired, desired, or despised for the accident of her physical appearance. All that was left of her was just a slip of a person with short black hair and a little white face. She dropped the sarong and kicked off the crocs. In her pink knickers and orange t-shirt she did for a man whom she didn't know and didn't trust, what Fletcher had been considered mad to do for a man he did know: she dived in to where Fletcher was struggling. The darling creature had the flapping fool brought to a buoy rope at the side of the media mogul's yacht within a few minutes. Suits, protesters, and presenters alike, applauded from the retaining chains.

Even coughing dirty Dublin water from every pore, Fletcher resisted efforts to pull him out. He clung to the rope and just kept sticking his head under to see if he could make Ryle out.

'Come now, Grattan,' said the young woman, staying with him in case he let go again. 'Your friend is gone. Don't follow.'

Grattan was silent and unsmiling, unrecognizable. He looked at her blankly.

'*When you look into the abyss ...*' she whispered.

Grattan came to and looked at her properly. 'Yes, quite. I'm sorry,' he said, his mind returning to dry land. 'Thank you so much.'

Yet it took another fifteen minutes before Fletcher could be persuaded to leave the water physically. He shivered as he crossed the yacht but refused a beach towel offered through one of the cabin windows. Back on the pier he tried to look sensible as he stood next to the girl, them both wrapped in gym towels, physical produce of financial services people, and steadied himself against the bollard, still gazing down.

The divers and the coastguard were getting geared to grapple for the body when a fresh faced chap of the suits, red hair cut short, asked, 'What's that?' He was pointing towards the South side. 'There's something moving on the water.'

'It's just a rat,' said one of the divers, expertly. 'They get big in these parts.'

Still and all, Fletcher, the girls, and some of the boys went across the Samuel Beckett bridge. It was not too far and it was a next thing to do.

'Fucken A,' said the red lad, getting ahead, 'I knew that was no rat.'

He was right indeed. It was nothing at all but the top of Ryle's head, covered in muck and swimming the estuary in large circles as happy as an otter. The bit of exercise had cooled him off and he was very relaxed, in no hurry at all to come out on the other side of things. Of course he did in time. What choice had he? And the days carried on as they always do.

Blood from a stone

Chapter XXIX

RYLE ENTERED HIS ALCOVE one morning only to come smartly out again and smack Fletcher on the back of the head, 'If you wanted me to get you Benadryl, you only had to ask, gobshite.'

Fletcher looked at him in bewilderment, he never having accepted Ryle's offer of a bottle for the journey. Ryle returned then, satisfied that it wasn't Fletcher who'd prized all his drawers open and messed things around. He rooted through each drawer again. All things bar one, disturbed. His cordless drill and his master key to every OPW heritage site were in the middle drawer instead of the top. His Slim Panatellas and open bag of liquorish all sorts, the other way. The CD with shop security dongle still in place was cast contemptuously on the floor with the cover cracked—a lesser man might have taken this personally. That disc contained Lynott and Moore playing Parisienne Walkways and was a memento from the last time Ryle had bothered pretending to have musical taste (excepting the periods of weakness for Shakira and Belle). In fact the only thing that was conspicuously left back in its exact right place was the rude little memory stick; you'll recall the dildo, that from which all of this flows. It rested in perfect innocence within the paperclip recess of the top drawer, reinforcing Ryle's suspicions that this wasn't earth tremor damage.

What would make a person of Mac Gabhann's calculating intelligence take this kind of risk? If you'd seen footage of a gnarly person you didn't know, reclining in your office, smiling at your cameras, arhythmically cracking the beading of your cherry desk with the leg of a chair, would you not do a lot of careful research and plan three times before launching a counter attack? After that process, surely you would not come up with the conclusion that best remedy entailed risking getting caught vandalizing, in return, that man's worthless little melamine desk and rifling through his bric-a-brac? What would make you think there might be something worth investigating on a sticky memory stick owned by such a man? All in all I think you'll agree that the rashness of these antics suggest panic. And the confused mental state can only have had one cause: belated realization of the existence of Ryle. Having blanked his mind for years to the other malign presence, Mac Gabhann was now seeing the little man everywhere. It was bad enough that he had formed some association with Fletcher. Worse that he'd been appearing in Mac Gabhann's office at night. But what troubled Mac Gabhann most immediately was the thought Ryle was on to him. That the intruding rodent had spotted Fletcher's castle folders stacked neatly on top of his stationery cabinet before they'd gone back to the basement; that Ryle had taken some evidence. Even with the IP rights signed over, Mac Gabhann was still intending to say that any similarities with Fletcher's work were coincidental. As it happens, Ryle was blind to heavy folders. But there was no way Mac Gabhann could have known that.

Ryle took the notebook and pencil from his inner jacket pocket and wrote a little note. He put the memory stick into his pocket. He said no more about it. He was the kind of card player who liked to do his own dealing. He left the locks as they were and headed out with Fletcher, who was a little puzzled when Ryle turned in the front garden and with a stretch looked boldly up toward the top windows showing a twist of teeth that might pass for a smile. Ryle rarely looked up.

Soon he and Fletcher were on the road again as if nothing had happened.

To where? Not to Westmeath this time. Off their own bats, Grattan and the Trinity woman who had pulled him out of the Liffey had recently got themselves in deeper, involved with a dangerous element. 'The Lost Ten Thousand,' they and the three other founding members were calling themselves. They were united in concern for the generation between theirs; those in their fourth decades who were being allowed to sink without a sound. The debt epidemic had been most virulent amongst the economically active with young families.

Everybody knows who it was that lost. In new homes of newly-weds and recently returneds the chocolates and roses stopped dead seven years back. Appalling tales of tumbled down promises unfolded untold behind the tarnished doors. That's how it goes. Everybody knows.

Grattan had been meeting this group off the books at night unbeknownst to Ryle (or to ourselves).

That morning, out of the blue, it blew up in Ryle's face. Their daily drive had brought them to a halt in front of a saluting man in a safari hat.

'I don't go in for pitch and putt,' lied Ryle as they drove through the great castellated nineteenth-century folly at the start of the winding driveway to the dour eighteenth-century house, now posing as the Kildare Manor Golf Estate and Spa.

Note: if there's one thing that unifies the traditions in this country, it's the tendency to make an elaborate entrance. *The compiler*

Ryle's coyness in relation to his enjoyment of the innocuous game of golf was born of the inverted snobbery with which a vocational schooling can leave you. In fact he played a mean 18-handicapper, always travelled with a 3-iron in the trunk and was as dangerous with it as he had ever been with a stout ash butt hurley. Fletcher, an unenthusiastic stand-in for the elite when it came to grinning and bearing all of Ryle's class grievances, ironically was more of a lawn tennis man himself.

'Enough is enough,' Fletcher told Ryle, who had again broken the 'don't ask' part of his policy of indifference in regard to Fletcher's daily intentions. 'The banks have sent out ten thousand letters pressuring people to give up their homes. We are here to confront a banker whom I've been informed plays here on Thursday mornings.'

'What's wrong with that?' said Ryle. 'Why should a man like myself who is in the clear with his house pay tax to cover fuckers who borrowed money they don't want to pay back?'

Fletcher reddened as they slowly crunched their way along

the gravel of the coyly curved driveway. 'You can't get blood from a stone,' he said, containing himself. 'The very people who hide behind the panoply of business-favourable law now want to bully folk into foregoing the few protections that the same body of law gives to the family home. Out of jail on technicalities, those who fuelled the frenzy preach to those who got crushed by it, about *moral* hazard of all things!'

'You'll need to change the name for one thing,' said Ryle, a good calculator. 'This outfit sounds too radical, even if you and I know it's just another talking shop. Granted, your voter likes to think they're descended from the dispossessed of Black '47 and the people wracked by evictions and emigration. But of course they are in their holes. They're descended from the few that survived and got the land of the evicted. When push comes to shove they're a sound conservative class of a person. They'll mouth off about this and that better than any. But on the day they won't vote for anything that sounds like it might rock the apple tart.'

That was where Ryle was wrong. Fletcher was gone past talking shop. 'Whatever,' he said, his language slipping uncharacteristically into the sloppy. The Lost Ten Thousand's program might not have been quite on par with the direct action of PETA or Sea Shepherd, but was a much more confrontational program of action than anything Grattan had hitherto associated himself with. His political development may now have been on a curve going somewhere. Who can tell and what does it matter?

If Ryle had thought Fletcher had no higher gear and was forever going to be a harmless talker, he had another think waiting for him in the slightly disappointing Vietnamese themed restaurant of that resort which otherwise would have enjoyed five-star ratings from TripAdviser.

'Also,' added Ryle, 'you need to be a bit wily about the shite-hawks who hole up in this particular safe house. Just remember some are currently the big swinging dicks of the State you're trying to be boss of. You'd do well to learn to suck them off. I suppose your pride will be your biggest obstacle on that. But my advice, take it or leave it: don't be like Blair pissing on Murdoch's rug while still wanting the Sky cameras to focus on his smile.

You can circle back for these bucks after you're in the throne and come down with the iron fist on their testicles as suits yourself.'

Fletcher wasn't hearing his adviser. 'They've gone too far,' was all he said, working himself up. Then he blurted, 'Philistines … flipping bloody flipping *cunts*.'

Ryle was a little taken aback at this new kind of fighting talk, as were some of the heads which turned from their green curry pasta as the last of Fletcher's words entered the room before him. The restaurant was full. Hired out for a private function, so they were told by the maître d' before they'd even asked for a table. The electronic boards in the clubhouse had indicated that The Free Market Think Tank had the place hired for a day long workshop.

Ryle could see there was going to be no sense talked here. His principal had himself too worked up. But, having done his best to put in the sensible word and avert trouble, he felt no further distaste for what may come, come what may. I hope it doesn't shatter any illusions for you to learn that the very same Suck Ryle was not a person who had fundamental problems with the fracas as a form of self-expression.

Fletcher was scanning the tables for his man. In the recessed area of the eatery, behind the business school lecturers, building society economists, aspirant apps developers, and a gym owner who'd come out to have themselves lionized up a bit by a cheery TV champ of the free market, he spotted the already made whales displaced to the private rear area for the day. They were looking trimmer for the moulting and were getting their sheen back. There were deals going down, green blood back in their veins, and competing offers being made to a waitress with a Krakow of a look about her. 'Mister Bob Barnaby!' says Fletcher in an elevated tone that was his best attempt at rough, 'Mister Barnaby, are you back there? Would you be so good as to come over here to speak to us?'

No stir out of the big men at the far side of the striplings. They were listening though. Hoping for a comic moment, another deranged egg-throwing shareholder, perhaps, whose antics could be added to repartee of a slow evening in Barbados.

But they were hedging their bets till they heard more. They didn't get where they were through impetuosity. One of them gazed, owing to a personal sensitivity about what was thought of him, and then fixed his stare like a limpet, owing to recognition. It was the Maltese media mogul again. For some reason his eyes were glued on Ryle rather than Fletcher. He paled. Not being an understander of the necessarily random distribution of coincidence in a disordered universe, his keen investment nose gave him the earliest whiff of a tear in the fabric of his existence.

No Bob Barnaby stood up though. Fletcher asked louder, '*Mr. Barnaby, the man who sits back there with developers and policy makers while his minions hound our Nation's young families out of their homes and their wits!*'

The maître quietly got on the phone.

'This seems like a bit of a misunderstanding,' said the TV guru from the foreground, a ferret with nasal problems. He swept his presenter's arm back across the room and smiled a brassy little smile as he raised his voice to presume to speak on behalf of all present. 'I would say that there is not a man or woman in this room who does not support assistance being given to those in *ginuine* mortgage distress.'

'Indeed,' said Fletcher, 'and also what about the small businesses that have struggled through the worst and are now, as things turn, being put to the wall by the banks?'

'When the tide comes back in you see who's been faking the breast stroke,' said the other, pleased with the laboured misquotation. It got a polite laugh. 'But it's also time to move on from focus on the problems and to drive the economy forward. We need solutions, not idle rhetoric.'

'Idle rhetoric indeed! Please don't bother me with arrant nonsense,' said Fletcher quietly and personably to the man in the foreground, not budging. 'Please stand aside as I have no quarrel with you or your guests. This is not your issue.'

'Let me guess now,' the showman continued pushing his glasses up on his sharp nose and rattling on a mile to the dozen as they tend to in Montenotte and Montserrat, 'you Gentlemen are from People Before Profit or the AA or some such outfit? And you're going to give us a little sermon peppered with *Tikettyisms*.'

'*Piketty* surely,' one of his delegates suggested. That didn't stop him. A little pot is soon hot. 'Am I right? Am I correct?' he danced from foot to foot. 'We all agree that everyone is entitled to his or her opinion. But you know the public is also getting a bit tired of the champions of woolly incoherence. Your kind of grand-standing sounds great but doesn't take us anywhere, only backwards into the abyss of quasi-socialism. We are where we are my curly friend, *we are … where … we … are*.'

'As things start to reheat, let us not choose to just turn our backs and pretend nothing happened here,' Fletcher said sombrely. 'How the Nation tore each other apart like dogs in the street. Nobody knows how many good people were broken, how many were put to the end of their road. How many people decided they'd rather be dead.'

'Well let me challenge you to debate on economics right here and now!'

Fletcher was as on for it as a mare in heat. He rolled up his Gore-Tex sleeves. So easily was he distracted from his mission.

Ryle was weighing things up. He was now certain there was going to be an altercation here because causing it was his only alternative to listening to what might come out of these two mouths. His problem was that he knew he couldn't get stuck into the TV man. Ryle always remembered the advice he got from an attorney he'd met in a pool hall while on holiday in The Bronx back in the eighties: *there's no way to look good when you pick a fight with a dwarf. If you beat him you look like a jerk and if he beats you, you look worse.*

'The blanket liturgy of the markets,' said Fletcher, 'these days makes its believers look cowardly as well as dull. Surely we have learned over the past centuries that intransigent literal adherence to *any* ideology or faith is hugely dangerous? Literalist fundamentalism of any variety speaks of fearfulness of spirit and a lazy or submissive conformist intellect.'

'Besides,' contributed Ryle, 'every self-made multi-millionaire is a person who was bullied at school. What else do you think keeps Branson, Murdoch, or O'Leary at it? A chip on the shoulder still making him try to get ahead to prove himself better than the honest schoolmates who pointed out his little faults.' The audience scratched their heads at this and then looked back to the two more mainstream oracles.

At the back roped-off rear section no man nor ligger stood to prevent the ferret from continuing to speak brashly on their behalf. One woman did, fair play to her. Everyone knew her. She had a bad reputation created by being rougher than the toughest in a man's world. She ran a chain of grocery shops and made her business on not paying anyone their due and stuffing the courts to a standstill with any of them that asked a second time.

'Did I not see you two drive up here in an OPW van?' she shouted across the room, shrewder than the average man after all. She came forward with a strong voice used to having to assert itself. 'Now isn't that ironic? The highest paid civil servants in Europe preaching socialism to the hard-pressed entrepreneurs who pay their salaries while still trying to keep this ship on the road. If you really want to do something about debt, why don't you forego your extortionate pensions? In the meantime why don't you get on back out to your van and twiddle your little mickeys while you pretend to be doing something useful in return for your shameless theft of public funds.'

Fighting talk. Ryle liked. He could see even more clearly now where this was going. 'Always picking on the low-paid public servant,' he said, 'as if we were the only freeloaders in the room.'

People involuntarily looked at their food. Ryle could have that effect.

'We are sadly well accustomed to divisive and belittling comments of that sort, Madam,' said Fletcher, 'comments from people absurdly positing that controls of the State should be handed over to business.' Fletcher spoke softly and slowly as he thought he was delivering a cruel put-down. 'A well-run society however is an orchestra within which your sector is just one component. Making, sadly, a rather shrill contribution of late. It would do you no harm to occasionally acknowledge that the sheet music set before other sections can be more complex than merely clanging repetitively your cymbals, profit and market.

Make no mistake though, it is we, all of us together in this room, who are accountable to society rather than the other way round.'

'What has your mate been snorting?' she said to Ryle, apparently not very put down.

'Quite frankly, madam,' continued Fletcher, 'your propositions are tedious.'

'Yes,' said Ryle, wanting to rile her up a bit more, 'you run the shop and leave us to run the street. How about that.'

'There is no call for that,' said the valiant ferret, standing in front of Fletcher, unhappy to have the defence of his realm interfered with by this woman. 'There is no need to be personal with Lady Mucher. She gives more to charity each year than you will ever earn in your life.'

'Besides,' said Fletcher, seeing a need to cut closer to the little man's bone, 'financial punditry and other financial *services* are much like the public services you deride, in that they were only ever intended to be that—enabling *services*. When they get control of the political system they too mushroom out of control, sucking all life out of the real productive economy which they hide behind.'

'The naked every day she clad, when she put on her clothes,' said Ryle, staring at the charitable lady and showing that schooling hadn't left him entirely unscathed.

'My friend has a point,' presumed Fletcher. 'Too many miss the essence of the third virtue. Giving without respect is charity hollowed out. Respect is everything between us. Withheld, every gesture is debased.'

'D'you know, I never got how that was such a terrible put-down—cladding the naked only after he put on his clothes?' said the ferret, a mediator of all ideas. 'I suppose it's this bogus perception that giving when you have plenty behind is somehow cheap egoism. But we live in a non-ideal world. In your guys' world, everyone is paralyzed. Only those with the purest altruism can do anything of merit. In my opinion however, those who do nothing at all should say nothing at all.'

'Agreed,' said Ryle, always ready to fertilize common ground, 'but the last thing you'd want to see before breakfast is some old coke rake climbing out of his Range Rover Evoque in gym knickers giving away his overcoats.'

'And by the way, your model was never more shaky than it is today,' said Fletcher, as if Ryle's contribution meant nothing to him, 'as we leave our under-25's behind. There is not going to be enough work to give everyone a real chance of a dignified role. Private or public. All of our children are in the one boat,' he concluded looking around the room inclusively, with a sweeping offer at a shared perspective. 'It's simple. Good people generally close their eyes and put faith in the unwritten contracts that bind us all together. Now too many people open their eyes to find it's all been pilfered; to find themselves locked out regardless of how much they study or volunteer. With betrayal on this scale, the contracts will break and there'll be hell for us all.'

'Aha, the *Lump of work* fallacy,' crows the patronizing falsetto, not at all lured by the brotherly compromising tones of Fletcher. 'Do I have to spell it out? The Luddites predicted the same at the time of the industrial revolution. *Oh no, don't mechanize, you'll take away our jobs!* Don't you even understand basic economics? Left alone, the markets naturally distribute the labour and ergo the income. More and more become middle-class, ever increasing demands for goods and services. Thusly there's more work for others in delivering those goods and services. As in Asia, then in Africa,' whined the little poultice, as if he was talking to the backward. (It's not for me to take sides here since I take care of my own concerns but there were times when you would sorely want Fletcher to be right.)

'It was never a fallacy,' said Fletcher, 'it remains basic logic, just delayed in reaching its always inevitable conclusion. Increasing consumption cannot indefinitely provide more jobs than increasing automation takes away. The former is constrained by a finite line item – how much stuff there is to consume. The latter now explodes at a rate no industrial era person could ever have imagined. We can't afford to walk blindly into this! Houses are being imported in panels from one-man factories in Germany. With thirteen staff Instagram was able to process more of our images than Kodak could with 160,000 people. We cloud click past the jobs of shop staff and await drone delivery. You are invoiced by email rather than via the postman. Our medical data is better analysed by software as is legal discovery. One person can farm a thousand acres instead of three men farming a hundred. Airlines, banking, taxation, and welfare services all employ more user interfaces than people. This needn't be bad. But we must fast find ways to de-concentrate the benefits from the hands of the few.'

Note: I can endorse Fletcher's scorecard on this. Just to put what I'm going to say in context, I am cornered into mentioning that I successfully completed a batch of multiple choice questions at the end of an online course in literary criticism during the heavy frost last weekend. (I have avoided saying this up to now as I wanted you to feel I was ordinary like yourself.) One of the learnings: generalism and being widely read is out. The monograph is in. So, I restrict my observations on this occasion to my own specialist area, paint men of fiction. Kennedy Toole's manager at Levy's Paints has various clerks, typists, and accountants. Kick on twenty-five years, same shop, same bloodsucking owner, and Vlautin's manager runs it alone. Only a tenth of that time after Vlautin I'm using an app to give the farmer the queer eye. We pick the colours together and the data goes to the cloud in real time enabling the very same Levy, richer than ever, to fly the paint direct to me from a mixing facility in Calcutta without lifting a finger. [fn] I'm no daw. It won't stop here. Soon the farmer will be able to plug the phone into the spray gun and get the whole job done automatically. My day will soon be done, just like yours is. *The compiler*

[fn] Footnote
Yes, we know! It was Pants. And the compiler gets his paint not from Levy, but from Amazon the same as everybody else. Integrity goes straight out the window when you're dealing with someone desperate for an argument of his own. *The Editors*

'Control of production,' Fletcher went on, 'now only requires control of finance and a few technologists. Labour, manual or white-collar, is neither here nor there. The real fallacy is for countries like us to play *I'm All Right Jack*; to sit back and think everything is fine just because we've got a little bit more than our share of the shrinking employment pie by bending a little further for Bezos and Blankfein. The corporations make just a little contribution here, which means a lot to us. You guys get to pretend that it's the taxes you avoid that are paying for everything. We all get to think we're so much better than the Greeks for a minute. Because we don't have quite half of our young people without decent work yet. But we should not gloat. No matter what new tricks a hooker learns, the clients will eventually move on.'

'So, not Piketty then,' mused the libertarian, scantily versed in his enemy's creeds it seemed, 'so what mishmash of theory have we then? A Trotskyist Accelerationist then? One of those who rationalizes his personal enjoyment of the fruits of capitalism on the premise that in so doing he is accelerating it to its inevitable demise?'

'Would you ever go away and fuck yourself like a good man,' said Ryle harmlessly out of the side of his mouth, concentrating ever more now on the lump of Mucher as she continued to work her way through the think tankers. Zero hour approaching. In the distance the other whales had gone back to their gaming of the waitress. As the old people used to say, neither great poverty nor great riches will hear reason. With sufficient fruits stashed beyond the avaricious reach of National governments and with adequate consideration given to philanthropic work, the big men found the ferret almost as tiresome as Fletcher. This kind of idle ideological talk was beneath them. Only the weighty media man kept a watery eye on Ryle, still feeling the sweet sweaty shadow of madness pursuing him.

'Willfull blindness!' said Fletcher more loudly, irritated, 'is what allowed communism to continue for generations after it was clear that its fundamental flaws were making life for ordinary people ever worse. We do not want to end up like that, requiring ever more surveillance and coercion to keep people from telling us the obvious: that our system too is flawed and needs fundamental reform. Seeking fairness is not weak, it's necessary for survival. Global organization in business is here to stay. There is no point in moaning about that. Global organization in broader human governance simply needs to catch up. *Gesellschaft* needs to move beyond National borders for communities to become healthy again.'

'Typical! Bloody civil servants now want a world government!' jabbed the Corkman to a laugh. 'Clichéd demonization of the successful corporations—in favour of government which is always a fail.'

'When did I demonize corporations?' said Fletcher reddening further, he liked a fair fight and hadn't enough guile for the other's elbows and nips. 'It would be as absurd to demonize them as to celebrate them. They are merely manmade social constructs run by folks who play by the rules we set them. Our job is to keep adjusting the rules as necessary so we can continue to harness the game to the service of the primary entity, a functioning society. Please understand, it's not the *Market* itself that is the force of nature, my friend. It is but one manifestation of the real immutable force behind all our best and worst endeavours, biological competition.' Fletcher looked around as though he expected nods for this obvious pronouncement.

'In the cradle Mother gets you to eat an extra spoon of puree by offering it to your sister. You devote long hours in college and then work, all to try to *get ahead*. In retirement you would like to grow the biggest pumpkin or get the best rating from your cookery circle. In hospital you are still taking some motivation from seeing someone worse off than you in the next bed. The same competitive force that the market harnesses is a fundamental in science and the arts too by the way, with entirely different rules for metering the rewards. Competition is the raw nuclear core of life and it is not only society's right but its *obligation* to vigilantly maintain the walls that contain it and to channel its motive force for good. We used to make and change that section of law that describes what companies may look like, as suited each society. Facing our responsibility to regulate them once more, now at an international level, is the only way back to having business work for societies. It's the only route to dignified roles, and fairly distributed leisure, for all of our children.' Fletcher spread his arms again in that open way he had, never quick enough to condemn even the worst sorts. It was the thing that Ryle resented most of all about him. As if prodigal enemies were just as welcome in his embrace as was a person who put up with him every day. 'Otherwise what we end up with is an Irishman putting ten thousand families on the street in the hope of a good rating from Wall St. And then going for a game of golf, feeling blameless. Defenders of capitalism should be aghast. Meltdown is where this blindness leads.'

'Laissez-faire capitalism, my simple friend, is what powers the diesel engine in your van and produces the hi-tech fabrics in your rain jacket.' Bringing the metaphors down to earth, the Cork City man patted the Dublin City man's jacket as if he had given it to him for his birthday and was reminding him he could take it back. It's what is reviving the tiger as we speak. This will always be unpalatable to the likes of you but the rich are actually the heroes.' He glanced back to the whales looking for the nod, seeming a little unnerved at their continued inattention.

'You'll need to learn a shitload of new tricks to compete with the Polish one for their affection,' said Ryle politely to the ferret. 'To start with, you'd need a bit of work done on the undercarriage. And you'd need to get the voice box tuned down. It's idling a bit high. That's only my opinion.'

The ferret looked at Ryle, not understanding him at all.

'Laissez-faire? *Laissez fucking faire!* Tell me this,' burbled Fletcher, further angered and punching wild like a nine-year-old now, 'how does it not stick in the gullet of an Irish person to parrot the mantras of Ayn Rand and Margaret Thatcher? Have you not one ounce of awareness of the history of this very ground we stand on? Do you not even know that the very same Malthusian mumbo jumbo allowed Trevelyan to think himself a sophisticated man as he choked the relief in '47? *There is to be no interference whatsoever in the laws of supply and demand.* Does that sound familiar? Like Cromwell before him and ISIS after him, he went forth maddened by a grey god, possessed of pure creed, dutiful in readiness to oversee the mowing down of the more colourful faiths. And of course with a desire for land. It is the faith that allowed him to wring his hands as he began the expunging of three quarters of the population of Ireland. Like you, he believed that equating his current rules of the game of commerce to the laws of nature, rendered them immutable and thereby rendered his class helpless to intervene. Hapless servants to the execution of God's work. All the while of course, making manly plans for the cleansed lands. *Shame! SHAME* on any Irish person who parrots from the same prayerbook from which the obituary of our people was read!'

The ferret took a moment. He was not sure how to respond to Fletcher now. In fairness, anyone who didn't know how easily Fletcher could move himself to tears might think his visible emotion a signal that they needed to take note; to think that this was one of those rare moments in their lives when they were hearing unprepared words that actually meant something to the person saying them. It caused a degree of restlessness in the audience, as some nodded with Fletcher. Or to him. But the little tiger recovered from the sucker punch and was clearing his throat to carry on with some response.

That was the kind of men they were, Fletcher and the Corkman. Ryle knew from unsweet experience that this class of bourgeois shadow boxing could go on for hours if he didn't break it up. He intervened to start the more direct action which he now agreed the campaign called for. He strafed a patent shoe in a downward direction along the shin of the ferret and as the squeal subsided, he admonished Fletcher, 'There was no call for that. The man was only trying to think of something to say.'

It didn't take too much further proxy provocation on his part to ensure that Fletcher had to deal with the raging presenter who had sprung like a bullfrog and dug into the big man with a kick that tried his cruciate, following up with a table knife attack. Fletcher pushed, shoved, tackled, mostly trying to keep the flailing man at a normal arm's length.

Ryle himself opted to get down to brass tacks with the well put together Mrs. Mucher who it turned out was, like himself, much fonder of action than talk. 'There's none so blind as them that cannot see,' said Ryle as he gave her the two fingers into her eyes. When she recovered some sight she showed that she knew how to take care of herself, I'll give her that. She had seen a few boxes thrown in her time. The two couples were rolling around the floor hammering each other with fists and kneeing each others' groins when the gate man who had touched his safari hat at them earlier, entered the room. He had with him seven men and a girl in Black Sheriff outfits. Ryle who had been giving the occasional glance toward the door was reminded of a previous experience with Schwarze Sheriffs as they cured the homeless of Munich by truncheoning them up and down the cleanly tiled tunnels of the Scheidplatz U-Bahn station. He thought it time to slip out. He apologized to the woman whom he had come to respect so much that he had developed a little horn for her. She wasn't on for letting her man get away and planted a diamond crusted fist into his temple, bringing no blood out of multiple gaping wounds. He made good his escape from the sheriffs on this occasion but not before taking a part of the grocer's cauliflower ear in his mouth, leaving her a van Gogh of her art, a Malchus of her creed, and a Holyfield of her Morriganism.

Fletcher got the worst of it. Not having had the fair weather eye out for the declining odds, he stayed to deal with both the The Free Marketeers and their bouncers. Thus compounded, the defence of libertarian capitalism proved more telling on that day, credit where it's due.

While Ryle waited for his boss, seated in the van giving his little mickey a bit of a twiddle, his mind turned to other matters. Who can blame him? Boredom finds few persons acting to their highest standards. He took out his phone. *Do you do pictures at all*, he said in his text message.

What now, Leonard, what do you mean? Surely you know that I'm not going to the movies with you. Not ever, came back the quick reply from Margot.

He responded, *WHAT! I haven't watched a movie since Dirty Dancing. Get with the times, woman. Personal pictures of course. Do I have to spell it out? Point the phone to whatever part you think might amuse me. I'm interested.*

That's it. I'm finally going to tell him just what kind of creature he's hanging out with, she replied after some minutes.

Ryle guessed she wouldn't but not the reason – that she wouldn't want to shake Fletcher further in his already unsteady state. Suck Ryle sent another message, *No need to be snotty. I'm only telling you what I want. Ask and ye shall receive. Did you never hear of that?*

No reply.

Would you at least set up FourSquare on the phone so your acquaintances can keep track of you? Ryle wrote, and left it at that. [fn]

[fn] Footnote

Have we in this country, one wonders, finally produced a work to fit the US censors' shameful dismissal of Joyce: *emetic rather than erotic? The Editors*

Fletcher was lorried out through the glass doors on a golf caddy. He was in a sorry state. Ryle tapped his fingers on the steering wheel waiting for him to make his way to the van. Ryle then spun the wheels on the gravel and jerked off even before Fletcher had the door closed. Ryle's momentos, a brass birdbath and sun-dial, rolled around in the back of the van as they took a shortcut through the rose beds.

They proceeded without much conversation, Fletcher reek-ing of disapproval. If only he knew how trivial were the minor disloyalties he disapproved of in his friend, compared to the ones he didn't know about.

The volumes unspoken were such that it was getting in on Ryle and as they came up along the South Circular he offered to put on a bit of music as a concession. From 98FM, the only station he could get on the OPW radio, Bruce again. This time he was belting, *my home town, This is ... My ... Home ... Town.* Over and over. Ryle started bopping.

Note: Ryle had time for Springsteen ever since he'd met him at the Ballsbridge Horse Show. In fact, Ryle had reached out with a few horse-trading tips so that he shouldn't get codded next time he was buying a show pony for his daughter.

'You know what hurts most,' murmured Fletcher, 'if I

examine myself honestly?'

'The broken snout?' said Ryle.

'None of the bruises,' said Fletcher. 'Not even your desertion. Forgive me for saying so, but I hardly expect better of you
anymore.'

'No bother,' said Ryle.

'No, it's the banal disappointment at the blurring. You'd
think at least the bankers and developers could be our stand-up
bad guys in all this. Until you realize those imps lost their own
money too. So they swallowed their own hype. Feet of clay are
a disappointment in our demons.'

Note: since I've previously summarized the musical inclina-
tions of the main characters to save you having to discover
the same over reams of pages, I can also give you a summary
regarding clay footings. Ryle's feet had been caked in it from
early on. Mac Gabhann, the Dub, had feet that had never
seen clay. Fletcher too, clayless. A very dainty size seven the
latter's were, by the way. An enigma in their own right. Like
a tall wall with a small foundation, the only wonder with
Fletcher was how he didn't topple more often. *The compiler*

As a further attempt at making up, and because he was running low on caffeine, Ryle pulled in next to the door of The
Craven Head for refreshments. 'You can go to the jacks in here
and wash the scabs off your face. Pamper yourself a bit before
you get back into the paperwork,' he said considerately.

The coffee and merlot at the ghastly pub were also mistimed.
Things were happening fast now.

They were stuck with a barman who wanted to talk about
Ireland. He was dry for the want of tourists and needed to inflict
himself on them instead. I'll summarize this buck as anything
more would only sicken you.

He is the kind of lad that goes to all heritage events. He is an
expert in stone work, wrought iron, and 1916. He has a scrotum
full of relevant tales about unknown men who fired shots from
various buildings in the immediate locality of the pub he works
in. He is fifty with a full head of blond hair and lives with the
parents. Though he is against most foreigners he latches on to

tourists. In short, he is like a Celtic Louis Farrakhan, prickly proprietor of Irish victimhood, his authority on most subjects stemming from his ethnicity, and hence trumping any Ph.D. from Boston. A self-appointed maker and polisher of pisrógs. Most years he lands himself a short affair with a person of the American diaspora who has hit middle age and found herself so lost that she could briefly listen even to the likes of him.

He was busy brushing the two bruised men up on what real Irishness means when all they wanted was silence. Oblivious to cold questions from Ryle about where he wanted to be buried, he carried on as if he was paying for the drink. 'We're great craic of course,' said the barman, 'though we hardly realize it ourselves. That's what keeps them coming.'

'You're great craic anyway,' said Ryle, eyeing the man up, not in a good way.

Not getting any traction on the tribal warmth front, the bad barman started on the foreign nationals. 'It's opened our eyes,' said he, 'having so many of them all of a sudden in our faces. I'm not prejudiced but I don't see why we should have to host them. We don't have a colonial past to make up for.'

The man then rested his elbow on the counter and made a fist for his fleshy chin in the manner of a person about to do a bit of thinking. He gazed at them before adding, 'Especially not the people coming here from parts of the world where there is a lower IQ, I don't care what anyone says. No continent mentioned.'

'You should care what anyone else says though, because that way you might learn,' said Fletcher, risen so soon again.

'The African just doesn't think beyond the welfare and rights,' he said.

'Straighten up, man,' said Ryle, 'you look like a fucken rodent.'

'Don't tell me you think that if you put a problem in front of a Nigerian you'll get the same result as if you put the same problem in front of a Chinese.'

'That's nuts,' said Fletcher, picking his scabs, distractedly. 'Of course some of the differences in outlook between any two people will have geographic and social influences. Therefore, of course it's trivially true to say that when confronted with a given situation people may be temperamentally inclined to following different thought tracks depending on origin and experience. The mark of genuine stupidity is to assume the other's way, stupid.'

'Stupidity indeed,' said the man, fuelled by instinct, 'and don't start me on the fucken Romanians. What will we have at the end of it all?'

'Harmonious integration perhaps,' said Fletcher, 'what about that?'

'Even if they all stay four hundred years their great great grandchildren still won't be Irish. We can't afford this. Remember, this is the land that has punched far above our weight in the arts. That will all be swamped to nothing. Besides, haven't we enough fucken gypos of our own.'

'Listen here you, you … you unpleasant man,' said Fletcher, roasting. 'Tone, Emmett, Davis, Yeats, Stephens, Beckett, all eternal foreign nationals by your calculus. They hadn't a drop of blood more *catholic* in them than Dame Barbara Longford who writes admiringly of Cromwell and Thatcher. I suggest you take as Irish those who take themselves as Irish and be proud that they wish to.'

'Ah, the Teutonic elites,' the barman warming at last, at home in a well-walked thesis, 'there's a funny thing about the Norman. Even as a renegade he owns everything he touches. Benn became lord of socialism and Dugdale, lady of Republicanism. The Bloomsburys told everyone they were in charge of literature. Yet he recognizes the poverty of his peoples' cultures. Whereas the Spanish and Portuguese brought their culture wherever they went, Algernon appropriated wherever he went, like … like, well like a culture sponge.' Blondie explained for the two men with interesting hand movements. 'He invents lineage to Arthur. He stuffs his writing with Greek allusion. He becomes expert in witchdoctor masks and Aborigine songs. He Frenchifies his surname. His beloved, Battleaxe Brittanica, boils sheep and pig, then serves mouton and porc. He eulogizes in placenames from Malahide to Manhattan those he wiped off the map. The likes of Yeats, that was just more of it. With his Celtic revivalism and occultism. Pulling the bleeding scalp of the conquered over his head to the point that the native becomes regarded a corrupter of his own culture.'

'What a cosy little living room you inhabit. You know what every other person is made of, by genotype, eh?' said Fletcher, throwing good talk after bad.

'Don't get me wrong, the ordinary Englishman I've nothing against,' said Blondie, 'he's just a good bloke like ourselves.'

'When you prejudge people you are the loser. I suggest you treat everyone with respect until they've done something to explicitly demonstrate they don't deserve that.'

'In your own case,' said Suck Ryle, to Grattan Fletcher, 'they'd need to shit directly on top of your head.'

'And in your case, my friend,' Fletcher turned, 'I rather fear that you start by prejudging *everyone* you meet and precipitously acting on the assumption that they're about to try to *shit* on your head.'

'And I am right more times than I'm wrong. Prevention is better than cure.'

The barman lost interest, saying, 'Personally, I don't blame that lamppost you walked into.'

A lull followed with each of the three looking down, none taking responsibility for any further conversation.

This was the lay of the land when in walked a prophet. A miserable streak of a chap barely twenty if he was barely a day. He approached the two customers after the barman was taken away by a mobile call. The seer pulled down his shitty grey hood and came over to light on them. It was Fletcher upon whom the pale stare settled. He saw something in Fletcher that nobody else had seen yet. Or so he seemed to think.

A bony white finger came out nearly touching the poor battered man. '*You!* I know *you!*'

'Go on away with yourself now,' said Ryle, 'before you get yourself into deeper water than you can float in.'

'*I know you!*' said the stinking wisp, unflinching, ignoring Ryle's advice.

'Yes, son,' said Fletcher, no bottom to his tolerance, 'you look like you are not taking good care of yourself. Here, have a seat. Would you like us to get you a sandwich?'

'*I know you!*' said the lad, with a madness in his eyes that five roped camels wouldn't hold down. 'You are a priest. You are the beast.' Clawing at Fletcher's shirt a hysterical desperation taking his voice ever higher, 'Show them, show them the brand on your belly!'

'Bye bybyby bye,' said the returning barman into his phone, in the conversation-terminating mannerism that had come to signify sudden extreme busyness amongst the lethargic. He leaned on the counter and took a look at the new situation in his parish. With the weary eye of seasoned hospitality worker, he assessed the situation before him, and said, 'Get the fuck out of here, you scumbag junkie.'

The pale boy turned a blank gaze at the barman, confused.

'Don't talk to him that way,' said Fletcher, 'this boy could be your child or mine.'

'Couldn't be mine,' said the leader in his domain, 'he's a bogger. Only bogmen and old-timers take serious drugs these days.'

'That's an absurd assertion,' said Fletcher.

The uninhibited thing inside the boy lit up again at Fletcher's voice. 'Absurd, abssertion,' frantic now. One part of him was shrewd enough to know that his allocated time was drawing to a close. 'I'll devilthefuckingdevil with you heel for heel and toe for toe. You don't scare me, scaramunctious old curly knobbed molester. I'll stab your eyes out.' He was reaching in his pockets, presumably for stabbing equipment. Instead of a little pocket knife or compass, such as might be the best you'd expect someone in such disarray to have been able to lay on for himself, he surprised them all by pulling out a decent little sword. He held it in his shaking hand. The barman jumped back.

Ryle on the other hand was thinking ahead. Malnourished though the chap was, the strength of a madman is something Ryle believed it best to be cautious around. Ryle was quick enough to observe the large nose that had been broken a few times, as well as the other scars scattered around his head, all indicating he was a chap who wasn't made only of ornate words.

Fletcher had an already bruised arm uselessly raised in a token defence of his already battered face. Some kind of rusty laugh was issuing from the boy. Though Ryle did also see a funny side of Fletcher's milky self-defence, and though he couldn't be accused of being personally concerned for Fletcher, he was a little concerned for the future of the campaign. It should be remembered he had a fair bit invested in the latter by now. So he came in from the side, invisible to the stare that was bolted onto Fletcher, unheard through the ridiculous laughing, and swung a barstool so that its protruding mahogany lip tapped firmly against the side of the patchy haired skull. This crack sapped the deranged determination of the boy.

As he lay on the floor the barman came back into the fray. He put in the boot a couple of times.

'There's no call for that,' said Ryle sending the blonde away with a return swing of the stool into his neck. The barman tried to pretend vertebrae weren't hair-lined at all as he retreated, recognizing he'd finally run into someone more ignorant than himself.

The chap sitting up on the ground now pointed to his own chest and said in a small voice, 'What about me? What about me?' His face crumpled and he started to cry.

Fletcher dialled 999 on his phone. Instead of asking for cops he asked for an ambulance.

The chap was coming around and looking at them in a foreign daze like a person returning from an epileptic seizure. His other voices exorcised at least temporarily, he looked at them for some explanation of who he was and what he was doing in this world.

'So you're the junkie's old fella and you've disowned him, eh?' the breathless barman read Fletcher. 'I don't blame you. It's the only medicine for them.'

'He's not a junkie, he's a nutter,' said Ryle, his recent heroism entitling him to more airtime than he usually sought. During his stint on the street, Ryle had become an ignorant man's expert in the various categories of ailment that could capsize a life. This he had found necessary learning if you wanted to rob fellow travellers from time to time without it leading to unforeseen fuss. 'I'll lay money. One day this was a nerdy son puffing a few joints out the bedroom window of his nice family's semi-detached and the next day the boy was gone, never more to be seen, replaced with a spitting psycho too dangerous even for others to rob from.'

Fletcher had got down on the floor to sit with the shaking lad who let him hold his hand. The barman stared blankly, 'You can't tell me my business, I see them every day. Fucking junkie.'

'I'd legalize the brown stuff any day but this stuff needs to be snuffed out before the country is entirely mad,' said Ryle, filling the awkwardness with the closest he would come to political speech. 'You can easy cure a man sick from want of heroin. Just give him heroin. Cheap and clean and he can live to old age boring as fuck. But today's skunk tippler is taking a five-to-one chance of going stone mad, never to come back. If you're going to play for those kind of stakes you might as well do it with a revolver. There's a better kick out of winning the real roulette and a smaller downside to losing.'

'You might have a point there,' said Fletcher quietly, looking up at Ryle almost proudly. 'My cohort in the judiciary think only of jolly days naughtily taking a couple of puffs of grass in the back of the college bar.'

Ryle couldn't leave it all well rounded like that of course. As the ambulance siren approached, he said, 'The only cure for this lad now is for them to put him down. Who wants to live in nightmareland with no waking up from it?'

'Get this scummer out of here,' said the barman to the ambulance men, reasserting himself. 'And take him to Dundrum because he's a fucking nutjob. A small crowd had stopped on the pavement outside. Fletcher helped the spent boy to his feet. The foul thing inside him gave out a little scream at the sight of the uniforms and flashing lights. He bolted, made for the other door with the agility of a feral cat, and was gone. His tormentors as supple, gone too, stuck to the poor lad like shit to a blanket. Fletcher wandered out on the street, looking after him in a daze, forgetting the bill.

Ryle sat down while he finished his coffee.

'That'll be a tenner on the nose there, friend,' gasped the barman, wiping a glass with his handkerchief, his head barely tilted.

'That'll be alright,' said Ryle, closing his jackets, 'go on with yourself now like a good man and don't worry about it.'

The barman took the advice.

When Ryle was leaving he picked up the sword. It was of soft plastic and bent easily as he slipped it inside his belt.

The company I keep

Chapter XXX

FLETCHER'S BOUNCE WAS VERY solid in this period. Rather than hampering him, the hammerings seemed to be burnishing him. The morning after the golf club beatings, Ryle came in to find the big man kitted with shades over the purple eyes, all fenestration reports written, daily request for further duties submitted, and ready for the road.

Ryle took the opportunity to bring focus. 'You will need to change gear while there's still good life left in you.'

'What do you mean?' asked Fletcher foolishly.

'You won't have legs forever,' said Ryle, exasperated that he should have to spell it out. 'All good runs come to an end. You've got comfortable in first gear revving high and covering very little ground. Now is the time to gear up.'

The Black Sheriffs' boot bruises on Fletcher's ears and neck came to the fore as Ryle's words set his head throbbing. 'For heaven's sake, Suck,' he said shortly, 'can't we for one day just enjoy the journey for its own sake?'

'Don't be ridiculous, boss,' said Ryle. 'You can't carry on like this, going around doing noble things for people who wouldn't do anything for you and who'll never thank you. Keep dribbling and the ball will be taken. It's time now to go in for the score.'

Fletcher stopped engaging. Ryle would come back to this. In his own head the path was clear. He had all the marketing collateral sketched out on a notepad at home. He was getting ready a list of quips he thought Fletcheresque so he could hit the ground running with a Tweet deck. More important, he was as always current with the nightfalls of every important citizen of the town. He would be able to call on all opinion makers and opinion publishers when the time was right. This data Suck Ryle had acquired naturally during his unseen nocturnal prowling of parks and lanes. (He didn't favour the high viz after dark.) And he fleshed his records out by keeping an eye on the comings and goings at the more upmarket massage parlours and bordellos. So Ryle knew which National broadcasters thought it necessary to be surreptitious about their liking for anal loving; he knew those of the Sunday newspaper columnists who conducted their car boot transactions in the deserted car park of Crumlin shopping centre; he knew who of the respectable Irish daily liked walking in Merrion Square with their petrified genitals hanging out; he knew those Oireachtas members who were the coke gluttons; and he knew those GAA managers who were spending their gate takings at the hold'em tables on Leeson St. And so on. Let's not bend to rake through any of the sad little specifics. The only one who appeared to have no undercarriage at all into which any kind of grappling hook could be jacked, was the O'Toole of Tara St. But Ryle wasn't worried about him. That fine man would be appetized by Fletcher's story, without condiment.

They now needed a date for the election. And that couldn't wait to the end of the first term of the little man who was currently holding up the post, in case his popularity went up. Ryle had just remembered the old saying, keep anything for seven years and you'll find a use for it. The man had to be ousted. Ryle was waiting only for the smallest flicker of a green light from Fletcher before going full tilt at that project.

Not even a flicker that could be interpreted as a green light came this morning.

'Suit yourself,' said Ryle. It was very frustrating to the loyal knave to see everything aligned but no grabbing of the moment by Fletcher. 'You're getting like an old bachelor. Full of bold chat for women, but paralyzed the minute one agrees to a shift. The kind who thinks his mother gave him the mickey for stirring his tea. Think it over. You don't even need to issue the instruction. It can be entirely arm's length. Let's say, if you are wearing that Wilsons fleece tomorrow I'll take it as the signal to execute Operation Evacuate D.' At times Ryle came close to giving away his military past.

'*What?* Just, OK, just …' said Fletcher, a little bit exasperated, 'let's have a nice day today, Len, how about that?'

'I read you,' said Ryle and put a note next to OED, saying *green light secured.* He put the notebook back into his pocket.

They took the Lexus because Grattan wanted to drive at a pace sufficient for them to get where he wanted to go. Though he was humming Richie Kavanagh's *The Borris Fair* he only belatedly mentioned to Ryle that he was thinking of Carlow again. They were just past the Red Cow when Ryle insisted that they pull in at a service station. He needed a bite to eat. While he went to relieve his little bladder, Fletcher ordered the baguette just the way the lesser man liked it. It was easier than arguing and losing good mood – that was how Fletcher rationalized this particular codependency of his. 'Yes, you will need to put on extra ham, and more blue cheese, yes, the fried eggs soft; and … no … yes, the spicy chicken; if you please, Roshan,' said Fletcher. 'Mayo?' asked the tired looking man whose gold name tag gave him away.

'Mayo fuck!' said Ryle still pulling at his zip as he returned, some of the denim having got caught. 'The name has caused too much pain to our people. When we are in charge, my friend, it will be scoured from the National memory banks.'

'Whatever,' said Roshan, closing the lid.

When Fletcher went to pay he was held up behind a man in a pleather jacket who was taking some time about picking his lotto numbers. Some old crone from the nearby office park.

'Fucksake, would you ever hurry up, you donkey,' said Ryle from a bit behind, the hunger getting the better of him now that the roll was in sight. 'No matter what numbers you pick you'll still be just as well able to fantasize about winning right up until you lose again.'

The man's hearing was alright. He turned and looked without an emotional response of any sort. He had a washed out face on him. 'Yeah, well,' he said and turned back to the assistant to start again with the numbers. He was changing his usual combination to include his son's birth year in it.

'And how is little Henry?' the assistant prompted, familiar with the man's sagas and angry on his behalf at the rude behaviour of the blow-in customer behind.

'He's doing much better, thanks,' said the watery voice, 'Martine's got him into a special school now. Expensive though.'

'And you, Richard?' asked Roshan, 'you're not looking well.'

'Fucksake, fucksake,' said Ryle from behind, 'cry me a river. You think Roshan here doesn't have his own troubles, four or five doctorates behind him no doubt and he working for minimum wage to feed a village back in Bangladesh?'

That was fair enough, until the man turned again and Fletcher said, '*Richard?* Jesus, Richard Toner?'

'Grattan,' nodded Richard as flat as if he'd seen him yesterday. These two had known each other well in Trinity. And not at all since. Fletcher paid for the roll and handed it to Ryle.

'This guy had everything, he was doing the real stuff,' gushed Fletcher shaking the wan hand vigorously, and looking around to see where Ryle was. 'He won International awards for discovering a unique genera of plants on the Bog of Allen.' Fletcher lacked the critical faculties to be able to see that all the gaunt man was doing now was jogging past an age when men should jog. 'How have things gone, Richard? I presume you succeeded in getting the WWF endangered species designation.'

'I did a bit of this and that. Not much out there for botany PhD's. Ended up with Fall Computers twenty years ago. And you?'

'Aha, so you're with the multinationals, the guys who are pulling us all out of the dudu,' said Fletcher, trying to reconfigure the enthusiasm he chose to have for his friend's success in life. 'Much more dynamic than anything I've done, I'm afraid.'

'Yeah?' said the man, thinking to go and then fatally deciding to stay talking. The Grattan effect, something you don't need me to identify for you at this stage. 'Dynamic? Yes that would be a word we hear a lot,' said the man, stealing a look at his watch. He slowly pulled the cork and anger started to fume out in every direction. There in that little convenience shop in which nobody had done him any harm, he said, 'I've worked twelve hours a day, six days a week for twenty years with three weeks off. I neglected my family and contributed to a pension fund that even before it was skimmed by hedge funds would have paid me half my current salary for all of two years after retirement. The elusiveness of the carrot, hierarchy and share options, becomes apparent to everyone after a while of course. If you're hesitant about make-work process improvements devoid of external logic, you're marked to make the bottom numbers in a numbskull's meritocracy chart. You will never even make bishop. My wife kicked me out three years back. I hadn't been attentive and she can get more for herself on the social as a lone parent. I live in a bedsit that they recently renamed a studio and doubled the rent for. I was doing very well in the work early on, going places, but helped too many young guys still eager to eat dog, to get past me. One of them is a senior manager now and is so stupid he thinks he's made it. He gets a laugh out of putting every doomed project my direction. I work harder to go backward. So, yeah Grattan, it's pretty *dynamic* alright. I'm hanging by my fingernails. And doing the lotto.'

'That isn't right,' said Grattan seriously. 'There are anti-bullying laws. Protections against ...'

'Come on away, you,' muttered Ryle, to his mentor, 'there'll be no good to come from being a windbag here. With this kind of mess, the more you stir, the more it will stink.'

'Don't,' said the guy putting up the palm of a small white hand to Grattan, but looking all the time at Ryle. 'Quite frankly, Grattan, I have too much on and I don't know you now. But I can only judge you by the company you keep.' He turned and then looked back with a dry laugh, 'By the way, they discovered that several species of my *unique* genera exist all around Galicia. They came here when our ancestors marched up from the Iberian peninsula it seems.'

After he'd gone, Grattan stood for a bit, clearly stung by not being taken seriously. He wasn't used to that. He did allow himself one angry look towards his companion, deflecting. Then he said, 'Right then, we're going back to Dublin.'

'You'll have to get over this public sector guilt, my friend,' said Ryle sagely. 'Those fuckers chose serfdom when it sounded glitzy. But so anyway, the Carlow mission is again still-born?'

'Carlow can wait,' affirmed Fletcher and then rather pointedly added, 'I'll let Richard know the kind of man I am. That I can't be judged by association.'

'*Oh?*' said Ryle, feigning hurt.

'I've got a friend who is a labour lawyer,' said Grattan, taking out the new phablet. 'Let's go talk to him.'

'I'm telling you right now,' said Ryle, 'you'll be better off leaving that fucker to get old and poor in his bedsit. Like an antelope when the lion has already chawed his backbone, he's standing stupefied, already resigned to his fate. Like every washed-up modern manager he's finally realized he's on his own. He's traded in friendships and interests for the striving and now it's dawning on him that there's nothing left of him. Trying to drum a bit of life back into him at this stage will only make it worse.'

True enough for Fletcher of course, an hour later they were sat on cheap furniture in an office suite near the Four Courts. Fletcher's friend wasn't able to get in on Fletcher's thinking. 'This is about procedurality, not justice,' he said. 'I'd guess they've probably done the CYA.'

'I'm sure there's something can be done where a dedicated man is getting a daily whipping for purely capricious reasons? Think outside the usual employment law parameters. Think class actions regarding pension erosion, incompatibility of US employment practices with Irish social protections, that kind of thing.'

'Good luck with that,' said the jolly lawyer, laughing. 'Out of bounds onslaughts will go nowhere. Everyone knows you don't blaspheme the inward investor. Nobody wants us to lose their Grace. And in the end what else have we? We can maybe take a little consolation from the fact that it's nothing personal. They treat their own very little better.'

'You don't seem to be doing too fucking bad out of it,' observed Ryle, who didn't care for lawyers, blaming them entirely for the short stay in Mountjoy that he still failed to see the positives of. And of course, he knew the cut of a Savile Row suit pants when he saw it, even when it was topped by an everyman open-necked shirt.

'I am getting by, right enough,' said the lawyer, knocked a

peg or two. He knew only too well that in this country it's still uncouth to let anyone see how well you were getting on. 'The slip-stream is where you want to be. Not the galley. That's the trick.'

'Keep an open mind on it,' said Grattan, to the man whose mind was clearly as open as a stable door on this matter. 'Can I book a first consultation with you for my friend? Decide after that.'

Back in the manse Grattan bombed off a note to Richard, with whom he had insisted on exchanging details. He was eager to have a go at his enslaved friend's despair. His report to Richard was somewhat more upbeat in tenor than the legal briefing would have merited. Grattan reached out with *various possibilities* for courses of action to improve the situation, to get recognition for tenure and expertise, to get the company to compensate for pension fund losses, and to bring the whip hand to order. He provided a couple of time slot options for the consultation and said the exploratory one would be free so there was nothing to lose. He CC'd the lawyer and said he would leave it between them but that they should call him if they thought there was anything further he could help with.

The next day, mercifully, Fletcher was away at the toilet when his phone rang. Ryle picked it up and said, 'Yeah?'

'I believe that someone picked up your email to me, Grattan. Richard Toner here.'

'Yeah?' said Ryle. 'Toner eh?'

'Well it wasn't good. This morning the HR Manager called me in and didn't refer to it directly of course. But she was clearly mad and asked me if I'm unhappy here. She asked whether I have an issue about the company's HR processes. She asked if I'd talked to anyone outside about internal company procedures. When I said no, she said that's good because we all have ND clauses in our contracts.'

'Of course she said *that's* good, you clown! It *is* good. Good for them,' said Ryle, who knew all you really need to know about labour law. 'What were you at, starting action against them and then denying it? What kind of gobshite are you at all? If you'd said that a complaint was already under way then the juice of getting rid of you wouldn't be worth the squeeze for them. They wouldn't do shit to you because they'd know you'd come back at them with a retributive dismissal charge. Instead you gave them a window to fuck you through before they officially know anything about said actions. So to speak. Do you understand?' Ryle quite liked paralegal roles when they were landed on him.

'I'm not an imbecile, of course I understand, Grattan,' said the man. 'But you will recall that I did not actually start any action against them?'

'That's not even a little bit fucking material to this,' said Ryle, 'do you comprehend me now?'

'For goodness sake, why am I talking to you,' said the man quietly, not having enough vim to continue puzzling the change of tone from Grattan. 'You should not have done this, Grattan.'

'What is the nature of your concern?' said Ryle.

'She then said they'd like me to be one of the applicants for a voluntary redundancy package that's just come on the table. I told her I couldn't. I'm institutionalised. I am expert only in their custom in-house language. Other companies looking for someone with no relevant experience can pick a less crusty specimen straight out of college. When that got no smile I told her I have a son with ongoing needs. I asked her to please pick someone else, *please*. More than anything in twenty years I regret speaking of my child in that room. She looked straight at me saying, if I need a counsellor to help cope with the adjustment or advice on how to pitch myself in the job market, the company would facilitate that free of charge. In short, I just had the most pathetic defeated moment of my life in front of someone who has been tutored in the right balance of professional concern and detachment to be displayed in such situations.'

'That's not so great,' said Ryle slowly, suddenly realizing that he needed to up his game. He had to protect Fletcher from talking to this fellow. Ryle, not entirely lacking in insight, realized that the campaign might take another setback if Fletcher came to see that he was after doing more damage. Ryle cleared his throat and burst his bollox to sound like Fletcher, 'Em, well well, I daresay they can't just force you to take a voluntary package though. We must fight this egregious thing together. Don't you worry your head about it, my solid buddy.'

'If I don't bite they'll come up with a selection process designed for me to fail. I know very well how it goes because I helped them get rid of others. I too have been on the other side feeling more immune for collaborating.'

'Collaborating, eh?' said Ryle mindlessly.

'The thing is, it was probably coming anyway,' said Richard after a bit, gone back to the beat up state that had been his equilibrium before meeting Grattan. 'I can't take any more whipping and I hate the place so much I'm not even going to fight them. That's my story up to now. We both know the rest of it.'

'Ehh, well that's that then. Game over, governor. Er, poverty is no disgrace but the hell of a disappointment, so the old folks used to say,' said Ryle. 'They're giving a bit of sun for tomorrow, that might cheer you up.'

'*What? Excuse me?*' said Richard, sounding puzzled.

'What class of a gobshite are you at all,' said Ryle, the act a little too much for him to sustain seamlessly, 'are we still talking about you?'

'Good day, Grattan. Please don't try to contact me again.'

'You can take that as fucking written,' said Ryle, his head aching. 'Good day to you too, sir.'

'Who were you talking to?' asked Grattan, returning.

'Nothing whatsoever to do with you,' said Ryle. 'I'm just handling one or two things for you.' Ryle was growing into the candidate-handling skills, growing in leaps and bounds.

The old dog and the hard rode

Chapter XXXI

AT AROUND THIS TIME the deplorable Charles Smith (a.k.a. an t-asal Mac Gabhann) walked in to his publisher's den trying to insist that a photostock image of a Welsh castle should not be used on the cover of The Castle People. He was already becoming proprietary about Fletcher's work.

'We see this kind of authorial concern about cover art and other marketing assets all the time,' Boland reassured Mac Gabhann over one or two Jamesons. 'You are very close to this material. Maybe a bit too close. The writer can't see the wood for the paper pulp, I always say.'

The show was on the road. The SEO strategies were in place. The 'coming soon' placeholders were already appetizingly arranged with all the e-book vendors. A preview had been sent to an Irish Times reviewer who was favourably disposed to Boland. More importantly, feelers had been sent, feeling up the Genealogy websites, the Irish Voice, the Paddylarkery sites, the wican blogs, and the Aryan forums—the white thinkers had yet to learn of the Milesian Sancho connection and were currently ranking the celt as the purest proto-European breed the earth had to offer.

The Gresham was booked for the launch. Mac Gabhann considered sending an invite to his full address book but then a chink of discretion tarnished his pride and he removed certain colleagues' names from the broadcast.

Mac Gabhann's relative pliability around his creative differences with the publisher arose from the fact that he had bigger artistic liberties to take that afternoon. Van den Heever had made it across the equator. She was waiting for him in Mulligan's B&B on the quays.

The young woman had triggered the trip on the very weak rationalization of wanting to impress upon the great man in person, the single editorial mark of significance that she wished he would accede to. In truth of course, both parties' understandings of the unaired reason she had travelled were destined to intersect at least briefly.

'Shit! Fucking rat hole!' he shouted when he banged his head on a low beam as he creaked up the narrow stairs. He passed a corporation notice declaring fire compliance issues. He had used the words *quirky* and *traditional* in recommending Mulligans, worried that she might expect him to spring for her accommodation.

The formalities were few as he entered. She was sunk in the stained and unsprung black leatherette couch with her hands on her knees. She was looking younger and less worldly than she would have liked. On entering adult life van den Heever had rejected the narrative of passivity as it had been handed down to her by a rigid Boer patriarchy. In all the affairs of her life she had determined she would drive. In the current situation however, she had failed to notice the control slipping out of her hands.

He had wine taken from his temperature-controlled cabinet that morning. Using a saucerless cup left out for Lyons tea, she got into that with some relief and appetite. Soon she had grappled her way back to the stable threads of their usual Skype-based interaction.

MacGabhann was caught on the horns of a dilemma when the South African woman said, 'The book is so extraordinary. I've never seen a manuscript that on its first edit needed only a few paragraphs removed. And those were only in the Introduction. You probably wrote that when you were in a brown patch. Mr. Boland agrees that we should rework that before it goes to the printers.'

'I thought we'd closed that subject, my dear,' said Mac Gabhann, peeved. He was torn between the desire to protect his illicitly gained access to her passions and his desire to finally take a stand regarding his creativity.

'Well, come on,' she said, 'pompous and archaic were the

words that came to mind. Who writes *"we shall henceforth observe..."* and uses an umlaut on coordinate?'

Mac Gabhann pursed his lips trying not to sulk right now.

'Come on,' she said a little playfully, 'perhaps you were off your nuts on something that night. No need to worry about shocking me. I've been around. I don't think anyone with so much beautiful prose under their belt needs to be sensitive to a small criticism. Let's be frank here. The Introduction is lacking any of the essence of the book.'

'And what might that be?'

'Fishing for compliments? You surprise me. Well OK then. As if you don't know. The essence of your book is that deep font of love for old buildings and your ability to divine the spirits of the people who passed through them. You bring us inside rather than imposing a cold architecture of historical fact. Your every word is anxious to share a delicate understanding of what is precious, what is crying out for us to value and preserve. You leave the reader so looking forward to your next work.'

'Next work?' said Mac Gabhann.

'Yes,' she said, 'come on, don't be coy. Have you forgotten that you let it out in your notes on the penultimate chapter? That you're now gathering material for a much bigger volume? Early Victorian Dublin?'

'I said that?' said Mac Gabhann. He had been so bored with the content by the time he was scanning the last chapters and hadn't paid too much attention. 'Er, I hope I didn't mention where I was keeping the notes by any chance?'

'Huh?'

'Well just scrap that footnote.'

'And the Intro too, OK?' she persisted, an Afrikaner bitter-ender after all it seemed. 'If you want, I'll ghostwrite that for you. I can only imagine how busy you are.'

Mac Gabhann had put his heart and soul into that introduction. He was a little insulted that this foreign national did not find even one syllable of it to be worth keeping. Still, literary pride was not yet stronger with him even than his weakish libido. A statement that does not by itself mark him as an imposter in the literary community. 'OK, you got me,' he said, laying his hands on her. Mac Gabhann considered himself well-read in the psychology of women. Thinking he could oil her up with a little jealous triumph he said, 'Rumbled! I allowed Fran to write that. But you can do it instead. Nuair a will shuck moore over hell. Anis, pull off the pants like a good girl and let me take a look at you.'

An attack of revulsion jumped up in her. But she suppressed it. Van den Heever was a cerebral type. She was subject to the folly of the intellectual: allowing reason to override what every better tuned organ was saying; landing them up in situations that in a late moment of realization could leave them utterly horrified and bewildered as to how they had got there. Resolute to her type, she let the mind drive on. She proceeded slowly with the undressing that just an hour earlier she had been persuading herself she would enjoy. Even though the heating was on full and the humidity was provided naturally by the damp walls, goosebumps were all that was aroused in her. She folded her arms over a slumped tummy and resumed wondering how she had put herself into this dark and lonely situation.

'What? Shivering? You miss the old Afrikaans heat, eh?' said the ignorant stalk of shit, Mac Gabhann.

The unfortunate person had a further flush of horror as he flashed his downy belly flesh, peeling off his shirt and jacket over his head. He had come without his tie. It was her first full-on look at the reality that Mac Gabhann was not the answer to whatever her question was. The devil had no solutions.

Then, attempting to lighten the moment, he took out his black leathery penis and recalled an ad for steaming hot Erin Soups, 'Here you go, darling, get this inside you. It'll do you good.'

There we leave them. Your guess is as good as mine in regard to what happened next.

Note: unlike the lesser Joyce of the prurient tomes, I am not the kind of writer that trawls any person's intimate mistakes or details the exercise of their bodily functions to give you cheap lifts. *The compiler*

Let it be enough for you now if I say that van den Heever's stubbornness to her embarked-upon trek proved stronger than the dry clench of fear that knotted her insides. And that the despicable Mac Gabhann was hardened to his cause by the very pheromones of her fright as they filled the air, in a way that no tender presentation would ever have floated his little bit of biltong. (Fran had discovered this dodge years ago. She now scuppered the scheduled conjugals, negotiated on her wedding day to occur on the first Friday of every month. These days, instead of waiting for him to get in bed behind her curled up form, looking for his dues, she now made a candlelit supper on the anointed nights and then went to his room in a negligee. That always flattened the little bit of manly mood out of him.)

Note: Fran had come into her own to some degree since discovering this impenetrable foxhole. Much to his disgust, she had got in bed with a literacy project for Roma women. There was a creeping return of her natural ebullience, which he thought he had quashed. He began to suspect she was taking cocaine and more with the director of the project—a man as weak as ditch water from being too long at the altruism game. I mention this for completeness, so you know that you are in the hands of a proper writer, a knower of every little nuisance detail, capable of allowing that even if you are the worst of cunts you may very well have troubles of your own. You can rest assured that despite seeing exactly what you are, I do not set myself up as your judge, but only as a neutral presenter of perspectives. I believe it was de Valera who said, 'The more eyes we can use to observe one thing the less castrated will be the intellect.' [fn]

And indeed I am not afraid of facing bare truths even when they are closer to home, of that I can assure you. Writing is like county championship games. You either come prepared to put it all out there or don't get on the bus. I will readily admit that you are right in what you are asking as you compare and contrast my own pair-bonding setbacks with those of Mac Gabhann. Is it better to be abandoned for being 'a bit of a non-entity,' or stayed with out of spite, for having been too much of an entity, you ask. I don't have answers but I will tell you honestly that it's a question that crossed my mind the day after Sarah moved on, especially every time she phones me having again lost the number of the man in Galmoy who services the Galaxy. He is a top man with a Ford, the same boy, I should say, though he operates from a cowshed and never bothered with the diagnostic software. Credit where it's due. Yes, 'I don't even know who you are,' she said, 'or why you don't have relatives or friends calling around like normal people do,' she added, in fact. A hard and slightly unnecessary put down for a writer, I felt. Was it not enough for her to be getting to leave me? And doing so, at that, when I was on the ball of my back in hospital, leaving the community with the harsh implication that she had needed to wait until I was incapacitated; when in fact all she'd been waiting for was to get off with someone better. Still, I took the hit and carry the limp and only comment on other people's affairs because it's my job, not because I set myself above them. I'll leave you to do that. *The compiler*

[fn] Footnote
Misattributions of misquotations, where would we even have begun with the editing. *The Editors*

As to the dismal situation that appended itself to the annals of human history already ingrained in the furry textured 70s wallpaper of the quayside hotel room, all I can further tell you is that due to a quirk of human composition, the law that makes our pride more rigid in proportion to the sogginess of the ground on which it is founded, our stand-in for the devil would get away with his crime. The hard dry rode daughter of Africa would later chalk the incursion of the old dog on her person, down to experience. That is easier than ever acknowledging you've been outright duped. The further pity is that the incursion, since it had to happen at all, did not last just a little longer. Due to the time that had elapsed since his last successful encounter with Fran, this event was tragically too brief to permit the boiling blood pressure evident in his reddening gills and snorting head to yield a timely rupture of a cardiac vessel such as could at least have given us all, including van den Heever, the last laugh. It wasn't to be. The vile bollox survived his little bursting coitus and was lying back lighting up a cuban when she sprung like a caracal with its hair on end and claws extended. Before he knew what was happening she had him scrawbed, bitten, and kicked out onto the landing with his underpants around his knees, his shoes and socks still on, and clutching his inside-out shirt and jacket with the coins he kept for restaurant tips dropping out of it and rolling down the stairs.

While van den Heever had indeed girded her loins for receipt of his crusty spawn, it seems her lungs had not been girded at all for receipt of his putrid greenish exhalations. No pleading or apology out of him would dampen her anger. She had strong views on the secondhand smoke issue. Which of us is not more peculiar than the next?

Mocking is catching

Chapter XXXII

A BIG WIDE PERSON with tufty brown hair and an excellent out-look stopped by the table where Fletcher was eating capers on water biscuits. The Department was having a tea party. The new man in HR aimed to build the sense of common purpose he imagined had been shattered by Josie's departure. Met Éireann, at least, had taken a favourable view—the sun was beating down out of the relatively high heavens and Grattan was all out in an off-white linen jacket over a festive green t-shirt and khaki ber-mudas. He beamed his welcome to her like she was chocolate. 'We haven't seen you in a while, old mate,' he said.

Mac Gabhann walked past Fletcher and the woman. His distrust of this woman as openly expressed as his disdain for Fletcher. He would not stop to be entangled in aggravating debates. He cast an eye over Fletcher's apparel and said in pass-ing, '*Senior management indeed!* Would you not make a bit of an effort?'

'Nonsense, Grattan!' said Sandy Hefernan. ' You're looking a million dollars. I was thinking of looking for the autograph of the most famous person I know. I saw you on Prime Time last week and I felt proud as hell. I said to my Mum—she's staying with me now, minding me again—I said, Grattan and me, we go back a way.'

'Get on,' said Fletcher.

'Hey Fletch,' she said, 'we'll have to get together soon again. You, me, Margot, and the others for one of those parties you used to have. Those were wild.'

'*Ha!*' said Fletcher.

Sandy was one of those people for whom, in younger years, the mantle of sexuality had never been a comfortable fit. Since achieving premature middle age the expectations had dropped from her like the shaggy hair falls from a May donkey. She had given up her previous rather energetic efforts in the erotic side of love; none having worked very well for her. She had come into her own, thrived and blossomed in every direction.

Note for the outsider: this island would long have been recognized as a concentration blackspot for the ambiguous human conformation. The type in question rarely cooperates with the hormones god or nature decided to squirt into their brains. The terms man or woman, the full package of attendant tendencies, styles, and proclivities as internationally decreed, are poor enough approximations for much of what you will find walking around this jurisdiction poorly kitted out in men's or women's clothing. Since the church gave up on them they don't even marry each other very much anymore, preferring to get on about their own business in whatever peculiar ways please them on the day. Studies attempting to definitively establish the cause of this phenomenon are still inconclusive, with the lines of enquiry having narrowed the possible causes to two. The first crowd from the romantic miserabilist branch of the biological sciences would put a fanciful victimized connotation on this, attributing it to the high levels of uranium in the water. Anyone with a stick of sense of course can plainly see that it's the other explanation which holds more water. (It may still have a few leaks, there being so much yet waiting for our researchers to reveal, but at least it's more basin than colander.) That correct explanation: the described phenomenon is simply due to an innate contrariness, a quality conferred genetically time and again across the length and breadth of this island, and the very same everyday cause of it being difficult to get any good of the people around you in any situation except where they've been duped into thinking that they're doing the opposite of what you require. *The compiler*

Sandy Hefernan was also the bursar in the Department of Heritage and Monuments.

The same stout individual didn't waste any time in her life.

She proceeded with the vigour of someone who understood the bargain: that she could die any day and her stint would be over. She was a hure to deal with as she always had five or ten birds lined up by the time she took one stone in her hand. She wasn't here just to say hello or to prolong an exchange of pleasantries, that much even Grattan knew. She was strict in her use of public time. She inveighed briefly against Mac Gabhann and the philistine path on which he had led the department, as was accepted handshake talk between senior members. Then she asked courteously, 'And how are Margot and the girls?'

'Only great,' said Grattan. 'Margot …'

Ryle moved away unseen from the table where he had been working his way through a plate of cocktail sausages.

'Very good, very good, delighted,' she cut him off. 'Listen, Grattan, I have to rush, but since you haven't attended any of the meetings and I'm guessing you haven't read any of the memos, I just wanted to let you know they've been doing a bit of reorganizing. Business jargon imported where it has zero applicability, adding the final façade of farce to what we try to do. They've made me a *service* director, whatever that means; and you are supposed to be reporting to me from now on, rather than directly to Mac Gabhann.'

'Oh,' said Fletcher, not listening. He had developed a profound deafness for the interior design changes that happened every couple of years.

'As an opening shot Secretary General Mac Gabhann has sent me a note that your salary is to be docked for absenteeism.'

Fletcher heard that alright. 'Oh,' he said in a higher tone. He was a little disappointed as he had been planning on taking Margot to Paris for her birthday. 'How bad? Mac Gabhann will not relinquish, by the way. You do know that?'

'Yes. Well, you'd get paid for just one day,' she said. 'The boss's memo says you've taken unpaid leave every day but one this month.'

Fletcher said nothing.

'But look, not to worry,' she said, 'the proper channels haven't been followed. Nor have I told him what those are. I just wanted to give a look in and check that everything is OK with you? You're taking good care of yourself? You're not succumbing to the anxiety bug that's going around the Service? If you come down with that miasma we're all doomed, Grattan. People count on you, you know? As a rock of sanity.'

Grattan went silent. A few responses passed over his face before he simply said, 'I'm as well as could be.' And then to change topics, 'Have you been South lately?' Sandy had a house in Cameroon where she had once been married for a month to a schoolmaster. She still went there once a year to teach maths to the seniors.

'Lovely, lovely,' she said, already moving on. 'Oh and there was another thing. I have a sister down New Ross way. She's in a bit of a pickle. Paid over the odds for an apartment at the peak. The building has flooded every winter since. They're all out of the building again after the rain last week. They may as well have been complaining to the wind for the past two years. Nobody is responsible, it seems. Insurance says it's a builders' indemnity issue. The council blames the developers. The developers blame the engineers and besides have gone out of business. The TDs for the area keep quietly looking into it. The people still paying an arm and a leg for the mortgages are at their wits' end and I was wondering …'

Grattan looked at her without a word.

'South of the Wexford border?' chirped Ryle, who had reappeared when he heard her change to the other foot and ask Fletcher for something. 'That people, the Wexican, is not even of this Nation.'

The scenario Sandy painted was a familiar one. Ryle yawned to no avail. Councillors had zoned a swamp and now the reality, an apartment block, was sinking in. No responsible party was to be found.

'Here's her mobile number,' said Sandy. 'The building is on Basin Street. It would mean a lot to her.'

'Fucking *Basin Street*?' said Ryle. 'Fuck me, what kind of imbecile is she?'

Sandy took one dismissive look at Ryle. 'Who are you exactly?

And why are you hanging off my lovely friend?' She turned back to Grattan, having said all she ever intended to say to Suck Ryle. She possessed a good nose.

'The man has a point,' said Fletcher. 'How did anyone get to build there?'

'A former minister owned a few of them,' she said, 'an environmental minister. I suppose people took reassurance from that. He managed to sell his but even after he got himself out he stayed slightly behind the campaign and is mildly outraged on behalf of the other owners.'

'Oh yes. The pure blooded Irishman can't resist thinking of himself as champion of the downtrodden,' said Ryle, 'even when he did a bit of the trodding himself.'

'Is there any way you could bring some ... profile to her case?' said Sandy, still staring straight into Fletcher's soft eyes. 'The media seem to be following you around now.' The way she said it was flattering. But it wasn't entirely devoid of mockery either. She had called on Grattan like you'd call on a homeopath or a faith healer—to give him a try when the serious options are spun out.

'Is this what I am now, a media clown?' said Grattan to Ryle after she had hurried away from the Herbert Park occasion in order to pursue other issues. 'Every little victory, a fool's triumph celebrated mockingly.'

'Mocking is catching,' said Ryle. 'Besides, if you ever bothered to listen to my strategy advice you wouldn't have them laughing at you. Your basic mistake is trying to help these people. You know they're all full of misplaced pride and with such types you have a better chance if you're asking a favour than offering one.'

'Even Sandy, the soundest person there is,' Fletcher continued, 'is talking out of the side of her mouth at me.'

'Exactly, a poor man's Joe Duffy is how she's treating you, indeed,' said Ryle thoughtfully. 'I hate that Sandy one too.'

'*What!*' said Fletcher. 'How could you hate Sandy? Why?'

'I heard that up till a few years back before she gave up the sex all she needed was one glass of bubbly and she'd get up on a gate post, male or female,' said Ryle, 'and her with some kind of a husband down in Africa. That's not right.'

'And you know this,' asked Fletcher, delicately, 'because she …
she made love to you too?'

'*No!*' said Ryle. 'Why do you think I hate her?'

Fletcher said nothing.

'So if we hit the road now we should be passing the Poitín
Still in time for a proper buffet,' Ryle said, gathering himself.
One proverb he had never bought into was the one that spoke
against the free lunch. 'These fucken sausages are giving me
heartburn. And then we could be with the swamp people by
half three.'

'Right you are,' said Grattan, pulling from his wallet the card
a reporter from RTÉ had given him, 'let me make that call.'

After arranging the rendezvous with Sandy's sister, Grattan
sat back in his seat and drove. He was dwelling, still stinging.
"Buffalo soldier" was *woy yoy yoying* from the CD stack in the
boot. 'What is that?' he said to Ryle. 'To be the source of amusement to people who are, at the same time, availing of what I
bring.'

'Well isn't that a service in itself?' said Ryle. 'Giving people
a laugh. They need that as much as they need blind courage to
face into the everyday misery of their lives. Otherwise the whole
thing would fall apart.'

'So my service, all it amounts to, all *I* amount to, is amusement?' said Fletcher near to tears. 'I really wanted … I really
want to do some little bit of good somewhere along the way.'

'A do-gooder is never liked, especially not a preachy one,'
said Ryle.

'Am I preachy now too, Len?' said Grattan, so disarmed as to
take in criticism that on better days he'd have known to not take
a blind bit of notice of. 'I didn't think I was ever that.'

'The Irish,' said Ryle, taking the mic when offered, 'are prud-
ish about personal pleasures and don't like to see a man getting
off in public on that kind of carry-on. Just listen to what they
say about that chap of the Hewsons and all his efforts at being
a big generous fellow.'

'It comes back full circle to there being only one way to
get involved without being regarded as some kind of futile

dilettante,' said Grattan. 'That's politics.'

'Exactly. Instead you can be regarded as a proper cunt. People respect that. They give lip service to benevolent thoughts on Sundays, Holy days and after eating well. But the overwhelming force of the world is not goodness and light. It's the other way. In politics you'll be taken seriously as someone whose job it is to get things done for yourself; someone with no serious pretence of high and mighty motivations. And you won't be ridiculed for fixing things only for them who are friendly, useful, or related to you,' said Ryle. 'So you're back in the race.'

'You know it was a flippant throwaway thought in the beginning,' said Grattan, 'and I discarded it as such. But yes. Funny how that happens.'

'Whatever you say, boss,' said Ryle. 'Welcome back to the right side of things. Now we'll really need to start looking at what promises to make and who to butter up.'

'What?' said Grattan resurfacing from the pleasure of stumbling upon the meaning of some other old aphorism. 'No! If by *right side* you mean the cynical and amoral? Nonsense, man! Even politicians mostly want to do good. Some may make a few too many compromises on the journey and become jaded. But only the true sociopaths align with your contention. And those are actually rare. Faith is the misunderstood virtue. Have faith in people and in yourself, my friend, and see decency and greatness flow from the most surprising sources. Without it, we all are nothing.'

'Keep that for the television debates. In the real world you have to trust only myself,' advised Ryle. 'Promises are piecrust, made to be broken. That was the one sensible thing I heard out of my grandmother. You see, boss, people want you to flatter them with the offer of perfectly baked promises. And then they like to feign outrage when you take the first bite of their pie for yourself. You get a few years to do what you want. When the next election is coming around you do a little act of contrition for them, maybe dance a jig. Then, you offer them more pie. That's the game we're in. It's called public service.'

Lord have mercy, wailed Marley.

◊

'We meet again, Mister Fletcher,' said the TV6 person prodding her big woolly mic at him, a dangerous change at the edge of her smile today. 'Is it true they're calling you the uncrowned King of *the Indig Nation*?'

Note: 2014 was getting on and by now there was a bit of a turn being heralded. So many voices were telling the people that we had reverted to being the best little people on earth. An astute commentator such as the reporter at hand needed to get ahead of this kind of thing. She would soon be back to covering the plush refurbishments of the well-to-do. Cracks were starting to appear in the little walls of protest. And she was onto it. *The compiler*

'What's that?' Grattan said. He was somehow distracted, not his usual solicitous self, not picking up that the angle of the camera was changing again. Those who knew him would have worried. After staring into space he said, 'The contract is breaking all around us.'

'Sorry, Mr. Fletcher, could you explain what that has to do with the flooded buildings?' she said. 'What are you proposing now? That the taxpayer must bail everyone out here too?'

'What's that?' he said again, somehow not noticing her backing him up into a corner. 'People are being left behind by the bucketful, the majority striving in a new kind of serfdom. Wrung dry at every turn. By all of the powerful institutions. The government at the head of the queue. Insurance executives just one more hand in people's pockets. Shareholders interests must be served. While family photographs float.'

'So, but … what are your demands then?' she said, determined to the baiting.

'Young people and old men, falling out of the system. Ever diminishing opportunities for meaningful contribution. Women left in impossible situations they never asked for. The system isn't working. Agency over one's life must be restored to the person.'

Ryle tried to move Fletcher away, with a mongrel's sense that all was not well with his master.

'Seriously Mr. Fletcher, you appear rather well-heeled. Are you not just one more iron Johnnie trying to ride people's rage to some destination of your own? What is your agenda actually, Mr. Fletcher?' she redirected coldly. Her nostrils flared, pale and refined, attuned to the delicate bouquet of blood in the water. 'We all know where a road paved with good intentions leads. Where might your road lead to, Mr. Fletcher?'

Fletcher looked into the puckered face for a moment and then he said, 'I'm a nonbeliever, Annie, but I can tell you that some of the best honed words of human comfort and wisdom come from the ancient books. Let's harden not our hearts.'

Ryle's aggravation levels soared at this for some reason.

'There we have it,' she said, turning to the camera with a hard smile, 'the ground floor is under a metre of water and the would-be leader is quoting from the Bible.' Turning back to him she said, 'I must insist though, Mr. Fletcher, the viewers might like to know who do you actually represent?'

'The Bible is at least folk wisdom filtered over thousands of years,' Fletcher was looking dizzy now. 'For example, the three virtues Jesus spoke of can bring peace to the hearts of all human beings. And, and, I would suggest that it remains today as hard for a man bonded to riches to find his soul, as for a camel to pass through a needle. Sorry, what were you asking?'

'We hear him here, we see him there,' the interviewer mocked openly now. 'What is it that *you* stand for? What's the objective of all your campaigning? What's the *point* of you, in fact is my question, Mr. Fletcher?'

'All the protesting, why? I'm not sure. Is it pointless?' Grattan asked the camera like a smitten child. 'I don't think it is pointless. Is it? People are just wanting to do better. They don't know all the answers. They don't even know if what they're trying for has any meaning. They're unsure and scared, protesting sometimes. It's cold to be on the outside of things. But they're trying to have some kind of say. Trying to change the costs calculus back in their favour – to make it cheaper for power to take their views on board than to trample them. And they're trusting that they're looking in a better direction. There's nobody with much of a right to disrespect them for that, in my opinion. Is there?'

'I mean *you*, Mr. Fletcher,' says she, seeing the hesitating abstraction and going in hard to bring the man down, 'not some abstract others. What is *your* point?'

Ryle wanted this case closed before the concussed babbling out of his full forward got any worse. In his haste, he again got caught in the corner of the lens. As he stepped behind the cameraman the interviewer noticed him and said, 'And you, sir? What is your role in Mr. Fletcher's organization?'

'Campaign executive,' Ryle grunted.

'Aha! Campaign!' she said. 'What campaign? So there we go. Mr. Fletcher is yet another one out to get a cushy seat in the Dáil.'

'We're not in it for the praise, so that'll do you now,' said Ryle. He lurched into his own man with a front-on crash tackle that landed him sorely on the pavement several feet back amongst the crowd, inadvertently ruffling the celebrity interviewer. He then whispered rustily to Fletcher, 'Pull yourself together for fucksake, you wouldn't win a fucking donkey derby with that kind of half-baked speechifying.'

'You little shit,' said the interviewer, tidying herself up and putting the microphone away. 'And what may I ask is your contribution to humanity, you poxy little fucker?'

Ryle, not being given to bragging, was not tempted to tell her that she would see later that evening what his contribution to this slice of humanity was. Instead he rubbed his smooth face and said, 'Here's my contribution for now. Every pawn likes to think of himself as more sinned against than sinning whereas in reality he does more harm than good. The reason the general person gets these sums wrong, you see, is that he is a little paranoid. So he counts every random event that he doesn't like as a sin committed purposefully by someone *against him*. Then he fires away on the sinning against others, thinking he's still in the black. The grand total is humanity. A plague of blackguarding lemmings.'

It wouldn't have mattered if this little oration had been about birds of paradise. It was the raw meanness of Ryle's tone and the sincerity of the intolerance it was laden with that signalled a tariff increase for proceeding. The astute crew's appetite for baiting Fletcher subsided. Their curiosity about small-town drama had never been very intense to begin with. They departed the scene in no time.

Fletcher could not be got to do the same. Sandy's sister had introduced him to the chairman of the residents, a tidy buck with hip-length silver grey hair and a brown horseshoe moustache. Fletcher had himself convinced that there was something he could do for this lot.

'There's a senior minister I've had dealings with,' he said. 'I'll get on to him this evening. And let's set up a Facebook appeal for support. Pictures and everything ...' and so on. He readily agreed to the chairman's request that he come with him to a meeting. The mayor had just heard about the TV cameras and had suddenly found a time in his calendar. Ryle could see there was no return to Dublin on the cards this evening and he was fairly disgusted.

'Thank you so much,' Sandy's text said.

Grattan called her. 'What do you mean?' he asked.

'I saw you on the early bulletin,' she said. 'Things will move now.'

'But they made a complete hare of me in the interview,' said Grattan. 'I made a complete hare of myself.'

'That doesn't matter, Grattan,' said Sandy, too honest to contradict him. 'What matters is you got them there and got the cameras on the situation and now there's a percentage in it for the politicians to line up on the people's side of the issue. It may even now be equitably resolved.'

'So you're saying,' said Grattan slowly, 'even if I came there dressed as a clown, you'd be thanking me?'

Hearing the hurt in his voice, she didn't reply. Perhaps she hadn't realized he wasn't just clowning around.

'So it's a fool's triumph,' he continued, 'celebrated mockingly.'

'That's not it, Grattan,' she said awkwardly, 'that's not it at all. And surely it's the result that counts.'

Fletcher's problem was that he didn't believe that.

Hardly an hour into the meeting in City Hall, the sirens sounded. There need be no mystery left about the cause of the conflagration on this occasion. I cannot tell you for sure that being a 'bug' was amongst the hobbies that Ryle had pursued in one of the earliest chapters of that wonderful little life of his, but I can tell you for sure that he gave every evidence of being an experienced hand when it came to the incendiary game. The blaze was expertly started in the middle flat in the second floor of Basinville and so had gained good traction before anyone noticed it. No amount of expensive investigation will ever find a trace of evidence sufficient to activate either of the exclusion clauses, foul play or act of god.

'Isn't that just terrible,' said Fletcher as he stood back from the families watching the final destruction of their homes, eerie glows cast on the dark billows by the cheery amber town lighting.

'What's your problem *now?*' asked Ryle.

'How can you be so cold in the face of further great misfortune befalling people already under unbearable pressure?' said Fletcher.

'There's no pleasing some,' said Ryle. 'I thought their problem was that the insurance excluded flood damage?'

A peculiar gawking confusion flushed over Fletcher. He was too nice a man to admit the realization that was knocking on the door. But despite himself he said, 'But not fire, eh? But still they've lost all their possessions.'

'You can't have everything,' said Ryle. 'Anything that was worth anything will be paid for. The rest is only pictures and memorabalia. The kind of shit they're better off moving on without. Now are you ready to go back to Dublin because I'll tell you one thing, I'm not missing another fucking card game on account of you.'

'What about your own homeplace?' tried Fletcher. 'Don't you ever go back there to be at one with the smells and sounds of your memories?'

No answer.

'What about your parents?'

'Both dead for twenty-one years,' said Ryle.

'Sorry to hear that, they died together then? How?'

'Smoke,' said Ryle.

'The curse, tobacco,' said Fletcher, 'but how sad you lost them both the same year.'

'Fuck no, the house burnt down.'

Fletcher retained the foolish disturbed grimace on his lips as they drove home that evening.

'You're not cut out for this kind of work, boss. Hose those people out of your head now,' instructed Ryle. 'You'll get the vote down there and never hear another thing from them. What more do you want out of a day's work?'

The better parts of valour

Chapter XXXIII

TO TELL THE TRUTH OF DUBLINERS, the alien ways are yet only skin deep with them. Word of death still gets to travel quickly through them and reaches the places it needs to reach in enough time for things to be properly attended to. Grattan got word that Emily Cassandra Esmond was dead, in good time for him to decide between the removal and the burial.

It was sudden with Cassie in the end. They had given her a year or better. Martin Fletcher had been planning to wrap things up in Manila and be back next month to stay with her for the remaining time. But the dank of that building had got into the poor little thing's chest over the weekend past. She had still had fight and determination to hold out. But a couple of fine nurses came, regular visitors to the old nuns now. Under cutback pressures they cut straight to the morphine drip to ease her breathing. Cassie went out like a light. A double mercy effected, they pronounced.

Grattan was very put out on getting the word. He decided in the end that he'd do both services. And so it was that himself and the runt headed out to Chapelizod for the removal. It wasn't to be a big journey. She was to be removed from the bedroom she'd been occupying only as far as the little chapel next door to it. With a bit more forethought the old sisters could surely have roomed her further from death's door.

Grattan approached the pedestrian gate, plain mid-last-century mild steel grill with praying hands and two off-centre fleur de lis tacked on in afterthought. Ryle walked behind. Each had his eyes on the ground, Grattan was thinking about what he was doing here and what he might say to the women, Ryle was scanning for lost property and thinking what he might say to the women.

From the carpark to the left there approached a camera crew, a sight that is getting to be a staple in this document. I'd have left it out on this occasion if it wasn't true. This time at least Fletcher had not heralded the exposure.

'Sorry to trouble you gentlemen,' said a pleasant man. 'I'm the producer of the BBC program, Searchlight. We wondered whether you could possibly arrange for us to come inside to interview the Reverend Mother? The elderly nun who came to the gate simply told us to go away and come back another day.'

'Sorry, folks, but you've come at a bad time,' said Fletcher. 'Give me your card and I'll ask Margaret to call you.'

The man explained that they had flights booked back. They were trying to wrap up a further exposé on laundries and the depravities of Ireland in the 50s. They wanted to give the sisters their say.

'Fine,' said Fletcher, 'but, seriously, this is a bad time.'

'We came here yesterday and got the same,' persisted the producer. 'There's never going to be a good time, is there? The truth has to be told.'

'I agree. Just, please come to find it another time.'

'Are you both priests? You are, aren't you? I am sure I recognize you, padre,' the man addressed Fletcher, trying a slightly more interrogatory tack. 'May I ask what order are you with and what is your connection with this case?'

'What bloody *case* now?' responded Fletcher intemperately.

'We can plainly see the smoke from the chimneys at the rear of the complex. I have to ask this: have you come here perhaps to help the nuns to burn *laundry* records?'

Despite how much he wanted to get on and ignore, Fletcher rose to angry words, 'Laundries, eh? Well yes. We took over the institutions you left us. And yes our post-colonial primates aped the values Victoria had left behind, values that were never ours before, values that culturally catholic Europe never shared. Yes, they continued the sadistic corporal punishments, the magdalenes, the baby exporting, and the mother shaming after even Britain started to get over its shame of sex. The meretricious dealings continued too, just with nuncio instead of King. The moral exemptions transferred to the strident new elite. As for our decades of prurience and wilful blindnesses, to our disgrace we were still in your shadow. It was Britain we continued to copy. From only a short distance. You banned Lawrence, we banned O'Brien. But, yes there's nobody here denying, there are indeed still many horrid stories that need airing in this country. Just, in this convent it has to wait for another day. Please, can you do that much for us?'

Ryle was entertained and not yet bothered at all. There would have been no problem if they hadn't turned the camera on him. There was no way for them to have known the bad history the man had with cameras. He stood alongside the cameraman and when he sensed the machine being turned again, he took a professional grasp of the double-breasted lapels of the man's three-quarter-length black coat. He pulled forward and then suddenly pushed back with the man's resistance, having thought to extend a little right leg behind him first. This may have been unfair given that the crew's own taxes had paid for the hand-to-hand skills deployed by Ryle upon them.

'Oh, very nice,' said the producer, observing the pile on the ground, 'way to go in defending the sisters. You do see how this could play if you don't get us access forthwith? *Investigative crew manhandled by priests.*'

'I apologize,' burbled Fletcher, his face purpled like a ripe bramley as he helped the cameraman up. 'But I've tried to warn you. Feelings are high today. And you've got the wrong Order by the way.'

Ryle stood back like a terrier looking for a chance to dig in from behind. 'You never had workhouses or borstals of any kind at all over in your own quadrant?'

'The man has a point,' said Fletcher, availing of a direction in which to vent a rage of pointed comment entirely disproportionate to the situation, and entirely alien to himself. 'Something I only learnt recently is that passionate blaming seems to often be founded in furtive self-exoneration. Leave aside the fact that the starting point of this laundry story is soiled with unnecessary slanders. Acknowledging all that as we finally do now, respectfully, do you guys not now also have fresher pickings for a moral hypocrisy epic on ground better known to yourselves?'

'Yes, yes, yes,' came a better voice. The voice of a Cambridge classicist, you know the type that can't stand Romans and is very selective about his Greeks. The presenter strolled casually now from the black Range Rover with genetic self-assurance. He was a taller, younger Jeremy Paxman, and owned every footstep he placed upon this earth. He had no doubt that whatever few words he might shortly set out would settle matters amongst the Englishmen and the Irishmen before him. He assessed who was least unworthy of address and made the common choice. He faced Fletcher. 'You don't think we've heard any of that guff before? Attempting to throw sand in our eyes?'

'You'd be better employed to tidy up any current business you have of your own,' Ryle jabbed vaguely.

'Indeed,' said Fletcher. It was no fault of the unfortunate TV crew, just going about their jobs, that some of the issues at stake here had been worked heavily through Fletcher's mind of late, catalysed by the sting of his cousin's words. 'Yes, indeed, while allocating the wrongs of the past, ought we not also worry about what will make people ashamed to look back on our own time in charge? In your country as in ours the very same generation that survived the childhood institutions is again orphaned by living families unable to find a way to keep them. In weakness again unwanted. Re-admitted to lovelessness in bully-ridden institutions. This time there will be no nuns for any of us to pin it on.'

'Closing ranks around a fallacious *tu quoque?*' taunted the evidently learned presenter. 'Frankly, I'm a little disappointed.'

Fletcher was not himself. He reddened further. He didn't want to be having this conversation. He wanted to be inside. 'Know me by the fights I choose,' he said, 'and by those I eschew.' He tried to edge past and reached for the gate bell.

'You must understand,' suggested the cool character. 'We came here to do a job. We insist on seeing it through, not least for the benefit of your country. I'm sorry to be the one to have to break this to you gentlemen, but your own countrymen are the first to cheer the exposition of your Church's hypocrisy.'

'Oh I do understand,' Fletcher's voice choked up in free

ranging anger. 'None of us very much enjoys having our parents judged by today's sensibilities. But rest assured I do *very well understand*. We already blame ourselves for *everything*. Respectfully, perhaps we need a little of your Nation's ability to forgive ourselves for everything. The Germans have managed their catharsis. The Americans publicly face their dark spots ad nauseum. Might I ask, when is it to be your turn? Was it not yourselves in the flipping BBC who contrived distracting scandals around adult affairs and feigned shock at politicians in bordellos, while you ignored whispers about boys consumed and extinguished above the mink halls of Westminster? And what about 80s London where being enlightened meant extending the same consideration to a gay man who took a vulnerable pubescent home as you had always allowed for a straight man doing so? Your chat show hosts were feeling up guests, gay bashing was a select workingman's sport, and Dick Emery was the hilarious poofter on TV. Until the nineties you could still go home after a few pints of bitter and rape your wife. Being gay in a hotel was illegal till 2000. You gave just a little air to those who still called *whitewash* in the case of Lord Saville but none to those who cried *beast* in the case of Jimmy Saville. *Spare me!* Now please just get the heck out of our way.'

'I believe you will find our reputation for unflinching self-criticism stands up pretty well the world over, not least in Germany and the US I might add,' said the resolute presenter. 'And I think it would serve us all rather well to tone down the histrionics now. What about we all try to focus on the matter at hand?'

'Unflinching?' said Fletcher, still looking for more sand to throw. 'So you've covered the invention of concentration camps, carpet bombing, and castration as twentieth-century methods of war?'

'Christ, please do not become tiresome,' said the presenter, finally showing a little flicker of exasperation. 'We are about uncovering new history rather than raking over novel interpretations of old stuff. The role that is required of you is merely to get us inside that gate. After that, you can keep your polemicizing for your parochial house.'

'What can get tiresome is forever being the foil for another people's refusal to confront its own history,' continued Fletcher, the windiness not even slightly removed from his sail. 'I'm truly not claiming that we are better than our British friends. Just asking you to consider whether we are really all that much worse.'

'There are of course a few other minor differences over the past half century,' said the producer now mildly stepping in for his tut-tutting presenter, 'For example, the small matter of women's reproductive rights.'

'Churchill cared about women?' intruded Ryle, a person well-read on breeding and gonads. 'Those old boys were into eugenics before Hitler could spell the word. The Tory has been pushing birth control and abortion up till a sprog can talk back only because they didn't have myxomatosis for the lower orders. You didn't see the queen taking the tweezers to any of hers and heading out to work.'

'All, er, *interesting* perspectives, no doubt,' the patrician, poise regained, resumed on Fletcher. 'That too, father, may I respectfully say, is entirely irrelevant to the job at hand. Had they taught you the first thing about syllogisms in the seminary you would not expose yourself with such hollow evasions as may perhaps earn you a pass from your own parish pump media.'

Fletcher went to speak and the words got lumped in his larynx. The corpse that he had to face was weighing heavy on him and he couldn't find his way through to her. The presenter didn't notice but his colleagues looked away considerately.

'Why don't you take a walk now, head,' said Ryle more plainly to the speaker.

'Oh,' said young Paxman, showing mild amusement, seasoned newsman to the hilt. He had faced Jihadi ninjas and was not fazed by Suck Ryle. He was ready for any change in direction his story might take, 'An interesting side angle emerges: the two priests diverge in anger, one avuncular and the other carbuncular.'

Ryle didn't mind about that. His voice turned quite suddenly to a bloodcurdling bitterness, 'Fuck you and the horse you rode in on, you squinty eyed cuckoo. I'll fucking hammer you into the middle of next week and you can phone me from there to tell me how logical it looks.'

The valorous jadedness instantly vanished from the presenter's face, and his colleagues' words of respectful discretion finally filtered through to him. It may have been the chainsaw-like whine in Ryle's voice that had brought this broadening of outlook. Or it could be that Ryle had already picked up a couple of handy sized lumps of granite. Only a man with a gun would beat Ryle when he was so armed, drilled as he had been in childhood turnip fields to understand that it's a disgrace to allow anyone with any lesser weapon, hoe, sword, night stick, or slash hook to put a scratch on you once you have hold of two good stones; the first one to floor them with when they enter a six-foot exclusion zone and the second to go down on them with after felling, pounding the nonsense out of them. All credit to Ryle though, he was fighting fair with this gentleman, offering a warning word before croosting.

'Well I can see that you men are a little overwrought,' said the bigger man receiving the advice in good part. He stepped back in some state of shock at this kind of issue from a man of the cloth, 'I am now concerned that we might not be able to do justice to the reverend sisters' side of the story with feelings running quite this high.' He then made the mistake of asking the others whether they'd got all that. A kilo of granite rocketed into the very fine digital Canon.

Luckily parochialism and incompetence were so firmly typed within the presenter's largely loving impressions of this island that he confidently advised the others that there'd be no point in calling *the Garda*. They'd adjourn to Templebar to meet the nicer Irish and possibly return another day.

'I'll be fucking waiting for you,' said Ryle unnecessarily. 'I'm the only fox gets into this henhouse.'

Inside, a little ancient person took them to the bedroom. The red deal wainscoting, darkened by years of varnish, absorbed Fletcher's whispers. Sunbeams showed the dust in the air suspended. A half full bottle of Lucozade, an open P.D. James novel, and red pajamas displaced as if only temporarily to a window sill, making room on her bedside table for the mundane equipment of mediation, a warping candle with bakelite rosary beads bundled at its foot.

Cassie was laid out on a single bed with a pine headboard. Impossibly, she had shrunk more. Now very little remained to show for forty-seven years of modest eating. There was a man sitting next to the bed keeping her company, a man who wasn't Martin Fletcher. He said he was her brother. A farmer of a fellow, he whistled involuntarily as he walked toward them with hand extended. He hadn't known her really, he supposed. He had been only a chap when she went out foreign, he said. Since the old people had died out, she hadn't visited much. 'We gets sent things her poor little orphans do make,' he presently continued. 'Ornaments and the like. We would have very little use for that sort of a thing but I do keep them all locked safely in the mother's press. You know, in case there was ever a call for them.'

That was just life for you. Still, he was showing his respects and he was taking care of her and seeing that everything was done right, even though the nuns had left nothing wanting, in fairness to them. There would be more of the family up the next day for the burial.

Fletcher stared at her face. It was still plastic smooth but for a little downturn at the edges of her pursed lips. She looked like she was still holding back what she really wanted to say. She was positioned left of centre. On the other side of her, farewell gifts. Knitted scarves. A real toy telephone—a big-buttoned cardboard Nokia. A wire car with toilet roll wheels. And a card with a big heart painted in felt pen saying, 'Please don't have a long holiday Sister Cas.' Apart from these, a canasta set from the sisters. Cassie had become a fiendish player in her last weeks.

An old priest arrived. He nodded to the assembled and shook hands with the three men, enquiringly. He then resigned himself to a decade of the rosary. An undertaker and his niece put Cassie into a simple box mounted on a well used trolley. Fletcher took a malachite ring from his right index finger. He had won it from Martin in a schnapps drinking contest at Clongowes. He put it in the coffin with her.

They followed to the chapel next door, Ryle trailing so he could quench an unnatural thirst that had come over him. He left only a dribble in Cassie's Lucozade bottle.

After keeping their hands clasped for another prayer they left the church. The boss woman, Margaret, couldn't tell Grattan whether Martin was coming home for the funeral.

The next day Ryle went with Fletcher again. Who knows why. He said it was that funerals loosened women up. That old desire to defy death by procreating in front of it. The thing that had stirred the slapping and riding contests in wakes of old. But that couldn't have been it as there was no nun there showing any signs of an interest in shifting Ryle. Fletcher fancied it was just that Ryle wanted to keep him company and couldn't admit to that. I have my doubts.

As the pre-burying mass ended the key woman rose awkwardly. It had all been going well until then. She was very shook looking. 'I received an email from someone who Cassie ... loved very much. I thought I would read it to you all,' she cleared her throat to give her voice more strength. '*Dear Margaret, I decided not to be there. There is nothing for us to do, only to die as we have lived. As you leave her forever in the wet yellow clay I will be refereeing a welterweight tournament. Kids sparring as if nothing else matters. Bless you and thanks for everything.*' She paused, needing to clear her voice again. Then she added softly, 'The sisters and I called on friends of ours to sing a song for our lovely Cassie and for her lovely lost Martin. Let us all keep him in our prayers.'

Two fairly substantial individuals stood up and were recognized. The one was in tuxedo and the other was well got out in a sequined black dress. He started,

Parigi, o cara, noi lasceremo,
la vita uniti trascorreremo.
De' corsi affanni compenso avrai,

Margaret buried her face in a big white handkerchief. When the woman joined in, the very marble pillars of that little church were set a tremble.

... Sospiro e luce tu mi sarai,
tutto il futuro ne arriderà.

Grattan had to leave again.

Out of respect, Ryle never looked at him until they were back in the manse. And then he decided to leave him be.

Fletcher sat with a blank email page open. Martin wouldn't answer the phone, that he knew. Just then a snippet from the bible came to him with a *ding*. A divine dispensation slipping through a porous spam filter. It had come not to comfort but to twist the knife in his heart, the regret at his own loss. How hard it went on him after all, a deeply connected human, to be disconnected from the comforting thoughts developed by humanity over all those millennia. Balms for every occasion. And here he was with nothing to say to his beloved cousin now. Even a low-brow misquoting evangelist spammer could have trotted out words profoundly more consoling. *There shall be no more loneliness, sorrows, and pains. He that sits on the throne, the King of Glory, remembers you. He will take away the hardship, sickness, and loneliness. He will never let you down. Your season is made. The battle is not yours.*

The battle is not yours alone, he borrowed in the end. *Ever since I met Cassie, you and she have been so much in my thoughts. My blindness fills me with despair. Please come home. Stay with us for a while.* As he wrote he knew he would never see his cousin again.

A minute later came the response.

'The wrong words, Grattan. When I was leaving she held my hand tight. She knew the doctors were wrong. And when I glanced back from the door I knew too. Even as I promised I'd be back at Christmas and stay with her then, I knew. Her brown eyes wet with fright. That's all I will ever be able to remember of her. And I will remember it every moment. That's what we do, isn't it? Ultimately we desert everyone who trusts us until we ourselves know what it means to cry out, *why hast thou forsaken me.*'

Grattan didn't turn to Ryle, who he sensed at his shoulder. He spoke slowly, and lowly, 'To tell the bare truth, just sometimes recently I feel like I'm sinking alone in a marsh and the harder I run to reach anyone, the deeper my legs go down into the black water.'

'You don't know the half of it,' said Ryle, like it was information.

Half a loaf is better than no bread

Chapter XXXIV

RYLE WAS OUT ON THE SALSA splattered North quays one sunny Sunday morning. He was mooching along savouring the superior pleasure, mean entitlement of the sober, taken during these quiet early morning respites in which the rest of the Dublin race is consigned to their beds with liver work aplenty to be completed.

He was also waiting for a woman. Someone from MarriedMattress.com. There was method in everything Ryle did. He knew they needed to survey him before approaching. That was because there was not the faintest fingerprint of a Leonard Cromwell Ryle anywhere else online. No profile and no networking. Nothing to substantiate the little white flies he was dangling on the cheating sites. Google asks, *Did you mean leonard cromwell rule?* And of course these days, not showing suggests abnormality or not existing.

So he held the shoulders back with hands behind his nice sky blue blazer as he strolled slowly and then stood nonchalantly for inspection. He had chosen a canary yellow turtleneck and he had the hair gelled subtly. He comprised a tidy little offering, he felt. He was fairly upbeat about this one. Recently married and probably nervous, she wouldn't be very judgemental. In her abrupt messages she had made it clear that by 'seeking intimacy,' she was not meaning anything too abstract. And though she was wordy, a teacher or a prison warden Ryle had decided, she was good at the conjugation verbs and used the future probable tense promisingly.

He assumed she was the kind who underrated herself, having warned him that she was not all that much to look at. 'I don't worry about that kind of thing at all,' Ryle had reassured her, 'half a loaf is better than no bread.' She had thereupon concluded with reciprocal latitude, a key ingredient for these kinds of flying trysts to get off the ground, that he was a humorous man. And she had agreed on this meeting. Given all of these circumstances, Ryle gave himself excellent odds of her showing up. In fact, she was probably already scanning him from across the river. He'd take six to five on it. He was already planning where he'd go for lunch in a couple of hours when she had gone back to toss a lunch salad for her family and he was free again from these mild and decreasingly frequent impulses of servitude to oestrus.

He stood there reflecting on how the arc of consumptive desire had mercifully become less acute than when he was twenty.

As the seconds of her indecisive surveying wasted themselves, he got tempted to peer across at the far wall of the river to see if he could spot her. That wouldn't do. By way of distracting himself he decided he could do worse than to appear to be looking into the window of a bookshop, conveniently there, the Winding Stair. He faced up to it with hands still behind his behind. He had heard it was supposed to be good, of its sort.

Note: I couldn't comment firsthand on the inside of this or any bookshop. You see, as a writer one should never enter any such place until invited in to sign or read. I might not have much but I do still have my dignity. *The compiler*

Ryle had his own reasons for having interests that had up to now kept him away from bookshop browsing.

There was a good lash of sunlight about the town that morning and mostly what Ryle inspected in the plate glass was his own reflection. However, after a minute of looking at this, the main display behind his reflection also caught his attention. 'Holy fuck,' he muttered.

There was a large poster taking up nearly half the display space. There were books stacked in front of it in an irregular structure that a bookish person may have thought pyramidical. Ryle did not recognize the castle on the cover of the book. But the title began a ringing between his little ear flaps. He had seen it before. Previous to their current campaign, Ryle had on occasion availed of Fletcher's absences to give a quick check of the great man's computer. There had been no mal-intent. Ryle, believer in rainy day provisioning, would just be looking for things that he hoped he would never have to use; in the way that you rarely need a thing once you have it safely in your possession. Bank passwords and the like. His eye had regularly been drawn to the largest subsection of Fletcher's documents folder. It, like the book before him, had been called The Castle People. He had never bothered to expand the folder, guessing that it contained only the mountains of notes that Fletcher had managed to manufacture after each visit to a damp pile of stone.

OK, now Ryle was one of the few who did have a native intuition about the nature of coincidence; that contrary to popular opinion, experiencing the occasional coincidence could not be used as evidence that there was a hand on your chain. Statistics dictate that any lifetime *must* have a light peppering of coincidences in order to give it the look of true randomness. Only a life devoid of coincidence or one that has them coming thick and fast should ever be considered suspicious or a revelation.

Note: Ryle, no more than myself, had never observed a life either devoid or peppered. Of course it's down to your own freedom of religion to make the call whether this consistently plausible scattering of coincidence is due to the planners being meticulous in the randomness department or due to them having gone for the natural effect by taking their hands off the chains altogether. I only present the established facts.
The compiler

When his glassy eye moved down the jacket onto the next coincidence, the author's name, Ryle knew straightaway that the probability of such a concatenation of high coincidence was far too remote to bother considering. Embossed, the eye was, by the name Dr. Charles Smyth. Mac Gabhann had thought the Anglo would get more respect for a job like this.

There was a subtitle, '*The definitive genealogist's guide to Irish Castles.*' And the poster the PR gurus had come up with advised viewers to, '*Establish Your Royal Roots.*'

Ryle did think of phoning Fletcher at that point. But then a woman in a thick brown trenchcoat and a Leinster rugby beanie began walking uncertainly across the Ha'penny Bridge.

Anyone watching would have to acknowledge the refinement of the software on the dating site. It was matching now ten times better than the human eye could have done. She limped over to where her counterpart stood and said in a hoarse smoker's voice, 'What kind of a mongrel are you? You look nothing like the picture. *Debonair* you said, huh? That's a fucking laugh.' She hadn't undersold herself after all, was Ryle's thought as he looked her over. Hazel was her name, a sturdy lump, and she had fallen quite far from the tree. She looked at him and mellowed a little, 'You didn't say you were also interested in books. That's nice.' He offered coffee but she said she hadn't time to waste on that kind of faffing. 'I've come the whole way in from Dun Laoghaire with my heart set on a shag so you'll have to do now.'

Ryle flagged a cab to take them to Donnybrook and he forgot all about the book issue until lunchtime. Then he decided not to phone Fletcher. He couldn't miss being present for the final explosion of a rage so long and unnaturally restrained. A dam wall finally bursting with a ferocity that would make the Lord drop his sole claim on vengeance. Ryle wanted to be present when Fletcher finally recognized that he was being destroyed by his antagonist and that all the mantras about mindfulness and controlling your own sensations of the world, were all so much shit when stacked up against an objective reality of being humiliated and robbed by a half-arsed hyena, insistent on being hated by you.

In order to facilitate this, Ryle was considerate enough to swing in via Dawson Street on his way to work on Monday morning. Sure enough Hodges and Figgis had the fine thing on display too. They were promoting it as a coffee-table offering. He picked it up. It was a solid kilo of Grattan's words and pictures. On the back were gushing quotes from Pat Kenny, Brian O'Driscoll, and Barack Obama exalting the stupendous work and predicting huge success for Smith with the book. Surely Mac Gabhann had forged those. Ryle wasn't entirely without admiration for our common enemy at that moment, it has to be said. Ryle could be a shallow individual at times. However, to tell the truth of him, he removed the tab and put the big awkward thing under his yellow jacket and walked out with it, rather than contributing to Mac Gabhann's fortunes. Then again, that was hardly a singularly magnificent gesture from a man who rarely bought anything, being invisible to CCTV cameras.

Anyway, when Fletcher arrived back from his second coffee break the stolen book was sitting on his keyboard and Ryle was coiled up in the alcove waiting for the detonation.

It was slow in coming.

'Oh Jesus,' was all. After a bit, 'Suck, come out here will you. I presume it was you who put this here?'

'What would be your estimate on the odds against that being what you think it is?' said Ryle sucking in his glee, 'with the same title as you would have used.'

Fletcher said nothing, offering the book back to its wrongful owner.

'I'd take a look inside if I was you,' said Ryle getting a little agitated that there was barely a seep out of the dam. He was committed now and he'd use semtex if he had to. 'See if any of it looks familiar.'

'No, thanks,' said Fletcher, his voice weak but the force with which he pushed the book into Ryle's chest, strong. Perhaps a crack emerging, Ryle felt.

'So,' said Ryle, 'do you think your friend Mr. *Smith* was doing the same research as you all that time? Or have you considered at all the possibility that he has finally put his Seán Tomás up to its hilt in your fluffy arse?'

Fletcher shifted uncomfortably but said nothing.

'Listen,' said Ryle, emerging from a brief round-trip to his alcove, now proferring an oak chair leg with a brass screw protruding two inches from the end of it, 'go up the stairs this minute and beat the daylights out of him. Be sure to target the knees so that arthritis has a good entry point in years to come. That way he'll get a little twinge to remind him of you every time a royalty cheque lands in.'

Nothing from Fletcher. He just remained motionless, standing with an elbow on the back of his chair.

'Do I have to do everything for you?' said Ryle, deciding to go himself.

Fletcher stood and blocked his way, 'I knew already,' he said softly, 'I figured it out a few days after he got me to sign a release that it turned out nobody else was being asked to sign. I stuffed up. *Ça va.*'

'And that's it? *Ça va?*' said Ryle, 'a ten-year labour of insanity, stolen. And all comes out of you is, *sa- fucking vacking?*'

'At least the work is out there for people to enjoy,' said Fletcher, 'so I can view this almost like publishing under a *nom de plume.* Even if the cover is an apalling barbarity.'

'Horseshit,' said Ryle. 'Nobody's pride is *that* castrated.' And I'd have to say, this being an area in which I have expertise, on this occasion the little globule of misfortune was dead right.

'So you know the corollary of realizing that we exist only through others we have reached?' said Fletcher lapsing into his faraway voice. 'You yourself are made up of the grand total of others who have touched you. Betrayal of one of those destroys an irreplaceable part of the betrayer. Yes, I'm hurt, but I'll get over it. But things can never be quite the same for Charles.'

'You can sing that,' mumbled Ryle, putting the furniture item aside and reaching into the inner jacket for the notebook.

'I will concede, it rankles again now, especially on seeing the final product,' said Fletcher then, looking away. 'How could it not? To get no acknowledgement for all that work. Though I loved doing it and all that.'

'Fuck the acknowledgement,' said Ryle, 'you'll get over that. Follow the money. That smeer will be rolling in it and you will go to your grave as poor as the spendthrift you are. Never able to give the lovely Margot the treats she deserves.' Smart comments indeed from the very man who trebled Fletcher's daily lunch bill.

'Ah well you're wrong there,' said Fletcher. 'That part doesn't trouble me. You don't write for money. Especially not factual books. If you're not in it for the love of the creation, then there's likely to be nothing in it for you.'

Note: Your compiler can vouch that Fletcher is the one who is wrong here. Factual books such as the one at hand can make lorry loads of money. [fn] *The compiler*

^{fn} Footnote
The compiler had not thought to discuss our distribution plans at this point. *The Editors*

'Clown!' said Ryle in disgust as he went back to his desk. He would wait for Fletcher's next toilet trip before phoning Margot. Which was when the alliance between Fletcher's right and left flanks were to finally get off the ground.

◊

When Fletcher returned from a toilet break, stepping airily like a kid pretending he could carry any load, Ryle was entirely calm. Pleased looking, in fact.

'What? Suddenly you've switched back to the cat that got the cream,' said Fletcher, sinking into his chair, 'What's going on now? You haven't done anything to him have you?'

'I've been here all this time,' said Ryle. 'You must have been very bound up.'

'What then?' said Fletcher dropping his own calm collectedness since it was wasted in this new situation.

'Everything comes when its name is mentioned except a fox and a dead man,' said Ryle. For some reason he did not like the neater modern form of this expression.

'What?' said Fletcher. 'Did Charles appear here while I was out?'

'No,' said Ryle.

'So you're just saying sayings for no reason?' said Fletcher, so easily sidetracked by idle words. 'What about this then,' he added when it was clear that no further explanation was forthcoming, 'Ar scráth a chéile a mhaireas na daoine.'

'What is that to me?' said Ryle. 'Maybe if you could put it in an intelligible language.'

'I suspect that the soundest wisdoms have been passed intact from when humans first developed language.'

'Do you indeed,' said Ryle, bored already. 'What has this got to do with your problem?'

Fletcher, sharpish: 'You remember that poor guy, the one in

Galway whose wife you took to the outhouse even though he and everyone else could see you through the window?'

'The Foxford alien gentleman?' nodded Ryle. 'I was trying to forget.'

'Do you remember the strange thing he said when he leaned into the car?'

'How could I pay attention with the platoons of bacteria marching off him in on top of me?'

'He said that life is the process of learning the meaning of old sayings. That's true, isn't it? For a normal person. You know it's true when you hear yourself saying something and you suddenly remember your mother or grandfather saying it. And you suddenly *really wholly understand* what they meant. Year by year you understand a little more of what ten thousand previous generations actually understood. What came with being human all the way from Africa. Isn't that something?'

Ryle was hopping a golf ball on the flat of the chair leg like they were magnetically connected. The latent talents of any person can surprise you if you give them time to come out.

'People live in each other's shelter,' translated Fletcher then. 'And do you know that a very similar expression still exists across Africa today? So central to being that no generation over a hundred thousand years missed its meaning and let it drop.'

Ryle missed the ball and watched it roll uselessly under Fletcher's desk.

'The Zulu version is *umuntu ngumuntu ngabantu* – a person is a person because of people. That's all there is wherever you are, whoever you are. We all learn it, some sooner and some later. Sadly for Mac Gabhann, he can grab and scheme for himself but always misses the simple gem of it all, there for the taking, the basic truth without which there can be no understanding or contentment. Yes, he can have his name on my book. But that's not anything in the end. Whose shelter does he live in?'

'The true nature of a cat,' contributed Ryle, edgy, 'shows in the way he uses his claws.'

Fletcher turned on him, a little raw, 'You know, Len, I've defended you against all comers. I've said there's a depth of character in you that doesn't meet the eye. But there's not, is there?'

'Oh, very good,' said Ryle, 'the coward's way. Instead of lambasting the enemy he turns his frustration on his near and dear. He shoots the messenger.'

'But you, Len?' continued Fletcher unfairly. 'What can we ultimately say about a man who knows the oldest of proverbs and recites them at will without ever giving the slightest indication of appreciating the meaning of any? What kind of person gets to the age of forty-five unaffected by any part of the human story?'

What kind of man indeed. Fletcher didn't know the half of it.

Each kills the thing he loves

Chapter XXXV

As to what use the following interlude might be to man or beast, well your guess is nearly as good as mine. But of course, I relate it. [fn]

[fn] Footnote
Of course you do! *The Editors*

A rip of curiosity buoyed Grattan a little on reading a request that had landed in his Inbox. Curtly, he was to go visit Clondangan Manor. Directions pared by the sender's essential form to two words, *Carlow border*, he did not need. Fletcher knew the place, having stood at its chained Coalbrookdale gates more than once. The house was a mid-nineteenth-century Dean and Woodward makeover of an Elizabethan seat, its granitic grounds full of acid lovers: specimen magnolia trees and ancient azaleas of East Asian origin, dating from the time when competitive horticultural exoticism was raging between the manor dwellers. Everything he'd read of Clondangan Manor, its curtilage and plantings, was irresistible to Fletcher. He had used the occasions of various surveys of National Monuments as pretext to take himself to the gates hoping each time they'd be open, incorrectly assuming the owners' phone numbers were unlisted rather than non-existent. However, he'd yet seen nothing but 1960s black and white pictures. The owners were reputedly reclusive and somewhat eccentric.

This summons was not from the Marquess of Clondangan himself. Nor from himself operating under any of his subsidiary entitlements, Earl of Tinahealy, Viscount Clondangan, or Baron Clondangan. Nor yet even from the less adulterated Michael

Cremeanglaise. Not even was it from plain Micky Custard as the owner of the estate had asked to be known in a mid 90s letter to the Times on the subject of bees—the *Crème,* a Francophile affect that had been granted along with the principal title and a herd of buffalo in return for an earlier Custard voting to muck an earlier Grattan, his parliament, and the entire Northside.

No, in fact it was the daughter, a very fine estate agent with McSharry Premier Properties in Dublin by all accounts, who had issued this shout-out to Fletcher. Nor did she waste words on explanation or persuasion. Sufficient argument for Fletcher to visit her home place, she felt was provided by the statement that she herself was at her *fucking wit's end. Someone to match father's obtuseness is required. I spied your name and notable noggin in a Journal.ie article and had an impulse that you might be the man.* She didn't mention how she'd got Fletcher's email address.

'You big bold thing,' said Fletcher as he considered how to reply. Ryle stuck his head out from his hole in the wall to see Grattan talking to his screen.

Dear Lily, Fletcher, two fingered his reply trying to get in on her tempo, *Might have taken you seriously did I not already know your flipping cast-iron cherubs do not part for the public servant. Warm regards, GF.*

She came back instantly, *Ooops, Mr. Fletcher, so sorry for the er flippant message. I was just doodling on my phone. Thinking what to do about Dad's … situation. Didn't actually believe I had a live email address for you. But hey, if you really could go visit that would be so so deeply appreciated. Just to have him meet an outside person especially one with a background in heritage and possibly a predisposition to sharing his appreciation of the place … All that's left of Dad is duty, you understand. He leaves the grounds only once a month—to try to sell poor paintings of his dog at the Tullow flea market. So, sorry for the presumption but I had just been imagining how he might let his guard down for the right person and permit himself to see things as they appear to a normal human being. Btw the cherubs are chained together only to try to prevent those, too, becoming the booty of bailiffs and plunder of pillagers ☺. Access is easy though—come on the side lane off the Tinahealy Road. I can meet you there if you'd like?*

'What the hey,' said Fletcher, leaning aside and scrolling to show the mail trail to Ryle, 'do people just think we float around the country by random request? She does not even say what the difficulty is, let alone what she thinks I should do about it … Much as I'd love to see that place … But no. This is just too arbitrary. We couldn't justify it. *Could we?* Do you think?'

'Don't be stupid, man,' said Ryle, with unusual enthusiasm. 'Read it again. That young one is all but mounting you. That's what her generation is like. She thinks you're famous and that's good enough for her. Besides it's way too fucken late to get selective about who you visit. None of this reverse snobbery shit. That placc is only a short hop down the road, and not the slightest bother to us to lend a Christian hand to a man in need. I wouldn't mind a spin. And to get away from the phone.'

'Yeah,' said Fletcher, with a note of admiration, 'I noticed you've gotten busy on the phone.'

True enough. Ryle had never had a landline call in his life but a week back he'd had Fletcher's line diverted. Fletcher hadn't yet noticed that the silence had been transferred to himself. Handling the calls from the CID boys was taking an increasing bit of effort from Ryle and he was keen on taking a breather. Especially since they'd just got off from telling him that they were coming in this morning for an interview regardless of his bowel issues and the suspected outbreak of MRSA in the return.

Ryle insisted that they take a van rather than the car. That's because he was intending to rob a few small items for himself, a practice he exercised at all stately houses. Since his illegitimate Grandfather Kox had left him nothing, and by the logic that the ascendency were all Kox's second cousins at furthest remove and therefore his own, he felt entitled to do his bit for redistribution where and when the opportunities arose.

'Where are you two headed?' asked McLean, who was entering the building with a jute sack over his shoulder. The others looked at the sharp outlines but didn't ask.

'Out to see The Marquess Cremeanglaise,' said Fletcher, 'want to come? You'd love the manor, it's a one-off.'

'Georgian bastardized by the Victorians? No disrespect, but a 30s corporation terrace tarted with 70s plastic brick facia is of as much interest.'

Fletcher looked disrespected.

'The Custard is not a bad sort though I heard,' added the big article, definitively. Then he tried to lighten things. 'Only here four hundred years. Do you think they'll mix, eh Suck?' He whistled off with himself up the stairs unaware that he had assaulted each of his friends' sensibilities in entirely different ways. Fletcher was left wanting to argue that it was nothing personal—that few escape the Norman caste phenomenon even to consider English co-religionists mixing material. Ryle was left unwilling to point out that they had mixed.

Ryle took Fletcher out Wicklow way without any thought for Public Works speed restrictions or indeed for snack stops. After not much with ninety minutes they were potholing along the back lane to a grassy disused stable yard as a Wexford-registered Hiace courteously waited to pull out via the same lane, right down on its springs with the weight of whatever was in the back.

Then they crunched the gravel around to the front of the edifice, courses of finely dressed granite interlayered with dark brown sandstone. 'Breathtaking!' said Fletcher, gazing breathless. 'Every bit as extraordinary as I've been led to believe.'

Indeed, it would have been a very fine structure if the roof was not widely ruptured and the windows in need of a lick of paint and a pane of glass. A mangy greyhound looked up from behind the cast poles that were barely supporting the creeping-virginia-laden porch.

'Ho ho, what the fuck kind of a place is this?' said Ryle, less enthusiastically. And he had not yet even seen the inside.

'You know,' said Fletcher, with his hand paused on the door handle, breathing deeply through his nose as he did when he had someone trapped in a moment with him, 'these buildings evoke such a mixture of feelings. For me, the fascination of Victoriana is always the least. The overriding essence, a feeling of leaden sadness for all of the souls who here remain entrapped.'

'It's true enough for you,' said Ryle intelligently, 'the gapers think they'd have been the lord or his lady, though ninety-nine point nine nine nine percent of them would have been queueing to get on the back stairs, their lives no story at all.'

They were crept upon by the Clondangan who had peeped out from behind a fine little paper-bark maple. He was small, balding, pale, about their own age, and remarkably gaunt for a living person. He wore a Lidl tracksuit that was well past needing replacing. He stood looking at the car not knowing whether to approach.

'Not even that so much,' said Fletcher. 'When you read Molly Keane, Elizabeth Bowen, or even Henry Green you feel the anger and frustration of people born into rigid roles. They were harder on each other than on anyone. You think of the childhood in a house like this where you were taught to suppress affection for parents whom you might only be permitted to meet at Sunday lunch. Feelings espaliered from the start so that you learn of sentiment as a corruption that would erode all that your kind has built. Brought up with a duty of superiority that cut off the possibility of seeking warmth or new direction from any of the surrounding humanity. Taught to march on with shoulders square to the world. The intensity of the only fully permitted outpouring of affections, on beloved dogs, echoes like a heartfelt cry from little pet graveyards.'

'Of course. Half them burnt the houses down themselves in the end,' said Ryle with a dangerous spark in his eye. 'We all know that but no one will say it.'

'What do you mean?' said Fletcher.

'More to the point,' said Ryle, looking the still uncertain marquess up and down, 'what the fuck kind of gazebo is this lad?'

◊

Custard, as he had them call him, was most pleasantly engaging, showing not a bit of the suspicion he reeked of. He held onto each of their hands in turn as he intently enquired who they were and how life was going for them.

'North Kerry sandstone, I see,' said Fletcher, nodding at a

brown layer of the house wall.

The man stopped in his tracks. '*Bloody heck!*' he said, light-ing up like a wick in a tube of oxygen. '*Well well! You don't say!* So my grandmother was correct. She always called it the Kerry stone. After years of the experts telling me she was talking rot! All those experts insisted that the masons would have drawn the sandstone from quarries down the road in Wexford. But are you sure, how can you tell? What did you say it is that you do again?'

'Pretty sure,' said Fletcher. If there was one thing Fletcher was always sure about it was stone. 'You can tell from that ever so slight green fleck.'

The man went over to the wall of his house and put his face right up to it. 'My God, you are absolutely right. I've never ever noticed. What does that tell you?'

'Some Saturday if you're free, my friend,' said Fletcher, 'it would be my great pleasure to take you to the very quarry. It's just out from Fenit looking out on the Dingle peninsula. Disused since before either of us was quarried. It's the only place in the country this stone could have come from.'

'Brilliant, wonderful,' said the man, delighted. 'I may just take you up on that some day. Come inside, please.'

'Don't I know you from somewhere?' asked Ryle, not budging.

'I don't believe I've had the pleasure before,' said the man. 'But I could be wrong. I have some rather hazy days in my past.'

'*Tragic Gash! Of course!*' said Fletcher also good on bands. Not even a hard-trying college punk band slipped his memory. 'You are dead right, Suck, he was the bass player in Tragic Gash.'

'Don't be ridiculous, man,' said Ryle.

'You guys played UCD,' continued Fletcher, 'when was it, 86? Whatever happened to your lead singer – Trevor Purgatory wasn't it?'

'Trevor, yes, he wanted to get real. He's still at it. Heroin and women.'

'A little part of us all admires a guy like that, I think,' said Fletcher, 'by now he's done everything there is to do.'

'Perhaps,' said the Marquess, 'or perhaps poor Trevor, like the rest of us, has just continued to do the same couple of things over and over again.' As they progressed toward the entrance he suggested tea. They passed beneath the gothic arched door lintels in silence.

'What a fine mind,' whispered Fletcher, turning back to Ryle, 'what a delightful and lovely little man.'

Ryle's disgust was complete then as the only thing that their eyes could rest comfortably on inside was a fairly intricate tiled floor. 'It's said,' said Fletcher, 'that a previous Lord Clondangan had this done by two Italian masters and that he chopped their hands off afterwards to ensure nobody would have a replica.'

'Bullshit,' said Ryle, not very interested. He was looking up at the mouldy cake icing ceilings and then toward the great Adams mantelpieces realizing there was none of it he could take in the Transit.

The sod bounded out from a scullery with Seville orange crates for them to sit on while he proceeded to set the kettle up to boil over a candle. 'Never got in the electricity,' he said sheepishly.

'Don't be shitting me,' said Ryle, 'we can hear the hifi going upstairs. Are you one of these poor mouth guys? We're not from the Revenue so you can show us where the furniture and ornaments are.' Indeed there was a bit of a concerto going on somewhere in the bowels, Ryle was right about that.

The man didn't respond.

'I suppose you read with the fucking candle sticking out of your arse too?'

'Good gracious no,' said the Clondangan, 'I have a perfectly good storm lantern to read by.'

'Things not going so well?' asked Fletcher delicately.

'We're just fine,' said the skinny man quickly, preparing to put a used teabag in the pot.

'Where is the daughter,' asked Ryle, 'I thought she was going to meet us here, she might at least be a bit easier on the eye.'

Again, the man didn't respond to Ryle.

When the Clondangan produced a plastic bag containing a mouldy quarter loaf of sliced brown bread and a dusty tin of sardines Fletcher saw the kind of miracle that was needed here and his heart went out to Custard the custodian. He knew all the signs of poverty, the dreariest thing. A person who has slid gradually into it doesn't notice the slow constriction of life. This particular species of it, the house and garden created with the assumption of a couple of score of workers and an ascendency income, now without lands, tariffs, or hands on deck, sucking the life out of the last man standing.

'Things have been better,' the man finally conceded to Fletcher's gaze. 'I don't go out a lot. So much to do here, trying to keep the old place going.'

'You might think of throwing a few slates on the roof,' said Ryle, 'and stopping the boys of Wexford robbing your furniture.'

'But I'm not winning, am I?' said the man.

'Have you considered,' Fletcher waded straight in, 'you know, offering it to the State? Let the taxpayer fix the roof and curtail the rhodos? Let them plant a few replacement trees where the skeletons of the wych elms lie. Maybe some zelcova.' Fletcher knew there was no point beating around the bush with this model of man.

'Aha, so there we have it, you are on a mission after all,' said the man cordially. 'Lily sent you? My daughter means well but you may as well know this: I'll be taken out of this place in a box.'

'Fairly soon too,' said Ryle.

'Well, you wouldn't necessarily have to leave ...' Fletcher thought he saw a glint of consideration in the Custard. He was reaching here. The Board of Works were several decades behind schedule with restoring the heritage structures they already owned and losing five further years with each new decade. Also, there was no money for acquisitions. But he was already form-ing the arguments he would champion for an exception to be made. An entirely unique building and garden that were quickly tipping beyond the point of recovery. Something had to be done with great expediency. A lease of some sort could obviate the capital outlay—this man didn't want capital. Divert some Local Leader funds and skills to the restoration in return for local input in the running. Custard to be kept on as curator as part of the deal. Give him a monthly stipend that would make him richer

than he'd ever been and convert one of the stables to a comfortable apartment for him to get plump in while Ryle's former colleagues put up the scaffolding around the house. Slightly devious
wheels were turning in Fletcher's head. Hadn't Sandy mentioned
something about being his line manager? He knew if he could
convince her, she wouldn't give a shit about the irregularity. She'd
have it signed through before Mac Gabhann knew a thing.

'Actually, I'm doing fine,' said the man then, retreating. 'But
thanks for coming and I do know your concern is genuine. I can
see that. It's just that … Well here we are.'

Fletcher stood, disappointed and walked over towards the
marble mantelpiece. 'How extraordinary it all is though,' he said,
running his fingers over it. 'All the more so when you think of
the limited tools they had.'

'Yes, yes,' said Mickey Custard, excited again now, the awkward subjects dealt with. He knew he had a fellow here, 'Come
with me, let me show you around the other fireplaces. The one
in the front room is even more splendid.' There was no time
though. All in sudden succession there was a creaking from above
where Fletcher stood and then a splintering and then falling
plaster, joist fragments, an upright piano, a stool and a woman.
The music stopped and Fletcher disappeared under the rubble
and flesh. Lily, up on Fletcher as Ryle had predicted.

Young Custard was shocked but fine, dust all over her striped
realtor suit. She rubbed her eyes and mouth and joined the frantic efforts of her Dad and the more methodical efforts of Ryle,
pulling aside the damp rotted joists. Luckily enough they found
Fletcher on the other side of the piano and he started talking
again the minute a few sections of the laith and plaster ceiling
had been cleared from him. He was in a bit of pain though, the
unfortunate. With almighty strength the two Custards managed to lift the piano off his lower right leg, with Ryle directing
Fletcher when to pull the leg out.

'Oh my, this is so terrible,' Custard senior kept saying, staring
at the protruding piece of tibia.

'It's just so lucky that only the leg is broken,' said Lily Custard,
having got Fletcher to move every other part of himself while

holding his hand and trying to provide the consoling distractions that it's always good to have at the scene of an accident.

Note: back when the compiler had his own workplace mishap, he could have sorely done with such a warm pair of hands shifting the locus of his concerns until tablets arrived.

The compiler

'It would have been a fair bit luckier,' Ryle corrected her, 'if you had left the piano behind when you were going down on him.' And then, gaping up at the hole with some expertise, 'A house divided cannot stand.'

As they were waiting for the medics, Mickey was torn apart with awakening. He couldn't forgive himself. 'How could I not have seen how bad things were becoming? What has become of us? What am I to do?'

'Each man kills the thing he loves,' gasped Fletcher, the shock starting to anaesthetize him. 'I give you my word that I will fast track assistance for you and that you will be kept here to your dying day. That at least is something I know I *can* do, even if I seem to fail at most everything else.'

'Don't talk nonsense, man,' said Ryle unnerved by the paleness of Fletcher now. 'You'll probably fail at this too. I wouldn't put it past you.'

As he was being stretchered into the ambulance Fletcher said, 'You remember, Len, when I said I wanted to be a catalyst?'

Ryle didn't respond.

'Well a catalyst is unaffected, so I'm not that.'

'I'm not affected,' said Ryle, never a truer word spoken.

2FM was playing in the ambulance as Ryle abruptly refuted the suggestion that he might like to accompany Fletcher. The celebrity news was interrupted with a breathless announcement about Rik Mayall's death. Suck Ryle nudged Fletcher, who was finally slightly sedated, 'Hey, you hear that bojangles?'

Fletcher had heard and was tight lipped.

'You and Margot are going to have to find a new *all-time favourite post-punk comedian* now too, eh?' prodded Ryle who had been dubious about the tear Fletcher had shed just a few months before on the news of Philip Seymour Hoffman's passing.

In this, Ryle was genuine. It was beyond him how anyone could care about the death of a person they'd never met. You have to remember, there were people he himself had met every day for years and never sincerely cared how or when they ended. 'You're not having a good year, are you, with all your *friends* dying.' I might add, Robin Williams was still alive and well at this juncture.

Fletcher turned his back on his nearest friend.

A person only through other people

Chapter XXXVI

MARGOT HADN'T EXACTLY agreed to an alliance with Ryle when he had phoned her that morning. He had opened by checking whether she knew about Mac Gabhann's publishing breakthrough and testing whether she shared Grattan's benign views on the matter. She had tried not to let Ryle hear the surprise and anger in her voice. Ryle had noticed only that she hadn't hung up. And that when he'd said there might be a way of causing Mac Gabhann a setback, she had stayed on the line.

'Of course,' she'd said, 'anything you suggest must be above board and we'll have to get Grattan's approval on it.'

'We'll see,' Ryle had responded.

'It's not that Grattan's running away from it, you know,' she'd said. 'He is no coward and that's partly what draws Charles onto him. Grattan bends but never stoops. Charles can't stand it. But now it's this *theory* he has. Which I get, you know, I really do. Kind of.'

'What fucking theory?' said Ryle, knowing right well but being a sharper man than most when it comes to fanning the first sparks of loyal criticism. That is, disloyalty.

'Well, that the only important thing is how we exist in other people's minds,' she said. 'That we are only a person through other people. I do get that in most things. But ...'

'But not on all things?' helped Ryle, his instinct in this as good as any ten-year study in philosophical logic would have equipped him with, telling him that such a theory is an all-or-nothing job. Establishing uncertainty about any aspect provided the undoing of the whole shebang. And Ryle, having never got much into doing, had connoisseurship in undoings.

'But just extending that to letting go of this? Nobody knows how much of him is in those pages.'

'But surely Grattan is right when he says that Mac Gabhann will be the loser in the end?' Ryle had stoked, enjoying himself.

'Grattan assumes that the loss of the love and respect of the people we *exist* through is the loss of everything,' she said, quickly then, forgetting who she was unthreading before, 'because it is so for him. And he cannot fully conceive of a person for whom it would not be so. A person who has never been loved and who really doesn't care. A person who will get off on humiliating Grattan and who will enjoy every penny of the royalties even more if he knows that people around him suspect he got it all by shafting Grattan.'

Ryle now heard the rage that paced behind Margot's barriers and felt as close to being understood as he had ever done. He paused for several seconds before responding. Then he said, 'Well then Margot, we'll have to do something about it. Won't we?'

'I don't know, Len,' she said, not rejecting the *we*, he noted. 'I just don't know.'

'Well you hold that thought, baby girl,' Ryle had added then, 'because you've taken the hard step of talking to the right man.'

'Excuse me?'

'And don't worry about a thing because I will be in contact with you again when the time is right. I always take care of my own. Up to a point.'

'What exactly are you talking about?' she'd asked, slipping back to reality.

It was only Ryle's impetuosity that caused her to finally drop the call. If he'd waited a bit longer before mentioning castration, she might well have consorted further that morning. That slip up aside, Ryle had taken it as written that he had a de facto alliance on his hands.

◊

Ryle was in a mood close to festive over the days after the verbal engagement with Margot. So agreeable that anyone less aristocratic than Fletcher would have smelt the rat.

If Ryle was patient about proceeding with what he saw as his end of this contract, trimming Mac Gabhann's wings, it was not only because of the meticulous protestant brain on him. It was also because he was relishing the prospect of a prolonged collaboration with Margot. He did not as a rule involve others in his work. But this time he was of a mind to make an exception. Nor did it ever occur to him to ask who was playing whom, a question that we can't so easily evade. The allure of a woman, how often has it contaminated the clear thoughts of a generally sound little man. His musings were so bloated in this scenario-planning dalliance that he never suspected that this weakness might be his very own horseshoe nail. Though it might not either, he should at least have suspected it.

Meanwhile, entirely unbeknownst to either of our main protagonists, Margot having never before formed an alliance outside of Grattan's knowing, was to develop a second one not so long after that call with Ryle. It never rains but it pours.

Hobbled or not, Fletcher had phoned her one evening with the now familiar story that he'd been unexpectedly called away. Again to Westmeath. Again, he was whispering on the phone. Again, Margot felt a pang of worry that he was developing unhealthy mental patterns. Margot was not to know that on this occasion Fletcher had actually fully intended to be home in time for their dinner appointment. And that he would most certainly have done so had he not got bogged down on a soft shoulder while waiting for the fracking people; and then been unavoidably detained in the company of Sergeant Geas and Garda Devine.

Just to re-calibrate you, you have now looped to where Sergeant Meg Geas has just pulled her pants back up after finding the frosting glass of Fletcher's side window a little sticky on her bum. Geas' recent ad lib performances on the primal dominance game were starting to worry Devine and he wasn't remiss in broaching the subject with her as they adjourned for their torchlit tea break. The very same break during which Fletcher briefly interrupted his existential exchanges with Len Ryle in order to phone in his excuses to Margot.

It wouldn't have helped for Margot to hear more than the

little she was told. She would still have been just as fed up with having to make last-minute cancellations of their engagements. So this time she did not do so.

She put on her new boho batik caftan bought from a website that catered exclusively to curvy women with a retro hippy aesthetic, her comfortable leather boots, and various other things that I won't pretend I would have made note of if I'd walked right into her on the street that night. She proceeded unaccompanied to the Ballsbridge home of Mary Krakton, the well-known oil woman. Margot didn't offer a bit of explanation to the hosts or other guests as to why the place next to her was vacant. She remained convinced that through casual determination, she could change the habits of a lifetime. There was going to be no more trying to smooth everything over.

Then another turned up partnerless, Donal Horace, the head of a forex empire. In his case apparently everyone knew the explanation and just asked politely how poor Sally was coping these days. He was set into Grattan's place much to Margot's displeasure. But she smiled politely and continued her new fight against her instincts. She didn't try to fix it. On the contrary, she talked away to Donal Horace like she was a person open to being flattered freely by his awkwardly exaggerated courtesies.

Margot had never known Horace before. As for Horace, he had known Margot before. They'd been teenaged at the same time in Kings Hospital School. She'd been ranked as classy by the prefect who got lucky with most girls. And then as iceberg. Horace hadn't even got around to talking to her.

Not at all icy, Horace now determined. He felt her avid eyes take in everything about him with the sure poise of a cat padding her way expertly toward engagement. He felt no ice either when they occasionally touched shoulders. But he also caught the tone of her occasional references to her husband and observed how her eyes closed for a moment with Grattan's name. He got it. Her flirting was only for Grattan. She had something she was getting around to talking to him about. Though Horace knew well that he too was not going to get lucky, he settled for the dance.

A lot of wine disappeared along their metre of the table. I can't say if it would have been considered too much as I don't know the protocols of a sophisticated life. (I know you might never have guessed that but I prefer to be upfront about these things.) As the others were sucked off to Mary's studio in the basement to get a sneak peek at some aggressively daubed canvasses that she was going to be exhibiting the very next week, Horace and Margot stayed at the table, neither with an appetite for art just then. Their eyes made many incidental contacts as various subject matter sloshed and rolled by them like waves off the side of an ocean liner.

At some point when she again made mention of the fact that Fletcher was engaged in various projects, Horace responded, 'Indeed. It sounds like your little man is brave. He's going headfirst at it—taking the present as the time to do or die. I'm intrigued and I promise you I'm going to do a bit of research on his stuff.'

Fletcher was not little. He was six-two if he was an inch. But Margot shrewdly let the ex-rugby man away with this small conceit.

Horace then gave a more sticky look at Margot as he revealed that he had been thinking about his own footprints during a recent stint in hospital, getting stents inserted in himself. 'What is your husband's plan?' he asked. Margot lit up, her instincts proven good. Even in drunk flirtation, worried thoughts for Grattan were clocking up. 'I think,' she said, having to think on her feet because recently she didn't know what Grattan was about, 'at heart I think … he's just wanting to do his bit to restore some decency. And such like.'

Margot was coming to the view that the best thing for her husband would be to get out of the Department. She hated how his dutifulness toward his family, trying to extend them a secure footing now for another generation, had allowed him to be handcuffed by Mac Gabhann; wilfully constrained, kept from any work other than that which was the most patently futile. And now there was the book.

So she dipped another cornbite in a horseradish sauce that

had soy sauce unnecessarily added, and put the thing to her lips. She was again rubbing shoulders with her neighbour because neither of them was small. She was estimating the touchline before she kicked. 'A solution to the nice man's predicament,' she said while politely closing her teeth on the unsavoury snack, 'might coincide with a solution to Grattan's then.'

'Explain,' he said, pulling back to look at her whole.

'Well have you considered hiring someone with whom you might be quite in tune?' she kept going now that she'd picked her spot. 'You know, to apply some of your clever winnings with equally astute conscience while you could remain at the main table a while longer, playing for the people who've come to depend on you remaining this *alien ruthless man* that you've created.'

Horace went quiet. He wasn't sure he liked her paraphrasing his sincerest disclosures so flippantly. But he got over it. 'OK,' he said, 'you know, maybe. Maybe not the worst suggestion in the world. OK? I'll think it over.'

That's the class of person Margot was. So overwhelmed by care of those around her that thoughts for herself never dominated. She didn't take anything for herself from Horace. There were exchanged looks that left no doubt about another way the evening might have proceeded.

Note: I can nearly hear you ask, what chance did Suck Ryle ever have when not even an International rugby billionaire could get more than a prolonged look out of Margot, even on a night when she was mouldy drunk and fairly pissed with Fletcher to boot? Let me tell you those odds would not have fazed the same bold little man at all. He didn't lack heart in that respect. *The compiler*

When the host's Bang and Olefson started issuing the plaintive heart plucking electrics of Eric Clapton at his best ... *this beautiful lady...* Horace looked embarrassed. It did not stop him mouthing, *you are wonderful tonight*. Margot got up to go. She and Horace held each other a second longer in the parting hugs, a briefly dwelt upon unspoken thing that is probably every bit as good as coitus for sophisticated people like Horace. None of the other guests noticed the lingering grasp.

Note: why would they? Even in the highest class of Irish company there are not yet standards and guidelines for the correct application of embrace and cheek kisses between acquaintances. Why, for instance, should a gay woman have to welcome the approach of a man's wet lips when she is every bit as revolted by the idea as I am myself? And how is the sensitive man not to feel left out when he doesn't get any bit of a cuddle from his best friends? I stay away from the whole thing myself. Not too hard for me of course, since in the areas I frequent, you don't get asked to cross that boundary even with people who might have given birth to you. *The compiler*

Don't mind your neighbour's garden

Chapter XXXVII

FLETCHER, LIKE RYLE AT LEAST in this, was in surprisingly good form those days, click-clicking around the place like he was born to crutches, not a worry lingering about how well he'd master marsh with them. The book thing had been weighing on him for a while. Perversely, now that his humiliation was out there for all to guess at, he was unburdened. He was not going to be devoting any minutes let alone years of his life to a quarrel. If he was going to be jealous about anything in his life from here it was going to be in guarding his mental garden and in weeding out that which could strangle preferred thoughts or deplete the soil of any molecule of nutrient. And so on, to that effect. In short, despite seeming weak to those around him, he was the strongest of them all because he ruled his brain with a gardener's obsessiveness. Or at least, he did so some of the time.

To make matters better for him, he got a call.

'Grattan?'

'Yes.'

'Donal Horace here,' said a voice which we can only assume was Donal Horace's. 'I got your number from a Traveller woman I met in woods down near Borris ... You helped her after her daughter got in trouble.' It was true enough about the woods and the woman. The odd woodland encounter coming so soon after he'd put Margot out of his mind, had startled Horace, a logical man, into reflections on fate.

'Ah,' said Grattan, relaxing, 'Margaret Collins. How is the good lady? Are you one of her family?'

There was silence for a second. Even though he was down with the altruism thing, Horace was not yet on to the purest form, the anonymous gig. He was accustomed to people knowing who he was before he set them at ease in conversation with him. He was not, on the other hand, used to meeting people who could tell no difference between a Clontarf accent and a tinker's. 'Horace,' he gathered himself, with a laugh, 'I captained the Irish team once or twice back when it was easy?'

'Ah,' said Grattan who kept only a very occasional eye on the rugby. 'Donal. How are you?'

'Not bad,' Horace laughed.

'From all I've heard,' said Grattan, 'you are a gentleman. How do you know Mrs. Collins?'

'That means much coming from you,' said Horace, knocked off balance by the direct turn from Fletcher. 'Mrs. Collins and I walk in the same woods, as it happens. Fellow travellers, you could say.'

'And fellow countrymen,' Fletcher came back.

'You are doing your bit to try to help people where you can?' said Horace. 'So I understand?'

Fletcher said nothing.

'A thankless task, skirting all the time on futility, do you not think? The closer you look the worse everything seems, don't you find?' said Horace. 'We really are such a horrible species, are we not?'

'That doesn't make sense,' said Fletcher. 'No species is good or bad. Ours just has more responsibility because of the power we have accrued.'

'So … the white man's burden extended to all of humanity, eh?' tried the other.

And so it went. The two of them got into tag tackling, each with enough respect for the other not to be immune to the jibes as well as to little bits of flattery from him. Horace heard himself confide that he was trying to get the measure of all things in his life. That he found himself increasingly overcome with the feeling that he had ended up where he was by a series of accidents. He was only happy these days when he was away in those woodlands that he had planted on the Southern slopes of the Blackstairs. But he couldn't find the courage to go there permanently. Too many people depended on him remaining the person he had created. And so the call. He had heard a little of Grattan's doings and he was riding an intuition that they might connect.

Though not a million miles off the whole truth, as we know, this was not quite that. Despite the level he had got to, Horace had never in his career actually had the courage to make a cold call, the bread and butter of all business.

Fletcher never even wondered how Horace had got his mobile number from the Collins lady who didn't have it.

By the time he ended that very first phone conversation with Horace, not ever even having had a lunch with the man, Grattan Fletcher had a potential benefactor and a job offer to consider. 'Every bard needs a patron,' Horace had just said to him.

'I'll have to talk to Margot and the girls about this,' Grattan had said, 'giving up the anchor of the pensionable job is not a decision I alone own.'

'The pension will be taken care of. So you do that,' said Horace, allowing himself a sly moment of satisfaction. It passed Grattan by. Horace had concluded, 'You go see what your lovely mainstay thinks and then please get back to me, my friend.'

Grattan's thought was that he was going to have to be very careful with himself about this. Asking at all would put Margot in an impossible position, he thought. Yet he was plain excited by the idea. You don't know how badly you're harnessed until you let yourself imagine just for a minute, being fully unyoked. How much more constructively could a working day be spent when you and your boss saw objectives similarly. He was already sure it would be like that with Donal Horace. There was an inexplicable connection. Besides, how could he turn away money that might change lives?

Over the next weeks Horace phoned every morning at about seven thirty when most other desks in both their offices were still empty. He wasn't putting pressure on. He was just wanting to talk shit about this and that. Grattan came to appreciate it at that particular moment in his life, more than he would have at any other. Two walkers of different universes. They had never met. Yet Fletcher felt the entanglement. It was very good. He looked forward to the calls. So he delayed telling the man that he wouldn't be taking his shilling.

No mistakes, the worst mistake

Chapter XXXVIII

WHEN RYLE AND FLETCHER headed out of a Tuesday in early May, one nearly as jaunty as the other, each had noticed the other's recently improved manners but neither guessed the respective reasons. What matter.

They walked out onto the wide Northumberland pavement and turned onto Haddington Road heading for the Argentinian restaurant (Ryle liked their beef). They nearly bumped into Ryle's limpy. She was in a suit, devoid of the rugby beanie, and had the hair nicely brushed. She was a Vice President with Chase Stanley Arbitrage, it transpired. She comes right up to Ryle, no bullshit, and says out in front of Fletcher, 'Are you fucking following me?'

'Do I know you?' said Ryle.

'Anyway, it's good we've bumped into each other, Michael, because I notice that your profile has been taken down from the MarriedMattress site.'

'What's good about that?' asked Ryle.

'Well it occurs to me now that I should tell you, you have been on my mind a bit,' she said, dropping the agro. 'It seems I quite like you. Hey, I'm as surprised as you are.' Another good match made.

This character, Noraid, she would be on a good salary and mighty bonuses, let me assure you. Nor was she any more married than he was – she too had lied. She had a half grown daughter and nobody else looking to share the teat. Suck didn't need anyone to point out opportunity—if he took up with her he'd be well-kept and could retire early. Yet this brave creature, exposing herself squarely in his face, was barking up the wrong tree.

'I quite like you too, as it turns out,' he confided, 'but I like not having you near me even more.'

She looked a bit crestfallen, as you would be when you get an insult you don't understand from someone you didn't think had a vantage from which to insult anyone. 'Nothing personal,' clarified Ryle. In fairness, his habits were very precious to him.

'It is though, you know,' she said, dwelling on the minor hurt, not realizing how light she was getting off. 'It's a little bit personal, Michael. Can you see that?'

'You are a shitty little man, *Michael*' said Fletcher disgusted, as he watched the good woman hop away with surprising briskness. 'Forget the beef now and let's hit the road.'

They proceeded to the Lexus and took off. They were going to meet two fishermen from East Cork who had had their boats confiscated as punishment for giving collateral cod to a nursing home instead of dumping it to rot in the sea. 'This is great all the same,' said Grattan, 'isn't it Suck?'

Fletcher's mobile rang. A number it couldn't pin a contact name to came up. He answered and groaned as the first sounds came through. With his usual unnatural timing, it was Mac Gabhann, the sluther. Starting always as though he was trapped in mid-conversation with Fletcher, '… most people defeat themselves of course. Like in a game of cards when they become convinced their luck has turned against them and they proceed to seek only bad luck and defeat as confirmation. A peculiar human trait, wouldn't you say? Linked to troupe subservience—resentments, regrets, and paranoia bring even the most ebullient into line in the end. Isn't that right, Fletch?'

'What is it you wanted?' asked Fletcher in depressed tones.

'Aha! Touched a little nerve have we? Have you considered SSRIs at all, Grat?' the sound bouncing from Fletcher's ear lobby into the car.

Mac Gabhann continued casually, 'You know, cut to the chase? There's no shame in it these days.'

Grattan's voice cold and hollow, 'So you think every phase and tidal movement in a person's life is a chemically remediable condition?'

'Perhaps, perhaps not,' was the considered response out of the foul mouth, 'but we're just talking about *you* here, Grat. You have the classic symptoms, you know. A sudden realization that the family you've overly vested in and the ideals you've blindly trusted in are dissipating into the ordinary mess of everyday things. So now you rush like a fool to find the relevance you had always assumed automatically accrued to you. Treading frantically to avoid the inevitable fall to earth. Alas Grattan, you can turn this way and that but you'll soon accept that the loftiest fall hardest.'

Ryle pulled up his collar—he knew as well as the next person that the bad thing about depression is that the wrong people get it.

'We are destined to fall every single day, Charles,' said Fletcher, quietly. 'It's when you decide not to get up again that you've lost anything worth anything.'

'Ease of mind not worth anything, Grattan, eh? Don't tell me you wouldn't give your right testicle to have a little of the contentment enjoyed by those of us better grounded?'

'Good day,' said Grattan, ending the call. Silence followed.

'And how are things with Margot?' Ryle chirped sometime later as they pulled off the motorway to head into a Tipperary town, Ryle having developed a craving for a rock bun.

'Good enough,' said Fletcher. They drove slowly along the main street on which little else moved. They stopped at a house on the outskirts where the gate was still swinging after the last person leaving. The sight of a new D reg had the remaining heads, zombies, spinning. News of the end of the recession hadn't reached here yet. One flagged them down and said, eying the car, 'Isn't it mighty for you coming down to sympathise with us, and you maggotty with money.'

They should have guessed by this eerie turn of events that their luck had turned against them. But then if you were to guess worse to come every time that a peculiar thing happens, you'd never get out of bed at all.

'Great,' said Ryle, after Fletcher had rolled up the window, 'give her my best.'

Fletcher decided to stay off the motorway until they hit a place with more heart.

Next they stopped at a warehouse on a bend in the old Cashel

Road. The hardcore had been colonized by willow weed since the last trucks had departed. Yet there was shimmering heat over the roof and so nothing would do Ryle only go in. Although the man who slid the steel doors open was Vietnamese, he was dressed like a native and it was plain that you might as well be talking to the wall as asking such a person about where you might get rock buns. Behind him, his fellow new Tipperary people continued diligently picking hemp leaves into baskets. 'Well boys, that's not too bad a day now, thanks be to god,' said the man in his badly broken English. 'Why are yez lookin for rock buns anyway, are the croissants beyond in Mary Willie's not good enough for Dubs now, eh?'

They drove off and hadn't got much further when they had to stop because there was a circle of crows on the road in front of them, refusing to rise up. One unfortunate crow in the middle was getting a dressing down for some misdemeanour and it looked like the others were set on being judge, jury, and executioner. So much for the old ways, put me in front of a modern court any day of the week, with its inbuilt sympathy for miscreants.

This sight made Ryle very nervous indeed. True, it isn't a thing you'd see every day. But Ryle was very yorky when it came to rooks. Poor old harmless Grattan merely thought it a wonderful spectacle. He took pictures of the dark, wily things on his Nokia product, placed on the dash for steadiness. The great corvidians looked back through the windscreen at him with cold pre-historic eyes. He then got out to shoo them off like they were dumb-assed chickens. They merely hopped to the side as one, eyeing him steadfast and without comment.

Unfortunately, as the ups and downs of life dictate, the two lads never made it to their rendezvous with the fishermen, nor even penetrated the vast hinterlands of the county of Cork, Ireland's Congo. Ryle was pale and in need of a pee after the recent sequence of events. He was thinking strongly that they must turn around and go back to Dublin and pull blankets over their heads until this day had passed completely by. It was to be one of the things that he would regret for some period, not getting around to saying this to Grattan.

They stopped into the gateway of a field of thistles within a stone's throw of Cashel, near the Devil's Bit to be precise. As Ryle went to get out, Fletcher again put his hand on Ryle's shoulder. The situation froze. 'I just want to say this, and I'm not sure why now seems like a good time,' he said in a fearful voice suddenly childish with vulnerability, 'do you remember that night we were bogged on the hill? Sitting ducks for our Garda friends? And you remember, you accused me of undermining other people's beliefs and all that?'

Ryle remembered only too well. This time he turned around and bit the hand that so often fed him, expecting to implant an incisive memory mark.

'*Ow!*' said Fletcher retreating, and shocked briefly into bluntness, 'You know, *I do get it, Ryle, you bloody, you, you* ... ? It's not impercipience, you know. I'm not absolutely thick. It's not that I hadn't *noticed* your personal barriers. I just haven't wished to leave you like that. My actual lack of perception has been in thinking there must be some level on which you are crying out to be reached. But I have been wrong, haven't I? A funny thing, that, from the person who clowns about existentialism as if it was an alien concept to himself. Yet you're the only human being I've ever met who could truly say without any shred of unappealing romanticized self-pity, that you are surrounded by uncrossable personal space, that you exist genuinely in that empty room and are truly unperturbed by the cold; that you go through all, out of reach to any other person. Where does that come from, Len?'

Ryle looked out the window, largely untouched, his point made. He didn't care either way.

'Anyway, as my dear friend, please tell me *you know* it's not like that. I'm not claiming I'm sure of the way, Len. You know that, don't you? I don't claim to understand. Not death. Not even life. I look in the eyes of our boxer and see a whole world of emotions beyond my touch. I am arrested by wonder at a little oak seedling knowing when to let go of its leaves. I find myself astonished at more each year, rather than less. The gap is too wide between my awe and the explanations received from biochemistry and probability. I see things far beyond my comprehension. I'm only trying my personal honest best to find a way that is alright in the end.'

'As Heisenberg said,' said Ryle, thinking this an opening for meaningless statements, 'you can't have your cake and eat it.'

Note: in case you think the tech education served him better than you'd been led by me to believe, the mention of Heisenberg came from a quiz book that Ryle had been brushing up on as they drove. *The compiler*

'Jesus preserve me, what am I like,' said Fletcher quietly, to himself, 'what on earth is the matter with me?'

'Dear friend now, eh?' Ryle reflected, a bit nonplussed all the same. Had he been any other kind of person he'd have regretted the blood flowing from Fletcher's knuckle. 'Come on here,' he said, 'I'm bursting.' They got out and crossed the gate as if they'd been doing it all their lives. Fletcher a bit slower, granted, with the plaster of paris on his left foot slipping off the bars.

It was a lovely day indeed for people taking an unhurried side step from their ordained trajectories, as it does us all good to do sometimes. There were a few black cattle a bit away in the field grazing contentedly on the docks and crow's foot buttercups. 'Kerry cattle,' Grattan announced, back to top form. 'The most ancient Irish breed and by the physiognomy, I'd say they came with us from Spain nine thousand years ago.'

Not everyone knows it, but there's a strain in the harmless looking little Kerry cow that is cracked to the world. Not even Ryle knew this, though you can be sure he'll remember it for the future.

Note: in case you don't understand genetics, how it works is if you have any people resurrected from only a handful of genes, like would be the case with many isolated and aloof peoples, you can get magnification of any little weaknesses they might have hitherto hidden. On this island one of the weaknesses common to the people and to their cattle was in the derailleur that controls mood. The human islanders can find themselves reeling freely between high and low gear sprockets without constraint, and so who among us can blame the cow of a

rarified breed who finds herself in the same predicament?
The compiler

Anyway so here we have the two indolent government men standing about twenty feet apart with a slight angle between the ways they were facing so neither should have to catch a glimpse of the other's mickey. Up comes one of the Kerry cows casually walking between them like she was more used to the company of people than of her own kine. She had none of the herbivore flight zone. From a hint of an in-heat lifting of her upper lip, it was clear she had noted the fresh streams of piss splashing on either side of her but seemed not bothered by that either. There wasn't a calf or dog in sight and so, unlike at the house in Walkinstown, there was no reason to blame Fletcher for not having sensed danger. In fact she looked as even-headed as an English cow, a Hereford or Sussex. This cow however was unstable as befuck, that's all. There's no way of knowing how she decided on Fletcher. Though you couldn't entirely eliminate the smell of his knuckle blood as a clinching factor. But having made her choice, it didn't help that his crutches were lying on the ground as he worked his zipper or that the rare breeds have a derogation in respect of keeping the horns. The ten-foot run from the midpoint was enough to drive the curly right spoke through the poor man's chest. As she turned her head toward Ryle he could see the black tip sticking out between buttons at the front of his cheesecloth shirt.

Ryle hurled himself at the cow, boxing and kicking her head and shoulders and smashing her arse bones with a handy rock as she shook her head to get Fletcher off the horn.

Fletcher didn't scream as he fell. He just said, 'Len, is it bad?'

'No, it's only a bit of a gash,' said Ryle as the cow stood back wondering what to do next.

'Len, I'm so afraid,' said Fletcher, holding the other's hand as the voice was fading.

'Whissht now,' said Ryle, 'I'm calling for the ambulance.'

'I'm done for, amn't I? Tell the truth please, Len.'

'A couple of stitches and no one will be any the wiser. Spare your breath now, there's enough of a leak.'

'I've made so many mistakes,' gasped Fletcher.

'The only way to make no mistakes is to do nothing,' said Ryle, finally not pushing Fletcher's hand away. 'The worst mistake of all.'

'Please tell Margot and the girls I love them and I will be with them forever.' Then he gave way to a low moaning that was the common language of many a dying mammal. The cow came forward again.

'Are you fuck done,' screamed Ryle, giving a reasonable impression of being perturbed, 'this is not on the fucking agenda.' In a single frantic movement Ryle then took out a fine strong Gerber knife from the inside pocket of the leather jacket, unfolded it, and jumped behind the offending lady to slash her hocks like a Whiteboy. She sagged at the back but didn't turn. She was intensely focussed on Fletcher. She had only one mission. As Ryle tried to roll the long bleeding body away, the heifer stumbled forward and knelt on Fletcher's poor bleeding chest, squeezing the last breath out of him. She exhaled warmly onto his face through her nose, now nuzzling him like a newborn. Hormones can go wrong. Too late, Ryle did what anyone would know he should have done first: brought the rock onto the back of the dome of her skull. She dropped off to die by Fletcher's side, doing a sad bit of moaning of her own.

I would have liked to write a different outcome but since I already told you I was at the funeral, there'd be no percentage in that.

Ours, not to reason why

Chapter XXXIX

No NEGATIVE COMMENTS were heard about refreshments being offered *before* the month's mind mass. It was appreciated how far people had travelled. Where else but in the Heyns place. Several bottles of Grattan's most prized malbec were offered around. What could you do out of respect for the man, but drink it? It wasn't too bad, I'd have to say, even though I wouldn't drink red as a rule.

The numbers were down on the funeral. The poorer showing wasn't necessarily evidence of fading memories. Most of Fletcher's crowd had reasonable grounds to feign ignorance of such traditions as mind masses. There were no straw boaters, no Nigerians, no camper vans, and no foxy alien. There were of course the bogmen. Also in attendance was one guard from the Crusty Squad. There too, a palefaced loner in a leather helmet and airman goggles uploading images of himself eating water biscuits and cucumber—he'll do as Daly, moved on to steam punk, I'd heard. Things change fast these times. He was failing the eye of a tall young one who was mixing awkwardly. The person in question spoke in a non-Trinity accent. She wore a charity shop greatcoat, a swimsuit under it, no doubt. Too late for rescuing Fletcher now.

There was a warm loud tufty haired woman, who I'll put down as Sandy. She stood herself next to the still stony-faced Margot. The latter was at the counter making sure everyone got the sandwich or strudel they wanted. Sandy occasionally put a hand on Margot's shoulder but that made no difference to her expressionlessness.

Ryle was there of course. The fluster of the funeral was well gone off him and the traces of black and pink colour completely retreated from his sallow canvas.

After that it was mainly just a gathering of arbitrary people of no relevance to you. We can put them down as the extended family, neighbours, and public servants.

I was there myself because I was getting through the notes by then and had already begun to develop half an interest in writing the man up. I was also a little bit curious as to how Margot was getting on since her marbled performance at the funeral.

I decided I'd take the opportunity to introduce myself properly to the lesser remaining half of the partnership whose work I had been studying almost non-stop some days for three weeks. (I had to take one week away to paint a lean-to for a little woman in Wicklow—a Presbyterian. They're very good to pay but I find you can't miss a date with them or they'll never call you back.)

I approached the little man who had gone over to the bar to stand beside a late arrival, a very big fellow. From the wild head and loud noise of the latter, I took this to be Connie McLean the raving archaeologist.

When I approached, they stopped whatever they were talking about, which some people would consider rude but which I very much appreciated. 'Well, how are the boys?' I said, in the very same bog bathos that Mac Gabhann had once so derided. No hair was turned by these men though they were native speakers. I took a ham sandwich from the plate they'd sneaked aside for themselves and added, 'It's no harm the pre-fasting died out anyway. Meat and mass make a man, so my Grandmother used to say, God rest her.'

'I'm not too bad,' said the big one non-committedly, 'and yourself?'

'What the fuck do you want with your big grey head on you?' said the small central man, pleasantly enough too. 'Haven't I seen you before somewhere?'

'Only at the funeral,' I said.

'No,' Ryle said, looking me up and down suspiciously, 'before that. I saw you before. You have the look of a loss adjustor. You are trying to implicate me in something. I'd know by you.'

You might not believe it, but at that exact moment the hotel sound system connected with the function room pipes and started to exhale Sting's stalker song into the assembled ears:

Every move you make

I barely joined in but upon seeing the involuntary movement of my lips, Ryle spoke to me in his flat faced manner. 'Fucking ghoul,' he said.

I glanced across at Margot. She looked straight through me as if I wasn't there.

We were then interrupted as the Garda came over and patted Ryle on the shoulder. 'Poor Grattan, he wasn't the worst,' said Devine. 'We miss him.'

'Not a bad turnout, Devine,' said Ryle, shouldering the hand off himself.

'To tell you the honest truth, he'd have had my vote for the Park,' said the Guard, an awkwardness creeping up in him by surprise and choking his voice. He wasn't used to looking for reassurance. 'Tell me ... Er, he did know of course that we were only doing our overtime jobs and personally had nothing personal against him or what he was doing? Lord rest the good man.'

I was impressed that at least there was someone amongst these subjects who was showing a bit of emotion.

Ryle wasn't as impressed. From the previously noted memory emporium, he pulled on Devine with, 'If they'd taught you anything about syllogisms in Templemore, bud, you'd know that fallacious *tu quoque* will get you nowhere. It's too late for your slobbering. Besides, you still haven't answered my question. How bad would a lad have to be to lose the stripes in Store St.?'

Devine just looked at Ryle in awe. It had become a matter of shared wonder between himself and colleagues that Ryle had been every bit as immune to having spots knocked off him as had Fletcher. Albeit for different reasons. Ryle was as bold as ever.

'Still not talking, fuckface, eh?' said Ryle in a comradely tone. 'Anyway, where is Sergeant Meg Geas this weather?'

'Meg? What made you ask that? What do you know about her?' said the Guard, striking a neurotic note, a nerve touched. Then he shrugged, 'Gone underground, so to speak. Disappeared the same day Grattan ... She had a hen party in Cashel ... Anyway, she hasn't been seen since the day of poor Mr. Fletcher's

incident. She had been going a bit wild anyway, the power of
the bogs corrupting her. Some say she went native, gone back
to Kerry maybe.'

'*Kerry*, eh?' said Ryle, reaching into his jacket.

'Ours is not to question why,' opined Devine. He wandered
off to shake hands with others.

'So you got in with Mac Gabhann's wife?' I resumed, stabbing
in the dark with an educated guess and trying to get away from
the subject of where Ryle thought he'd seen me.

Ryle scrutinized me again. 'Who exactly are you and what
do you know about my business?' he said, making a grab for my
testicles but only getting the keys of the Passat.

'I'm going to guess you were not shy about letting Mac
Gabhann know the fox had been in his particular henhouse
too?' I added. 'And I happen to know that you led Margot to
believe that it was Mac Gabhann had sent you and her husband
on that last mission.' That got his attention. I wrapped it by
saying, 'I am the man who knows your whole story. So a bit of
respect wouldn't go astray.'

'Since you know so much,' he said, not all that put out after
all. He nodded to the non-descript Beyron driver who I hadn't
noticed eating Taytos on his own in the corner, 'Since you're so
great, tell me about Fletcher's secret friend.'

'What would you like to know?' I said obligingly.

'How much money did he give my man?' said Ryle, getting down to brass tacks. 'Was it put in a trust or paid direct
to Fletcher's AIB account? Also. Did my closest friend Grattan
leave a will at all? Or did he think he was going to live forever?'

'Even if I knew the answers to those questions,' I said professionally, 'breaching ethics to tell you would imply a warmth that
I do not feel for you as a character.'

'So tell me then, what's going to happen next,' asked Ryle, a
little rattled, I'd like to think.

'I'll tell you that if you fill me in on what has happened in the
past month,' I said. I did also take the opportunity, in case the
conversation ended abruptly, to get in a mention of the business
that had brought me into this mess in the first place. I said to

Ryle that his brother-in-law owed me a few bob going on for six
months now and that it would be no harm for him if he would
give me a call about settling it up.

'Now I remember where I saw that big silvery nut before,'
said Ryle.

'You saw me at the funeral,' I repeated.

'No, before that,' he said. 'On a bog road at midnight on the
bad side of the Shannon.'

'There's a lot like me,' I said.

'And spilling diluted paint onto the roof of a trailer,' he said.

The big fellow looked bemused. 'What the hell is this charade
about,' he said. 'I'm sure I saw the two of you talking like old
friends at the funeral.'

That was a bit close to the bone. 'I haven't got all night,'
I said untruthfully. 'Before we get sidetracked onto harmless
reminiscences I'd be eternally grateful to you two fine people
for an update on what's been going on in Fletcher's world. I'm
interested in this Grattan Fletcher character.'

'Are you indeed,' said Ryle, pointlessly raising his voice. 'It
may be of interest to you also then to note that I have no sibling
or wife and therefore no in-law who you can threaten into paying you for painting any hayshed in this world. Or for painting
any robbed lorry for that matter. So I'm sorry to have to tell you
that your time has been entirely wasted. You are on to the wrong
man. You have now attended one funeral more than you needed
to in your life and as a result of that careless bookkeeping you
have gotten yourself wrapped up in the affairs of people whose
business need be none of yours.'

'Show a bit of respect for the occasion,' said the big lad quietly to Ryle. 'What harm? Tell him what you know and I'll tell
him what I know.' McLean then put his mouth near my ear
after his large mad head had looked around suspiciously in the
manner of any man who has visited a fairy fort once too often.
'*I am with Fletcher,*' is what he said.

Ryle left his indignation to one side and proceeded to provide
me with the few further sparse details, interspersed with pieces
of nearly pure conjecture from the big lad.

◊

After the hotel pleasantries on the one-month anniversary of Grattan Fletcher's departure, people moved through the drizzle and darkness to the chapel so as to get the mass out of the way.

One bad, the other worse

Chapter XL

BEFORE THE MIND MASS is said I'll relate to you what I pieced together about the happenings of the intervening month.

By now you will have become accustomed to a high-fidelity record. You no doubt have come to take for granted unflinching accounting that avoids the flaws so widely evident in contemporary historical work. Few traces of revisionism, recentism, or holism here.

Unfortunately, a Faustian moment has now been arrived at by myself, as it is (arrived at) much earlier in the careers of all the big names in writing; that moment when they turn their first trick for for a glint of appetite from a publisher or a satisfied sound from a reader. I'm weakened by awareness that you may feel that you might as well have got no bread as have been given half a loaf. So I risk my reputation to feed you the remainder. I would have you at least line your stomach with a caveat before you go at it.

Note: I must remind you that while I will do my best to untangle all and plaster over the missing bits of the month up to the month's mind for you, the primary sources were solely Suck Ryle and Connie McLean, one of whom is bad and the other worse when it comes to reliability. *The compiler*

You don't need detail of the tearing and wrenching still going on in Grattan's daughter and granddaughter since the terrible event. The two unfortunate creatures were entirely unprepared for discovering with each passing day the true meaning of words that had been mouthed by every previous generation on the subject of death. The wounds that would continue to tear a little more every time they looked like scarring over.

On other fronts the funeral had been followed by reckoning.

Margot either had no weakening reactions or she had them so well hidden as had the same external effect. There wasn't a minute of crying out of her and she gave a hard shoulder to those who wanted to comfort her. Ryle, also burying his loss in process, had reached her in this state. He saw what it was. She was in his territory now, a place where anger calmly nurtured was an exhilarating expression of being alive.

He started calling to Rathmines in the evenings. No physical relations developed. Their engagement had moved into a different realm. And besides, she had issued certain cautions. She allowed him to stay late though, drinking tea at the kitchen table, solid elm from a tree killed by the dutch (there was nothing in the house that didn't speak of Fletcher), talking first about the great things the great man had done and then quickly diverting back to the subject on which they both chose to dwell, the wrongs that had been done. That was the new reality of their world, the passive Christian and the active antichrist allied in consumptive thirst to avenge the dead atheist.

Soon enough there was a small frenzy starting to ignite in the way that creatives touching shoulders can often spark off each other. Ryle was empowering a whirlwind of rage and vengeance in Margot that made her feel the strength of the wilds in her brain and the ferocity of our rivers running free in her veins.

The tantrum started quite justifiably with vehement thoughts on the subject of Mac Gabhann. Ryle could tell he had tapped into a gusher. At the first mention of the name he had seen dark response break the strange composure from every square millimetre of her countenance. Like any good mental professional, having found the wound that would keep him in business, Ryle was not remiss in reopening it at every opportunity. He was rewarded by seeing the neuralgic reaction only grow to anaphylactic proportions.

In this state Margot quietly absorbed most of what Ryle told her. He mentioned that Grattan had been ordered to the lethal location on that fatal day. That Mac Gabhann had produced an ordinance survey map with a black X showing a stone they were to survey in that brutal paddock. That Mac Gabhann had sent them off with the words—*you will see what becomes of men who think themselves outstanding in their field.* She didn't even blink when Ryle added that he had concrete information that other forces of the State had come in behind Mac Gabhann, not prepared to wait for his popularity to get to the point where he was too big to fail.

All that was inside the music teacher was being funnelled into one singular rage that banished her powerlessness along with her considerateness and deferred her loss along with her recalibration.

Ryle did not have reason to curtail his intervention or to keep his scope narrow. He was not a prudent person in that way, in fairness to him. He was envisioning an orgy of vengeance of which he would be the agile enabler. As she came fully into his domain he would empower her. He would nurture every predisposition. And soon he would have her reddening the institutions of the partial Republic that had trampled Fletcher's campaign and Ryle's career aspirations along with it. Ryle's conversations were not idle. He made notes. After Mac Gabhann was floored and Margot's taste for power whetted, he calculated on moving on initially only to those for whom he was sure Margot already harboured negative sentiment: squandering leaders, rackrent landlords, smug jesters, hate mongers, embedded journalists, and possibly celebrity chefs.

Whatever the little man's own dreams, and the way they had a habit of getting dead-ended, we can say for sure that Margot got off to a good start.

Mac Gabhann became unnerved when things started happening. Sudden gusts of wind disturbed the blinds in his airtight office. Mould grew overnight on his leather inlay. A coffee cup parted from its handle and emptied itself into his leather satchel. His biography of de Rossa fell off the shelf and lay open at a page with the plot to assassinate de Valera highlighted in yellow.

Mac Gabhann referred feebly to the open source movement when the Minister asked about his relocation to the open-plan area on the second floor of Northumberland Manse. Then all of the files deleted themselves from his laptop before his eyes. Gone from all his backup devices and the cloud at the same moment.

His Facebook timeline terminated and his page was memorial-
ized. The biography video had him in the opera suit remarkably
well photoshopped into dogging movies. He developed a shake
and the decomposing process that in most people progresses
slower than the eye can see from the age of twenty-four, accelerated in Mac Gabhann to a rate where each day underlings would
whisper about some new deterioration: the halving of his mass,
the blackening wrinkles of his pelt, the upturning of his toes.

Then word came in that an asymmetrical pyramid of the
castle books had spontaneously combusted at a shop in Finglas.
That got the booksellers a bit nervous, but they put it down to
environmental factors. It was alright until the exact same thing
occurred at Lysarts in Dundrum. This being a branch of a multiple, paranoia spread systemically.

> Note: 'Master the Novel in 7 Steps,' that was the manual I
> worked from when I taught myself writing. I never mind
> sharing. Be warned though, it was wrong in one or two
> things. Principally I recall it boldly states in the final slide,
> *Manuscripts don't burn.* Clearly the instructor had never heard
> of Cambodia, where the Chinese outsource their production
> to. The paper made from Khmer rubber trees apparently finds
> certain combinations of words inflammatory. *The compiler*

All the other shopkeepers quickly sent their stock back to
the publisher. Boland, a man who had heard from his father
about book burnings, felt that the immolations were punishment for the suspicions he had repressed about Mac Gabhann's
creative capacity. In turn he sent his remaining stock back to the
printers in Ghuanzhou. Then, demonstrating the literal meaning of the old expression, too little too late, the short fat fuck
slumped against a stud partition and died. He did so in front
of his assistant following his return from lunch at Devitt's on
the Tuesday after his castle dream collapsed. The cause of death
was unknown, certainly to myself, as I didn't ask. Another little
publisher gone to the wall.

> Note: of course I remain neutral on all reported events.[fn] But
> as the ancient Chinese used to say, if you sit on the river bank
> long enough you'll see your enemy float by. *The compiler*

[fn]Footnote
If mendacity had currency, our compiler would possess wealth in all denominations. *The Editors*

One evening when Mac Gabhann was out for his walk in Bushy Park, skirting an escalonia hedge still recovering from the bad frost back in 2011, the bush parted before him. Nothing visible emerged. The two inbred russells, weak headed though they were, had the sense to wrench themselves from their association with this man and fled in every direction.

Some time later two joggers tried to skirt around a whimpering heap. When they couldn't get past without going on the grass they tried to help Mac Gabhann to his feet. But they found he couldn't be sustained. There were cuts in his chinos. A white boy, he kept saying, had run a blade across the backs of his knees. Ex-cruciate, the man was in a degree of pain and it was starting to dawn on him that his troubles were only beginning. On the positive side, he would never have to go through the knee operations.

Saoirse, a circumspect girl at the best of times, never spoke to Ryle. She worked around him in her mother's kitchen in the evenings. She would keep padded white earphones on her head as she made asparagus soup and Turkish coffee, then prepared little Margot's snackbox for the next day, and headed back to her room without a word.

Ryle perceived this matter but took not a blind bit of notice since he had no interest in flighty young ones.

'You could at least acknowledge the man's presence occasionally,' Margot said to her one night after Ryle had left.

'What does *that guy* even want here?' said Saoirse. She associated Ryle with her father's death and that was hard. Young though she was, she had insight. She knew in her bones from the first time she saw Ryle that he was the kind of man who would always want something for himself. That there would always be a price to pay for any favour.

'He was your father's friend and he is just helping me with some things,' said her mother, shut off from reason.

'*Otva'li!* I won't ask what kind of things Mum, but …' blurted Saoirse, who was showing some of the father's form. She'd rebuffed suggestions about college. Too stuffy for her. But here was the fine young thing studying classical Russian out of passing interest, 'Do not call a wolf to help you against dogs.'

'I'll bear that in mind, sweetheart,' said her mother, well used to Saoirse's immersive engagements. She spoke in dead blank tones that Saoirse found frightening and annoying in similar quantities.

'By the way, Mum,' Saoirse said wickedly, looking for any kind of reaction, 'I'd been thinking of going to Melbourne for a bit. Get some restaurant experience instead of sitting on my ass waiting for things to pick up here. I've some friends there and there's lots of work.'

The offering had the desired effect on Margot's composure. At least for a moment. Her UCD 1990 mug slipped from her fingers to the floor. It turned out she hadn't been keeping anything of that sort from Fletcher.

'It's OK, Mum, it's OK,' Saoirse tripped over her withdrawal, 'I've decided against it. With all this. And the school Dad got Margot into, well I have to admit it's kind of perfect for her. I probably shouldn't take her out.'

'Did … Did your Dad know this, Saoirse?' Margot asked slowly, regaining herself.

'No, Mum,' Saoirse said, her face dropping with the sudden extra worry, still a baby herself. 'No. I don't think so. Could he have? I would have gone months ago but I couldn't figure out how I'd tell him.'

Margot just looked at her daughter and then at the coffee and delph scattered on the Liscannor flagstones.

◊

Mac Gabhann was somewhat emotionally perturbed by all that was going on. One evening he took the bold step of coming to Margot's house. Maybe he thought he would be able to clear the air. He didn't know who or what was behind the concertinaing of his life. But he'd taken a notion that if he talked to Margot about his regrets his ease would return. She met him at the door and he immediately said, 'There are things I want to talk about with you, Margot.'

She said, 'Get away from this house.'

'Ah now,' he said. 'Listen, Margot, I remember one thing that Grattan said often. He said, *Harden not your heart.* Remember old times, Margot.'

She smiled and the coldness of the winter night at his back set a violent shivering into his bones. 'It's too late for that, Charles.' She quietly closed the flawlessly restored Victorian door on him. He watched her wide shadow retreat through the etched butterflies of the stained glass panels.

As he turned on his walking frame he had the further misfortune of seeing a figure behind him at the gate. Ryle had come about the evening business but was delayed as he tried to close the latch on the misaligned cast-iron gate. There was nothing about a historic house that Ryle appreciated. He didn't even look up from his work on the hinges as he said, 'A dog always returns to his vomit.'

'Jesus! What are *you* doing here?' said Mac Gabhann, unable to help himself.

'You know,' said Ryle, straightening to cast an eye over the diminishing frame, 'you know that you told the great man that the atheist devil wouldn't care.'

'*What the fuck!* How do you know about that?'

'Well he may,' said Ryle with indifference, and opened the gate for Mac Gabhann. 'That devil may care.'

Note: you might wonder which use of the word 'may' was intended here, the English or the South Leinster. Given the origins of the issuer and remembering that the indefinite is not a form of speech we have heard much of out of him, I'd say he meant *may* in the common sense. That is, rather than indicating uncertainty as to the devil's likely state of mind, he was indicating that in his view there was now an onus on the same elegant gentleperson to take an interest in these matters. This *may* was a *must. The compiler*

And then there was Fran. Grattan's death had thrown all

of Fran's carefully minded arrangements into disarray, broken her walls. She re-established her coffee dates with Margot, who didn't want them anymore but who was so unnaturally calm that she was able to cater to other people's losses. Over beverages of various sorts Fran did the grieving, beating herself up for the years of friendship she had let herself be deprived of. Margot measured the pace of her advice and soon enough Fran started herself on the process of moving out of Mac Gabhann's circle of purgatory. That wasn't enough for Margot. On the evening that Fran first met Ryle at the Fletchers' house she downed enough gin to make her see crooked. She took it on Margot's ungodly suggestion that she could do worse than let Ryle drive her back to her marital home, in the garage of which Mac Gabhann was painfully moving his speakers to lower shelves. She went in as bold as anything in narrow daylight and led the degenerate to her bedroom where she engaged him in exercise, wave after wave of rutting, an animated symphony of solid spite. The cripple stayed in his shed until the faint light of a summer dawn was starting to appear out toward England, and Ryle walked out onto the pavement leaving the modern front gate wide open behind him.

If the month's mind mass had taken longer to come, there's no telling how much damage would have been done in that little city as Margot and her agent widened their scope. But it came when it was due, as often happens in fact.

A story is good until another is told

Chapter XLI

THE AFFRONT TO FLETCHER's disbelief was whittled down, a month after his death, to a single continuous drone of concatenated words, a bloodless resurrection of the Latin incantations, out of the mouth of a single old priest with a lonely alcoholic head on him and not even enough life force to pull a few vestments over himself for the occasion.

On their own in the front bench were big Margot, the frail wafer that was Saoirse, and little Margot looking all around her with her granddad's red cheeks and lovely big head of curls. On the seat behind, never sure when to stand or kneel, was a scraggy-bearded scrap of a chap in purple pants trying to come good for little Margot. He periodically put a hand on the little girl's shoulder.

Ten minutes into the mass, in arrived a figure twisted around a zimmerframe. I hardly recognized him. The priest paused in the childlike un-self-conscious manner of the soft leftover men to whom home parish duties have now been defaulted. Everyone else turned to look as the crooked man cranked his way slowly up the aisle. By Jesus if it wasn't the same fellow who had spent hours disposing of good whiskey and dispensing bad advice to me in the fine country Hotel just four weeks back. Secretary General Cathal Mac Gabhann had aged a millennium, and bear in mind he'd been looking fairly shook to begin with. If I hadn't believed half of what Ryle had told me up to then, I started to half-believe it at that moment.

Having not yet at that point in time undertaken the bit of further research necessary in order to enable me to wrap up this chronicle, which I think I owe you very little on now, I started wondering if guilt and regret alone can beget such harrowing

411

effects on the health of a person.

A very pleasant looking woman in a summery lime green dress came in after Mac Gabhann. She walked like someone getting used to being looked at. She spread her bottom at the far end of the pew from him. I saw Ryle give her the nod and she responded with a bold smile in full view of the ailing husband. Fran had indeed been letting the hair down, I confirmed.

It was at that moment that I decided to write the foregoing.[fn]

[fn] Footnote
Difficult to resist observing what a pity it is that the compiler didn't instead forego the writing. *The Editors*

The holy show that was the entry of Mac Gabhann and his wife at the month's mind wasn't the only interruption to the ceremony, by then looking to drag on a fair bit longer than I'd allowed for. The priest had barely found his spot in the relevant letter of St. Paul to the Corinthians when another cold gust was admitted from the swinging main door at the back of the holy building. This time there was a collective gasp and some people took hold of each other in unabashed fright.

Up the aisle progressed the visage with the characteristic rolling Fletcher walk and a big red face that smiled even in his great trouble. The greying curly black mop was as wild as ever.

The figure faltered only at the middle of the church on catching sight of Sister Margaret. Nodding then, he walked further. The place remained in frozen silence as he stopped again at the front pew. The Fletchers, Margot, Saoirse, and little Margot, slid up and let him sit next to them. He put his hand on Saoirse's. Then he had to stand up again nearly immediately as he went up to help the priest who was trying to find his homily. From the pulpit Martin Fletcher looked down on Margot in silence. Then he said softly, 'The battle is not yours alone.' He paused and looked across the assembled. He swept his arm over all of us in an amiability so familiar that even Ryle changed the foot he was propped on and let a little grunt of fetid air escape from him.

'I'm with Grattan,' said Martin quietly. There was a general murmur. In that moment I have to say I even saw myself nodding. I was with him too. 'He lives through us. He walks among us.'

That was the end of Margot's war. Her shoulders slowly collapsed, she heaved, and began to melt. All the 'holding up well' was suddenly flooding out of her. Martin came back down to sit with them.

'Fucksake,' said Ryle the unregenerate, staring in at Martin Fletcher in polite resignation. He zipped up the Pakistani lamb leather, and then Velcroed the high viz over it, 'what is that scuttering muppet on about? That's that then.'

He had the old ways in him all the same, I noted. He stayed until the consecration, on the dot, so nobody could say he hadn't done the mass. Maybe it was just habit, of course. The font in the side porch where we were leant again was dry and so I can't tell you if he'd have blessed himself if there'd been water to do it with. But I can tell you he knew there and then that Margot had lost eyes and ears for his ways as suddenly as she had found them. I could see the reorganization writing itself across the calm yellow leatherette as the hazel eyes darted around, re-configuring with no time wasted on minor recriminations. He was going to be left to finish Mac Gabhann on his own. No better man for that job. I hadn't a bit of doubt that the same bad bastard who had thought he was pulling a stroke on a harmless bogman when he gave me his card in a hotel lounge bar only a month before, and whose hock problems would soon be put in perspective by bigger difficulties, was only still alive because there was one little party who wanted him to go slowly.

Ryle would not be easing off. He was a person of hermetic commitment to any task he had set himself in the way that all successful people are, their lives pivoting around some early traumatic realization of inadequacy that makes them less secure even in serial success than the awestruck onlooker is in regular failure. Yes indeed, Private Cromwell Ryle would keep marching to his own drum.

'Prick,' Ryle nodded to myself then, the last I'll ever see of him, I trust. He wandered off from that church, joining up with McClean who had stayed on the outside—Cornelius

McLean was steadfast in his sceptical stance on all non-indigenous superstitions.

Ryle was doing a bit of travelling with the same large fairyman these days, having found the alcove suddenly a bit too quiet for him. The Land Cruiser would stop on the road outside the Manse. Ryle would climb in without anyone behind him knowing or caring. The two would disappear off to various parts of the country that nobody has heard of.

McLean, a freelancer by disposition and an archaeologist by nature as well as by trade, couldn't let sleeping dogs lie. One of his life chores was to dig up the bones and other possessions of dead Vikings, which he felt had no place in Irish soil. (McLean was also busy with a parallel project, restoring and reinstating without requisite permissions, the souterrains of certain ring forts. The less said on that the easiest mended.)

There's one thing you could be sure of, no good would come of the Viking enterprise though.

Note: there's bitterness in my own family going back to Clontarf. It wasn't often we agreed on anything. As the old saying goes, one nail drives out another. But I can tell you this much, we were united at Clontarf. And it wasn't on the side of the so-called *High King* of Ireland that we picked up axes. Like three-quarters of the country, we have a crow to pluck with the same Boru and his Munster Danes. We still wait for the history books to be revised. *The compiler*

Ryle of course was still prevented by union rules from direct participation where a spade or shovel was involved, but he was able to give helpful advice and increased McLean's monthly outgoings.

Before I leave him, I should also mention a small happy note in relation to Ryle. He did something for himself on the equine thing. I understand that he has taken a few acres in Kildare for himself. On them now stands an animal with a fair bit of black ink in her pedigree, bought for very little because nobody but Ryle likes a chestnut mare.

If you are not relieved by these small digressions I'd respectfully suggest to you that have not been to mass in a while.

I thought better of it and shouted discreetly after Ryle, 'When you have your current assignments wiped up you can give me a buzz.'

Ryle nodded and got into McLean's old jalopy.

The mass proceeded.

Getting on toward the end of it Fletcher stood again. He looked all around. Then he started with a soft humming. This gave way to a full issuing of "Starry Starry Night" in the sweetest tones you could imagine. He cast a spell on all present and even I myself was not entirely unscathed.

When that died out he closed his eyes and eased into "Last Rose of Summer," perhaps knowing how Grattan had thought of Moore and loss. When the last echoes were faded from the majestic cavern built by generations of these people long gone, the audience sat small in their seats. Nobody wanted to move from the magic communion of this moment onto the next solitary thing in their lives. They were waiting for more and he was stuck to the spot as he had cued up nothing else vaguely suitable. Then he thought of something. 'Back in school, Grattan and me had a band ...' he started to explain. Then he just got on with it ... *Redemption songs.* Appropriate enough. I stepped inside and looked. The church-sanctioned accompanist, having failed on the other songs, took up a creditable finger dance on the upper keys of the organ.

A song of freedom. The choice shouldn't have been a surprise to anyone who knows anything about the Fletcher mindset, always pushing forward.

Martin Fletcher was taking a break from the Asian boxing, so I heard after. And the religion. He was going to work with Horace, the man who ran the Bughatti out of a few acres of scraggy forestry down near Borris. Though none present could foresee this, there was in the fullness of time going to be a foundation named for Grattan and chaired by Margot. The tagline would be contended between Martin's *Ar scráth a chéile* and Horace's take, *The House of Many Rooms*.

As you can imagine yourself, with three renaissance people at the wheel instead of one, there's going to be more to tell. But a story is always good until another is told and so there's no percentage for myself in going on and on.

As Mac Gabhann crawled his way out past me ten minutes later I caught the corner of his eye. 'That was a fair turnout,' I bade him civilly, my only intention being to properly wind up the exchange of funereal courtesies we had started a month earlier, 'considering it's such a miserable old evening. Though I think they're giving it to get worse by Saturday.'

'*Don't talk to me about weather!*' spat Mac Gabhann. 'And do not presume to be my friend!'

'Right so. The deceased was a very decent skin, all the same,' I said, not sinking to his level yet. 'It was a great shock to you all, I'd say.'

'What kind of man are you at all and where do you come from?' said Mac Gabhann stopping the crab-like movement for a minute. The face was not as barbarous looking as I'd remembered, pain becoming him. 'From the first day I clapped eyes on you back in that gank hotel, I called it. You were involved in the plotting! I should have had absolutely nothing to do with you. Absolutely nothing.' If I didn't know better I'd nearly say there was a hint of respect for myself in his eye, behind all the regrets that were just for himself. I had to appreciate that, as I don't get it from everyone I meet.

'Nevertheless, do you know it's a shame so many thought of you as the devil himself,' I came back at him.

'*What?* What on earth do you mean by that? Bloody madman!' he said to me and then added without rhyme or reason, 'Anyway, do you know, you fit the description of the man they say has been stalking the dead man's wife?'

I let that observation pass, chalking it down to his state of mind.

'I suppose your own one is off in Turkey with a toy boy like the rest whose men can't even keep them at home,' he rasped, the bile not yet entirely squeezed out of him it seems. 'Ha! You didn't think I noticed you were only talking to voicemail back that day in the bar? So what's wrong with you that you weren't able to keep yours at home?

'You don't think you're the first to ask me that, you fatuous fraud,' I said, not very fazed.

Note: a peculiar learning given rise to by my personal loss is that people are always looking for deep explanations where there are obvious shallow ones that need no further exploration. *What complicated thing had gone so wrong*, they always want to know, and who was to be sided with, indeed. Meanwhile the obvious reason for that good woman moving on didn't seem to satisfy anyone: that she had chanced on a better man. More power to her. *The compiler*

'An artist, wasn't it?' he grimaced. 'Well if you've read any of the notes I referred you to on that secret Internet blog, you might be able to join the dots. You yourself should take heed of what a mid-life epiphany can lead to.'

'I'm not sure we read the same pages.' I was surprised to hear myself rising to Grattan's defence.

He was knocked off balance, clearly not used to the robust tackle. He squinted at me with his wandering eye and, albeit with a shake in his voice, he eventually resumed the theme which I took to indicate that he did not have many to choose from. 'A sudden burst of interference in the ways of life will be vigorously resisted by the system trying to correct itself. It's the second law of thermodynamics that killed Grattan Fletcher. Best to keep on a path of making very little difference. A path I would say that you, by the looks of you, are well acclimatized to.'

'That's where you're very wrong,' I responded without hubris. 'An idea, you see, is made up of nanoparticles. And it has recently been proved just down the road in Geneva that those very same little articles when tormented with lasers are not subject the second law at all. That's why a good idea doesn't die and never killed anyone.' And then I added, in case he needed help with his own dots, 'But do tell me now, which natural law is it that you think is propelling yourself to the exit, you a person clearly dying on your feet?'

'Don't you too now start to develop a holy show!' said Mac Gabhann. 'Grattan may have been … whatever he was. But I am sick of people no better than me, only whatever worse, basking in Fletcher's glow.'

'I don't know,' I said, 'I may as well tell you I was regarded as a saint when young.'

'To my point,' he cut me off, sharp enough. 'Young saint, old …'

There came Fran and shut him up with her glowing presence. She was in a strange mood. Any church worth its salt, I suppose. 'A person is a person because of people,' she quoted. She touched Mac Gabhann's teapot-handled arm in an extension of personal shelter that nobody would have expected of her. He got past me and started to tediously work his way down the elegant bull-nosed granite steps, grunting and gasping as though he was the first person to ever feel agony.

Disclosure: at this point you may be asking whether Mac Gabhann's was truly the evil shadow that stalked Grattan Fletcher through the foregoing episodes. Had he been anything but a showman you would expect him to have side-stepped the few harmless snares that Ryle laid on for him. You justifiably ask, was Mac Gabhann in the end nothing more than an average hateful old bollox. I'd have to concur, on reflection, that Mac Gabhann's offences were mostly venal. He may have merely considered murder (evidence on the actual execution of Josephine Sloane points elsewhere) but that hardly distinguishes him from the average person such as yourself, if you are honest for a minute. True, he brazenly stole Fletcher's work. But he was not the one who took Fletcher into that field. He has certainly exhibited seven minor cancers of personality, the seven little atrocities so pervasive in the patterns into which the lives of most ordinary, decent people descend: corrosive envy (which it's easy to criticize only if you have a lot going on yourself), angry besting, stingy avarice, misplaced pride, horning after young ones, slowness of wit, and gobbling the biggest slice of every pie within reach.

So I can see now that I have not pinned any primacy on him. I have not nailed him for being more than an ordinary practitioner. Only an insipid shadow after all. Too late to fix that now though and even if I had time to go back and turn all my work upside down for Mac Gabhann, why would I. The downside of being an unlikeable character is that nobody is going to bother to lift a finger to get you out of a hobble. The book is written. Minor errors and inconsistencies can be ironed out in later editions. And may I conclude by sharing a wisdom a grandaunt of my own passed on. I hope that it may resonate soberingly with you at some time in the future: if you have to spend much time wondering who the worst cunt is, it's probably yourself.

It was then I indulged in a little crime of my own. Not alone did I fail to put a stop to Ryle's plans for this ordinary man's slow death, but I pulled on Mac Gabhann myself even though I knew I was crossing every boundary of good workmanship. Fraternizing with the characters and interfering with the course of history is usually beneath me.

All I said to Mac Gabhann was, 'Here, before you are gone altogether, sign this.'

I saw one foreleg of Mac Gabhann's walking frame go out over the lip of the top step as he turned to look.

'I think it might be a rare thing in a month's time when copies of your signature are even harder to come by than copies of the tome.'

I came forward offering a gold MontBlanc pen I had won in a quiz. On the other hand I had Conwy Castle. I opened my own copy of The Castle People at the blank Acknowledgements page. That I was the one who seemed to lack fear of incineration may have been the far-fetched first thought of the unfortunate frightened fellow then. Again, the simple explanation eschewed—it never dawned on him that I'd turned off the heating since Sarah left and the house at home had become so cold and damp that after a week in it the Cambodian paperwork could not have ignited itself even if it was bathed in petrol. He retreated a fraction. That was all. I never laid a hand on the man. The steps, finely bush-hammered and all as they were, went from under him in the drizzle.

It was a harmless transgression enough when you look back on it, though it mightn't have appeared that way to the stickler, Martin Fletcher. Moving with Grattan's family down the central aisle at that very time, he happened to glance across toward the side door where my own little event was unfolding. No doubt, to the causality-craving eyes of a former churchman, the little rib jab from my book and the tumble down the steps were connected. Fletcher looked at me and shook his head in a kindly way that turned my stomach. I thought back on the aloof disapproval Ryle too had put up with from a Fletcher, in the execution of those little bits of behind-the-scenes dirty work that somebody has to do in order to keep any team winning.

It took Fran a while watching her husband pick himself off the tarmac below before she went down after him and bundled him into the low passenger seat of his seven series, put some Mamma Mia on his MP3 player and circumlocuted off with other stragglers to have one or two pints for herself before couriering the crocked dependent back to Dublin.

The Fletchers proceeded out the main door. They never came near me or cast another look in my direction. I was glad of that as I knew there was trouble waiting at the back of the chapel. Two great lumps of McClaferty headmen had seen Martin going in and thought he was the Fletcher. Detecting pumelling anger at the latest insult added to their injuries, I had side-stepped them like most decent people would. Some said Fletcher had got too familiar with the tinkers and so brought this kind of thing on himself. No sense of protecting his own patch of sanity. As if all the words in the world could bring life back to any of their eight fat in-foal cobs that had been run into the ground and shot by County Councillors going tough on Travellers for the elections. Some things never change.

Even a wavy line takes you to the next point, in the end. Anyone could do my work here now. Regardless of whether you have nothing better to do, I have a couple of other jobs on my books.[fn]

[fn] Footnote
And there you have it. What further could we add? He'll never write another word in this town, of that we feel certain. *The Editors*

Tom O'Neill has written since he was given a pencil back in Carlow in the early 60s. His creative efforts have rarely impacted anyone as much as they do himself. Writing educational materials is what has kept the pot boiling. Then he met a man from Dalkey Archive Press who told him to write what he knows about. He doesn't know a lot about anything. But he cares quite a bit about family, fiction, development education, pisrógs, bio-sciences, farming, heritage architecture, new technologies, old wisdoms and being of Ireland. So now he has migrated to Kilkenny (via Galway, Cork, Munich, Kimberley, Durban, Dublin, and Cape Town) and writes mostly about what he cares about.